JUST THE SIX OF US

T0352373

Laurie Ellingham writes romances that centre around family and second chances, adding humour to the everyday moments of life. Before becoming a full-time writer, Laurie studied a degree in psychology and worked in public relations in London.

She now lives with her family in the Suffolk countryside, alongside a cockerpoo called Rodney, and two guinea pigs. Laurie also writes psychological suspense as Lauren North. Readers can follow Laurie on Twitter @LaurieEllingham and Facebook, searching for Laurie Ellingham Author.

JUST THE SIX OF US

Laurie Ellingham

An Orion paperback

This edition published in Great Britain in 2022
by Orion Dash,
an imprint of The Orion Publishing Group Ltd,
Carmelite House, 50 Victoria Embankment
London EC4Y 0DZ

An Hachette UK company

1 3 5 7 9 10 8 6 4 2

Copyright © Laurie Ellingham 2022

A CIP catalogue record for this book
is available from the British Library.

ISBN (Paperback) 978 1 3987 1061 0
ISBN (eBook) 978 1 3987 0999 7

Typeset by Born Group

www.orionbooks.co.uk

For my daughter, Lottie.

And for all the parents who get up every day and try their best! This one is for you. xx

February

February

Chapter 1

Jenny

Thirty-nine is too old to have sex in the back of a car. This is the thought that strikes Jenny as her elbow clonks against the hard plastic of the door. If there ever was an acceptable age, it was at least two decades ago and yet here she is, on the back seat of a Vauxhall Estate that smells of strawberry body spray and popcorn. Parked up in the middle of nowhere, with the seatbelt connecter jamming into her right bum cheek, fumbling in the pitch black with Dan, lovely Dan, kissing her in a way that makes her want to throw off all her clothes despite the biting February air.

She will die of embarrassment if someone sees them. OK – so not actually die, but close enough. They might be a mile from the nearest house, parked in a lay-by on an unused lane, but it would be just her luck to be spotted by a dog walker or a late-night runner. And, of course, it would have to be someone she knows – one of the snooty mums from Jack's class that she's never clicked with, even after sitting through six years of assemblies together.

Jenny searches for Dan's face but it's just a shadow, a feeling of heat and that buzz, that delicious zing. She can't see his hazel eyes with the flecks of green or his George Clooney smile, as Jenny likes to think of it. George Clooney when he played the cheeky Jack Taylor beside Michelle

3

Pfeiffer in *One Fine Day*. All lip-twitching smirk and crinkly eyes, that's Dan's smile.

But the smile is where the similarity to George Clooney circa 1996 ends. Dan's hair is light brown, a touch of grey on the sides. He's tall, a good half a foot taller than Jenny. He has frown lines on his forehead and a small dad paunch that Jenny doesn't mind. If anything, it makes her feel better about the extra inches around her own waist, not to mention the way her boobs have started drifting towards her armpits when she lays flat.

Thirty-nine! What on earth keeps possessing them to do this?

Jenny knows the answer. Of course she does. It's the same thing that makes her grin ear to ear when Dan texts her. It's Dan. It's lust. It's them stepping off the parenting rollercoaster and forgetting, even for the shortest of times, about all the things – the endless bloody jobs – they have to do. Living in the moment, having fun, that's what this is.

The warmth from the heaters has long gone and a shiver runs over Jenny's skin from the cold pushing into the car. Dan's fingers slide beneath her bra, his lips move to her nipple and for one delicious minute Jenny stops thinking about the wobbly bits and the car and the cold. Then the pain hits. A cramp in her leg.

Ouch! Ouch! Ouch!

Her foot is jammed underneath the driver's seat and she can't get it free. Not unless she can just . . . that's it, a little wriggle and . . . 'Shit,' she hisses, the cramp clutching at her calf muscle as she yanks her foot free, her knee jerking up and slamming into Dan's side.

'Ow.' Dan's cry is followed by a clonk against the roof of the car. The light springs into life, illuminating their half-naked bodies in an alarmingly bright look-what-we're-doing light.

'Turn that off,' Jenny yelps, scrambling to cover her chest.

'Sorry.' Dan flashes her a grin. 'My head hit the switch.'

Dan flicks the light off and reaches for her hand in the darkness. 'You OK?' he asks.

'Yeah, sorry. I got a cramp in my leg.' She wriggles upwards until they're sat beside each other.

The mood between them, the desire that drove them here and made them scramble into the back seats like a pair of horny teenagers, fizzles – flat lemonade at the end of a kids' party.

Jenny fumbles with her top in the darkness, her fingers running along the sides, searching for the label. Rebecca is a great babysitter. The boys have known her since forever and love her to pieces, but Jenny doesn't fancy trying to explain to the fifteen-year-old of her best friend, Nicola, why her top is on inside out again. The last time it happened Jenny had pretended she'd accidentally worn it inside out all night and not realised. Nicola had phoned the next morning in fits of laughter and there was no hiding the truth from her.

'Shall we . . . do you want to . . .' Dan says, his hand drifting up Jenny's thigh.

There's a pause, a beat where Jenny feels as though they're looking straight into each other's eyes in the darkness.

'The moment's gone, hasn't it?' he says before Jenny can form the words to tell him exactly that.

'I think so. This isn't working, is it?' She pulls a face.

'What?' Dan's voice is no longer soft but panicked. A second later the light is on again. 'What isn't working? Us? But I thought—'

'Not us,' she laughs, throwing her top at him and waving her hands in the air. 'This . . . sex in the back of your car. We have to find a better solution.'

He laughs too, rubbing a hand against the side of his face where a line of stubble has started to form. 'I thought you meant—'

'God, no! I just meant the car sex. I like having fun with you.'

Jenny reaches for her top and pulls it over her head, but not before she catches the strange expression on Dan's face.

'What?' she smiles.

'Nothing.' He shakes his head. 'I'm really sorry you couldn't come to mine tonight. I thought the girls . . .' He sighs. 'They were supposed to be sleeping over at their mum's.'

'Don't worry. I get it.' She really does. One hundred per cent.

'I had this perfect night planned out for us.'

'Really?' A grin spreads over her face.

'Oh yes. I cooked my famous beef bourguignon – from scratch. And bought us a very nice bottle of wine. I thought we'd go for a walk around Wellesley and stop at the pub for one of their Valentine's cocktails.'

'That would've been amazing.'

'I know.' He sighs again. 'It's been a crap date, hasn't it?'

'No, don't say that,' Jenny says, even though it has a bit, and yet she's still laughed, hasn't she? Still had fun, which is the whole point of this, of them.

Dan looks at her with knowing in his eyes.

'OK,' she admits. 'The Horse and Hound was a bit naff, but it's not your fault we had to change plans at the last minute and couldn't get a table for dinner for love nor money. I've still had a good time tonight.' It's the truth and yet Jenny feels a longing for her PJs and snuggling with the boys on the sofa, not caring if her mascara has smeared around her eyes or if her brown curls are untamed and pulled into a messy ponytail.

She has a sudden image of the boys on one side and Dan on the other, all squished up watching *Britain's Got Talent*, booing at Simon Cowell when he presses the red buzzer. She wonders what it would be like to have someone else to laugh with at home, to help do the million and one things she has do every day for the boys, even someone to help her do up her necklace, so she doesn't have to twist herself like a contortionist every time she needs to find the tiny sodding clasp.

She shakes the image away. That's not what this is. That's not where this is going. The very last thing Jenny needs is someone else in her life. Necklace contortion aside, she's fine on her own. Better than fine, actually.

A dull ache spreads over her chest. A hurt of another life. Paul and what he did. Never again will she let herself get hurt like that. There is only one person Jenny can one hundred per cent rely on to turn up every day – sleeves rolled up, big girl pants on – and that's herself, which is exactly how Jenny wants it to stay.

Sure, she likes Dan. A lot. More than she thought she would when they found themselves side by side at the school's adults'-only bonfire quiz night four months ago. Bunched on the single parents' table like they were contagious. Heaven forbid they get too close to the couples and spread their singlitus. When he stopped being a dad with a daughter in Ethan's class, and became Dan, lover of quizzes and drinker of unpronounceable European lagers. And made her laugh until she cried by whispering silly comments in her ear about the head teacher's inability to read out the quiz questions properly.

That first night in November they'd said goodbye in the darkness of the school car park, both a bit tipsy, huddling under Dan's umbrella from the misty cold drizzle while they waited for Jenny's taxi to arrive. And Dan had leaned in and kissed her. A proper, hands in hair, bodies pressing against each other, kiss. It had been unexpected but not as unexpected as the tingling pleasure that shot – no, burned – through her body. And all that was before she discovered that Dan understood her life. He totally got it. All the single parent stuff. Dan has the same baggage she does and there's something so reassuring about that.

Meeting him awakened something inside her, a realisation that it was OK, it was time in fact, to put herself first just a little bit. And that's what she's done, what they've both done. This thing with Dan isn't going anywhere. It won't be messy. She won't get hurt. It's a no-strings attached, leave the baggage at home thank you very much, kind of relationship.

Are you sure about that? a voice asks in her head. Nicola's voice, obviously. *What about the thing?*

Oh god, she promised herself she wouldn't think about the thing. She's never been the regular-as-clockwork type. It doesn't mean anything, just like it doesn't mean anything that her hair is a little greasy, the curls laying flatter than usual.

So yes, yes, she's quite sure.

'I can't believe we've been seeing each other for over three months and you've not seen my house,' Dan groans. 'I feel like a teenager again.'

'I will one day, when our days line up and both exes have the kids at the same time.'

'I hate going two weeks without seeing you properly,' he says, buttoning his shirt. 'Do the boys ever stay with your ex on a school night?'

'He leaves for work too early to get them to school.' There's more Jenny could say about Paul and her past. The words shove their way forward. Like how he's a good dad. The best really. Hands on from the very first exploding nappy. Always cheering the boys on from the sidelines of their football matches, clapping and proud no matter what the score. Like how laidback he is. Never stressing out when Ethan forgets to pack things or loses a shoe, which he does on a weirdly regular basis. Paul is so laidback, in fact, that he spent most of their marriage horizontal in bed with other women.

But Jenny keeps the words in. She doesn't want to taint her nights with Dan with the bitterness of her past, and she's pretty sure Dan feels the same because he only mentions his ex in passing when he's talking about the girls.

Dan nods. 'Ginger is the same.'

They fall silent and Jenny hears an owl hooting in the distance. She shivers again. It's too cold to be sat here like this.

'Jenny,' Dan says, squeezing her hand. 'Why don't you and the boys come over for Sunday lunch this weekend? That way you can all see the house and I can finally cook something for you.'

'What?' She feels the surprise register on her face. 'Are you serious?' He can't be, she decides, her heart thumping in her chest.

He laughs and she wonders if he's nervous too. Then he shrugs. 'It's only a lunch. I want to spend more time with you, and I want to be able to do it without feeling like I'm ditching the girls. It's the next step, isn't it? Otherwise, what are we doing?'

'Having fun, I thought.' An itchy panic crawls over her chest. He can't be serious. This was not part of the plan.

'Yeah, we are. But why can't we keep having fun and have a lunch with the kids?'

9

'Can I . . . do you mind if I think about it?' she asks, her voice sounding so cautious, so slow after Dan's. 'For the boys, I mean. It would be a big deal for them. Can I let you know tomorrow?' She cringes, knowing this isn't the answer he wants to hear.

'Of course that's fine. Tomorrow, or Sunday morning even. I only need to know how many potatoes to peel.'

Jenny looks into Dan's eyes for any sign of annoyance, but all she sees is that warmth, that 'I get you, Jenny Travis' look he has, and Jenny can't stop the smile from stretching across her face. It's the goofy one that makes her look a bit mad, but, god, this man!

And just for a second she feels the simplicity of it, of them. Dan likes her and she likes him. And they want to spend more time together. The feeling – sugar-fuelled butterflies break-dancing in her stomach – is a relic from a time so long ago, Jenny can't even remember, but it's there and just for that one second she lets it stay.

Then the boys crash into her thoughts. Jack. Precious, sensitive eleven-year-old Jack who cares too much about making others happy, who worries about every little tiny thing from where the lost socks have gone, to whether the icebergs really will melt one day. And Ethan, who is eight and Jenny's tornado of energy and cheekiness. She thinks of them in bed, begging Rebecca for one more story, and Jenny knows there is nothing simple about this.

'There's no pressure, Jenny,' Dan whispers, brushing a curl away from her face. 'It doesn't have to be a big thing. It's just a lunch.' His lips find hers and a spark shoots through Jenny's body. She reaches up to turn off the light and this time there is no cramp or discomfort, there is only Dan.

Chapter 2

Dan

Disaster! That's the word that springs into Dan's mind as he watches Jenny walk up the path to her front door. That date was an absolute disaster. Or as Amelia likes to say in the voice of Craig Revel Horwood from *Strictly Come Dancing*, 'a disa-rrr-ster, darling,' and yet he's smiling, isn't he? Grinning even. Like Bryony does when a chocolate fudge sundae with a double shot of chocolate sauce is placed in front of her.

Jenny, Jenny, Jenny. He can't get her out of his head. Man, she's beautiful. That hair. Soft, zany curls that tickle her shoulders until she swishes it away or up into a bundle on top of her head. Huge brown eyes and a smile that lights him up inside. She is beautiful and kind and funny, and yet Dan is quite sure Jenny is utterly clueless to all of this.

With a final wave, Jenny disappears into the house and Dan pulls away, driving past the glowing red lights of the twenty-four-hour garage on the corner. Red roses sit in tubs on the forecourt, wilting in the fumes from the petrol.

The first drops of sleet patter on his windscreen and he flicks on the wipers.

All he wanted was one perfect date with Jenny on Valentine's Day, to show Jenny his house and take a tiny shuffle forward in their relationship. But he didn't know how to say that to her and now he's put his foot in it and suggested a lunch with the kids, which he's really not sure they're ready for. Except the invite is out there now. He can't exactly take it back.

He should've known Ginger would throw an almighty spanner in the works, should've known her offer to have the girls for a sleepover was exactly that – an offer and nothing more.

There is a special kind of disappointment – a jaw-clenching, teeth-grinding anger – that rises up when someone lets down your kids. He always thought he could protect the girls from anything, but he was wrong. He can't stop them being hurt when someone they love disappoints them.

Ginger was late to collect them, of course. Pulling into the driveway in her soft-top Fiat with a breezy, 'the traffic was crap' just as Bryony's bottom lip was wobbling and she was clinging to Dan's side, looking up at him with wide-eyed expectancy as though he had a magical power to fix everything. Everything except Ginger, who leaped from the car, arms open wide for the girls to rush into, filling them with promises of Pizza Hut and a midnight feast.

How many more promises are you going to break, Ginger?

The question leaves a bitter taste in Dan's mouth as he picks up speed on the main road. The turning for Wellesley comes into view and Dan flicks on the indicator. He spots the church tower in the distance – the sign he's almost home. The grey stone clock tower is lit in a yellow glow like a beacon against the night sky.

Two hours Ginger had the girls for. Two hours before she was pulling back into the driveway with an exasperated eyeroll. 'Change of plan,' she said when Dan opened the door. 'The girls have decided not to stay with me.'

Dan looked down at Bryony's tear-streaked face and Amelia's slumped shoulders, and knew, he just knew, there was another side to this story.

'They decided that, did they?' Dan asked when Amelia and Bryony were lugging their overnight bags back to their bedrooms.

'Of course.'

'And you didn't say anything to convince them?'

She sighed, running a hand through her blonde hair. Was it him or had it grown ten centimetres in the week since he'd last seen her? 'Of course not. I simply mentioned the burglaries we've had in my apartment building. I wanted them to be careful and not leave their things lying around. I had no idea Bryony was going to get so scared.'

She's seven years old. Of course she was scared. Dan clenched his jaw and kept the comment in along with the questions jumping like popping candy in his mind. *Didn't you try to convince them? Didn't you want them to sleep over?*

Ginger strolled up the three steps to the front porch and leaned against the white door frame, plucking at a leaf of ivy from the bush that keeps threatening to take over the house. 'Before you say anything,' she said, holding her hands up in an 'I come in peace' gesture, 'I know you've got plans tonight. The girls told me. I'll stay here and babysit while you go out.'

I don't think it's called babysitting when it's your own kids. It was a struggle to keep the comment in, but he did. It's part of their unspoken deal – don't argue, don't react, don't scrape beneath the surface.

Dan drives through the narrow country lanes, slowing the car to a crawl as he weaves through Wellesley's sleepy high street. The awnings of the dark shop fronts flap in the wind. Soft orange light spills from the pub on the corner and Dan imagines the hum of voices bouncing around the oak beams, the wood floors, the village dad crowd supping their craft beers that Dan has never felt part of. Probably because he's taught most of their kids over the years.

Dan winds down the window, letting in the cold air so he can breathe the smell of the firewood from the chimneys. He turns the final corner into the cul-de-sac, his mood plummeting with the thought of facing Ginger again.

He stares up at the house as he kills the engine. It's big – four bedrooms, five if you count his dad's old study in the loft, but Dan never does. It still doesn't feel like his, really – the house. Even with the new kitchen installed and the wall he knocked through into the dining room. Even ripping up the carpets downstairs and restoring the wooden floors didn't help make it feel like it was their house – his and the girls. Fresh paint and new bathrooms aren't going to change the fact that this will always be his parents' house, and the only reason he can afford to live here is because both his parents died. That thought is a constant hurt that haunts him every damn day.

Their unwavering rock of love and support; he'd felt his whole life disappear almost overnight, it felt. Losing his parents changed something inside of him he can't explain. One, two, three years later and the loss is still a burden of hurt and sadness threatening to engulf him.

It happened the year after Ginger left, when Dan was still drowning in a thick swamp of single parenthood and teaching full time. His dad went first – heart attack in the Frozen aisle of Tesco, clutching at the last of the two-for-one arctic rolls. His mum followed a month later from a stroke. Christ, he misses them.

Dan unlocks the front door, closing it carefully behind him so not to wake the girls. He finds Ginger stretched out on the sofa in the living room, bare feet tucked under a cushion as she swipes through her phone.

The image is jarring and, for one single moment, one fleeting second, an old familiarity wraps itself around him and he could almost believe that this is the woman who stood by his side on a beach in Barbados when they promised to love each other for ever. The woman who gave birth to two bright, wonderful girls who are, and will always be, the centre of his universe. The woman who slept on a tiny stretch of floor in-between the girls' beds for a week when they were ill with chicken pox, back when they were living on top of each other in the poky terrace house on the other side of the village. A happy family, or so he'd thought.

But this person in skinny jeans and a top that clings to every curve is not his wife. This person before him is his ex-wife, and those two people are not the same. This person walked away from him, from their beautiful girls, something he's never been able to understand.

'Hey.' Ginger stretches her arms above her head as he steps into the living room. 'How was your night?'

'Fine, thanks.'

'I like what you've done with the bathrooms,' she says. 'A touch too white for my liking, but a hundred times better than the beige your parents had. It's a nice house.'

'Thanks,' he says.

'The girls are lucky to live here now.'

Dan frowns. How the hell does Ginger do that – line up just the right words to use, the exact tone so it lands like a compliment and yet somehow isn't? He looks at her. Really looks at her. Past the make-up and the hair, and stares into her eyes. Was there a note of bitterness in her tone? Blame, even? As if he wouldn't move back to the terrace in a heartbeat if it meant his parents were still alive, still showering the girls with the love and attention their own mother rarely gives them.

Would things have been different for Ginger if this had been their house from the start? Dan doubts it. Ginger would still have missed Ipswich and her old life, the one she had before Amelia was born and they'd moved back to the village where he grew up because it was such a nice place to raise a family.

Sometimes he wonders if moving away from Ipswich was the very first nail in the coffin of his marriage. Other times, he rakes over the memories of their time together and thinks it was doomed from the start.

For a moment, the weight of all the questions he's never asked, the truths they've never spoken to each other, hang in the air between them. Dan nudges it away. What good will dredging up the past do? Ginger left four years ago. Talking about it now will only lead to arguments and accusations, and he can't allow that. He has to stay on good terms with Ginger for the sake of the girls.

'Where did you go tonight?' Ginger asks.

'Just for a few drinks in the Hound and Horses,' Dan replies, dropping into the armchair on the opposite side of the room. He wants Ginger to leave now. He wants to go to bed. It's a full morning of dance classes tomorrow that Ginger was supposed to be taking Bryony to.

Ginger laughs. 'Bloody hell, Dan. You know how to treat your dates, don't you?'

His jaw tenses. 'It wasn't exactly the evening I had planned.'

'Ah.' Ginger has the decency to look sheepish. 'Yes, I saw the casserole. I didn't realise you had plans to stay in. So who were you trying to impress?' Ginger's eyes are sparkling with mischief, but they're questioning too as they stare into his.

Dan thinks about being vague, sticking to their deal to stay out of each other's lives. It isn't any of Ginger's business what he does or who he sees, but then he checks himself. His first reaction to anything Ginger says or does is generally never the one that will help the girls maintain a relationship with their mother.

'Her name is Jenny. She has a son in Bryony's class.'

Ginger's lips stretch into a smirk. 'I'm surprised it took you so long. I thought you'd have one of those PTA busy-bodies moved in by now, doing your cooking and cleaning, washing your pants for you. A girlfriend is cheaper than hiring help, eh?' she laughs.

A hot lava thrashes through his veins. Heat burns his face. 'I've not dated anyone since you walked out four years ago, and you know that.' The words, the anger, fire out before he can stop them. 'I don't comment on the company you keep, and I'd appreciate it if you didn't comment on mine.'

The smile slides from Ginger's face. 'I'm sorry. It was a stupid joke. I'm glad you've met someone, Dan. I hope you'll both be happy.'

Like I wasn't. Dan fills in the words Ginger doesn't say.

She glances at her watch. 'I'd better go. I'm meeting some friends in town.'

'It's gone ten.'

'Still early then,' she grins, slipping her arms into a cut-off denim jacket that looks like something Amelia should be wearing.

'How did you arrange to go out if you thought the girls were sleeping over?' *Unless that was never the plan,* Dan thinks. *Unless she knew all along that the girls wouldn't be staying. But not even Ginger would be that cruel, would she?*

17

'It's Friday night. There are always people out.' She scoops up her bag and moves towards the door.

'Ginger, hang on. The person I'm dating – Jenny – I've asked her to meet the girls. Just as friends. It's not serious or anything yet.' The yet surprises him. Does he think it will be serious one day? He enjoys spending time with Jenny, but they both agreed to keep it light.

'Fine.' Another shrug from Ginger. 'I really need to go. And you probably want to say goodnight to the girls.'

'Say goodnight? Are they still awake?'

'Sure. I said they could play on the tablet together in Amelia's room until you got back. I knew you wouldn't be late.'

She strides out the door, calling a 'Bye, girls,' as she leaves.

Not late? he wants to shout after her. *It's hours past their bedtime. Bryony is seven years old. She has an hour of ballet followed by an hour of tap tomorrow morning. They need to be out the door by 8.30am. Of course it's late!*

He heads for the stairs, squashing down the anger. He can't let the girls pick up on his mood.

Dan opens the door to Amelia's bedroom. It's dark, but from the light in the hall he can see the two forms of his sleeping daughters, side by side in Amelia's bed, the tablet still resting between them.

Dan moves the tablet before lifting Bryony into his arms and carrying her to her room.

'Nighty-nighty, Daddy,' Bryony mumbles, her eyes still closed.

'Sleep tight-y,' he whispers in her ear. 'Don't let the bed bugs . . .'

'Bite-y,' she says, finishing the rhyme they say to each other every night.

As Dan climbs into bed he thinks about Jenny and the invite to lunch, turning it over in his head. Is it too soon? Maybe.

Maybe Jenny will cancel and he won't have to worry that he's made a mistake.

Chapter 3

Jenny

'Right,' Jenny says, herding the boys through the front door, the three of them squashing together in the narrow hallway to hang up their coats on the hooks. It's just as cold as the grey outside and Jenny silently curses the old boiler and her landlady, Mrs Hannigan, who seems as likely to book an engineer as Jenny is to book a five-star cruise around the Caribbean.

'Football kits straight in the washing machine, please. Jack, have a shower. Ethan, get changed and feed Hulk before he has guinea pig food rage, and I'll make us a quick lunch.' Before she has full-blown spent-all-morning-running-around on-half-a-bowl-of-Ethan's-leftover-Rice-Krispies food rage.

'Oh, Muuuum,' Jack says, dragging out the final word in the same way Ethan drags his feet at bedtime. 'Do I have to have a shower? Ethan isn't.'

Jenny glances at Jack's eleven-year-old face, glowing red after an hour of football training. His brown hair is damp at the edges and there's a sheen of sweat on his frowning forehead.

'Yes, you do. When you get older, you sweat more and that sweat starts to smell. Do you want to be known as the smelly boy when you go to senior school in September?' The moment the words are out Jenny wishes she could snatch them back. Jack's face takes on a deer in the head-lights fear and she knows he's thinking the same thought as she is – how the hell is he going to cope at senior school? As her anxiety twists into nausea, Jenny pastes on a smile and gives Jack her best 'you'll be fine' hug.

'I'm going to feed Hulk now, Mummy,' Ethan says then, hurrying down the hall and leaving a trail of damp sock prints across the pale laminate.

'Plus,' Jenny says, 'you and Ethan are going to a party in . . .' She checks her watch. 'Less than an hour, so go go go, I need to make you a quick lunch.'

'But it's a football party. I'll be sweating there too. So why does it matter if I smell?'

'It matters. Stop arguing and get in the shower.'

A moment passes between them. A mini stand-off. Jack says nothing, but he's thinking about it. Jenny can see it in his eyes, can almost hear the retaliation. Then his face softens, and he sighs. 'Fine.'

Her eldest son has always been a pleaser. Even when he was three years old, Jack would be at Jenny's feet with a duster while she cleaned, or fetched toys for Ethan when he cried. She knows it's connected to the worrying, the fear of being told off or letting someone down, and while she's never had to tell Jack two, three, ten times to do anything the way she does with Ethan, she wishes he'd relax a little, be more carefree.

'By the time you're washed and dressed, lunch will be ready.' Jenny nods to the stairs. And then she needs to talk to the boys about Dan's offer of lunch, and then Finley's mum will be here to collect the boys for the party . . . and then she needs to do the thing. Nervous energy froths – a fizzy bath bomb – inside her. At least Nicola is popping over for moral support, whatever that means.

Lunch first, Jen. Get the boys out of the way. And she's got to wrap the sodding presents for the party. Jenny closes her eyes. She has one hundred and twenty cupcakes in the kitchen that need to be iced this afternoon too. A last-minute wedding anniversary order that someone is collecting at three o'clock. She tries not to think about how easily that money has gone. Petrol for her dilapidated Ford Fiesta, birthday presents for the party, the test (when did they get so expensive anyway?) – and poof, it's gone. The worst kind of magic trick.

And that's before she's even thought about the small fortune she spent on Christmas a few months ago, not to mention the extra cost of paying Rebecca to babysit, and buying some much-needed new underwear. Until her third date with Dan, Jenny spent most days wearing a sports bra and her comfortable but hideously unsexy post baby knickers. Why is it the smaller the knickers, the higher the price? Kylie Minogue's tiny bottom must cost her an absolute fortune.

Jack disappears, feet hammering on the stairs with the same force as an elephant running up them and Jenny steps into the kitchen. It's small and narrow, like the rest of their rented house. There's a sink and a wooden back door at one end that sticks in the winter, and a table and chairs at the other. Sure, it's small and the boys have to share a room and the kitchen tap drips and the boiler rarely works and the kitchen cupboard by the fridge keeps falling off its hinges, but it's home and a home she can afford at that.

Mortan is nowhere near as nice as Wellesley where Dan lives and the boys go to school. Mortan is not a tourist spot so much as a petrol station and a mini supermarket that someone in the sixties decided to build a load of houses around and call a village. But there's a park too and it's quieter than living in town, and only a ten-minute drive to school, twenty minutes to Paul's. Besides, Nicola lives just around the corner and Jenny loves that they're in and out of each other's houses now, just like they were when they were kids.

The jittery nerves return as Jenny tips two tins of baked beans into a saucepan and runs through her to-do list again, adding a food order to her endless jobs. Where is the live in the moment, have fun, don't think about the thing feeling she had last night? Smothered, she decides. Crushed under the weight of the Saturday morning routine and standing in the middle of a boggy field, the wind and rain pummelling her face and knotting her hair so she comes home looking more like an extra in *Fraggle Rock* than anything resembling a human.

Maybe she should wait another week. Until she's properly late. The thought elbows its way into her mind, settling itself between the school uniforms she really must put into wash and the cake order she has to finish.

Five minutes later, Jack wanders into the kitchen, odd socks on his feet, hair slick against his head and dripping onto his t-shirt. She spots a smudge of mud on his knee and rolls her eyes.

'Is lunch ready? I'm starving.'

'Hey, Jack, I really have to tell you about this crazy new invention called a towel,' Jenny says with a smile just as the toaster pops. 'It's madness. Honestly, you wouldn't believe what it can do. You rub it on wet skin, hair, anything, and it dries it. Actually dries it.'

'Ha ha.' Jack pulls a face, sticking his tongue out at Jenny.

'Where's Ethan?' she asks.

Without bothering to turn his head or take a step away from Jenny, Jack opens his mouth and hollers for his brother. She winces at the noise.

'I'm here,' Ethan says, appearing at the back door.

'Ethan, what have you been doing? You should be changed by now. Up you go, now please. And hurry up, lunch is ready.'

'I'm so hungry.' Ethan clutches his stomach and scrunches his eyes shut. 'Can I change after lunch?'

'Go on, Mum,' Jack pleads. 'Ethan can change in a minute.'

'Fine, but wash your hands and don't rub the dried mud off the clothes.' She concedes too soon as usual. Bending her own rules like they knew she would. But Jack could have been grumpy then, pointing out the unfairness of his shower when Ethan hasn't even changed, and he didn't.

Both boys are the spit of Paul, as Nicola likes to say. If Paul had Jenny's shock of brown curls and hadn't lost ninety per cent of his hair by the age of twenty-one, anyway. But whereas Ethan lives in his own bubble of football and Hulk and playing tag with his friends, like most kids his age, Jack has an awareness of others which is more than just being a few years older. It's a quiet thoughtfulness that takes Jenny's breath away sometimes.

'What are we doing tomorrow, Mum?' Jack asks when they're all at the table. 'Can I invite Finley over?'

'Um . . . maybe.' Jenny slides the plates of food in front of them. 'There was something I wanted to run by you actually, about tomorrow.' She swallows hard. Testing the water, that's all this is. She's not said yes yet.

'Are we going on holiday?' Jack asks.

'What?' Jenny frowns. The questions the boys ask never cease to amaze her. As if they'd be going on holiday tomorrow.

'Are we?' Ethan bounces in his chair, spilling a forkful of baked beans onto the floor. 'Can we go to Centre Parcs? Like when Dad took us last year.'

'It's not a holiday,' Jenny says quickly before the idea can settle in their heads. 'And if it was, it wouldn't be Center Parcs.' *Not unless a money tree suddenly shoots up in the garden.*

'What then?' Jack asks.

Jenny shoves a fork full of beans in her mouth, buying herself time.

'Are we going to see Uncle Peter in Southend?' Ethan asks. 'Can we go to the fairground there? I bet I'm tall enough for all the rides now.'

'Don't be an idiot.' Jack nudges his brother gently. 'The fairground is closed. It's winter.'

Ethan laughs, the noise hyena-like. 'Oh yeah.'

'Don't call your brother an idiot,' Jenny says, the words automatic, said a thousand times at least, and a thousand more no doubt.

'Is it a trip to Legoland?' Ethan mumbles through a mouth full of lunch.

'No, it's not that. It's . . . look, you know Bryony Walkers's dad?' Jenny says before Ethan and Jack drag her veering into a conversation about holidays she can't afford.

'Yeah,' Ethan nods. 'Bryony is in my class.'

'Well . . .' She takes a deep breath. 'He's invited us for lunch at his house tomorrow.'

'I wonder if the whole class are going,' Ethan says at the exact moment that Jack asks, 'Why?'

'It's just going to be us.' Jenny looks from Ethan to Jack and back again. 'It's because . . . because Dan, we . . . we met at the quiz night. You remember me telling you that and we—'

Ethan fidgets again, bouncing. Ants in his pants, Paul always says. Ethan's knife clatters to the floor. 'Is he your boyfriend?' he asks as he scoots under the table to fetch the fallen cutlery.

'Er . . . we're just friends,' Jenny says, regretting the lie the moment it leaves her mouth, but she doesn't feel able to use the word 'boyfriend'. *Gah! This is awful.* Jenny can almost hear the hiss of the can of worms she's opening.

'Will Bryony be at the lunch?' Ethan's head appears then his body as he slides worm-like onto his chair. 'We play together sometimes when I don't want to play football. She's got a guinea pig too, although hers is a girl and everyone knows girl guinea pigs can't do as many cool things as boy guinea pigs.' Ethan's words come out a mocking sing-song.

'I'm quite sure girl guinea pigs can do just as much as boy guinea pigs,' Jenny replies, wanting to stay on topic but unable to let Ethan's comment go. She will raise two feminists if it kills her.

'And yes, both of his daughters will be there. Amelia is the year above you, Jack. She's already at the senior school. I just wanted to see how you felt about a lunch. We don't have to go if you don't want to?'

'So no one else from school will be there? No one from my class?' Jack asks. He's still eating but his eyes are narrowed, his face set in concentration.

'No, just us,' she says, wishing there was a manual for this kind of thing. There probably is. She'll google it later and no doubt she'll find a parenting guide, a how to introduce your new sort-of, but not quite, boyfriend to your children.

'Are they going to live with us?' Jack asks, and Jenny can tell he's thinking of Paul moving into Lilly's house last year with Cookie and Crumble – Lilly's two beige pugs that Ethan and Jack love so much.

Jenny laughs, the sound falling flat as she prods a fork at her half-eaten slice of soggy toast. Her appetite disappears.

'No. Definitely not. This is just a lunch,' Jenny says, gulping back a mouthful of water.

The doorbell rings and a split second later the door flies open. 'Only me,' comes Nicola's voice from the hall.

'We're in the kitchen!' Jenny shouts.

'Hello,' Nicola calls, breezing into the kitchen with the giant handbag she takes everywhere. It knocks against a pot of felt tip pens on the counter, sending them toppling over and rolling to the floor. 'Oops. At least it wasn't a wine bottle this time.' Nicola scoops her black bobbed hair behind her ears and winks at Jenny just like she's done a thousand times before, ever since that first wink across the classroom in year seven Geography when Mrs Greggs caught them both daydreaming. They've been best friends ever since.

'Blimey, it's cold in here. I've brought extra icing sugar,' Nicola says as she scoops up the pens. 'And I know we said one-ish, but Ryan is watching the footie and Rebecca has gone into town with her friends and I had nothing to do. Literally nothing.'

Jenny grins at her friend and wonders what 'nothing to do' feels like and if she'll ever get to that point in her life.

'Aunty Nicola,' Ethan says, scraping the last of his food from the plate. 'There's a girl in my class called Bryony. She lives with her dad, not her mum like us, and we're going to their house for lunch tomorrow.'

'Are you now?' Nicola leans over, kissing both boys on the tops of their heads.

Ethan nods. 'Yes. Mum says Bryony's dad is not her boyfriend but Mr Adams and Miss Hatton said they weren't boyfriend and girlfriend at school for ages and ages even though we always asked them, and then they got married in the summer so they were.'

'Really?' Nicola grins, winking at Jenny.

'We were only talking about going for lunch,' Jenny says. 'If you're not sure then—'

'I want to go,' Ethan says.

'Jack, what do you think?' Jenny asks.

Jack shrugs. 'It's OK, I guess.'

She studies Jack's face. Is he just saying it's OK to make her happy? Does he hate the idea? When did Jack become so hard to read?

'Look, it's a stupid idea, let's—' Her words stop short as the doorbell trills again.

'Clare's early.' *Shit!* Jenny leaps up, snatching up the wrapping paper and pushing it at Nicola. 'Wrap these. Jack, shoes on. Ethan, run, and I mean run, upstairs and get changed. Finley's mum is here to take you to the party. Go.'

Three minutes later, in a flurry of Sellotape and scribbled gift tags, and the fastest outfit change known to man that sees Ethan leaving the house with his t-shirt on back to front, the boys pile into the pack of Clare's car and are gone.

Jenny leans against the front door and closes her eyes, the silence ringing in her ears. How is it only 12.30? She feels like she's run a marathon. At least she has three hours of peace to ice the cakes and tick everything from her to-do list before she has to pick up the boys.

'Are you ready, then?' Nicola's voice calls from the kitchen.

'Actually, I was thinking, I'm going to leave it another week. There's really no way it can have happened. I'm just—'

'In denial about being pregnant?' Nicola appears in the hall, one eyebrow cocked. 'You are doing the test and then you'll know and can stop freaking out.'

'When have you ever known me to freak out?' Jenny pulls a face.

'On the outside, never. You have your shit together more than anyone else I know, but inside?' Another cocked eyebrow and Jenny closes her eyes, pressing her hands to her face. There is no way she is going to win this argument with Nicola.

'Come on then.'

Chapter 4

Dan

Dan opens the washing machine and winces at the sharp twinge snaking across his stomach.

What the hell possessed him to do a hundred sit-ups yesterday?

The answer is obvious – Jenny. Or, more accurately, the lie Dan told Jenny on their first date when he'd been trying to impress her. 'I try to keep fit. Fifty sit-ups and fifty press-ups every morning, and two runs every week.'

Does it count as a lie if he means to do it? Would do it in fact if something didn't always get in the way. Like last week, when he was ten sit-ups in before Bryony screamed the house down because Poppy had jumped out of her arms and was hiding under the summer house, and he ditched the exercise to become chief guinea pig rescuer.

He's still looking good for forty-five, isn't he? He still has all of his hair, and he plays football with the old team on Sunday mornings when the weather is nice and the girls don't mind playing in the playground for an hour. It's not quite the vicious, sweat-inducing dive into every tackle game it used to be, but they come off the pitch feeling good. It's been a while since they played in matches though. After that jibe from the Clacton team about joining a walking football league: 18–0 they lost that day. The score and the comment still smart.

Dan pushes in the bedding, squeezing in an extra towel he knows doesn't really fit before forcing the door shut anyway and turning it on.

The radio is playing in the kitchen and Dan sings along, murdering the verses to Adele's 'Hello' as he cleans the kitchen, rubbing at a smudge of butter that dropped from the knife Amelia used to make toast yesterday and has dried a hard yellow on one of the cupboard doors.

Dan runs a cloth across the worktop and surveys the kitchen, thinking of Jenny. He wants Jenny to admire the modern white cupboards, the dark worktops. There's an island in the middle where they eat breakfast and across the room where the dining room used to be is a long table and a sofa facing the patio door and the garden. The sofa is still piled with the year ten books he needs to mark.

Dan's eyes pull to the window as though he expects to see his dad in the garden wearing his white bobble hat, digging or weeding, or doing one of the thousand jobs that always needs doing.

But the garden is empty.

Of course it is, mate.

A sadness sweeps over him. He bites down on his bottom lip. His fingers itch to pick up the phone and call his parents. They'd always come on the phone together, his mum from a handset in the kitchen and his dad from the phone in his study, so they could speak to him together, to hear his news. Even if he was just calling to say hi, they'd both pick up.

He wishes they were at the end of the phone right now so he could tell them about the girls. How Amelia has settled well into senior school. Top sets for everything, but he isn't sure she's happy. He passes her in the corridor sometimes between classes and her head is down, her face

31

unsmiling. Maybe it's just the uncoolness of seeing her dad in school every day, but he worries it's more. And how Bryony no longer clings to his legs in the playground when he drops her to school, only showing that wobble before or after a visit with Ginger.

He sighs and turns back to the kitchen.

Grief is love that has nowhere to go. Dan read that on a Facebook post once, all swirly letters written over a cheesy image of two people hugging, but the words stuck.

'Dad?' Amelia's voice carries through the house.

'Yeah?' Dan coughs, sweeping the sadness away, hiding it under a flimsy rug until the next time it slips out.

'Can I go to Chelsea's house?'

'Do you think you can come into the same room as me if you want to ask a question?'

He catches the loud sigh and footsteps pounding the stairs.

A moment later, Amelia appears in the kitchen doorway, breathless, her expression urgent. Her hands are hidden inside the sleeves of a black Hype hoody – a Christmas present she's worn after school and every weekend since. 'So, can I?'

'When?'

'Now.' She nods her head for emphasis.

'Has she invited you?'

'Yeah. Course. Vicki is going too.'

'How long for?'

She shrugs. 'She didn't say.'

'What did she say?'

His question is met with an eyeroll. Amelia pulls out her phone from the back pocket of her jeans, seeming so much older than twelve. Twelve. It still seems too young for a phone, but he knows from teaching that they all have phones when they go to senior school. And Amelia wanted to be able to text her mum too, which Dan couldn't stand in the way of.

'Do you want to come over to mine this afternoon? Vikki is coming too,' Amelia says, reading out the text.

Dan rubs at the stubble on his face, feeling the overwhelming sense of new territory he's wading into. 'Should I call Chelsea's mum?'

'Dad, no.' Indignation rings in Amelia's tone. He feels like he's just suggested accompanying her to a disco. 'Can you take me?'

'Where does Chelsea live?'

'I've told you. She lives in Great Wellham.'

'OK. Give me ten minutes.'

Amelia's face falls.

'Two minutes? Can you let me put a jumper on and some socks at least? It's freezing outside.'

'Two minutes.' She grins before tapping out a message on her phone.

'Bry?' Dan calls into the living room. 'We need to pop out and drop Amelia at a friend's house. Get some shoes on please.'

'Can we get me my new school shoes while we're out?' Bryony shouts back.

School shoes. *Shit.* He'd meant to order some online. Her old shoes are only five months old. He bought them at the start of the new school year, but her toes are already pressing at the ends and she needs a new pair.

Dan pictures Clark's on a Saturday afternoon. All those parents. The sodding ticket system. And there he was thinking they were having a quiet afternoon.

'Vikki's mum says she'll drop me back before dinner,' Amelia says, and then, 'are we going?'

33

Dan nods. 'Bry, get a pair of school socks and we'll pop into town.' Pop? Ha! 'Amelia, call me if you want collecting earlier or if anything changes, please.'

'Sure.'

It's only when they're walking to the car that Dan remembers the reason he wanted a quiet afternoon with the girls. He wanted them relaxed and happy when he told them about Jenny and the boys coming for lunch. And now they're rushing and Amelia is going to be out all afternoon.

Maybe it's better this way, he thinks. It's just like he told Jenny. Lunch. No big deal.

'Girls?'

They turn to face him as they reach the car.

'Um . . . Lunch tomorrow. I've invited someone.'

'Who?' Amelia asks, her eyes narrowing.

'Ethan and Jack's mum, Jenny. We've been . . . dating.'

'Gross,' Amelia replies, looking back at her phone.

'Jack and Ethan are coming too, of course.'

'Yay,' Bryony says. 'Ethan is so funny. He put a pea up his nose in reception and his mum had to take him to the doctor to get it removed.'

'Right.' Dan makes a face at Amelia, expecting her to laugh, but she's still looking at her phone. 'Amelia, is this alright with you?'

'Yeah. Can we go now?'

And it's done and it's fine. Good, even. Dan smiles as he climbs into the car, pushing away his own nerves and thinking how good it feels to know he's seeing Jenny tomorrow. He's glad he suggested it now. It's only a lunch. What can possibly go wrong in one afternoon?

Chapter 5

Jenny

With Nicola's hand on her back, Jenny steps into the tiny downstairs toilet, aware that if there was even a smidgen of extra space in the room, which she's sure started out in life as a cupboard, then Nicola would be pushing her way in too, offering to hold Jenny's hand, or the stick itself.

Jenny slides the lock across and smirks at a memory of lying on the floor in Nicola's bedroom, her friend beside her, the pair of them sniggering over *More* magazine's Position of the Fortnight. God, they loved that magazine. It felt like a rite of passage into a world of relationships and adulthood they didn't have the first clue about.

Focus, Jen. It's Nicola's voice, and for a moment Jenny doesn't know if it's from inside her head or outside the door.

'Are you peeing? I can't hear peeing.' Nicola raps on the door. 'Stop dilly-dallying.'

'This is so stupid,' Jenny calls back, shimmying down her jeans and unwrapping the plastic cover for the pregnancy test. 'We always use condoms.' But she sits on the toilet anyway and positions the stick between her legs. She never thought she'd be doing this again. Not ever!

She waits a beat. Nothing happens.

Come on, relax.

With a long sigh, Jenny feels the first trickling and begins the surreal game of catch the pee on the stick.

A minute later, Jenny unlocks the toilet door and almost laughs at the expectant look on Nicola's face.

'Why do you look so excited?' Jenny gives a shaky smile. Her gaze goes to the sink and the stick waiting to be read. She forces herself not to look. Two more minutes.

'Are you kidding? This is the most excitement I've had since Tom Hardy started reading Bedtime Stories on Cbeebies.'

'Isn't Rebecca ten years too old for that?'

Nicola laughs. 'Oh my god yes, but I am most definitely not too old.'

They fall silent. Nicola glances at the test. 'Are you going to look?'

Jenny swallows hard and turns, the room spinning with her. The only sound is the thud, thud, thud of her heartbeat banging in her ears. It's like a car crash by the side of the road. She doesn't want to look, and yet she can't help it. Her eyes are moving down the wall, past the tap, around the sink.

Thud, thud, thud.

She stops breathing.

Thud, thud, thud.

Then it's there, right in front of her. Pregnant. Jenny feels her entire life tumble downwards – a Jenga tower crashing to the floor.

'And?' Nicola asks.

'I'm pregnant,' she whispers. Her voice is flat and the complete opposite to the panic charging through her.

Nicola nods. No jokes or quips now. This is serious. 'How do you feel?'

'Er . . .' Jenny draws in a shaky breath. 'Shocked. And old. Really old. I'm too old for this.'

'Oh come on,' Nicola soothes. 'Loads of women have children into their forties now. If anything, you were just young the first time around. Are you going to—'

'Keep it? Yes.' A lump forms in her throat and easy tears fall down her cheeks. There is no doubt. 'I couldn't not. But the boys,' Jenny cries. 'Ethan will take it in his stride, but Jack will freak out. You know how he gets with change. He'll worry constantly. He'll think . . . he'll worry I won't love him as much.' She gulps back the fear threatening to overtake her.

'Jen, you're crying. What the hell? You never cry. You didn't even cry in *Paddington 2* when Aunt Lucy arrived, you heartless bitch.'

Jenny laugh-cries, the noise ending in a sobbed hiccup. 'I can't . . . I just can't believe it. It's like I've rolled a double one and landed on the go back to the start square.' She pauses, raking a hand through her hair. 'I mean, I've been there, done that and got the stretch marks, haven't I? Twice. I have two wonderful, amazing children to show for it. Jack is going to senior school in September. I can't start all over again now. I can't. I'm forty in August, for Christ's sake.'

'Why don't you go and sit down on the sofa. I'll make us a coffee.'

Jenny shakes her head. 'Sit – yes, but in the kitchen. I still have to ice the cakes.' And put the washing on and collect the boys from the party. And she's pregnant with Dan's baby. This really, really can't be happening.

This wasn't the plan! The one time, the first time in fact, in seven years since she kicked Paul out, that she tries to grab a little adult time, a little fun, to feel like a woman

37

again, a human being even, and suddenly no-strings attached has become a knotted mess she can't begin to untangle.

They fall into an easy silence as Jenny mixes the first batch of butter cream icing into silky perfection and Nicola makes two cups of coffee. Decaf for Jenny. She feels a sudden pang for the caffeine and wine she can no longer have.

Jenny makes a list in her head of things she needs to do:

- Book a midwife appointment
- Phone Mrs Hannigan about the boiler again
- Create more Facebook Adverts for Cake-i-licious
- Start a savings pot for when she won't be able to work
- Tell Dan
- Tell the boys

Fresh tears well in her eyes. How is she going to do that last one?

Only when the icing is ready and they're both sat at the table with 120 cakes between them, does Nicola break the silence. 'What are you thinking?'

Jenny shakes her head. 'I'm thinking that I can't believe it.' Pregnant. Jenny thinks back to her last period. It was . . . the birthday party at the soft play. A friend of Ethan's. Jenny remembers digging out a battered tampon from the bottom of her bag. But that was over two months ago. That can't have been her last period. Oh god! What's wrong with her? She's not a teenager anymore. Could she really be two months pregnant already? 'How the hell did this happen? Dan and I, we're careful. Condoms are like 99.99 per cent effective.'

Nicola raises an eyebrow in that knowing way she does. 'When used correctly,' she says. 'And I think it's only ninety-eight per cent.'

'What do you mean, when used correctly? We're not kids. We know what we're doing.'

'I somehow doubt that condom companies measure their effectiveness based on two people shagging in the dark in the back of a car.'

'You're right.' Jenny shakes her head, unsure whether she's going to laugh or cry.

'Are you OK?' Nicola asks, pressing a warm hand over Jenny's.

'Yes and no and who the hell knows.'

Cakes. She should focus on the cakes. *Breathe and focus, Jen. Add to list, tick things off.* That's how she'll cope, same as always.

There's a tremor in her hand as Jenny picks up the piping bag, but the simplicity of the job she loves, the beauty of transforming a plain sponge into a stunning cupcake, is calming and she loses herself in the task.

'Hey look, I've finished one.' Nicola lifts the single cupcake in the air, brandishing it like a trophy as Jenny places her tenth cake in the box.

Jenny bites back a laugh, unable to stop her lips twitching. 'Er . . . thanks.'

'What?' Nicola's eyes narrow but she's grinning too.

'Nothing.'

'Tell me.'

'It's . . . well it's very nice.'

'If nice means?'

Jenny cringes. 'If nice looks like my right boob when I got mastitis feeding Ethan and spent two days with half a savoy folded inside my bra.' Even now the smell of cabbage makes her nipples wince. Something else she never thought she'd have to face again. 'I'll just pop it at the back here.'

'Cheeky cow. I come over here to help and this is the thanks I get.'

'You came over here to revel in the disaster that is my life. Sometimes I wonder if we're actually even friends. I mean, you were only nice to me to start with because you had a crush on my brother,' Jenny smirks, making a gagging face.

Nicola laughs, a cackle-like sound that transports Jenny to park benches and drinking sickly sweet alcopops on Friday nights when they should have been at home revising for exams. 'Only while he had those gorgeous brown curtains. The minute Peter got his hair cut, I went right off him.'

'Thank goodness for that. But maybe for the sake of my reputation, er . . . maybe don't do any more cakes.'

'Fine. I'll sit here and drink my coffee. You can talk about Dan and how you think he's going to take the news.'

A crushing panic whips through Jenny's body. Her phone buzzes from the counter. An international dial code. She pulls a face. 'It's Mum.'

Anyone else and she'd ignore it, but ignoring her mum sets in motion a series of panicked calls from her mum to everyone else she knows in England to ask if they've heard from Jenny.

'Answer it,' Nicola says. 'Before she calls me instead.' Nicola grins, scooping up her coffee and sitting back in her chair.

'Hi, Mum,' Jenny says, pressing the phone to her ear.

'We've got another tax form, Jennifer,' her mum's voice wails down the phone. 'It's the third one this month.'

'OK.' Jenny rolls her eyes, staying silent and thanking her lucky stars that her mum is a thousand miles away and no longer turning up on her doorstep with whatever the crisis of the day is.

'What does it say?'

'I don't know. It's all so confusing.'

'OK, Mum. It's going to be fine. You knew this was going to happen after Brexit. You're not the only one going through this. Can you talk to one of the other British residents on the complex?'

Her mum gasps. 'No. I can't. They'll laugh at me.'

'They won't, Mum,' Jenny says, trying to sound soothing. 'What does Dad say?'

'I can't tell your father.' Her mum's voice jumps several octaves. 'You know how he worries.'

Jenny bites back a retort and lets her mum talk. It's the only way, like a balloon deflating. Her mum needs to get it all out.

'I'll speak to Barb across the road,' her mum says at last. 'She used to work for HMRC.'

'Good idea. Look, Mum, I'm just icing some cakes. I've got to go,' Jenny says before her mum can launch into another crisis. There's no way Jenny can listen to another of her mum's rants about the neighbour who is feeding the stray cats again. 'I'll call you Tuesday night when the boys are out.'

They say their goodbyes and Jenny sits back in her chair, exhausted.

'How's Phyllis?' Nicola asks with a sympathetic smile.

Jenny picks up another cake. 'Flapping again.'

'Nothing new then.'

Jenny laughs. 'Nope.'

'Are they still talking about coming back?'

'No, thank goodness. I'm not sure I could cope with their worries on a daily basis. And Peter has threatened to jump on the first plane to Australia the second they set foot on British soil again.' Jenny sighs. 'I love them. They're my parents. But—'

'They're flappers and you are the opposite of a flapper.'

'I'm not sure that's true right now.'

'Good point. You were just about to talk about your plan for telling Dan you're pregnant.'

Jenny groans. It's not just Dan. It's the boys too and how monumentally this will change their lives. She can't think about that right now. 'Oh god. Do I have to tell Dan? Maybe you could write one of your notes like you used to when you'd pretend to be our mums and get us out of PE?'

'This isn't school, Jen.' Nicola laughs again. 'You'll have to do it.'

'I know. But he's going to freak out. I know he is because I am. I mean, we've both got kids already, and we're not even dating. This was just supposed to be—'

'Jen,' Nicola cuts in. 'I swear if you tell me that you and Dan are nothing more than no-strings-attached fun one more time, I'm going to throttle you. I've never seen you so happy. Every time Dan texts you, you go all gooey-eyed, lovesick teenager on me.'

'But the kids,' Jenny cries, ignoring Nicola's comment. 'Jack and Ethan, and the girls. We have our own lives. And I happen to like my life exactly how it is.' She takes a calming breath. 'I'll tell Dan and he can be as involved as he wants to be, but I've been a single parent for seven years, I don't need him to do this.'

They fall silent. Jenny focuses on the cupcakes, ignoring the pointed look Nicola is giving her. She loves Nicola, but her friend has been happily married for eighteen years. She has no idea what it's like to be on her own. How good it feels to know that no one is going to let you down, no one is going to forget to do the washing or fall into bed with your hairdresser.

Jenny is perfectly happy relying on herself. However Dan reacts to the news, it doesn't matter. She doesn't need him.

Chapter 6

Dan

Dan scrapes the potato peelings into the bin and turns on the radio to listen to Steve Wright's Sunday Morning Love Songs. The kitchen is warm from the oven, and the smell of roasting meat reminds Dan of a thousand Sundays spent in this very kitchen with his mum singing along to the radio. But it's a nice feeling today. Comforting. He won't let the grief seep out today.

He can't wait to see Jenny, hold her, kiss her. He can't wait for the girls to meet her. They will love her.

Love.

The word makes his stomach knot. It's way too soon for that, and yet he thinks . . . maybe . . . this thing between them could be something more. Not now. But one day in the future, maybe they could be a proper couple. Today though, it's just lunch, meeting the kids, keeping everything relaxed. It's all fine, he tells himself again as a wave of nerves hit.

The thought lands at the exact moment the kitchen door opens, and Dan turns to see a tearful Bryony still in her polka-dot pink dressing gown. Her light-blonde hair is brushed and pulled into the high ponytail she asked for half an hour ago when he turned off the TV and sent her to get dressed.

Her pale face is blotchy red and there's no sign of the wide smile and bubbly chatter he's used to from his seven-year-old daughter.

'Hey—'

'Daaaaddddyyy,' Bryony wails.

Dan turns off the radio, plunging the kitchen into silence. 'What's going on, Bry?'

'Daddy, my tummy hurts. I feel sick.'

'Really? You were fine ten minutes ago. Are you sure you're not just a bit nervous? Because there's nothing to be nervous about. It's just Jenny, Jack and Ethan coming for lunch.'

She shakes her head, pushing Bear Bear to her nose. The old polar bear used to be soft white but is now a worn grey. They got it from the zoo the same month Ginger left, and for years it barely left Bryony's tight grasp. It lost an eye in the ball pit of the soft play centre a while ago, and it wasn't until Dan spent a painstaking hour sewing on a new one that he realised it was a different size. He'd meant to replace it, but Bryony didn't want Bear Bear to undergo any more operations and so one eye is now bigger than the other.

'Feel sick,' Bryony mumbles through the fur.

Dan's heart sinks. He can't bear seeing Bryony upset. She's been through so much already. He wonders briefly if he should cancel, but they'll be here in an hour. It's too late.

'Bryony, sweetheart,' Dan crouches down to the floor in front of his daughter. 'There's nothing to worry about. OK?'

There's a beat of silence where Bryony's eyes fill with tears and her bottom lip wobbles. 'I don't like *Power Rangers*,' she wails. 'It's scary and stupid.'

44

Dan bites back the desire to smile at Bryony's strange outburst. 'That's fine. Don't watch it.'

'And I don't want to stop dancing to play football on Saturdays. Football is boring. And . . . and I don't want to sleep in the room with the washing machine. It's too dark,' Bryony says with a hitching sob.

'Bryony, what are you talking about? You're not moving rooms or stopping dancing.' Not after the money he's spent on leotards, tights and ballet shoes this year.

'But Amelia said that you're going to marry Jenny and then you won't have time for us and we'll have to do what the boys do and watch what they watch and . . .' She gasps again. 'And Jenny will give my room to Ethan. I don't want them to come today, Daddy.' Bryony flings herself into Dan's arms, her tiny body shuddering under the weight of her sobs.

'Bry, baby, stop crying now. Let me talk to you.'

Bryony pulls away and stares at him with her huge blue eyes. Ginger's eyes. He smiles his I'm-going-to-fix-everything smile. 'Who said anything about getting married? Jenny, Jack and Ethan are coming for lunch. That's all. I like Jenny a lot. We like spending time together and we want to do that with you and Amelia and Jack and Ethan.'

'I don't want to play football.'

'That's OK. You don't have to,' Dan soothes. 'You're going to really like Jenny. Do you know what her job is?'

Bryony shakes her head.

'She bakes cakes. Big, tasty cakes, and I bet she's going to bring one with her today.'

'A chocolate one?'

'Maybe.' He smiles.

'But Amelia said—'

'I'll talk to Amelia. Now go and wash your face. They'll be here soon. Are you going to wear your new red dress?'

Bryony nods, the shadow of a smile crossing her face. 'I'm going to introduce Ethan to Poppy. He's got a guinea pig too.'

'That's a good idea. Come on then.'

Dan's doubts disappear as Bryony races up the stairs and into the glowing pink of her bedroom. Pink walls, pink bedcovers, pink carpet, pink curtains. 'It's like a unicorn vommed in it,' Amelia loves to say, usually with a theatrical gag.

Dan finds Amelia sitting on her bed, a schoolbook resting on her knees and three more surrounding her. She's wearing her hoody again with a pair of jeans with rips in the knees that Dan hates, mostly because he had to fork out thirty-five pounds for trousers with holes in them.

Amelia's room is a large square with built-in wardrobes and a window that overlooks the garden and the park beyond. The walls are a dull pale blue and covered with posters of star constellations and the Northern Lights.

'We need to get you a desk,' he says. 'And a fresh coat of paint in here.'

'Dad,' Amelia begins, tilting her head as she looks at him in a way that makes him start shaking his head before she's said another word. He knows what's coming. 'Just hear me out,' she says, scooping a strand of dark-blonde hair behind her ear.

He feels the familiar tug at his chest. Amelia is growing up so fast. He stares at her face, searching for signs of the little girl with the blonde pigtails and button nose who used to beg him for one more bedtime story, and put on dance shows for him and Bryony to watch. He still sees that cheeky girl sometimes when Amelia laughs suddenly or first thing in the mornings when she's sleepy and her hair is a mess.

'Grandad's old study would make a much better bedroom for me,' she says. 'It's bigger for a start, and—'

'Amelia,' he tries to cut in.

'And much quieter up there so I won't be interrupted when I'm doing my homework. Plus it has its own bathroom, which is sitting unused right now, which is stupid, and would be good for me . . .' She pauses, cheeks flushing. 'I'm growing up and my own bathroom would be really good.' She finishes by clasping her hands together, her whole body pleading with him to say yes.

He wants to tell Amelia that he would say yes if he could, but that room, it's his dad's, and it's the one part of the house he can't bring himself to change. But how can he explain it to Amelia, when he doesn't understand it himself?

Dan blows out his cheeks. 'Can I think about it?' He's aware he's giving the ultimate parenting cop-out answer and giving hope when there is none, but it's the delaying tactic he needs right now.

'Yes, think about it,' she says with the same excitement as though he's agreed. 'Thank you, Daddy.'

'Are you almost finished?' he asks, nodding at her books.

'Just maths to do later.'

'That's good.' Pride swells in him. Amelia was only a little older than Bryony is now when Ginger left, and it hit Amelia hard. She picked up some bad habits, including winding Bryony up, but one thing that has never changed is Amelia's focus, her desire to work hard at school.

'What day is Mum coming over next week?' Amelia asks. Her eyes remain on the pages of the book as though the question is casual, the answer unimportant, but he glimpses the tension in her face.

'I'm not sure yet.' Dan keeps his smile easy. It's well practised, well honed. He'll groan later when Ginger doesn't answer the phone, and will have nothing but vague answers for the girls until whatever day she swings by with her bags of chocolate and raucous laughter.

Dan worries sometimes that they're getting this all wrong with Ginger flitting in and out of the girls lives whenever she chooses. Maybe something structured like what Jenny has with her ex – every other weekend and one evening a week – would be better. But it knocked Dan sideways when Ginger packed her bags and walked out. No warning. No thought to the aftermath. One day she was there. The next she was gone. All he wanted to do was make it as easy as possible for her to see the girls whenever she wanted for fear she'd never come back.

But now Ginger gets all the best bits with none of the parenting – the homework help, the bedtimes, the school shoe shopping, the mad dash to ballet on Saturdays, the rush to breakfast club before school. And then there's the fact that he invites Ginger into his home like it's completely normal for a divorced couple to have dinner together. Dan hates that Ginger has no idea what it costs him to play Happy Families with the woman who broke his children's hearts.

'Are you alright about Friday night?' Dan asks, sitting on the edge of the bed. 'I know it must have been disappointing that you didn't get to sleep over at your mum's.'

'I told you yesterday, I'm fine about it,' Amelia replies, her voice bright. Dan suspects he's not the only one well practised at ignoring Ginger's flaws. 'Mum played on the Wii with us for, like, ages. She's really good at *Mario Kart*. It was fun.'

'When is Jenny coming?' Amelia asks then.

'Eleven-thirty. Crumbs, I need to put the potatoes on.'

'Better get on with it then.'

'Just quickly,' Dan says, remembering the reason he came to see Amelia in the first place. 'Bryony's a bit upset. She seems to think that I'm going to make her give up dancing and sleep in the utility room. Any idea where she got that idea from?'

A look of innocent confusion crosses her face. 'I didn't say that. You know what she's like, Dad. She blows everything out of proportion.'

'You didn't tell her she'd have to watch *Power Rangers*?'

'No,' Amelia laughs. 'I just said that Jack and . . .'

'Ethan.'

'Yeah, Ethan will probably want to watch boys' stuff on the TV and since they're the guests, we should let them.'

'Right.' Dan stares at Amelia a moment longer before letting it go. He has a niggling feeling that there is more to this than Amelia is letting on.

'I'll talk to Bryony and say sorry for upsetting her,' Amelia adds, sliding off the bed and disappearing into Bryony's room.

Dan heads back to the kitchen, pushing thoughts of Ginger out of his head.

49

Chapter 7

Jenny

Jenny pulls into a small cul-de-sac with four large, detached houses and finds Dan's driveway – a long stretch of gravel that leads to a house with big bay windows, a porch and bright-red door.

Bloody hell, this house is big.

Nerves bubble and twist in her stomach as her wheels crunch slowly across the gravel. She can't shake the feeling that this is a colossal mistake. Dan and her – it's barely a relationship. Last night she clocked up how many hours they've actually snatched from their lives to spend together over the last three months. It barely equalled twenty-four hours. This was always supposed to be a passing thing, something fun before they got on with their lives again. It won't last.

So what are they doing here? At least a dozen times today, Jenny has picked up the phone to cancel, but something stopped her. Those two pink lines on the test yesterday.

'It's like the *Home Alone* house,' Jack says as Jenny parks beside Dan's estate car.

'Yeah, but the garden is giant,' Ethan chirps as they climb out.

Jenny follows Ethan's gaze to a long garden visible from the side of the house. It makes Jenny's garden look like a weedy grass verge by the side of the road.

She suddenly wishes she hadn't told Dan on their second date that the walls of her house are so thin they can hear her elderly neighbour, Doreen, fart when she wakes up in the morning. The trump alarm, Ethan calls it. She cringes at the memory of them laughing now. What must Dan have thought, knowing he was coming home to this?

'What if they don't like us?' Jack asks, his voice barely a whisper.

'They will,' Jenny reassures him, wishing like she always did that Jack could find an outlet for his worries, a way to let them go somehow. She doesn't want him to grow up like her parents, freaking out over every letter that comes through the door and thinking all the neighbours hate him.

'There are a lot of trees.' Ethan skips around Jenny's legs as she moves to the boot and retrieves the triple-layered chocolate cake she baked at 5am.

'Just remember not to climb higher than your head, OK?'

'I remember,' Ethan says, hopping on one leg.

'I'll keep an eye on him, Mum,' Jack says, appearing by her side.

'Thank you.' She leans over to kiss his cheek, but he takes a sidestep and grins as her lips find nothing but air.

'Too slow.' He laughs.

'Right, no cake for you.' Jenny smiles. 'Fancy trying to dodge your sweet mother's kiss.'

'Old mother, more like,' Jack cackles, dodging a playful swipe from Jenny.

Old mother. Is that what people will call her? *Shit, shit, shit. I'm pregnant.* The thought hits with a fresh wave of panic.

'I'm going to ask Bryony to show me her guinea pig and see what tricks she can do,' Ethan says then.

'Guinea pigs can't do tricks,' Jack says, and the boys launch into a discussion about Hulk that Jenny doesn't hear. She sucks in her lips, rubbing at the lipstick she put on just before leaving the house. It feels too much now.

Jenny tugs at her knitted grey dress, suddenly conscious of how it's clinging to her stomach.

The door opens before they reach the top step of the porch and Dan appears wearing jeans and a polo shirt beneath a hot-pink apron with the words Dan's Kitchen written across it.

'Hi,' Jenny says, taking in Dan's crinkly-eyed smile. Something inside her melts and she can't stop the grin from spreading across her face. How is it possible for something to feel so terrifying and to still be bubbling with goofy, mushy happiness?

'Hello,' Dan calls. 'Come in, come in. Hi, Ethan, Hi Jack.'

Jenny steps into a wide hallway with varnished wood floors and high ceilings that wouldn't be out of place in a home furnishings catalogue. Dan even has a special shoe storage unit by the door, the one that has all the shelves perfect for a dozen pairs of shoes, the same one Jenny wishes she could fit in her pathetic excuse for a hallway. Her eyes move to the kitchen at the end of the hall. It's gleaming and white and at least three times bigger and nicer than her own. There's no way she can invite Dan and the girls to her house after this.

There are two other rooms that lead off from the hall. The first is on the left at the bottom of the staircase. Jenny glimpses chunky brown leather sofas, an entire wall of bookcases and a piano. It looks like the kind of room where drinks and sticky fingers should be forbidden, unlike the other room Jenny can see with its IKEA storage units and pink toy boxes tucked inside, a big TV and a squishy sofa.

Ethan giggles, covering his mouth with his hand. 'Hello, Dan.'

'Hi,' Jack adds in a barely there voice before shoving his hands into the pockets of his jeans and inching closer to Jenny.

'Lunch is about half an hour away,' Dan continues, smiling between Jenny and the boys. 'I've put up the rope swing in the garden and there's a football goal too.'

'Yesssss!' Ethan leaps in the air.

Dan leans on the banister and shouts up the stairs, 'Girls, they're here. Come down, please.'

A door bangs and then Bryony and Amelia appear in identical purple onesies. Amelia takes the stairs first, then Bryony, a miniature version of her sister with the same blonde hair and big blue eyes.

'What happened to your red dress?' Dan asks Bryony as she reaches his side and ducks behind his legs. The smile on Dan's face slips for a moment and Jenny wonders if he's nervous too.

'Changed my mind,' Bryony mumbles.

'Well come and meet Jenny, and you know Jack and Ethan of course.'

No one speaks.

It's like someone has pressed a mute button. The air feels charged with a nervous energy that crackles between them.

'Hi,' Jenny says, looking from Bryony to Amelia, her voice too loud in the silence. 'It's nice to meet you both. Your dad has told me so much about you.'

'Hi . . . Jenny?' Amelia replies, pausing as if she isn't sure she has the right name. 'Dad hasn't mentioned you at all, but it's nice to meet you too.'

For a moment Jenny thinks she catches a mocking in Amelia's sweeter-than-sweet tone. Jenny ignores the thought. Amelia is twelve not sixteen, and Dan is always saying how kind she is.

'Hi, Bryony.' Ethan waves his hand in the air before dropping it suddenly as Bryony clings to Dan's legs.

'I love a PJ day,' Jenny says, feeling suddenly desperate to escape this hallway, this lunch. 'I'm in mine all the time, aren't I, boys?' She looks at Jack and then Ethan, trying to convey a silent message for them to say something.

Ethan nods. 'Yeah. *All* the time.'

'Yeah,' Jack mumbles.

'Hi,' Amelia replies with a friendly smile, but Jack dips his head, face aflame in a way that makes Jenny's chest ache for him.

'It's not PJs,' Bryony says, reaching out to take her dad's hand. 'They're onesies.'

'Oh, I see. Well, I baked a chocolate cake for pudding.' She hands the tin to Dan, their fingers brushing against each other, warm and electric.

'What a treat. What do we say, girls?'

Bryony and Amelia mumble a 'thank you'.

'Can we go see the rope swing?' Ethan asks.

'Good idea, Ethan.' Dan smiles. 'Why don't you all go outside? Jenny and I can get the lunch ready.'

'Dad, it's, like, freezing outside,' Amelia says, wrinkling her nose.

'It's either cold or it's not. It isn't *like* anything,' he says with a grin that no one returns.

She huffs. 'It is freezing outside.'

'Good job you asked for that ridiculously expensive coat last month then, isn't it?'

Amelia sighs but she walks away, Bryony, Jack and Ethan trailing behind. Just before Jack disappears, he throws her a look, his face etched with worry and questions he's not voiced. She gives him her best 'trust me' look and wishes her own nerves would dissolve.

They stand frozen – Jenny and Dan – waiting for the kids to disappear, waiting to breathe again, it feels like to Jenny. Even her middle-of-the-night worries weren't as awkward as this.

'Hey, you,' Dan whispers, slipping his hand into hers. 'Are you OK?'

Jenny nods. 'Yep, totally fine.'

He fixes her with a look. *I see you*, it seems to say. 'I'm a bit nervous, to be honest,' Dan admits, and his honesty makes Jenny feel better. They're on the same page at least.

'Me too,' she says. 'I . . . I almost cancelled.'

Dan laughs. 'Me too. Why didn't you?'

'Because I . . . I . . .' *I'm pregnant*. The words push against her, ready to be set free, but she can't. Not now. They have to get through lunch first. Jenny shakes her head. 'I don't know really. Like you said, it's only a lunch.'

'The kids will be alright when they've had some fresh air and a play.'

'I know. And I made a cake.' Jenny cringes. 'I've said that already, haven't I?' The words spill out, sounding jittery even to her. The feeling is familiar. The nervous, skittish energy pulsing in her veins. A memory pushes itself to the front of her mind. Paul taking her to meet his parents for the first time. His mum cooked duck à l'orange and some special mash that Jenny hadn't heard of before, and she was so nervous.

At twenty-five, Paul was the first man Jenny had met who seemed to have his life together, running his own electrician business. He made the few men she'd dated before him seem like boys, and she desperately wanted his parents to approve of her. Not that Paul cared either way.

He was his own person. He never worried about what others thought, never dwelled on decisions he'd made, worrying they were wrong.

After years of trying to calm her parents' anxieties, Paul's attitude was refreshing. It drew her to him. But Jenny couldn't stop herself caring what his parents thought of her. Her nerves made her drink too much wine and blather on about baking like a deranged loon and how she was going to quit her boring office administrator job one day and set up a cake-making business. She was gesticulating widely as she spoke. Until the inevitable happened – she knocked over a glass of red wine. Rich dark liquid spilled across Pam and Reggie's best white tablecloth and dripped in puddles on their cream carpet. Cream! In a dining room! It was asking for trouble.

After that, it didn't matter how many uneventful lunches that followed, or how much Jenny did for Pam and Reggie. It didn't matter that Jenny followed every single one of Pam's suggestions for the wedding and even got married in a stuffy old church instead of the outdoor wedding Jenny had wanted. It didn't matter that Paul cheated on Jenny. Just like it doesn't matter now that Jenny is a good daughter-in-law and makes time for Pam and Reggie to see the boys anytime they like, whether it's Paul's weekend with them or hers. To Paul's family, she'll always be the woman who drinks too much, talks too much, and spills her drinks. Even now, Pam will only give Jenny half a cup of tea in one of the old mugs, the ones Pam reserves for workman.

Dan slips his arms around Jenny's waist, drawing her back to the present with a gentle kiss. 'I'm glad you're here.' Jenny breathes in the smell of Dove soap and the woody scent of Dan's aftershave. 'I wish you could have come over on Friday night,' he whispers, his lips tracing the line of her neck, sending shots of desire through her body.

'Are you saying that you don't think the back of your car is a romantic hot spot to get into my knickers?'

Dan laughs and pulls away. 'Come on,' he says with a grin. 'It wouldn't make a good first impression if I burned the lunch.' Dan grins. 'And if you're very good, I'll let you be chief pot washer.'

'Oh wow, thanks,' Jenny laughs, her nerves forgotten. She won't think about the pregnancy now. She can tell Dan later. She just has to find the right time.

There's a twinge of something in her chest – regret, she thinks. The moment Jenny tells Dan about the baby, their no-strings fun will be over. They won't be able to go back, but there's no way forward for them either. Once upon a time they might have stood a chance. Not now, though. Their lives are too set, too weighed down. It took Jenny a long time to move on from the hurt of Paul's infidelity. She has her own business, her own home – which despite the dodgy boiler, she's very happy in. She has her boys, her own life. Whatever happens, she doesn't need anyone else and she never will.

Chapter 8

Dan

Dan runs through the mental checklist in his head – meat done and resting; potatoes and stuffing cooking; gravy made; vegetables to boil. He turns to the hob and twists the dials for the pans of peas and carrots.

'When did you learn to cook?' Jenny asks, hovering by the sink, glancing between Dan and the garden where the children are now playing on the rope swing dangling from the huge oak tree that sits at the bottom of the garden.

'After Ginger left, my . . .' The word sticks in his throat for a moment. 'My mum became a meals on wheels for a while, but one day she turned up with the ingredients in a bag and made me do it myself, flicking me with a tea towel whenever I tried to rush a step. I wished I'd learned earlier now. It would have been a big help to Ginger when the girls were little.'

Dan feels the familiar pang of guilt. The ache in the old wound of his failed marriage. It's not that he wants Ginger back. That ship sailed long ago, but it doesn't ease the guilt. He let Ginger do too much. Nappies, night feeds, cooking, cleaning. She didn't ask for help, but he didn't offer as much as he should have either.

He checks the potatoes, opening the oven door and releasing a whoosh of hot air into the kitchen, blowing away thoughts of Ginger from this mind.

'It smells delicious. You have an amazing house, too,' Jenny says. 'This is pretty much my dream kitchen.'

Dan smiles. 'I can't take credit for any of it. The kitchen was designed by a man called Philip, who pretty much told me what I wanted. And the house belonged to my parents. They died three years ago and I'm an only child so . . .' A lump forms in his throat. He coughs, wondering if it will ever get easier to talk about.

'Oh, Dan, I'm so sorry.' Jenny steps close, a hand touching his arm. 'That must have been so hard.'

'It was. It still is to be honest. They were amazing parents. The best. Really supportive and loving. I grew up knowing I could never disappoint them. Even when I told them that Ginger had left and I was getting divorced, my mum phoned Ginger to tell her that she'd always be family and could count on them. My mum never said, but I always felt that perhaps Ginger wasn't the daughter-in-law my mum would've wanted, and yet she still treated her like her own daughter.

'They were always there for me. And then they weren't.'

'It must be bittersweet living here. Is it hard?' Jenny asks.

He nods. 'Yes. Sometimes I think I should've sold the house, but . . . it's where I grew up. It's where my mum and dad lived for fifty years. I couldn't give it up, and I knew . . .' He pauses, emotion pushing to the surface.

Jenny slips her arm around him and he feels the warmth of her body. 'It's OK.'

'Sorry.' Dan clears his throat. 'I didn't mean to lay this all on you. Anyway,' he continues, getting a hold of himself, 'I knew my mum would be happy to look down and see us in the house she loved.'

There's a pause, a silence Dan doesn't know how to

fill. He's never told anyone this stuff before. 'You must miss your parents too,' Dan says. 'How often do you see them?'

Jenny snorts, leaning against the counter as Dan stirs the gravy. 'Only once every few years normally. My parents are nice people, don't get me wrong, but they are pretty exhausting too. I felt like I spent a lot of my life growing up talking my mum down from a panic and trying to convince my dad that the neighbours weren't spying on us.'

'Sounds tough for you and your brother.'

Jenny smiles and shakes her head. 'Peter decided the best way to deal with them was to ignore their worries. I always thought I could help. It wasn't a bad childhood or anything. We went on holidays. We did normal family stuff, but the worry was always there. It made me and Peter pretty resilient. It was easier to deal with things ourselves than stress them out. I worry Jack's inherited it though. He's so shy and overthinks everything.'

Dan nods and thinks he understands Jenny a little better now. 'For what it's worth, I see that a lot in school. It's mostly a lack of confidence. Once they've been at senior school a while and have found their feet, they're different kids. Seriously, you wouldn't believe the chatty year nines who wouldn't say boo to goose two years ago.'

'That makes me feel better, thanks.'

As Dan gives the gravy another stir, he catches the opening beat to George Michael's 'Faith' playing on the radio. He turns to Jenny with a smile. 'I love this song.' He steps forward, dancing a little as he moves.

'What?' He grins, catching the smirk on Jenny's face.

'You dance like a dad at a wedding.' She laughs.

'Hey!' Dan pulls her into his arms. 'I'll have you know all the girls wanted to dance with me at school discos when

I was young. I played guitar and everything.'

'Oh well, now you've mentioned the guitar, that totally makes up for the dance moves,' Jenny teases.

'I bet you had all the boys asking you for a dance,' he says, kissing her neck and feeling the familiar desire stir inside him.

'Ha! I was more of a hang around the back of the hall with Nicola trying to smoke cigarettes I'd stolen from my brother.'

Dan gives a mock gasp. 'No.'

'It's true. I was definitely not a dancer.'

The song ends and they pull apart, laughing, smiling. It's exactly how Dan had imagined it would've been if Jenny had come over on Friday.

'Right,' Dan says. 'I just need to whack up the temperature on the oven for a few minutes to get the potatoes extra crispy and we're all set.'

'You didn't need to go to all this trouble for us,' Jenny says. 'A sandwich would've been fine.'

'Dad cooks a roast most Sundays,' Amelia says, appearing in the doorway to the mud room. Her hair windswept, cheeks flushed with cold.

'We'll be around more often then,' Jenny smiles.

'You have to be invited first,' Amelia replies with a pout that is so Ginger that a sudden welt of anger rises inside Dan.

'Amelia,' Dan says, adding a warning to his tone. 'That was rude. Please apologise to Jenny.'

'Sorry,' she says in a voice filled with contempt.

Dan is about to tell her to try again when Amelia speaks first. 'Ethan is stuck in a tree,' she says, still with the attitude – pinched lips, raised eyebrows and that defiant tone that makes him despair – so it takes him a moment to register the words Amelia is saying.

'Oh no,' Jenny groans, running to the hall for her boots.

Dan abandons the lunch, rushing to shove his feet in his wellies before running into the garden. The cold blows over his skin and he's instantly freezing in his t-shirt. 'Which tree?' Dan calls out.

Amelia points to where Jack and Bryony are standing below the oak tree. The very large and very tall oak tree.

Jenny appears beside him, sprinting towards the tree.

'Muuuuummmmeeeee!' Ethan's voice carries on the wind, sounding far away.

Dan scans the top of the oak tree. The rich-green leaves that cover the branches in the summer have long gone and Dan spots Ethan's cobalt-blue coat halfway up the tree. It's high. As high as the second-floor windows.

'I'm coming,' Jenny calls out behind him. 'Don't move, OK?'

'I'll get the ladder,' Dan calls, running towards the shed.

'It's fine,' Jenny replies. 'I've got this.' A second later she hoists herself up and into the branches.

As Dan watches Jenny climb effortlessly from one branch to the next – calculated and steady, confident in a way he's never seen her before – he realises two things:

One – Jenny is like a real-life Spiderman. Seriously, how can any normal person climb a tree so easily? He half expects webbing to shoot from her hands.

Two – He might have stronger feelings for Jenny than he's admitted to himself. She didn't so much as blink before climbing the tree to rescue Ethan, even in a dress. And she's funny too. Always making him laugh. Yes, he likes her. Really, really.

Get a grip! Dan tells himself, taking a steadying breath and glancing at Jack. The boy is frowning, looking so much like Jenny with his curly brown hair. 'You OK, Jack?'

Jack nods, gaze fixed on the ground.

'Your mum certainly looks like she knows what she's doing.'

Jack says nothing for a moment, kicking the ground with his shoe. 'There was this time in the park last summer when Ethan managed to climb so high someone called the fire brigade,' he says, voice barely audible. 'But by the time they got there, Mum had already got Ethan down and he was eating an ice cream.'

'Is he going to fall?' Bryony asks, her voice a whisper. She dips her chin inside the top of her coat as though trying to hide herself and there are tears swimming in her eyes.

'No way. Ethan never falls.' Jack pats Bryony on the shoulder. There's something brotherly about the gesture which makes Dan think – hope – that this lunch can still be salvaged. 'My mum will get him down.'

Bryony whispers something and pushes up against Dan.

'What was that sweetie?'

'I said I wouldn't play with Ethan and that . . . and that he couldn't hold Poppy, but I changed my mind,' Bryony says quickly, her voice higher than normal. 'I was going to play with him.'

'It's OK. It's not your fault.'

'Dad?' Amelia says from beside him.

'Not now, Amelia. And don't think I've forgotten what you said to Jenny a minute ago. That was rude and you know it. I want you to apologise properly.'

Amelia rolls her eyes dramatically. Dan's glad to see that four years of taking Amelia to theatre school, not to mention the thousands spent in fees, hasn't gone to waste. 'What? Like now? She's up a tree, Dad.'

'When she gets down.'

'But, Dad, there's smoke coming from the kitchen.'

'What?' Dan spins around. Even in the seconds it takes his eyes to spot the smoke he's hoping, praying, Amelia is joking.

She's not.

The potatoes. He cranked the oven up for the final two minutes. Except it's been way more than that. And didn't he leave the stuffing and the sausages in as well?

He sprints across the lawn, clomping strides that steal his breath. He really does need to start exercising.

By the time he reaches the kitchen, the piercing beep of the smoke alarm is ringing in his ears and the delicious smell of roast dinner has been replaced with the gritty odour of burned food.

Oh crap! Way to go, Daniel!

He throws open the window and turns off the oven as smoke billows out the sides. He slips on the oven gloves before opening the door and grabbing the pan of potatoes in one hand and the stuffing and sausages tray in the other. The smoke stings his eyes and claws at the back of his throat.

Everything is black. Indistinguishable charred, inedible, lumps. The skin on his fingers tingles where the heat of the pans is scorching through the gloves. He needs to put the trays down. Dan's eyes dart around the kitchen, searching for a space on the worktop, but there's nowhere free and the pans are really hot now.

'Ah,' he says. 'Ah aaaa, ouch.'

In the old kitchen, he would've dumped them straight in the sink, but the heat will ruin the porcelain of the Butler sink. He remembers the cost and swallows back another 'ouch'.

Where can he put it?

His hands are throbbing. The gloves feel as useful as a windbreaker in a hurricane. And bloody hell, that alarm is going to deafen him.

Outside, he decides. He can dump them in the garden. Dan rushes towards the mud room at the same moment that Bryony, Amelia, Jenny, Jack and Ethan appear, blocking the doorway. Bryony covers her ears with her hands and frowns.

'Ah,' he says again. The tingling in his fingers is now a white-hot pain. It's too much. He spins a final time around the kitchen, desperate to put the pans somewhere, anywhere. His elbow knocks against something on the side and there's a crash as it hits the floor, but his thoughts are on the pans, the pain. He can't take it anymore.

The potato tray slips first – a clatter of metal on the tiles. Coal-like chunks scatter across the kitchen. The second pan follows.

The smoke alarm gives a final screeching beep before stopping, throwing the kitchen into silence. Dan drops the gloves and runs his hands under cold water. Only when the sting has eased does he turn to survey the mess and see the thing he knocked on the floor – Jenny's cake tin. It's upside down, the lid off, the cake now a cow-pat splat beside the brittle chars of roast potato.

Chapter 9

Jenny

The house is freezing. A cold wind whips through the kitchen from the open back door. They're all in their coats, all except Dan who is still wearing his apron. He has a smudge of black on his forehead and a smear of chocolate icing on his arm from her cake. Her lovely cake that is now ruined.

It was an accident. A domino effect from Ethan climbing the tree, which was her fault really because Jenny should've known the moment Ethan ran into the garden that he would be eyeing up the trees, completely ignoring her reminder to stay on the lower branches.

And the cake is nothing compared to this – the silence around the table, the awkwardness. The only sound is the clink of cutlery on plates as they tuck into a lunch of roast chicken sandwiches and overcooked vegetables.

She glances at the faces of the children. Little Bryony with her red eyes and little button of a nose, who looks one more soggy carrot away from bursting into tears. Beside her is Amelia, who looks up then and smiles at Jenny.

You have to be invited first. The comment echoes in Jenny's head. Amelia didn't mean it to sound so cutting, Jenny is sure, and so she smiles back warmly.

'I'm so sorry about your cake,' Dan says for the third time.

'Honestly, it's fine.' Jenny's voice is all wrong. Too high and try-hard. She wants to rewind this day, to cancel when she had the chance, to be at home right now, just her and the boys. Another half an hour, she tells herself.

'This is still a great lunch. Isn't it, boys?' Jenny says, trying to fill the silence. 'Better than the beans on toast we had yesterday.' Jenny glances at Ethan and then Jack. Neither of them leap in to agree. There's something odd going on between the boys that Jenny can't read and neither of them look up from their plates.

The conversation she and Dan need to have, the words she needs to say lurch forward in her thoughts, but as her gaze moves from one unhappy face to another, Jenny isn't sure she has it in her to do it today.

Chicken! Nicola's voice whispers in her mind.

It's not that though. It's the day – this lunch – the children. It was a mistake to bring them and the sooner she can get out of here, the better.

'Had enough, guys?' Dan asks a few minutes later.

Four heads bob around the table.

'Why don't you put the telly on while we tidy up. We'll see if we can salvage some of Jenny's delicious cake.'

'Thank you for lunch,' Jack mumbles.

'You're welcome,' Dan replies in a cheery voice.

'Thank you,' Ethan says just as quietly as Jack.

Both boys hang back, waiting for Amelia and Bryony to go first in an unspoken understanding that this is their house, their TV, their rules. A second later the noise of American voices fills the silence.

Dan tilts his head to the side and frowns. 'Another disaster?'

Jenny pulls a face and nods. Emotions bubble to the surface. She feels herself teetering on the edge of a coin. Heads she laughs, tails she cries.

'I'm sorry,' Dan says, stacking the plates into a haphazard pile before moving them onto the kitchen worktop.

'Don't be. It was my child who got stuck up the tree and ruined the potatoes.'

'A very impressive rescue, though. I can see where Ethan gets his climbing skills from.' Dan looks up and catches Jenny's eye. The intensity of his gaze unleashes the crazy break-dancing butterflies all over again. She's suddenly hot in her coat and doesn't know where to put herself.

Tell him!

'He needs to work on his descent,' Jenny says at last, picking up a dish of untouched peas from the table.

'Has anyone ever told you that you could be Spiderman's stunt double?'

'Every day,' Jenny quips. 'In the supermarket, at the bank, it's all anyone says, in fact.'

They laugh, the sound pushing away the lunch, the silence of the kids, the burned food, the ruined cake.

'Do we risk looking at the cake tin now?' Dan asks.

Jenny drops her head into her hands. 'I don't think I can bear to.' The sight of it on the floor earlier was enough. Dan had scooped it back into the tin and slid it on the side with a hopeful 'Three-second rule?'

'I'll do it,' he says. 'You're not the only brave one here.'

'I didn't see much bravery when it came to holding those roasting tins.' Jenny grins.

'Hey, they were burning.'

'You need better oven gloves.'

'Believe me, I know.' He blows at the tips of his fingers as though they're still hot before prising off the lid of her cake tin.

'How's it looking?'

'It's . . .' He pauses, and Jenny can't stop herself leaning in. The contents look like it's been attacked by a blender. Jenny frowns and picks out a fleck of burned potato.

'I bet it still tastes amazing,' Dan says, scooping a blob of icing into his mouth before nodding effusively. 'Which is more than we can say for my lunch. Maybe we just give them four spoons and tell them to go wild while we hide in here.'

Jenny laughs. 'No way. I definitely need cake too.'

'Good point. We'll give them ice cream and we'll eat this.'

'Better,' she says.

Dan catches her hand as she dips a finger into the icing. 'Jenny?'

'Mmm?' Rich chocolaty heaven explodes in Jenny's mouth and all of a sudden it doesn't seem so bad that the cake fell on the floor.

'I'm sorry today hasn't gone as well as I'd hoped.' Dan moves closer, his eyes looking into hers. 'I thought . . .' He shrugs. 'I like you. The truth is, I can't stop thinking about you.' Dan leans close, his lips brushing against her cheek, his hand reaching to touch her hair. A charge of electricity passes between them as Dan's hands touch her face. Her mouth goes dry, her legs wobbly. This is the moment. Say something, she wills herself.

Tell him!

Dan pulls back. His eyes, his lovely eyes, are searching hers and she feels it, that pull he's talking of, she feels it. 'I'm . . .' Her voice is a whisper and her heart thuds in her chest, but, before she can say another word, a scream from the living room pierces the moment – a needle to a balloon.

'Get off!' she hears Ethan yell.

Another scream, then a thud on the floor.

'Stop it!' Bryony squeals. Jenny pulls out of Dan's arms, dashing towards the shouts. Dan is one step behind her.

Jenny dashes into the room, her feet stopping dead at the sight of Jack and Ethan brawling on the carpet like wild dogs.

Her boys. Kind and thoughtful Jack. Ethan, the cheeky joker who always makes her laugh. Her boys who never fight – never ever, not even play wrestling – are scrambling on the floor, their arms and legs lashing out as though they're trying to kill each other. It takes Jenny a beat too long to process the scene, but Dan assumes his teacher role and steps around them, his voice commanding.

'Boys,' he says in a tone Jenny has never heard before, 'Stop.'

The change is instant. Dan's two words throw the boys apart; her two red-faced, scowling children panting and poised, waiting to see if the other will attack again.

'Jack? Ethan?' Jenny says, dropping to her knees on the rug, throwing out an arm to each of them. Jack leans in first, his body hot, his t-shirt damp with sweat. 'What's going on?'

Ethan dives against Jenny's other side, burying his head in her dress. 'Jack hit me really hard,' he says, his body just as warm as Jack's and shaking with sobs.

Jack shuffles away, sitting back against the sofa, looking as stunned as Jenny feels, as though he has no idea what happened. A wall of tears builds in his eyes.

'Jack,' Jenny says. 'What's going on?'

Jack shakes his head and crumbles in a way that makes Jenny's heart ache with his hurt. An anger rises up – hot embers – inside her. This is on her. She put the boys in this situation. Of course they fought. Of course they lashed out. Dan is a stranger to them and she brought them to lunch without any real warning or explanation, any thought to how weird it would be for them, especially Jack.

Jenny promised herself a long time ago, after Paul broke up with girlfriend number two and it was Jenny who comforted Jack, rubbing his back as he cried himself to sleep thinking it was his fault, she promised she'd always give Jack and Ethan stability. No matter what. And she's just ruined that.

'Mummy,' Ethan sniffs. 'Can we go home now?'

'Good idea,' she whispers, scooping him into her arms. Jenny glances up, just for a second and sees Bryony crying on the sofa. Amelia is stoic beside her sister, her gaze focused on the TV. Dan is standing over them, his face pleading.

'There's no need . . .' he starts, but she shakes her head and he doesn't finish the sentence.

'Go get your shoes,' she tells the boys, releasing Ethan to the carpet.

'It was nice to meet you, Bryony and Amelia. I'm sorry about this.' She waves her hand across the room.

'Bye, Jenny,' Amelia says, her smile sweet. 'Thank you for coming.'

'I'm sorry,' Bryony wails.

Jenny crouches down so she's level with Bryony, her desperation to leave forgotten for a moment. 'Hey, this isn't your fault. It's my silly boys that were fighting. They don't normally fight. This lunch has been a bit weird though, hasn't it?'

Bryony nods.

'I'm going to go home now, but my cake is still in the kitchen. It's a bit squished but I bet it still tastes yummy. Make sure you have an extra big slice, OK?'

A faint smile appears on Bryony's face as she hugs an old polar bear teddy to her chest. Jenny can't bring herself to look at Dan as she hurries the boys to the front door.

'Jenny, wait,' Dan whispers, his hand touching her arm as she opens the front door.

'Go get in the car, boys,' she says before stepping outside and breathing in big gulps of cold air.

Jack falters on the porch for a moment, his head hanging low. 'Thank you for having me.'

'That's OK. It's all OK. I'll see you soon, Jack.'

'Bye,' Ethan says, hiccupping between sobs and sprinting to the car.

'Jenny,' Dan starts when the boys are out of earshot.

'I'm sorry,' she snaps, her voice so sharp the words fall flat. Meaningless. An anger builds inside her. She's so mad at herself. What is she doing here? What is she doing with Dan? Her life was settled, calm. Why did she think she deserved to put herself first? This is all her fault. And it's Dan's too, Jenny thinks then. It was his idea to have this stupid lunch, his kiss in the car park of the school all those nights ago that started it all. 'I need to go. They've never been like this before.'

'I know,' he says, his tone every bit as pleading as hers is barbed. 'You've told me all about the boys, remember? I know they're good kids. They just got carried away. The girls haven't been themselves either. Look.' He steps forward and takes her hand. 'Maybe this was a mistake. Let's forget the kids for a while. Go back to just us. In a few months, we can see if it feels right . . .' Dan's voice trails off. 'I'm sorry. I feel like this is my fault. Let's forget this happened and go back to how it was, OK?'

Jenny stares at Dan's face, his pleading eyes, his down-turned lips. The words build inside her, flying out in a hissed whisper before she can stop them. 'I'm pregnant.'

For a moment, a beat of her heart pounding loud in her chest, they stare at each other. She thinks of the kitchen, two minutes, five minutes, a lifetime ago now. *'I can't stop thinking about you.'*

Dan's expression changes. His eyes grow wide and the colour drains from his face. From pleading to confused in a split second. He laughs – a single ha. 'But I already have children.'

His words hit like a slap. Sudden tears teeter on her eyelids, threatening to fall. She scrunches her eyes shut, forcing them back before spinning on her heels and hurrying to the car. This is what she wanted, wasn't it? To be alone again, no one to let her down. She can totally do this on her own. She doesn't need Dan or anyone else for that matter.

Chapter 10

Dan

Dan stands on the steps of his porch, his mouth opening then closing, a flailing fish, as he watches Jenny half walk, half run to her car.

Jenny is having a baby. His baby. The thought swirls through his mind – autumn leaves caught in the wind. He can't catch hold of it.

He takes an unsteady step forward. The ground feels as though it's moving beneath him. He calls her name again, but his voice is lost in the slam of the car door, the sudden hum of the engine.

She pulls away and he knows he should run, but he can't move. Can't even blink. Can't breathe.

Jenny is pregnant.

But it was only ever meant to be fun. The thought slides into his head, lying next to the comment that flew from his mouth before he could stop it. *'But I already have children.'*

The reality blindsides him, a whop to the side of his head, like the jolting impact when the dodgems collide at the fair.

Oh god. Oh god. Oh god.

React, he tells himself. Do something. Anything. Breathe. Definitely breathe. Dan sucks in the air and blows it out. *Great! You sound like a panting dog, Daniel.*

He can't leave it like this. Dan leaps from the porch and sprints down the driveway, but it's too late. Jenny's car is all the way at the end of the road. He waves his hands in the air, but if she sees him, she doesn't stop.

He slows down. Stops. Turns back to the house. His heart is racing as much from the run as the thought of how badly he has just messed this up.

What should he do?

Pregnant.

A baby.

Just a bit of fun.

Thoughts bump against each other. He remembers the defiance flashing across Jenny's face and the split second just before when his words landed and he saw the hurt they caused. The memory is crushing. He can't think beyond the immediate – talking to Jenny, making sure she's OK.

Dan jogs into the house and snatches his mobile from the kitchen counter. He finds Ginger's number, willing the phone to connect faster.

The noise of laughter and clinking glasses drowns out her hello, and Dan knows before he's even asked, that the answer will be no.

'Can you come and watch the girls? It's important.'

'I'm sorry, I can't,' she replies immediately. 'I'm out with friends for Sunday lunch and I've already had two glasses of wine. If I'd known, I wouldn't have drunk.'

Dan sighs. As much as he wants to, he can't blame Ginger for this.

'Do you want me to ask Kate?' Ginger asks as the background noises of the pub replace with the noise of a road.

'No, it's alright. I can ask her.'

Dan hangs up, heart pounding as his finger hovers over Kate's number. His sister-in-law is the best aunt the girls could wish for and yet he hates landing them on her like this. Kate has Gregory and Max, twin toddlers who keep her rushed off her feet. Plus managing the livery yard connected to their house.

He closes his eyes for a beat and considers taking the girls with him, leaving them in the car so he and Jenny can talk. He shakes his head. It won't work. Bryony will want to see Ethan and Dan won't get the words out he needs to say to Jenny to make this right, not that he has the first clue what those words are yet.

Dan holds the phone to his ear, relief sweeping through him when Kate readily agrees to have the girls. 'The twins are about to have a nap. Drop them round and they can help me groom the horses.'

'Thank you. Thank you so much. It's only for an hour.'

'Don't mention it. And hey, nothing is ever an hour,' Kate replies, and he can hear her smiling. 'Why don't they stay for tea? It's pizza night and I know the twins would love to see them. The girls can wear them out for me.'

'You're a lifesaver, Kate.'

'So true. Is everything alright? You sound a bit frantic.'

'It's been a crazy day. Can I explain later?'

'Of course.'

'Great. See you very soon.'

'Girls,' Dan calls as he hangs up, 'Aunty Kate's invited you over to help groom the horses.'

'Goody,' Bryony sings from the corner where she's pulled out one of the toy boxes and is building a purple Lego house.

'When?' Amelia asks without looking up from the TV show she's watching. Dan's eyes stray towards the screen where Sarah Michelle Geller is wielding a wooden stake and karate kicking a teenage boy.

'Is this Buffy?' Inside he's shouting at himself not to say anything, to just get the girls out as fast as he can and get to Jenny. The more time that passes, the more she'll hate him. He's sure of it. And yet, he can't help it.

Amelia shrugs. 'So?'

'So maybe this isn't age-appropriate for your sister.' *Or you.*

'She's not watching it.'

'When are we going to Aunty Kate's?' Bryony asks.

'Right now,' Dan replies, making a mental note to revisit the topic of Buffy later.

'Yaayyy,' Bryony says, her face brightening.

Amelia pulls her gaze from the TV to look at Dan. There's something accusing in her look. 'Where are you going while we're at Aunty Kate's?'

The lie is on the tip of his tongue. The same one he's been telling Amelia and Bryony for months, or a variation of it anyway. *I'm popping out for a few pints with the football lads,* or *it's a school meeting, seeing some old friends.* When all the time, he's been seeing Jenny. He thought he was protecting the girls from any more hurt. But after today's lunch, he's not so sure. Maybe if he and Jenny had been upfront with the kids from the start, the lunch would have gone a lot smoother.

'I'm going to see Jenny,' Dan says instead.

'You just saw her, like, ten seconds ago.'

'Lunch didn't exactly go as I'd hoped and I want to check she's OK.'

'So you're still together, then?' Amelia asks, her face contorting into such disbelief that Dan laughs.

'Yes,' he says, hoping it's true. 'Why would you think we'd break up?'

She shrugs. 'Lunch was, like, really bad.'

'There'll be other times.'

'But why?' She's still frowning and the look sends a thread of unease through him.

'Because we like each other and we like spending time together.' He doesn't mean for it to sound so much like a question. 'Is that OK?'

'Sure,' she says. The frown disappears and she smiles. 'We'd better get dressed.'

'Great. We're leaving in five.'

The girls race upstairs and Dan hovers by the door, eyes on the clock. Five minutes pass, then ten. The knots in his stomach tighten with every passing second. What must Jenny be thinking right now?

Should he call her? Would she even answer?

He could text. And say what? He still doesn't have the words, but he knows if he can just look into her eyes, he'll find them.

It's fifteen minutes before the girls are dressed and Dan's redone Bryony's hair into two plaits because . . . because, he has no idea, only that it was very important, and quicker to agree than to argue.

Dan drives slowly, normally, fighting the desire to put his foot down.

'Where does Jenny live?' Bryony asks.

'In Mortan. It's not far.'

'Do you think Ethan is OK?'

'I'm sure he is,' Dan replies.

'Can you tell Ethan I'm sorry for not playing with him and that I promise I'll play with him next time?'

'Of course I will. Why didn't you want to play with him, Bry? That's not like you.'

'I just thought—'

'Oh, Dad,' Amelia says then. 'Don't forget I've still got my maths homework to do, so you can't be too long.'

'There'll be plenty of time. Don't worry.'

'And I don't know my spellings for tomorrow either,' Bryony wails suddenly and they spend the rest of the journey trying to remember them and practise.

Only when the girls are cuddling their Aunty Kate and waving him off does Dan's mind turn back to the pregnancy. He swallows and tries not to think about how many minutes have passed since he uttered those stupid words. Jenny will forgive him though, won't she? The question leaves an empty feeling in his stomach as he puts his foot down and drives towards Mortan.

Chapter 11

Jenny

The anger remains as Jenny drives home. It crackles and spits, a raging bonfire.

She pictures the colour draining from Dan's face. The almost comical expression of surprise, and then those words. That instant dismissal.

Why is she so angry? This is what she wanted, expected even.

She's raised two boys alone, and she's done a pretty damn good job of it too. She can do it again.

A sudden hurt cuts into her. She thinks of Dan and dancing in the kitchen, how easy it was to be with him, how much she'll miss him, but she swallows it down, focusing instead on the heat throbbing in her temples.

'Mum?'

Jenny jumps at the sound of Jack's voice from the back seat as they turn off the main road. 'Yes?' The single word is snappish and she wishes she could reel it back in, coat it in sugar and try again.

'We're sorry for fighting.' His voice is still quiet, still not her Jack.

She takes a breath. The fury whipping around her is desperate to get out, but it's not the boys she wants to shout at. It's Dan. It's herself. It's the sodding universe.

'It's alright,' she says with another breath, another sigh. *Come on, Jen. Calm down. For them.* 'I know you didn't mean it. What happened?' she asks, her tone finally normal.

'I don't—' Jack begins as Ethan leaps in.

'Amelia called me a baby and told Jack he should hit me.'

'Is that true, Jack?' Jenny asks, glancing in the rear-view mirror. 'Was Amelia joking, do you think?'

'I don't know,' he says. Their eyes meet for a second and Jenny catches the frown, the how-do-I-answer-this look he gets sometimes when he doesn't want to land Ethan, or anyone for that matter, in trouble.

'I think she meant it,' Ethan adds, his tone insistent. His tears have dried and his mood has lifted in the way it always does – fast, the hurt forgotten.

Jenny thinks of Amelia's comment about the invite to lunch. Jenny had thought at the time that the girl hadn't meant it to sound as nasty as it did. But now, Jenny wonders if Amelia wanted to sabotage the lunch from the start.

Jenny shakes the thoughts away. What did it matter now anyway? Based on the lunch and Dan's reaction to the pregnancy, they won't be seeing Amelia or Bryony anytime soon.

Tears threaten behind her eyes again. It's a fight to keep them at bay. 'Lunch was a bad idea,' she says. 'I'm sorry I put you through it.'

They pull into their road of little terrace and semi-detached houses in pale brick, and Jenny has never felt so relieved to be home. She wants to throw on her PJs, hide under a blanket and pretend this day never happened.

'Dan was nice,' Jack says, climbing out of the car. 'It wasn't all bad.'

Jenny forces a smile, pulling Jack into a hug, grateful he doesn't resist this time. 'Are you really alright?' she whispers.

His head bobs up and down against her chest. 'I'm really sorry about fighting with Ethan, Mum. I'll never do it again. I promise.'

'I know you won't.' She holds him tight for another moment before they walk into the house. 'Right, who wants to watch a film?'

'Meeee,' the boys say in unison.

'Can we have some chocolate?' Jack asks sheepishly.

'If we can find any.' Jenny's gaze lands on the pile of school shirts on the back of the sofa waiting to be ironed and the clothes beside them that need to be folded. So much for hiding under a blanket.

Sod it, Jenny thinks, reaching for her phone. The ironing can wait.

Nicola arrives ten minutes later in a new activewear set Jenny hasn't seen before.

'Don't,' Nicola laughs, her hand waving over her leggings. 'Ryan has gone on one of his fitness drives again, so obviously I have to up my game too. Or pretend to, at least. If he asks, I only popped in after my 5K run. Now, what's going on? I've got reinforcements,' she adds, waving a bag of giant chocolate buttons in one hand and two tubes of Smarties in the other.

Ethan appears in the hall, leaping up to grab the chocolate. 'Aunty Nicola, I got stuck up a tree and me and Jack had a fight.'

'And Dan set fire to the kitchen,' Jack shouts from the sofa.

'And he dropped Mum's cake on the floor. It went splat.' Ethan looks from the chocolate to Jenny, fist pumping the air as she nods.

'An eventful lunch then,' Nicola says, raising an eyebrow at Jenny.

'Can we start watching a film now?' Jack calls.

'Yep,' Jenny replies. 'I'm going to chat to Aunty Nicola for a bit and then I'll join you.'

As the opening music of *The Incredibles* carries through the house, Jenny makes two cups of tea and pours out the whole story.

'And you just drove away?' Nicola asks when Jenny finishes. There's an incredulous tone to Nicola's voice that makes Jenny squirm in her seat.

'Did you not hear the part where he told me he already has kids? As in, doesn't want any more, as in doesn't want this baby,' she whispers, emotion blocking her throat as a hand reaches for her stomach.

Nicola fixes Jenny with a hard look. 'Jen, be fair. What was the first thing you said after taking the test?'

'I don't know,' she shrugs. 'Something about rolling a double one?'

'And going back to the start. And how you'd already been there and done that.'

'But I never said I didn't want it.'

'Nor did Dan. Don't forget you've had – what – a week wondering about whether you were pregnant before finding out? It was already in the back of your mind. Whereas Dan got it thrown at him, completely out of the blue after a terrible afternoon, and his reaction was exactly the same as yours.'

'Except he didn't then say he was OK with it.'

Nicola smacks a hand against her forehead. 'Because you ran off without giving him the chance.'

Jenny wishes she could ignore her best friend's words, but they seep in, ice to the heat still simmering inside her. Everything Nicola is saying is true, but her best friend wasn't there. She didn't see the look on Dan's face. The horror.

'He isn't Paul,' Nicola says, voice soft, eyes glancing to the door to make sure she's not being overheard.

'I know he's not Paul. He's nothing like Paul.'

'Exactly. So from everything you've told me about Dan, he doesn't strike me as the type who's going to run for the hills the moment things get tough. Just give him a chance.'

'Paul didn't run for the hills,' Jenny says before lowering her voice. 'He ran into other women's beds.'

'I know, and I also know you're scared to get hurt here, but running away, backing off, whatever you call it, because you think Dan's about to do the same, is only hurting yourself.'

Jenny's cheeks flush pink. 'That's not what's going on here. Dan and I . . . it was fun, but we both have our own lives. I have Jack and Ethan and he has the girls. What we had wasn't serious and a baby isn't going to change that.'

'Maybe you're right,' Nicola says, 'but whatever happens, nothing will change if you don't let it or want it.'

'What do you mean?'

'I mean—' Nicola's words stop short as the doorbell trills through the house.

Chapter 12

Dan

'I'm sorry,' Dan half shouts as Jenny's door opens. Except it's not Jenny standing in front of him. It's someone else. Someone in fitness gear with short dark hair.

He frowns for a moment. 'Nicola?'

She grins. 'Hi, Dan. It's nice to finally meet you.'

'And you,' he says with a smile. 'I've heard a lot of good things about you.'

'Likewise.'

'Is Jenny here?' He bites his lip. The question he wants to ask lurking just behind it. *Will she speak to me?* He feels like a teenager again. Heart in throat, trying to convince Louise Fellgood's dad to let her come to the park with him.

There's a knowing in Nicola's eyes that makes Dan cringe inwardly. His face grows hot. 'It was a shock,' he says.

'I know. Come in.' She waves him into a small hallway that smells of clean clothes and Jenny. 'Why don't you say hi to the boys. I'll grab Jenny.'

Dan steps into a square living room with a grey corner sofa taking up most of the space. The boys look up briefly from a film they're watching and Dan raises his hand in a wave. 'Hey, guys. Glad to see you got some pudding,' he says, nodding to the bags of chocolate sitting between them.

Jack's face turns red and Dan gives him a reassuring smile.

'Ethan, Bryony wanted me to tell you she's sorry she didn't play with you. She said she'll play with you next time though.' *If there is a next time.* The thought flips through him, fear and hope.

Ethan nods, his eyes remaining fixed on the animation. A minute passes before Nicola appears with Jenny in tow. 'Right, off you go. I'll stay here with the boys.'

'What?' Jenny says, glancing at Dan before looking quickly away.

'Go and take a walk or something. Talk.'

'Please, Jenny,' Dan adds as nerves hit him again. Talk. Except Dan still has no idea what he's going to say. He wishes they could jump forward, skip the chat altogether and be in a place where everything is alright. He wishes he could take Jenny in his arms and they could kiss instead and she'd know all the things in his head that he can't get out.

She sighs, the determined look on her face half killing him, but she nods too and a few minutes later they're wandering along the road in the direction of a small woodland.

There's a damp mist in the air, like rain that's not falling. It makes Jenny's curls spring tighter. They walk in silence and for the first time since sitting beside Jenny at the bonfire night school quiz, Dan feels awkward. He shoves his hands into his pockets, hoping it looks like it's the nip in the February air and not because he doesn't know what to do with his hands.

When the pavement gives way to a dirt path and soggy, long-forgotten autumn leaves, Dan reaches out for Jenny's hand, pulling her to a stop.

'I was an arse,' he says.

She lifts her head for the first time. Her expression is a hard mask.

'I'm so sorry,' he adds.

'Do you think I wanted this? Do you think I planned this? Do you think I've done this to trap you? I'm already a single mother. I've raised Jack and Ethan alone since they were babies. Jack is going to secondary school in September. And I'm forty at the end of August. I thought I was done with babies, but it's happening and I'm scared and happy and—'

'I know. Me too. I'm sorry. I was an idiot. I didn't mean to sound—'

'Like a dick?'

'Exactly.' Dan gives a small half-smile. 'It just . . . it was the last thing I expected you to say. Lunch was terrible and you were mad and my head was focused on trying to fix it.'

Something in Jenny's face softens. He moves closer and she doesn't back away as he takes her hand in his, desperate suddenly to hold her, to not let her go.

'Can we try it all again?' he pleads. 'Pretend like you've not told me. I'll get it right this time, I promise.'

'I'm sorry too.' She lifts her head and their eyes connect. 'For throwing it at you like that. I was freaking out too.'

He wraps his arms around her and they stay like that, holding each other for a minute, the only sound the wind shaking the branches, the rustle of undergrowth from somewhere nearby. Dan tightens his hold, pressing his face into Jenny's hair, breathing in the coconut scent of her shampoo. 'How about we mark today as the lunch from hell, let it go and move on?'

'Move on to what, though?' Jenny's voice rings with emotion. 'What we had before was fun, it was great, but—'

'We can't go back to that,' Dan says, realising what Jenny is saying. 'But we don't have to decide everything this second, do we? Maybe we could just . . .' He shrugs. 'Try.'

'Try?'

Something sparks in Jenny's eyes. Dan thinks he might be starting to understand that look. Jenny's barriers are going up, and he hurries to say the right thing. 'At us, I mean. At this,' he waves a hand between them. 'Take every day as it comes. I know it's not some grand romantic gesture I'm making here, but I like you and I think you like me and we get on well . . .' *God, this is so hard.* 'And you're having our baby.'

Dan studies Jenny's face, watching the hesitance as she takes in his words.

'What I'm trying to say,' he jumps in before she can speak. 'Rather terribly, I realise, is Jenny Travis, would you be my girlfriend?' The question is ludicrous but it has the desired effect. The moment it's out, the tension between them disappears. Jenny bursts out laughing and Dan grins as the sound rings in his ears, filling him with hope that he's not completely messing this up.

'Did you seriously just ask me that?'

He laughs, rubbing a hand against the stubble on his face where it's starting to itch. 'Yes, I did.'

'Even though I'm knocked-up and nearly forty?'

'You know I'm six years older than you. Nearer fifty than forty. And I think I need reading glasses. Either that or that sign over there really says conversation arena, not conservation area.'

Jenny rolls her eyes, but they're dancing with amusement too.

'Hey,' Dan says with mock hurt. 'Mentioning reading glasses is one of my best seduction lines.'

'Um . . . I'm not exactly feeling like seducible material right now.'

'You are kidding?' His eyes trail to her cleavage, the dress that clings to her so perfectly and he feels desire stirring inside him. He swallows hard. 'If it wasn't broad daylight, I would totally be taking you for a drive in the love wagon.'

She looks into his eyes for a beat before they both burst out laughing. 'I think your love wagon has got us into enough trouble, don't you?'

'Oh god, don't.' They fall silent for a moment and then he says, 'Jenny, did you have something you wanted to tell me?'

She throws back her head and laughs. 'Oh right. Yes. Dan . . . I'm pregnant. We're having a baby.'

'What?' Dan yells with a wide grin. 'That's fantastic news. I'm so excited. How are you? Do you feel OK?'

Tears pool in Jenny's eyes, but she's smiling too. 'Tired but OK. Scared. Really, really scared.'

'Don't be. I'm in all the way.'

'Really?' she asks.

'One hundred per cent.'

They walk again, taking a path that leads deeper into the woods. There's a frosty feel to the air despite the daffodils poking through the ground, the promise of spring. The sun is starting to set, casting its sleepy orange rays through the trees.

'So is that a yes?' he asks. 'Can we try this? Us, I mean. No pressure.'

'No pressure except a baby,' Jenny says with a wry smile.

His chest lurches at the words, the craziness. Maybe it would be better if they went to being just friends. What if it doesn't work out and they end up hating each other? Dan isn't sure he's got it in him to play nice with another ex. He forces the thought away and tries to focus on Jenny and how much he likes her. It's enough for now. 'One day at time,' he says as much for Jenny as for himself.

She gives a slow nod. 'No pressure,' she repeats without conviction as though the word is a new top she's trying on for size.

Something zips though him – sparking nerves. He'll need to think about how to tell Amelia and Bryony, he'll need to wrap his head around the idea of nappies and sleepless nights and dribbly noses and mushy food, but right now all he can think about is holding their baby – his and Jenny's – in his arms and that thought excites him more than he could ever have imagined.

'So, what do we do now?' Jenny asks. 'With the kids? Should we keep things just us for now?'

Dan thinks for a moment then shakes his head. 'The problem with just us is that we barely see each other. If we're trying this, then we need to include them at least some of the time. Besides, they'll be sharing a little brother or sister in nine months.'

'Actually,' Jenny pulls a face. 'It's more like seven months.'

Dan gulps down an incredulous *seven* and takes a breath. 'Even more reason to then. How about we start being honest with them about us. I guess we really sprung today on them, didn't we?'

Jenny nods. 'So, no more secret dates?'

Dan gives a rueful smile as they reach the edge of the woods and find themselves back on the road where they started. 'A trip to the playground instead?'

'And crazy golf? The boys love crazy golf.'

'Ah, I warn you now, I'm a pro at crazy golf.'

'Well, if your pro crazy golf is anything like your pro roast potatoes then I guess I have nothing to worry about.'

'Ouch.' Dan throws a hand to his chest in mock hurt. 'What are you doing next weekend?'

'Ethan and Jack are with their dad until four on Sunday, so—'

'Ginger has the girls on Sunday too. She's taking them to a family lunch. Let's spend the day together. We can try this whole girlfriend, boyfriend thing.'

'Should we tell the kids about the baby?' Jenny asks as they reach the end of her road. Dan can see the uncertainty returning.

'We're going to have to at some point, but maybe we get them all together a few times first.'

'What if they freak out?'

'Then we'll deal with it,' Dan says, wishing he could be half as certain as he sounds.

He leans down and kisses Jenny, long and searching until she is all he can think about.

Chapter 13

Jenny

The house is freezing again. Jenny doesn't have to put her hand on the radiator to know the heating hasn't clicked on again. But in bed, under the covers with Dan, on this grey Sunday afternoon, it's warm and cosy and delicious.

Her stomach growls softly beneath the duvet. She should eat something too. The sandwiches she made for lunch are still sitting on the kitchen counter, untouched and forgotten. She should get up. She should fold the clothes, iron the shirts, pack the school bags, check her ingredient stores, do all the other hundred jobs she normally does to prepare for the week ahead.

Should. Should. Should. All the things she should be doing, would normally be doing on a Sunday when the boys are with Paul, and yet she's in bed instead, Dan's leg hooked over hers, fingers laced together, talking and laughing.

When they're together like this, all her fears dissolve and everything feels so simple. Boyfriend and girlfriend. Just the two of them. It's when she's alone again that the doubts return. No, she thinks, it's not doubt, it's certainty – certainty that her and Dan can't last. There's too many things against them, and Jenny will be a single parent again, which is totally fine. She'll be totally fine.

'What are you thinking about?' Dan asks, his voice low as he traces a line of kisses along her neck.

The baby, them. It's all she thinks about. But aside from Dan asking how she's feeling, they've avoided the subject today. It feels to Jenny like a baby-shaped elephant in the room and so instead she says, 'I was thinking that we should really get up.'

'But?' he says hopefully.

'But I don't want to. I think this is possibly the best way to spend a Sunday.'

The stubble of Dan's almost-beard rubs against her skin and she senses his smile. 'I can't believe we found a child-free afternoon for once. We should do it more often.'

Jenny laughs and touches her stomach. Nearly twelve weeks' pregnant according to the dating calculator she found online. She'd typed in the date of her last period and gasped at the result, feeling that panic, that disbelief, all over again. Jenny likes to think there's a bump now, a small curve, a change in her shape, but it's probably just the cupcakes and countless chocolate bars she's eaten every day this week. The sugary treats are the only thing that stave off the exhaustion, the constant feeling that she's one blink away from collapsing on the sofa.

'Aren't you forgetting something?' she asks.

A hand reaches over hers. 'Ah yes. Good point.' He pauses, the silence hanging between them. 'Can you believe we're having a baby?'

'No.' Jenny shakes her head. She really can't.

Then what?

After the trip to the playground and a dozen other outings together, when Ethan and Jack and Bryony and Amelia are used to the idea of their relationship, when Jenny's belly is huge and she's a waddling duck of a thing, then what? How the hell are they going to navigate this pregnancy with four kids, let alone the birth and actually having a baby together? The answers feels out of reach, an entire world away from her warm bed.

'Are you sure you're OK for tomorrow?' Jenny asks. 'Because I don't mind—'

'I'll be there - 8am in the hospital car park. I'll drop Bryony at breakfast club and drive straight there. Amelia gets the bus to school anyway. Apparently, driving in with her dad is lame.'

'It's the first scan appointment of the day so it shouldn't be late.'

'It doesn't matter if it is. I've got my classes covered until lunchtime.'

Nerves bubble in Jenny's stomach. Fiery hot then ice cold. Her age, nearly forty, and pregnant. There's so much that could go wrong.

Please, please, please be healthy. Please, please, please let there be a heartbeat. It's the same silent prayer she's been saying to herself ever since the midwife appointment on Tuesday when the midwife had laid out the risks of being an older mother, berating Jenny for even suggesting a home birth at her age. Jenny had sat in the chair feeling scolded and small and like she might cry.

'I need to collect the boys from Paul in an hour,' Jenny sighs. 'We really should get up.'

Dan scoots to the edge of the bed and appears a moment later with his phone in his hand. 'Sorry,' he says, glancing at the screen before throwing it back to the floor.

'No calls?' Jenny asks.

'Nope. It's not like Amelia to be ill. I still feel bad leaving her but she's not texted me to say she's still poorly so she must be fine. Ginger's taken them for lunch at her sister Kate's house.'

'You don't mind missing out on family time?'

He shakes his head. 'I get on well with Kate. She's really been there for me and the girls since Ginger left, but it's Ginger's side of the family and there's no need for me to be there as well as Ginger. It's good for the girls to spend time with their mum.'

Questions surface in Jenny's thoughts. Why did Ginger leave? What would make a mother walk out on her children? Jenny can't imagine it. She wants to ask about Dan's marriage too. Where did it go wrong for them? They are questions Jenny didn't have two weeks ago, when everything was just for fun and it didn't matter about their pasts. She hates that it matters now.

Jenny starts to move, wriggling her way to the edge of the bed and trying to climb out with as much confidence and dignity as she can scrape together while naked.

'Hey, where do you think you're going?' Dan reaches a hand across the bed, pulling her back into the heat of his arms. 'We've still got plenty of time.' A half-smile pulls at his lips that makes Jenny forget the questions, forget everything but Dan. She leans closer, pressing herself against him as they kiss.

Her body stirs again. The longing spreading through her as Dan's hands roam her body. And then there's a noise. A click and then a bang.

Jenny freezes. Dan's hands stop too.

Why did it sound like the front door of her house just opened and closed? She's holding her breath as she listens. Nicola has a key, of course, but she's visiting Ryan's family in Wales this weekend.

Who else would let themselves in? There's her landlord Mrs Hannigan, but in the ten years Jenny has lived here, Mrs Hannigan has always called if she wants to stop by and considering that Mrs Hannigan hasn't responded with anything more than an 'Oh dear, I'll look into that,' for each of the dozen times Jenny has called about the hot water and the heating, the kitchen tap, the broken cupboard, the flickering landing light, it seems unlikely that she'd stop by on a whim now.

Of course there's Pam. But it couldn't be. No way. Why would she come here, now of all times?

It couldn't be.

'Coo-ee,' a voice calls through the house. 'Jenny, love, are you here?'

It is. Her ex-mother-in-law is downstairs. And upstairs Jenny has a very naked man in her bed.

A heat spreads over Jenny's body. She cringes, and just for a moment, one tiny little moment, she closes her eyes and wonders, if they're really quiet, if they don't make a sound, maybe Pam will simply go away.

'Who is it?' Dan's face is a mix of puzzlement and amusement.

'My ex-mother-in-law,' she hisses.

Dan scoffs a laugh. 'You're kidding?'

'I wish I was.' Jenny swallows back the giggle fighting to get out and throws off the covers, her eyes darting across the floor for her knickers.

Don't come up the stairs!

'Jen-ny,' Pam calls again, stretching out the name in the sing-song way she does. Her voice now sounding a lot closer than it did before. 'Are you up there?'

Oh god, she's coming up. This cannot be happening.

'Yes,' Jenny shouts out, her voice shrill. 'I'm just . . . I was just having a lie-down. Be with you in a sec, Pam.'

'A lie-down? Are you ill?' Pam's voice sounds danger-ously close to the top of the stairs.

'No, I'm fine. Would you pop the kettle on, please? I'll be right down.'

'Alright, then.'

Jenny spins towards the bed, one leg now stuffed into her favourite skinny jeans. She hops around the floor, almost losing her balance. 'What are you doing?' Jenny whispers, taking in Dan's shaking shoulders. 'Get dressed.'

'Sorry,' Dan says, gasping for air.

'This isn't funny.' Jenny bites back another peel of laughter.

'I know, I know, except, it is a bit, isn't it? How on earth does she have a key?'

Jenny rolls her eyes. 'She borrowed it once years ago and I've been trying to get it back ever since. Have you seen my jumper?'

Dan reaches under the covers for a moment before pulling out Jenny's jumper and throwing it across the room. Jenny pulls it over her head, catching the mingling scents of her perfume and Dan's aftershave in the fibres of the wool.

'Jenny?' Pam trills. 'Do you have any milk?'

'It's in the fridge, Pam. In the door.'

'Will she mind me being here?' Dan asks.

And now it's Jenny's turn to laugh. 'You know Pam, Gavin's mum in *Gavin and Stacey*?'

Dan grins, his body visibly relaxing. 'Yes.'

'Well, this Pam is the exact opposite of that.'

'Oh shit.'

'Exactly. Now get dressed. I'll keep her talking in the kitchen while you sneak out the front door.'

'Sneak out?' Dan grins. 'How old are we?'

'Shhh.'

'Are you serious?'

'Deadly,' Jenny says, the laughter finally taking over. 'There is not even the smallest part of me that can imagine introducing you to my ex-mother-in-law. She didn't like me much when I was married to Paul so I doubt meeting the new boyfriend is going to help matters.'

Dan stops moving, his eyes finding Jenny's, a wide grin stretching across his face.

'What?' she asks.

'You called me your boyfriend.'

Jenny huffs an exasperated laugh but smiles too. 'For God's sake, get dressed.'

'OK, OK,' Dan leans over, kissing Jenny. 'But you owe me another afternoon in bed.'

'Deal. And remember—'

'Silence.' Dan clasps his hands together, his face serious as he bows. 'I'm as silent as a ninja.'

Jenny laughs. 'A naked ninja.'

'Right. Good point.'

Jenny rushes from the room, finding Pam halfway up the stairs, a bottle of milk in her hands and a pair of tartan slippers already on her feet. Who turns up unannounced at someone's house and brings their own slippers with them?

'Oh, Jenny. Is this off, do you think?' Pam sniffs at the bottle before wrinkling her nose.

'Shouldn't be.' Jenny takes the milk and guides Pam into the kitchen.

'Are you alright?' Pam asks, eyeing Jenny with the same disapproving look Jenny remembers from the first time they met. 'You look . . . flustered.'

Jenny rakes her fingers through her curls, pulling them into place. 'Yes, I'm fine. I'm just surprised to see you here, that's all.'

'Why? Paul told you I was coming, of course.'

'Er . . . He must have forgotten to mention it.'

Pam tuts her Silly Jenny tut and tilts her head to the side. 'I'm sure you've just forgotten. Paul is meeting me here with the boys so I can see them. I've got a little present for each of them. Apparently, Lilly's family are visiting her today so it would've been a bit cramped at their house.' She casts her eyes around Jenny's narrow kitchen, and Jenny can almost see the thought entering her head. *Not much better here.*

'I see, well, that's nice.' Jenny is going to kill Paul when he turns up.

The creak of the stairs sends a jolt of panic shooting through her body. She claps her hands together. One, two, three times until Pam is staring at her like she's a loon. 'So anyway, Pam, how have you been?'

'Fine, thank you. Maybe I should get the presents set up in the living room. The boys will be here any minute.' Pam turns towards the open kitchen door just as Dan appears on the stairs.

'No!' Jenny yelps. 'Let me. You're so much better at making tea than I am.'

'Perhaps if you didn't spill so much of it,' Pam titters, but she moves back to the kettle as Jenny hurries to the door, cursing Paul again for inviting his mother here without telling her.

'See you tomorrow,' Dan mouths as he picks up his trainers and reaches for the front door. 'Oh.' He smirks and points at one of his feet. 'I've lost a sock.'

Jenny stifles another giggle and shoos him with her hands as he leans in and kisses her.

Dan is opening the door when Jenny catches the shadow of movement on the path outside.

'Wait,' she hisses, but it's too late. The door is open and it's Jenny and Dan on one side and Jack, Ethan and

99

Paul on the other, their hands full with bags from their weekend together.

'Hi, Mum,' Ethan says. 'Guess what Dad got me? New football boots. They're so cool. Can we go to the park and try them out? Hi, Dan. Do you want to play football too?'

'Hey, babies.' And despite the situation unravelling before her, Jenny lights up inside at the sight of Jack and Ethan.

'Hi, boys,' Dan says with a wave. 'Good to see you again. I was just leaving, but football another day would be great. Me versus you and Jack?'

Jack looks from his dad to Dan before giving a shy shrug.

'Hi, you must be Paul,' Dan says, holding out his hand. 'I'm Dan.'

'Hello.' Paul shakes Dan's hand but his gaze flicks to Jenny, throwing her a quizzical look. The hallway feels suddenly too small, the walls closing in around her.

Pam appears from the kitchen and the boys race towards her. 'Granny!'

'Hello my three angels,' she coos. 'Oh, Paul, who's your friend?'

'That's Dan,' Ethan says. 'He—'

'He'll be one of Jack's teachers when he goes to senior school in September,' Jenny jumps in.

'Oh hello,' Pam steps forward, her voice now prim. 'Nice of you to drop by.'

Dan flashes Jenny a look which can only be read as 'HELP!'

'He's Mum's boyfriend,' Ethan shouts before collapsing into a fit of hyena-like giggles that makes Jenny wonder how much sugar Paul has given him today. Too much is the answer.

'I'm going to go,' Dan says. 'Nice to see you all.' He backs away, mouthing a final 'good luck' to Jenny before disappearing down the road.

'Boyfriend?' Pam mutters as Paul steps into the hall and Jenny closes the front door just in time to see Pam's eyes turn to saucers as she looks from Jenny to the stairs. 'Oh my.'

'Hiya, Mum.' Paul wraps his mum into a hug.

'Oh, my darling boy. It's so good to see you.'

Paul releases his mum from a hug and turns her gently towards the living room. 'Why don't you sit down with the boys and Jenny and I can make the drinks.'

The minute they're in the kitchen together, Paul turns to Jenny, eyes wide and questioning.

'What?' She shrugs.

'Don't what me. Who is Dan?' Paul smiles, amused at her discomfort.

'He's . . . a friend.'

Paul raises an eyebrow.

'More importantly,' Jenny says, desperate to change the subject. 'How come you're here? And how come Pam is here? I thought I was picking the boys up from you.'

Paul throws his hands up, rubbing at his shaved head in the way he does when he's just remembered something. 'Sorry,' he says. 'I meant to text you and ask, but my house—'

'Lilly's house,' Jenny corrects before she can stop herself. She doesn't know the ins and outs of Paul's relationship with Lilly, or any of the women he's lived with in the past decade, but she'd bet anything he doesn't pay rent.

'Whatever. It's mad. Lilly's parents and brother are visiting. They've brought their bloody dogs with them. Six pugs. Honestly, Jen, the house is chaos and stinks of dog farts.'

'What's that got to do with me?' she asks, hiding a smirk. 'Why couldn't you meet at your parents' house?'

'Dad's painting the living room today and Mum wanted to see me and the boys. You know how she is.' Paul gives her a knowing smile and Jenny softens. It's impossible to stay mad at Paul.

'Insistent.'

'Exactly,' he nods. 'And I thought, this way, you won't have to come collect the boys.'

'How gallant of you.' There's laughter and shouts of joy from the living room. Jenny reaches for another cup and sighs. There is no point trying to pick a fight with Paul. The boys are happy and they're home.

'You look good by the way,' Paul says as he hands her the milk.

Jenny stops, narrowing her eyes at Paul. 'Er . . . Thanks?'

'Like you've spent the day in bed.' He winks.

'Cheeky sod,' she says.

He grins and moves towards the living room, but Jenny stops him. Now is as good a time as any with Pam entertaining the boys. 'Actually, Paul, while you're here, there's something I need to tell you.'

Paul nods, leaning against the kitchen counter, hands cupped around the mug of tea Pam made.

Anxiety flutters through her, but however much she doesn't want to tell Paul, however much she wants to pretend it has nothing to do with him, it does. 'It's a bit . . . unexpected, but I'm pregnant.'

'Wow, Jenny,' Paul does his half-frown, half-smile face. 'Congratulations. When are you due?'

'Early September, I think. I've got the first scan tomorrow so I'll know for sure then. I haven't told the boys yet. I want to give it a few weeks.'

'Of course. Good idea,' Paul nods. 'If you want me to be here when you do, let me know.'

'Thanks.' Jenny takes a breath, relieved. She should've known Paul would take the news in his stride, the same way he does everything.

'Jack might take it hard,' Paul muses. 'Have you noticed that he's been worrying a lot recently. Yesterday he was nearly in tears because the traffic on the way to training was heavy and he thought we'd be late.'

Jenny's heart aches at the thought of Jack's worry, especially if she's going to be the one causing it. 'I think his teacher leaving last month has thrown his confidence a bit. You know how he adored Miss Thorne.'

'That's true. Well, if you need anything, or want me to have the boys while you go to appointments – that kind of thing, just let me know.'

'Thanks.'

'I assume you and Dan are planning to live together at some point?'

Jenny pulls a face. 'No. The pregnancy has been a bit unexpected. Dan and I, well, we haven't known each other that long and he has two daughters, so we're taking it slow.'

'Paul, darling?' Pam's voice carries from the living room followed by a 'Daaaad.'

Paul flashes Jenny a smile and disappears, leaving Jenny to collect her thoughts, or try to at least. Her head is suddenly spinning with her past and her future. Paul is a good dad. A good man in so many ways. He never misses his every other weekend with the boys or his Tuesday pick-up from school, dropping them home after tea, full of sugar and excitement, and always takes them on holiday for two weeks in the summer holidays. He's there for every parents' evening, every problem, and the boys adore him.

Guilt sloshes inside her. Paul hadn't wanted to separate. It was all Jenny. Sometimes she wondered what would've happened if she hadn't picked up Paul's phone that day and seen the message from a woman called Denise that shattered her life.

Paul admitted to the affair and apologised, and Jenny was just wondering whether she could forgive him when she found out about the others – the neighbour when she was pregnant with Ethan, the Saturday lady at the Co-op, a mum from the playgroup. Jenny had been glad her parents had moved to Spain before her life imploded. It was hard enough without the 'how will you cope' questions on top of the heartbreak of ripping up her family.

Jenny coped the only way she knew how. By making lists, ticking things off, gritting her teeth and working hard. She created Cake-i-licious and it wasn't long before a handful of orders each month became enough work to live on, as long as she was careful with her spending and the maintenance money from Paul.

But how will she work and look after a baby and the boys alone? The question twists in Jenny's stomach and for a moment it all seems impossible. Then she takes a breath and starts a list in her head. She's done it before and she'll do it again.

March

March

Chapter 14

Jenny

Mrs Hannigan's bright hello greets Jenny as she answers her phone, tucking it between the crook of her shoulder and her ear so her hands are free to lift Fiona Kimber's nineteenth birthday cake from the oven, sliding it carefully onto the side. God, she hopes this works. Creating a cake in the shape of a Hermès bag is a new one for her.

'Hi, Mrs Hannigan, how are you?' Jenny asks, waiting for the usual stream of health complaints and excuses for why the boiler can't be fixed yet. Jenny pictures the spiky purple hair of the yoga-obsessed landlady and imagines her sitting crossed-legged on a mat in her living room.

Nicola is always telling Jenny to kick up a fuss and demand more from her sixty-five-year-old landlady who inherited the house when her brother passed away and really doesn't have the first clue what she's doing.

But Jenny has lived in this house, ever since she kicked Paul out, and couldn't afford their old house on her own. This house was the only one in Mortan she could afford and she was proud of herself for going it alone. It wasn't perfect but it was their home – the boys' home, and besides, Mrs Hannigan hasn't increased the rent the entire time Jenny has lived here. There is no way she can afford anywhere else now that rental prices have sky-rocketed.

'I'm very well thank you, Jenny,' Mrs Hannigan says in a bright voice, which surprises Jenny. 'In fact, I have something to discuss with you. Is now a good time?'

'Of course,' Jenny replies, turning off the oven. 'Is everything OK?' Her heart flutters in her chest as she drops into a chair. She had enough money in her account for the rent this month, didn't she? It hasn't bounced.

'Yes, yes,' Mrs Hannigan exclaims. 'Better than alright, I think. I've just received a lump sum from my pension and thought it's time I sorted your house. I'm going to put in a new boiler and kitchen and new flooring, and have the place decorated. You've been so very patient with me, Jenny, and I appreciate it.'

'That's great news,' Jenny says with a smile, thinking of all the cold showers she's endured this month alone.

'I've found a building firm. Two men who seem to know what they're talking about and will coordinate all the jobs. They can start around the middle of May, so I just wanted to check you and the boys have somewhere else to live?'

'Somewhere else?' Jenny frowns. 'Can't we stay here?'

'Oh, Jenny love, there'll be so much dust and noise. You'll not be able to bake any of those delicious cakes of yours and there'll be no heat or water or electrics for a little while.'

'How long is it going to take?' Jenny asks, hiding a sigh. This is the last thing she needs right now.

'Only four weeks. Not long and of course I won't charge you rent. You have somewhere you can go?'

'Er . . .' No, is what Jenny wants to say. Nowhere at all. But that's not the answer Mrs Hannigan wants to hear and not the answer which is going to get Jenny a new kitchen and hot water on a regular basis. 'I'll find somewhere.'

'Wonderful.' Mrs Hannigan launches into more details – her plans for the kitchen, the colour scheme, the type of boiler. Jenny finds herself tuning out, her mind already formulating a list of options.

- Cheap bed and breakfast. No kitchen, which means no work for a month.
- Hotel. Too expensive and no kitchen again.
- Airbnb?

When Mrs Hannigan finally says goodbye, Jenny searches for places to stay. Anywhere close to Wellesley and the boys' school is eye-wateringly expensive. Frustration fizzes through her.

Jenny grabs her phone again and fires a text. Ten minutes later, she throws open the front door, practically falling into Nicola's arms as her friend steps inside. The urge to cry, to sob, to wail on the floor, full-blown toddler tantrum-style, takes hold of Jenny. She has a cake to make in the shape of a very specific black handbag, and now she has to find somewhere else to live too. At least Paul has the boys this weekend, so she doesn't have to pretend that everything is fine, totally fine, nothing to worry about here.

Everything had been going so well. The last five weeks have flown by. The twelve-week scan, her and Dan, days out together with the kids. They've all had fun, but Jenny should've known it wouldn't last. Should've known the universe would lob a Mrs Hannigan-shaped spanner into Jenny's bubble of happiness.

'I'm here,' Nicola pants as though she's sprinted the three roads from her house to Jenny's. She probably has, Jenny thinks, feeling the tinniest bit better with Nicola beside her. 'What's the emergency? I bought wine and chocolate.' Nicola holds up a carrier bag. 'The wine is for me, obviously, but I'm willing to share the chocolate.'

Jenny takes in the gym kit, the red face and messy hair of her best friend and realises that she didn't even ask Nicola if she was free.

'I'm sorry,' Jenny groans. 'Did I drag you away from something?'

'Saved me more like,' Nicola laughs, tucking her hair behind her ears. 'Ryan and I were doing a YouTube workout with that hotty instructor who's everywhere at the moment. That man is like a Rampant Rabbit.'

'Don't you mean a Duracell Bunny?'

Nicola bursts out laughing. 'Oh, Jenny. Poor innocent Jenny. I definitely mean Rampant Rabbit. If only he didn't have such a nice arse – the instructor, I mean. Not Ryan. Now, tell me, what's going on?'

Jenny's throat tightens. Panic spins tornado-style in her belly. 'Mrs Hannigan wants to replace the boiler and kitchen and decorate the house.'

'Oh my god, Jenny, this is terrible news,' Nicola cries out in mock horror. 'How will you cope with hot water again?'

'If you let me finish,' Jenny laughs, punching her friend playfully on the arm. 'I have to find somewhere else to live for four weeks from the middle of May.'

'That's easy, stay with us.'

Gratitude wells up inside Jenny. 'I . . . I can't. The boys and I—'

'Can bunk down in the spare room and you'll have run of the house during the week to bake.'

'It's a month, Nicola,' Jenny reminds her, thinking of the week they spent in a hotel room in Malta together when they were twenty-one. Jenny loves Nicola, but she's not sure living in the chaos of Nicola's house for a month will do their friendship any good. 'And hasn't Rebecca got her exams in May?'

'Oh shit. I forgot about Rebecca's GCSEs. I'm a terrible mother. You're right. Sorry, I can't help.'

Jenny leads the way into the kitchen, and, a few minutes later, they're side by side on the sofa. Jenny looks from Nicola's glass of wine to the wee-coloured herbal tea in her hands and feels her mood plummet further.

'Any woman who insists on being called Mrs Hannigan by their tenant is clearly a Froot Loop.' Nicola takes a gulp of wine. 'Is there no way they can work around you?'

Jenny shakes her head. 'Apparently not.'

'So you need to rent somewhere short term then, like a holiday cottage or something.'

'Yes, but I looked and they're all really expensive and I don't have any savings right now.'

'Jenny, noooo! How many times have I told you to build a nest egg?'

Jenny places her mug on the table and covers her face with her hands. 'About as many as I've told you that between my cake business and Paul's maintenance, I don't have the spare money for a Cadbury's Mini Egg kind of nest egg.

'Every time I manage to keep something back at the end of the month, something comes along like the summer holidays, or birthdays or Christmas.'

Shit! Shit! Shit! She has nowhere to go. Her parents are in Spain. Her brother has a studio bachelor pad an hour away in Southend-on-Sea and there's no way he'd want her and the boys cramping his style.

'Have you spoken to Dan?' Nicola asks, taking another sip of wine before placing it on the coffee table and rolling up her sleeves.

Jenny shakes her head. 'No. He's taken the girls shopping to Westfield today.'

'Brave man.'

'Besides, I'm not sure how talking to him will help.'

Nicola fixes Jenny with a look. 'Oh come on. Surely you and Dan have spoken about moving in together at some point in the future? In case you haven't noticed, you're having his baby. From what you've told me, he's got the space. A spare room for the boys and a large kitchen. Your dream kitchen, if I remember correctly. Wouldn't a four-week living together trial be a good thing?'

'Honestly, it's not come up. We're definitely not at the moving-in-together stage of our relationship.'

'So what's the plan, then? You're going to be together, have a baby together but live apart?' Nicola asks, adding a voice to the *then what?* questions gnawing at Jenny's thoughts.

'I don't know,' Jenny says with a groan. 'I don't know anything. But it all still feels so new for us and for the kids. We still haven't told them about the baby.'

'When are you next seeing each other?'

'Next Saturday. We're taking the kids to that crazy golf place near Kesgrave.' Despite everything, Jenny feels a smile tugging at her lips at the thought of Dan. She has to admit things have been going well between them. She thinks of the evenings when the kids are in bed and they FaceTime, chatting about their days, laughing at silly things Dan's students have done or the bizarre cake requests Jenny gets for hen dos. It's nice to have someone to share her day with, to share more of herself with, even if it is on a screen most of the time.

'And are you going to tell them?' Nicola glances at Jenny's stomach with a raised eyebrow. 'No offence, but

I'm not sure how much longer you can keep that particular cat in the bag.'

Jenny laughs before nodding. 'I know. We're telling them next Sunday. We're going to do it separately in case the kids freak out.' Jenny's voice rises to a squeak. 'I can't begin to contemplate living together on top of everything else, even just for a month.'

Nicola holds up her hands in defeat. 'I know you well enough to know that you have a list, so what else is on it?'

A faint smile touches Jenny's lips. 'Paul's friend has a caravan in Felixstowe. He took the boys there for a weekend in the summer last year. I was thinking of asking Paul to ask his friend if it's free for us to rent for a month.'

'A caravan in Felixstowe?' The look on Nicola's face says it all.

'I know it's nearly an hour away, but it'll be cheap.'

Nicola pauses, looking at Jenny for a moment as if deciding to say something. Then she takes her wine from the table and raises the glass. 'OK then. A caravan in Felixstowe, but you'd better come back soon or Ryan is going to cotton onto the fact that my long runs are actually me hiding out here.'

Jenny laughs. 'Oh don't worry. I'll be back before you know it.'

'Just promise me one thing,' Nicola adds.

'Sure.' Jenny takes a sip of tea and grimaces. It tastes as good as it looks.

'Talk to Dan before you do anything, OK?'

Jenny nods despite herself. Nicola is right. Of course she is. Nicola is always right. Jenny will speak to Dan about the renovations, but there's no harm in making enquiries. Whatever Nicola thinks, Dan would be as freaked about living together for a month as she is.

Chapter 15

Dan

'But why?' Amelia flops onto the sofa in the kitchen, burying her head in a cushion. 'Why can't I?' she asks for the tenth time in as many minutes.

'Because you're not old enough, that's why.' Dan clicks down the lid on the plastic tub of Bryony's sandwiches and searches the kitchen for any sign of fruit. He finds a forgotten satsuma in the bottom of the fruit bowl and tucks it into her lunch bag. He doesn't know why he bothers. He'd hoped Bryony would've grown out of her aversion to fruit by now, but they're still doing this dance. He hates to admit it, but he only puts the fruit in her lunch so the midday assistants don't think badly of him.

'Are you ready for school?' Dan asks, glancing over to Amelia. 'Is your PE kit all packed? I left it folded in your room. You need to leave for the bus in five minutes.'

'Yes,' she sighs. 'Dad, please, come on. Like, all of my friends are going. I'm the only one.'

'Is there any way we can have this conversation tonight?' Dan asks as he steps into the hallway. 'Bryony,' he shouts up the stairs. 'We're going.'

There's a yelp of a reply. 'I've not done my hair.'

'Bring your brush down and I'll do it.' Why do Monday mornings always feel so rushed? Dan gazes out the window

114

for a moment, taking in the spray of red tulips swaying in the morning sunlight beside snowdrops, dainty and white, and a dewy lawn.

Nearly the end of March already. Time is galloping forwards, leaving Dan with a panicky breathlessness he can't explain. The Easter holidays will help. Only two weeks until them. Dan tries not to count down the weeks of term, but it's hard. Relentless marking and lesson planning, coursework to mark too. Next term his year eleven students will take their GCSEs, which means extra revision classes and essay marking until his eyes blur.

He thinks of two weeks off, of a trip to the seaside with the girls if the weather is warm enough, Jenny and the boys too. The last month has gone by in a flash of trips to the park, a trampoline centre and roller skating.

No one needed to be rescued.

No one fought.

No one burned anything.

In fact, Bryony and Ethan are the best of friends. Jack is still very shy around him and Amelia has been a little surly, but he thinks that's hormones as much as anything. Dan gives a sideways glance at Amelia. She rarely complains about their plans, but he knows she's missing her mum.

She better not let them down on Sunday. The girls need to see her and, besides, Sunday is the day he's telling Amelia and Bryony about the baby and that means telling Ginger too. He closes his eyes for a moment, picturing like he always does the image of the baby, their baby, on the screen at the twelve-week scan. His stomach twists as he tries to imagine Amelia and Bryony's reactions. They'll be fine, won't they? Excited, even? Once the shock has worn off, anyway.

'But I need to tell my friends today if I can make it,' Amelia says, dragging his thoughts back to the kitchen. She appears beside him, her pleading face Oscar-worthy.

'I've already told you the answer is no, so you can tell them today.'

'Daaad. All my friends are going,' she says again as though Dan didn't hear her the first time around.

'And that's good for them, but I don't want you going shopping in town alone.'

'I won't be alone. I'll be with my friends.'

'Without an adult,' Dan sighs. 'You're too young. I'm sorry, Amelia. I know it's hard, but I'm trying to protect you. If you want to go shopping then I'm happy to take you another time, or we can ask your mum or Aunt Kate if you don't want to be seen with your loser dad.' He flashes a smile as Bryony appears with a hairbrush in her hand.

'Go get your shoes,' he says to Amelia as he scoops Bryony's tangled hair into a ponytail. No time to brush out the knots this morning.

Amelia mumbles something under her breath as she skulks down the hall. 'Where are my school shoes?'

'Wherever you left them on Friday.' It's a lie. Amelia left them kicked off by the front door like she always does, and Dan moved them to the shoe cupboard.

'Found them.'

'Anyway,' he adds, fastening the last hair bobble into place and leaning down to kiss Bryony's cheek. 'Go get your shoes on,' he says before continuing his conversation with Amelia. 'You're not free on Saturday. We've got crazy golf, remember?'

'You have. I never said I'd go.'

Dan frowns. That attitude again. He pads down the hall before remembering the lunch boxes on the kitchen sides. 'Of course you're going. It's family time.'

'Dad,' Bryony says. 'You've done my ponytail too tight. It's hurting.'

'Have I? I'm sure it will be fine,' he says, watching Bryony press at the lumps he's not brushed out properly. It's not too tight, it's just a bad job and, even at seven, Bryony doesn't want to tell him that.

'Let's try again,' he says, dropping the lunch bags to the floor and biting back the desire to sigh.

'It's not family time if they're going to be there too,' Amelia says as they hurry down the drive a few minutes later.

'Who's they?' Bryony asks.

'Jenny, Jack and Ethan,' Amelia sighs. 'Who else?'

'Amelia,' Dan snaps. 'What's going on? I thought you liked Jenny? Your attitude at the moment is not acceptable.'

'I do like her, but that doesn't mean I want to play boring baby golf. Why do we have to do stuff with them, like, all the time.'

'It's not all the time. We didn't see them this weekend. It'll be fun,' Dan rallies. 'And we'll get hot chocolates afterwards.'

Amelia pulls a face. 'Yay,' she says, her tone dripping with sarcasm.

'That's enough.' His tone is hard and he instantly regrets it.

'I wouldn't have to come to all this stuff if I stayed with Mum more.'

Dan feels Amelia's eyes on his face. A bolt of panic surges through him. *Be cool, Daniel. Be very cool.* 'You know your mum works full time. And we'd miss you.'

'I can look after myself,' she huffs.

'I know you can. But being able to do something and having to do something are very different things.'

'I've literally no idea what that means. I'm going to be late. Bye,' she says, striding down the drive.

Dan helps Bryony with her seatbelt and they drive down the road to Bryony's school. It's only a six-minute walk from the house to school, but this way Dan can drive straight on to school in time to make a cup of coffee before his form group descend on the classroom.

Amelia gives a reluctant wave as they pass and Dan has the sudden desire to pull over and talk to her, tell her he loves her, but he's pretty sure that such things are high on the lame factor.

'Dad,' Bryony says as they pull up outside the green school gates.

'Yes, sweetheart?'

'Where's my lunch box?'

Dan glances to the empty seat beside him and groans. 'Looks like we're having school dinners today.'

As Bryony scoots off to play with the other breakfast club children, Dan drives away, breathing in the final moments of calm. It's not even 8.15 on Monday and already he feels exhausted from the weight of Amelia's attitude on top of the everyday rush of their lives. He hates arguing with her, hates saying no to her requests. It knots in his stomach, the feeling of letting her down.

How the hell did his parents make it look so easy? They rarely fought or disagreed, never raised their voices. Dan wasn't a perfect kid. He tested them with the usual coming home late and a bit of underage drinking, but he can't remember them ever being mad with him.

He needs to try harder, Dan thinks. With Amelia and Bryony and with Jenny and the boys too. Even Ginger. He has to keep the peace, starting with crazy golf on Saturday. If there is even a chance of things working out with Jenny and the baby, then he's going to do everything he can to make that happen.

Chapter 16

Jenny

Jenny parks up beside Dan's car and glances down at her stomach.

In the last week, it feels like she's gone from an I've-eaten-a-full-stuffed-crust-pizza-and-a-tub-of-Ben-and-Jerry's-Cookie Dough-ice-cream look, to a distinct bump. Even Ethan asked her last night why she was getting so fat. At least she's not feeling so tired, or so desperate to stuff her face with sugar this week.

A sudden burst of nerves hits as she glances around the car park of the Congo Adventure Crazy Golf. Tomorrow afternoon Dan is going to tell the girls about the baby and Jenny is going to tell Jack and Ethan. That can of worms is about to spill everywhere.

She's worded and reworded it in her head for weeks now, trying to get everything she wants to say in before the questions start. She needs to reassure them that nothing will change when everything changes. She needs them to know that they are still her whole world.

'I see them,' Jack says, pointing to a small queue by the golf kiosk.

'Let's go then,' she says as Dan and Bryony wave. Amelia is staring at the ground, hands in her pockets, and hasn't seen them yet.

The sun is out but there's a cool breeze blowing the blossom from the trees around them. Jenny is grateful she has an excuse to wear a jacket and hide her stomach.

'Can I go first?' Ethan asks, bouncing towards Dan and the girls. Bryony's face lights up with a grin as they approach and she rushes towards Ethan, whispering something in his ear that makes him nod and giggle.

'You sure can,' Dan says.

'I'll go last,' Jack says as they collect their clubs and balls. 'Gives me a chance to assess the competition,' he adds, voice barely audible, but Jenny smiles at him. Is it a sign his shyness around Dan and the girls is lifting? She hopes so.

'Our dad brought us here last summer,' Ethan says. 'It's really good, isn't it, Jack? Hole nine has this volcano that really explodes when you knock the ball through the middle.' Ethan swings his club in the air and dances around.

'Sounds fun,' Jenny says, followed by a 'Be careful with your club, Ethan.'

Only Amelia hangs back as they approach the first hole. She's quieter today, sighing every time someone speaks. She's wearing black leggings today and a cut-off pink t-shirt. Jenny can see goosebumps on her arms from the cold and resists the urge to offer Amelia her rather uncool but practical mum jacket.

A pang of sympathy hits Jenny. She remembers being twelve. That awkward not a teenager, not a child age. All Jenny had wanted to do at that age was hang out with friends. She would've hated being dragged to play crazy golf with her family, although with her family, Peter would've tried to whack the ball over the wall while their mum asked the assistant ten times how often they cleaned the clubs, and all of them telling their dad to shush every time he started on about being burgled while they're out the house.

It wouldn't have been anything like this – a gentle competitiveness, a bit of fun, but still Jenny feels for Amelia.

'Your hair looks nice, Amelia,' Jenny says, admiring the two intricate braids that travel from the top of Amelia's head, right down to her shoulders. 'Did you do that yourself?'

She shrugs. 'Yeah, my mum taught me.'

'Amelia is going to try it on my hair soon, aren't you, Amelia?' Bryony says.

'Maybe,' Amelia replies, lining up her first shot and ignoring the look of disappointment on Bryony's face. 'Why are we doing this?'

'For fun,' Dan replies. 'Come on. Have a go.'

Amelia mutters something under her breath and takes her shot. The ball curves round a palm tree and rolls straight into the hole.

'Hole in one!' Ethan whoops, throwing his hand up in a high-five gesture. For a moment, Jenny thinks Amelia will ignore it, then she smiles and reaches out to slap his hand, and something in the atmosphere changes.

By hole seven, Jack and Amelia are fighting for first place. Dan is next, then Ethan, then Bryony, then Jenny, who is trying hard to be terrible to save Bryony from last place.

Between each hole, Bryony hovers close to Jenny until eventually she asks, 'Can I hold your hand?' and Jenny smiles and nods and slips Bryony's warm little hand into hers and listens to her talk about school and friends and guinea pigs and a TV show about a ladybird and cat superheroes that Jenny has never heard of.

'What's this place called again?' Dan asks as they reach hole eight, a runway-like start that shoots the ball into the air and over a stream before it lands on the other side. He nods at the fake palm trees and giant plastic animals.

'The lost Congo,' Jack says.

'Do they have dinosaurs in the lost Congo?' Dan asks Jenny with a wink.

'And gorillas in green jumpers?' she grins.

'It must be very deep in the Congo if they're wearing jumpers.'

Jack points to the next hole. 'There's a kangaroo over there in a yellow and blue scarf.'

'Of course there is,' Dan laughs. 'Everyone knows kangaroos are native to the deepest corner of the Congo.'

'Kangaroos wearing scarves,' Jenny adds.

'Your go, Bryony,' Ethan says, leaping back and forth over the stream.

'Please don't do that, Ethan,' Jenny calls out. 'You don't want to spend the rest of the day with a soggy foot.'

Jenny's heart melts a little as Jack steps up to Bryony and points at where the first part of the hole slopes into a ramp. 'Give it a really big whack,' he says. 'So it can jump over the water to the hole on the other side.'

Bryony nods, tongue sticking out in concentration. The club swings forward and the ball flies up, but the trajectory is all wrong and a moment later it lands in the water with a loud plop.

'My ball!' Bryony cries. 'I won't be able to finish the game.' Her bottom lip starts to wobble and Ethan hurries over to her side.

'You can share mine,' he says, holding up his green golf ball to her.

'No need.' Dan gives an exaggerated bow. 'You may have superpowers when it comes to climbing trees, Jenny, but I'm the master of getting golf balls out of water.' Dan grins as he climbs down the bank to the stream.

'Are you sure?' Jenny frowns. 'It looks kind of slip—' Before Jenny can finish, Dan's head disappears.

'Whooooaaaa.'

Something lands in the water with a splash and they rush forward to find Dan crouching on the bank, one foot dry, one in the stream. He reaches down and plucks out Bryony's ball. 'There we go,' he says. 'Easy-peasy.'

Jack chuckles and then Ethan lets out a high-pitched giggle and then they're all laughing, even Amelia.

'Oh my god, Dad. You are so embarrassing.' Amelia covers her face with her hands as Dan limps towards them with one squelching foot.

'You got wet,' Ethan howls, doubling over, tears running down his face like he's never seen anything so funny in his life.

'Thank you, Daddy,' Bryony grins, taking her ball. 'Is your foot very wet?'

'Yes,' Amelia laughs. 'It is.'

'And there I was,' Jenny says, 'worrying about an eight-year-old falling in and all the time I should have been keeping a closer eye on the forty-six-year-old.'

Dan laughs, throwing an arm around Jenny's shoulder and kissing her cheek. She glances at the kids. Ethan is now re-enacting Dan's limp from the bank, making the others giggle.

'Whose turn is it, then?' Amelia asks. 'I'm freezing.'

'I did tell you to wear a jumper,' Dan says, earning an eyeroll from Amelia.

'Bryony's,' Jack replies. 'She should get another go.'

'Jenny?' Bryony says. 'Can you help me get my ball over the ramp?'

'Sure,' Jenny smiles, stepping away from Dan.

'I'll do it, Bry.' Amelia steps forward, reaching Bryony before Jenny.

'You OK?' Dan asks, his voice low in her ear.

She nods. 'Nervous about tomorrow and telling the kids.'

'Me too.'

'How do you think Amelia will take it?' Jenny asks, flicking a glance to the girls, now both whacking at Bryony's ball.

'Oh she'll be fine. They all will be once it's sunk in.'

Jenny isn't so sure but she keeps the thought to herself. Dan slips his hand into hers. 'I've missed you this week.'

She gives an exhale of a laugh. 'We've spoken every night.'

'It's not the same.'

He's right, Jenny thinks as a knot tightens inside her, longing and fear tangling together. She's enjoyed their late-night chats and found herself missing him too, but would they be talking this much if it wasn't for the baby? Jenny doesn't think so, but what does that mean? Is this even real? It feels to Jenny sometimes like they've stepped – no, galloped – over the early stages of their relationship without stopping to ask if it's the right thing.

They finish the final hole and it's Jack who wins. He grins at Jenny and accepts a high-five from Dan as they stroll back to the cars.

'Who wants cake?' Jenny asks when they reach her car. 'I've got some pretty tasty chocolate and vanilla cupcakes in the boot.'

'Me!' Bryony and Ethan shout together before both rushing up to Jenny.

'Just don't let your dad hold the tin.' Jenny turns to catch Dan's eye and grins. 'We don't want them all over the floor again.'

'Hey,' he says in mock hurt. 'That was an oven glove emergency situation. I'll have you know, I used to be able to juggle.'

'Did you really?' Jack asks.

'Yep. Still got the juggling balls somewhere. I'll dig them out and you can have a go.'

'Cool.'

'Amelia?' Jenny holds out the tin of brown and white cupcakes, topped with thick chunks of fudge and swirls of chocolate sauce. 'Would you like one?'

'I'm not hungry.'

'Amelia.' Dan's voice carries a warning. 'Where are your manners?'

Jenny cringes inwardly, wishing Dan had said nothing. There's no chance of Amelia warming to Jenny at this rate.

'No, thank you,' Amelia mutters.

'Not to worry,' Jenny smiles but Amelia's eyes are on the ground.

'Wow,' Dan says with a mouthful of cake. 'These are amazing.'

'Thanks. I made a batch for a birthday party. These are the cast-offs, I'm afraid.'

'Jenny?' Bryony licks a lump of icing from the corner of her mouth. 'Can you make these for my birthday party?'

'I'd love to. When is it?'

'It's not for ages,' Dan says. 'July the tenth. We're having it at home and the whole class is invited,' he adds with all the enthusiasm of Jenny being forced to attend a PTA coffee morning.

Ethan whoops from beside Jenny, pumping his fist in the air.

'Would you like me to make you a birthday cake as well?'

'Yes please,' Bryony replies, her eyes like saucers. 'What will it look like?'

'How about a surprise?' Jenny whispers, tapping the corner of her nose, her mind already constructing a huge guinea pig cake to look like Poppy.

'Eeeee,' Bryony squeals. 'And you can come too, Jack.'

'Er . . . thanks,' Jack says before giving Jenny a do-I-have-to? look.

'Must be fun living in your house with all these cake cast-offs,' Dan says to Jack and Ethan.

'But we're moving,' Ethan replies, his face falling.

'What?' Dan's gaze lands on Jenny.

Her cheeks flush and she fiddles with the lid of the cake tin. Every night this week, she'd meant to tell him about the renovations, but somehow the words never came. 'It's only temporary,' Jenny says, trying to sound casual. No big deal, is quick to say. 'Just for four weeks while the landlady has the boiler and kitchen replaced.'

'Where are you going to stay?' Dan asks.

'Dad's friend has a caravan,' Ethan answers as though the question is for him.

'A caravan?'

Jenny can see what Dan is thinking – a caravan in her condition. She bristles. Plenty of people live in caravans all year round. This is just for four weeks. If Dan is worried, then clearly he doesn't know her at all.

'It's near the sea,' Ethan sing-songs. 'It's going to be like a holiday except with school too.'

'Felixstowe,' Jenny adds with a shrug.

'That's an hour away.' Dan frowns. 'How will you get the boys to school?'

'We'll leave early,' she says, aware of the irritation in her voice.

'Can we go now, Dad? I'm cold,' Amelia cuts in and for once Jenny is glad. 'Hey, Bry, I'll do your hair when we get back, if you like?'

'Yesssss. Can we go now, Daddy? Can we?' Bryony dances at Dan's feet.

'Um . . . OK,' he nods. 'Why don't you get in the car. I'll be just a minute.'

'You too, boys,' Jenny says, and a moment later they're alone.

'I can't believe this,' Dan says the moment the children are out of earshot. 'When did you find out?'

'Last weekend,' Jenny admits, her face reddening. She should've told him.

'Why didn't you say anything?'

'I don't know. I just didn't. I'm sorry. I didn't want to worry you. It's not your problem, is it?' Jenny has said the wrong thing. She can tell the moment it reaches Dan's ears.

'Right,' he gives a tense nod. 'So we've spoken every night this week and you didn't think to mention the fact that you're moving an hour away?'

'It's only temporary.'

'And you didn't think I could've helped you find somewhere or just talked things through?'

'I was handling it on my own. It's sorted.'

There's a tension in the air. Jenny knows she's in the wrong. They're supposed to be in a relationship, supposed to be able to rely on each other. And yet, she didn't. Couldn't, maybe. She doesn't need him to help her. She's fine on her own.

Jenny waits for him to say the retort which is so clearly etched on the creases of his face and yet he swallows and shifts his feet instead. 'Well,' he says eventually. 'Let me know if I can help with the move.'

They fall silent and Jenny senses Dan is holding back. It's the screeching beep of his car alarm that breaks the moment.

'The girls must have pressed the wrong button,' he says.

'It's OK. Go,' she says, relieved. 'We'll talk later.' She turns to leave.

'Jenny, wait?' Dan calls after her.

'Yeah?'

'It's going to be alright,' he says over the noise.

Jenny isn't sure if he means telling the kids about the baby or her temporary move or them. She isn't even sure if he's trying to convince her or himself, but she nods, ignoring the doubt rising up. *Is it?*

Chapter 17

Dan

Ginger leans back against the kitchen worktop and folds her arms. She's wearing an off-the-shoulder jumper and ripped jeans which are more rip than actual denim as far as Dan can see. He feels old looking at her, which is ridiculous – they're the same age. 'Well, you did always want more kids,' she says with a short ha-like laugh. 'Good luck.'

Dan screws up his face and feels the familiar rise of frustration snapping at him, desperate to be unleashed in a flurry of hissed words. *Why do you have to be this way?*

He swallows hard, trying to bury his feelings, but it's not so easy this time. First Ginger brings the kids back two hours late. Then he finds out that she took them to McDonald's, conveniently forgetting that he'd told her he would be cooking dinner. Now she's not even taking his news seriously. It's like he's told her they're getting a puppy.

Cool it! She wants to wind you up.

It's working.

He takes a long breath and thinks of the girls upstairs in their bedrooms and the enormity of what he needs to tell them tonight. And it has to be tonight. It has to be now before they fall asleep. Jenny is telling Jack and Ethan, and if he doesn't tell the girls then Bryony will find out at school tomorrow and he can't let that happen. But he has to tell Ginger the news too because Amelia will want to call her mum, and it's better Ginger hears it from him.

Dan focuses on scraping the uneaten pasta sauce into a Tupperware pot, taking a moment to breathe, to collect himself. Jenny fills his thoughts. He didn't call her last night and he should have done. They need to talk.

Is he mad at her? A bit. Surprised more than anything. Hurt too. He gets that Jenny has been doing things on her own for years now, so has he, but to not tell him about something as important as moving into a caravan an hour a way for a month when they're trying to build something together feels like a gut-punch, a reality check. He was starting to think he could see their future, see where their relationship was going, but now he's not so sure.

But the baby. They're having a baby. The thought drags him back to the kitchen.

'Ginger,' he says, drawing in a long breath that does nothing to soothe his frustration. 'I never said I wanted more kids.'

'I'm sure you did.' She shrugs.

Not for the first time, Dan wonders how they can remember their marriage so differently. It makes him feel horribly sad and confused and angry that they never talked about this stuff at the time.

'Look,' he sighs. 'I just wanted you to know before I tell the girls because it's going to be a big deal to them, a big change. Especially for Amelia.'

Ginger nods, her smile gone. 'I know. Has she mentioned anything about her friends at school to you? She said one of them took her PE kit and threw it into the boys' changing room the other day.'

Dan's heart sinks as he shakes his head. 'No, she didn't mention it.' But hadn't he worried just the other day that she didn't seem happy at school? 'I'll talk to her later.'

'Thanks.'

Ginger hesitates like she's going to say something then seems to change her mind. 'I'm happy for you, Dan. I'd like to meet Jenny at some point.'

'Would you?' He frowns, surprised.

'Of course. She's going to be in the girls' lives more now, isn't she?'

He nods, ignoring a sudden squash of uncertainty.

There's an awkward silence before Ginger scoops up her bag from the floor. 'I'm sure the girls will love having a little baby brother or sister.'

There's a noise from the hallway. A yelp, a cry. Dan freezes. He knows what's coming but it still cuts him to the core when Amelia's scream pierces through the house. 'HOW COULD YOU?'

Damn it! He thought she was doing her homework. He'd been so careful to check, to close the doors, so determined to listen for movement from upstairs. Amelia used to listen outside doorways a lot when she was younger. A habit she developed after Ginger left. Dan always thought it was insecurity, a desire to know bad or good news before being told. He thought she'd grown out of it.

'Amelia, wait.' Dan throws open the kitchen door, but it's too late. Her footsteps stomp up each stair with enough force to make the glasses in the cabinet chink and rattle.

'Give her a minute. She'll be alright,' Ginger says.

Dan isn't so sure. He wants to ask her to stay. Surely she knows she could help smooth things over with Amelia, but he can't find the words and when Ginger steps into the hall and asks if she should get out of his way, he grits his teeth and nods.

There's another pause. 'Tell Amelia she can call me to chat anytime,' Ginger says eventually. 'And Bryony too, of course.'

Chapter 18

Jenny

Jenny's hands shake as she points the remote at the TV and pauses the *Star Wars* cartoon the boys are watching.

'Oh, Mum,' Ethan says with an exaggerated groan. 'This is the best bit.'

'You can carry on in a minute,' she replies. 'I just want to talk to you both.'

She places herself on the sofa between them, one arm around Jack, the other around Ethan, who squirms into her – a wriggling worm – and pictures the bullet points of her list in her head:

- Baby
- Still love you
- Nothing will change

Emotion clogs her throat. She should have told them earlier. Got it out the way. A plaster being ripped off, but each time she tried, something got in the way. First it was football. An entire morning spent watching back-to-back matches. Both teams lost and there was no way she could tell them after that. Then it was Ethan's homework project – a family tree, of all things. Then a friend invited Jack to play and then it was dinner, and suddenly Jenny has run out of time. In ten minutes it will be time for bed.

Get on with it, Jenny. They'll be fine.

God, she wishes Nicola was here right now. She'd know how to explain to the boys that everything is changing but that it's OK. Nicola offered, of course, and Paul, but however nervous Jenny feels, this is something she has to do alone.

'There's something I need to tell you, and at first it's going to seem like everything will be different, but I want you to know that I love you both and that we're a family, no matter what. You boys are and will always be the most important things in my life.'

Jack tenses beside her. 'Are you and Dad getting back together?'

'What?' Jenny lurches to the side and stares at Jack, wishing she hadn't heard the hope ringing in his tone. 'No. Why would you ask that? You've never asked anything like that before?'

Jack's face falls. He looks suddenly caught out. His cheeks flush. 'Doesn't matter,' he mumbles.

Jenny closes her eyes for a beat and sighs inside her head. This is not how this was supposed to go. How can she tell them now? How can she not? 'The thing I wanted to tell you is that Dan and I are having a baby. I'm pregnant. It wasn't planned but we are happy that there will be another boy like you both or a girl like Amelia and Bryony, a brother and sister for all of you. I still love you so much and will always be here for you.'

A stunned silence fills the living room. Jenny takes a shaky breath.

'Seriously?' Jack asks.

Jenny nods.

'Where's the baby now? Is it in your tummy? Is that why you're getting fat?' Ethan asks.

Jenny gives a short huff of a laugh and touches her stomach. 'Yes it is, but I'll be getting a lot fatter.'

'How?'

She should have expected the question, but still. 'Well, when a man and a woman love each other . . . Er . . .' Jenny feels Jack fidget beside her, his face turning as red as hers. 'They have a special cuddle and . . . er . . . that makes a baby.'

Ethan shakes his head. 'I meant, how are you going to get fatter? Won't you pop?'

'Ooooh.' Jenny laughs with relief. 'I won't pop. The baby grows slowly, and my skin will stretch out, I promise.'

'But you're not married.' Ethan's forehead furrows into a scowl. 'You said you have to be married to have children.'

'I don't think I did.'

'You did.'

'I'm really don't remember—'

'Will you get married?' Jack cuts in.

Jenny shakes her head. 'No. Dan and I are very good friends. It's hard to explain. We like each other a lot but our main priority is to you and the girls. Right now, we're just having a baby together and even though things will change, you are still the most important things in the world to us.'

The silence stretches out again.

'Does Dad know?'

Jenny nods. 'Yes, he's happy for us and for you both. You can call him if you want to talk to him.'

Jack's nose wrinkles as though he's not sure he agrees, and Jenny tightens her hold on him, hugging him closer. What if something goes wrong?' Jack asks, his voice suddenly small.

'Like what?' Jenny hugs him close, hating the anxiety she feels vibrating out of him.

'What if you die? Or the baby dies?'

'That's not going to happen.'

'What if you and Dan break up and he takes the baby from you and keeps it like he did with Amelia and Bryony?'

'Jack!' Jenny exclaims. 'Dan didn't take Amelia and Bryony away from their mum. Ginger wanted to work full time and live in Ipswich and they both agreed that the girls' main home should be in Wellesley with Dan. Ginger sees the girls all the time.' It's a white lie. Jenny knows that Ginger's visits are sporadic. A dinner here or there, a cinema trip. Nothing like the routine Jenny and Paul have.

'This baby,' she continues, patting her stomach, 'will stay with us. We can visit Dan and he can come here.'

'Why don't you just live together?' Ethan jumps in, bouncing on the chair like he's just suggested living at a theme park.

'Where would *we* live, idiot,' Jack says, giving Ethan a playful push.

'I'm not an idiot. We'd live with Dan too. His house is huge and then Hulk and Poppy could be best friends.'

They fall silent, waiting for Jenny's answer. How does she explain that she and Dan don't want to live together, that they're not ready for that? They like their own space. Plus the whole boyfriend, girlfriend thing on top of the pregnancy is hard enough.

Jenny still wonders if Dan is mad at her for not telling him about the renovations. Last night was the first night they didn't speak on FaceTime in weeks. Maybe she should have called him. She thought about it, but something stopped her – an invisible barrier.

'Having a baby is a big thing,' she says at last. 'And for now, that's enough.'

'Mum?' Ethan asks.

'Yes?' Jenny prepares herself for another difficult question.

'Can we watch TV again now?'

'Sure,' she says with relief. 'But if you have any questions later or you want to talk about it again, just ask.' She presses play and snuggles with the boys to watch the final ten minutes of their cartoon.

Inside, her body tingles with panic, with all the questions she doesn't have the answers to.

Later, while the boys are in the bath, Jenny texts Paul.

I've told them.

The reply is instant. A thumbs up. Then another message: *How did they take it?*

OK, I think. Jack had a few questions but they seem fine.

Another message appears from Paul: *Are you OK?*

Sudden tears sting the edges of her eyes. Three words that cut so deep. The same three words he'd texted her the night he'd left, after she'd seen that message while he was in the shower. He'd stepped out of the bathroom and she'd thrown his clothes at him and told him to get out. He'd tried to reason with her, to plead his case, but Jenny had refused to listen and he'd packed a bag and gone to his parents' house, waiting a few hours before texting her.

A familiar anger slides over her like a perfect-fitting glove. She hates that he's asking her this question now. Hated it then, too.

Sometimes, not often anymore, sometimes she wonders what would've happened if she hadn't picked up his phone from the nightstand, hadn't seen the message appear from a woman called Denise with kisses at the end, hadn't unlocked his phone to find more of the same; worse – an affair, a massive cliché.

Because they were happy – Jenny and Paul. They argued a little here and there. Whose turn was it to get the milk? Who didn't shut the fridge properly? But what couples didn't bicker? Especially with a baby and a toddler to care for. Paul did his fair share with the boys, which was more than a lot of men, Jenny knew from talking to the other mums at the playgroups she went to.

There was no sign, no doubt or niggle before she'd picked up his phone. He was just as attentive and loving as always. And yet she'd still looked at that message.

Jenny knows she would've found out eventually. If not Denise then another woman. Paul may be a great dad, a great guy, a lads' lad – the kind of man people are drawn to, including her once upon a time. The kind of man who captivates a room with a story or befriends groups of total strangers in a pub. Everyone likes Paul. But he is incapable of being faithful, a fact which destroyed their marriage and every relationship he's had since, and will no doubt spell the end of Lilly one day soon.

It's taken Jenny a long time to accept that Paul is both good and bad. The truth destroyed her at the time. It broke, shattered and obliterated a part of her she's never got back. It's not just the trust, but a faith in something – love? Romance? Jenny isn't sure.

After Paul left, Jenny spent days and days crying whenever the boys weren't in the room. Her and Jack ate nothing but cheese on toast and cereal for a week. It was Nicola that pulled her out of it.

'You are too strong to let one stupid idiot man be the end of you,' she said, appearing at Jenny's door one evening with two bottles of wine and an entire carrier bag of chocolate. 'So we're going to drink this wine and you can cry and rant as much as you want, and then tomorrow you're going to start putting yourself back together again. Take all the time you need to do it, but it starts tomorrow.'

And that's what Jenny did. Her start was setting up a Facebook business page for Cake-i-licious and throwing herself into baking.

Jenny is stronger now than she ever was before. She doesn't need anyone. She'll never be hurt or crushed like that again because she'll never allow herself to need someone like that again. The thought feels like a scratchy blanket against her skin. Her go-it-alone ethos has been great when she's actually been alone. But she's not alone anymore. There's Dan. Jenny has no idea where they are going, but she knows that if they are ever going to be more at some point in the future, Jenny will have to find a way to trust him, and she's not sure she can do that, or if she even wants to.

Chapter 19

Dan

As the front door closes, Dan turns, taking the stairs two at a time, only stopping when he reaches Amelia's door. He can hear the soft beat of music coming from the room.

This is bad. Really bad. Epic fail, as his year eight students would say.

He takes a breath and knocks. 'Can I come in?'

'GO AWAY!' Amelia screams. 'This is the worst news ever. How can you do this to me?'

Dan rubs a hand over the back of his neck and wishes with every fibre of his being that he could rewind the last ten minutes and do it all again.

Too late for that now, mate.

From behind him, he hears the familiar creak of Bryony's door.

'Daddy, why is Amelia upset?'

He opens his mouth to reply, but Amelia gets there first. She throws open her door, eyes wild, cheeks red and stained with tears. 'Dad's having a baby with Jenny,' she shouts at Bryony.

'Amelia, calm down,' Dan says, keeping his voice calm. 'Let's talk about this, please?'

'Talking is what people do before they decide things. Don't pretend you care about my feelings now.' The door slams shut.

Dan turns to look at Bryony. Her mouth has formed a little O just like the time at the funfair last summer when Dan suggested going on the upside-down rollercoaster.

Without a word, he opens his arms and Bryony launches herself into him, firm and warm.

'You and Bryony are my world, Amelia,' Dan says. 'You know that. I'm sorry you found out like this, but I was going to tell you both this evening.'

'Is Jenny really having a baby?' Bryony's face is puzzled as she looks up at him.

'Yes,' he nods, crouching, then sitting on the floor and moving Bryony to sit on his lap. 'Jenny is pregnant. The baby is due in September.'

'So Ethan will have a little brother or sister?'

'You will too, Bry.'

Dan watches her mind process this information. 'Can we play crazy golf again? It was so funny when you fell in the water.' Bryony giggles.

He breathes a little easier and hugs Bryony to him. 'Yep. I was thinking of a trip to the beach if the weather is nice in the Easter holidays.'

'Yesss.'

'Are you and Jenny going to get married?' she asks.

'Oh . . . er.' Dan coughs and glances at Amelia's closed door. 'I think the baby is a big enough step for us.' Last week he might have added in a 'for now' or 'maybe at some point in the future', but he feels less sure of everything this week.

Bryony nods, her face serious. He can see the news sinking in and tightens his hold on her.

'Are you OK, Bryony?'

Bryony gives a slow nod. 'Can you ask Jenny if she can bake some cakes with me?'

Dan smiles and plants a kiss on Bryony's head. She smells of raspberry shampoo and that soft scent that is just Bryony. 'Of course. I'm sure she'd love that.'

'Oh goody. So when Jenny has the baby, will that make me a big sister?'

'It certainly will. How do you feel about that?'

'I won't be the youngest anymore. I like that.' She smiles.

'That's true.'

Bryony rests her head against Dan's chest and gives a long yawn.

'Bedtime for you, I think,' Dan whispers.

Bryony nods before clambering to her feet. 'Nighty-nighty, Daddy.'

'Sleep-tight-y,' he says in the silly voice he uses that always makes Bryony giggle.

'Don't let the bed bugs—'

'Bite-y,' he finishes, reaching to tickle her.

She gives a delighted scream before running back to her room.

Dan smiles after her before knocking again on Amelia's door.

There's no reply this time, no screaming anger. He takes it as a good sign and opens the door. He finds Amelia, face down on her bed, sobs shaking her body. He can't remember the last time she cried like this and it's a knife in his chest to see it now.

'Amelia, can we talk?' he asks.

'No.'

'I realise that this is a shock and I am sorry you found out the way you did, but I hope you'll be happy about it when you've had a chance to get used to the idea.'

'I won't, but whatever.'

141

In three steps, he's at the bed and sitting beside Amelia. He rubs her shoulder. Her body tenses for a moment before she turns and pulls him into a hug.

'It's a big surprise, I realise that. It was for me and Jenny, too.'

'Was it?' Amelia asks.

He nods. 'But then I thought about how much I love you and Bryony, and how much I'll love another baby too and it felt like . . . a gift, is the best way I can describe it. A surprising gift.' Amelia sighs but says nothing.

'Will you do something for me?' he asks.

'What?'

'Sleep on it. Once the news has sunk in, you might feel differently about it.'

'I won't.' Despite the words, something in her face softens and Amelia wipes her face and snuggles down under the covers.

'Nighty-nighty,' he says.

'Dad,' Amelia groans, a smile twitching on her lips. 'I'm too old for that.'

'If you're too old, what does that make me?'

'A dinosaur.'

'Well then, nighty-nighty,' he says with his best dino-saur roar.

She huffs but a moment later she says, 'Sleep tight-y.'

'Don't let the bed bugs . . .'

'Bite-y.' She rolls her eyes but smiles at Dan as he stands from the bed.

'I love you, Amelia. I meant what I said: you and Bryony are my world.'

When he's sure the girls are both asleep and he's marked the final homework book, Dan lies on his bed and reaches for his phone. A weary tiredness circles his head, and yet he's wired too.

Jenny answers on the second ring. 'Hey, how did it go?' she asks, her voice quiet. On the screen Dan can see the shadows of Jenny's bedroom and a face lit by the light of the phone. Her head is resting on a pillow, hair a mess of curls around her face. He has a sudden longing to be there with her.

'OK.' Dan rubs his hand across his forehead.

'Just OK?'

'Ginger dropped the girls back late and I ended up telling her first, but Amelia overheard.'

'Oh no, Dan, I'm sorry,' Jenny says, and he can tell she means it.

It's a moment before he realises that despite the events of the evening, he feels better from hearing her voice.

'She was a bit upset. I'm sure she'd have taken it better if she'd heard it directly from me. She's OK now. She just needs a bit of time to get used to the idea.'

'And Bryony?'

Dan smiles. 'She's excited about not being the youngest anymore. How about the boys?'

'They're fine too, I think. Ethan asked if that's why I was fat, which you know, always feels nice to hear, and Jack was worried something would happen to me, but he told me just before bed that he'd help me bake cakes when I get too big to do it myself. I think they think I'm going to be the size of house in a few months.'

'Well, for the record – you're not fat, and if you do become the size of a house then you will be the most gorgeous house in the world.'

Jenny laughs. 'Cheesy, but thanks.'

They banter back and forth, teasing and laughing in a way that has started to feel familiar to Dan.

143

'I'm sorry I didn't call last night,' he says when they've both stopped giggling.

There's a pause.

'I'm sorry too,' Jenny says just as Dan asks about the caravan.

'You go,' they say in unison before laughing again. It's awkward this time.

'I should have told you about the house renovations,' Jenny says. 'I'm just . . . used to doing things on my own and I know you would've wanted to help me find somewhere—'

'It is really annoying when people want to help you. I get it,' Dan quips with a smile.

Jenny huffs a laugh, shaking her head. 'But there is nothing you could've done. A caravan is the only temporary accommodation I can afford.'

'And there's nothing closer?'

Jenny shakes her head.

Felixstowe isn't the other side of the world. It's barely an hour away, and yet Dan suddenly hates the thought of the distance, another barrier to the relationship they're trying to build. A running-out-of-time feeling is pumping through his blood, but he doesn't know why.

'I just have this feeling like we're running out of time,' he admits.

'Time for what?'

'I don't know. Time to get this right – us – before the baby arrives.'

Jenny sits up, pulling at the curls of her hair. 'It's not like a deadline though, is it? I mean it is, but it's not like a fairy tale where if we've not kissed by midnight, we'll never be together. We'll have time after the baby arrives as well.' There's a hesitance to Jenny's voice and he wonders if she's thinking like he is about sleepless nights and exhaustion and how much time they'll really have.

The pressure bubbles and froths and there's more he wants to say but doesn't know how.

They move on to easier things then. Jenny talks about the caravan kitchen space, joking about needing acrobatic skills to squeeze into the space. He laughs at the right moments but inside all he feels is the feeling that he has to get this right.

Jenny, the baby, moving away, Amelia, Bryony, Jack, Ethan. They spin in his head.

So what are you going to do about it?

He doesn't know.

April

Chapter 20

Jenny

The whoomph whoomph of a tiny heartbeat fills the ultrasound room and finally Jenny breathes.

'Everything is hunky dory here,' Sandra, the sonographer, tells them, patting Jenny's leg. 'You looked awfully worried when you first came in, Mum, but you can relax,' she adds. 'I'll just take a few quick measurements, but development-wise everything is looking perfect for twenty weeks. If anything, I think you might be slightly ahead.'

Jenny closes her eyes, taking a long in and out breath. The fear that has dogged her thoughts, hounded her sleep for the last few weeks, slips away. The baby is OK, she tells herself, feeling the ache of emotion in her throat.

'It's amazing,' Dan says, squeezing her hand. She opens her eyes and finds he's smiling. A proper ear-to-ear smile, a megawatt goofy beam of a smile that makes her think of the boys on Christmas morning. 'We're having a baby,' he whispers.

'Yes.' She smiles too, tears pricking at the edges of her eyes.

'Would you like to find out the sex?' Sandra asks.

'Yes please,' Jenny replies at the exact moment Dan says, 'No.'

Sandra's tinkling laughs fills the room as they turn to look at each other. 'You'd be surprised how often that happens,' she adds.

'You don't want to know?' Jenny asks. Her cheeks flush as she glances from Dan to Sandra. They really should have talked about this beforehand.

Dan gives a half-shrug before lifting her hand to his lips and kissing it gently. 'If you really want to know, then I won't stop you. I just think . . . it doesn't matter, does it? As long as you and the baby are healthy.' His face softens and he looks from Jenny to the screen and she feels the heat of his hand, the love pouring out of him.

'No, it doesn't,' she says.

'Alright then,' Sandra says, her fingers tapping on the keyboard. 'I must say, I do tend to agree with you. I'm not one for all these gender reveal parties. All a bit much, if you ask me.'

Ten minutes later, Jenny and Dan step outside the hospital, blinking in the bright sunlight. There is a nip of cold in the air that makes Jenny wrap her cardigan around her body. Ahead of them, a man in a green uniform is mowing the lawns of the hospital gardens and the scent of cut grass is rich in the air, carrying a promise of warm days ahead, of sticky ice creams, picnics and paddling pools.

'You're amazing,' Dan says again. 'Thank you for making me the happiest man in the world.' He pulls Jenny into his arms and kisses her long and deep until Jenny's body pulses with desire and someone heckles them to 'get a room' and they leap apart, laughing and embarrassed.

'Shall I play hooky for the rest of the day? I could take you out for a late lunch or home to bed.'

She laughs. 'I hope you're joking, Mr Walker. You've got lessons to teach and I've got a farewell cake in the shape of the Statue of Liberty to finish and I've got to start packing up the essentials for the move. I can't believe it's May next week.'

Something changes in Dan's face, like Jenny has said the wrong thing, but doesn't know how to undo it. She knows moving further away isn't ideal, but it's only for four weeks.

'Hey,' Dan says after a pause. 'What about you and the boys coming for a sleepover this weekend?'

'Really?' The idea takes hold. A sleepover. It could be fun. The last month has been sucked away in a whirlwind of trips to the cinema and the playground. Neutral territory where the kids can get to know each other better. It's been action-packed, but exhausting, and the idea of a cosy Saturday night at Dan's sounds perfect. Maybe they'll even get some time alone together.

Ha! Wishful thinking, Jen.

'We'll watch a cheesy movie and eat too many sweets. We'll let the kids sleep in the living room and slope off to bed.'

'Um . . . yes, I'd like that.' She grins, the buzz of happiness pushing through her. She wishes she could bottle this feeling, the ease of being with Dan, but no matter how hard she tries, it always fades when she's alone and the doubt returns again.

'You'd better go,' Jenny says, reaching up to kiss his cheek, breathing in the scent of his aftershave.

He sucks in his lips, frowning for a moment, looking suddenly nervous.

'What is it?' she asks.

Dan takes a breath. 'The thing is . . . I don't want you to move to a tiny caravan an hour away. I know it's all you can afford, and—'

'And it's only temporary,' Jenny says. 'We'll be back in Mortan before you know it.'

'Exactly.' Dan gives a slow nod. There's a nervous energy to him which makes her heart race.

'Exactly what?'

'What I'm trying to say is that you and the boys should come and stay with us while your house is being renovated. We've got the space and, like you keep saying, it's only for four weeks. It will be a chance for us to get to know each other even better and it's really close to the school. You'll have loads of room in the kitchen to bake all the cakes you want, although I will need to eat some myself—'

Jenny laughs at that and feels Dan's excitement catching hold of her.

'And it's close to the school.'

'You've said that one already.'

'I know, but it's a good one. What do you think?' His brown eyes gaze into hers, questioning and intense.

'I . . .' Jenny starts, but no more words come.

'Don't forget my really big kitchen.'

Jenny laughs again. As Dan's offer sinks in, she feels herself torn. 'I don't want us to stay with you because it's something you think we have to do, because we don't. There's no rush.'

'No rush!' Dan cries out, pulling out the scan image from his pocket. 'I get what you're saying, and you're right, if we weren't having a baby I might not be asking – although I'd like to think I would – but we are having a baby and so maybe it's OK to rush this a bit, maybe it's the best thing that could've happened. This isn't just about you needing somewhere to stay for a month, this is about us, about being a family, getting to know each other. Please, Jenny.'

A cool wind brushes over Jenny, carrying the scent of blossom and a future staring her right in the face. She closes her eyes and breathes it in as a single tear rolls onto her cheek.

She can't find the words. She can't explain the fear that holds her so tight sometimes when she thinks of Dan and the life they're trying to build out of cardboard and sticky tape it feels like sometimes.

Jenny looks into his eyes and feels herself waiver. Dan's optimism is intoxicating. It's swirling through her thoughts, brushing away the doubt. 'I guess it's only for a few weeks and then the boys and I will be back in Mortan.'

Dan's face lights up into the half-smile that flips her stomach. 'Is that a yes?'

Jenny bites her lip and nods. 'OK. Let's do it. If you're sure?'

'Yes. Completely.' Dan wraps his arms around Jenny, warm and strong, and just in that moment the fear lets go of her and she feels Dan's happiness mixing with her own.

Chapter 21

Dan

Dan pulls the car into the empty space by the school bins and kills the engine before reaching for his phone.

There's an energy jittering through his body, but he's smiling.

In a few weeks Jenny will be living with him for four weeks. He can't mess this up. The realisation is a gut-punch. Every mistake he's ever made pushes to the surface, burning in his cheeks.

It's not just the baby they are having, or Amelia, Bryony, Jack and Ethan. It is those things, but it's more than that. It's the two of them – their relationship that he doesn't want to mess up. The more time he spends with Jenny, the more he thinks he's falling for her. Dan closes his eyes for a moment, wishing he could call his parents right now and tell them about the scan – the little arms, the long legs; tell them about Jenny, too, and the boys. He's sure they'd have loved Jenny and, oh, how they'd have doted on the boys. The grief is a dull ache, but he won't let it take over today.

He picks up his phone and finds Jenny's number before he can change his mind.

'Hello?' Jenny's tone is questioning, and he can imagine the half-smile, half-frown she does when she's confused.

'I have to tell you something,' he says. From the corner of his eye, he spots a group of year seven kids by the gate. They watch him for a moment and one of them waves, before turning inwards into their group, their own world.

'You know we only just saw each other twenty minutes ago, right?' Jenny says. 'I've only just got back.'

'I know. I'm in the school car park. I've got about sixty seconds before the bell goes and I have to be in class, but I've got to tell you something.'

'Something you didn't think to mention during the two hours we've just spent together.'

'I wanted to, but I chickened out.'

'OK,' Jenny says, uncertain now.

'The thing is . . .' Dan pauses. The words are there. I'm falling for you. But the nerves return. It's all moving so fast. He's suddenly not sure he trusts his feelings, not sure what Jenny will say. 'I've lied to you,' he says suddenly. It's not the confession he intended but it's a confession of sorts.

'What about?' Jenny asks and Dan can sense her bristling, preparing for the worst.

'Remember on our first date when I said I did press-ups and sit-ups every day and run 5K around the park twice a week?'

'Yes.'

'Well, I don't know how to say this, but it's a lie, Jenny. I wanted to impress you. I'm sorry. I've been trying to find a way to tell you and I figure you're going to find out pretty soon when you come to stay that I don't do any of that stuff. I mean to, but then, I don't know, life gets in the way and there are always other things I would rather do.'

Jenny's laughs rings in his ears. 'Oh my god, Dan, do you think I hadn't guessed? And by the way – what a relief. A long walk in the countryside is as energetic as I get.'

'I can think of another energy-burning exercise.'

'I'm hanging up now. You are such a doofus, Daniel Walker.'

'See you at the weekend?'

'Yes, now go.'

Dan tucks the phone into his pocket and sighs as he climbs out of the car, stepping through the doors to the school just as the bell rings for the end of lunch. He'd wanted to say so much more and he hadn't. Then he remembers the photograph tucked in his jacket – the black and white image of their baby. Yes, he chickened out of telling Jenny how he feels, and yes he's about to give thirty-four groaning year nine students a pop quiz on key battles of the First World War, but he's not going to let anything get in the way of the joy he feels thinking about that image – their baby wriggling around in Jenny's stomach, Jenny brimming over with love and emotion, and he felt it too and it was perfect and . . . and magic, Dan thinks.

Thousands of people might lie on that bed in the ultrasound room every year. Thousands of dads might perch nervously on the plastic chair, eyes glued to the screen, but today – Jenny and him – that was magic.

Chapter 22

Jenny

'Muuuum, I can't find my toothbrush.' Ethan's voice rings through the house.

Jenny turns to Jack, sitting on the sofa, his rucksack on his lap, shoes on, ready to go. 'How is it not in the bathroom?' she whispers with an exasperated smile. She catches Jack's eye and waits for him to laugh. He doesn't.

She's at the foot of the stairs when Ethan calls again. 'Oh I found it. It was by the sink.'

'Great,' Jenny shouts. 'We're leaving in ten minutes.' She checks the time, knowing that they should have left ten minutes ago, but the day has run away as it always does – football and homework and a trip to the park.

You're dragging your feet!! Nicola's voice sing-songs in her head.

Am not, she wants to say back, even though she really should've asked Ethan to pack his overnight bag for their sleepover at Dan's house an hour ago, instead of letting him play with Hulk.

Jenny wants tonight to go well, and yet there is a tiny voice in her head, a whisper, telling her it would be easier if it didn't. Then she and the boys could stay in the caravan like they'd planned. Just the three of them. Simple.

It's a stupid thought. Jack and Ethan hadn't groaned at

the tiny caravan or sharing a room the size of a wardrobe when Jenny had sold them the idea – an adventure she'd called it. But when she'd casually mentioned that Dan had invited them to stay with him and the girls instead, both boys had whooped.

'The caravan was yucky,' Ethan said.

'And really far away from Dad and school,' Jack added.

They were right on both accounts and she'd already said yes to Dan, but Jenny can't shake the knots inside her, the voice whispering, 'He'll let you down.'

God, will he, though?

Yes. Probably. There's a chance, she knows that much. And yet, Jenny has to try this thing with Dan, doesn't she? No matter how capable she is on her own, how happy her and the boys have been just the three of them, she knows for the baby as much as herself and the boys, she has to try.

Jenny collects her thoughts and drops onto the sofa beside Jack. 'How are you doing?'

He shrugs, burying his chin in the neck of his hoody. 'Jack?'

'Are we definitely coming home on Sunday?' he asks.

She frowns. 'Yes. This is just a one-night sleepover and then in a few weeks we'll stay for a month while they fix this house for us, and then we'll come back.'

'We're not staying with Dan for ever?'

Jenny's heart clenches. This worry she's caused. She takes Jack's hand and smiles. 'It's just a sleepover tonight. If you really don't like it then we'll go to the caravan instead. OK?'

Jack thinks about it. Jenny can see more questions forming in his thoughts. Then he nods.

'Is there anything else going on that you want to talk about?' she asks.

He sighs. 'I miss Dad.' Easy tears well in Jack's eyes and Jenny pulls him against her, hugging him tight, shielding him from seeing the surprise on her face. Where is this coming from? Jack has never said he's missed his dad before.

'You saw him on Tuesday,' Jenny says, 'and he'll pick you up from school next Tuesday and you'll see him next weekend too, just like always.'

Jack nods his head against her, but says nothing.

'You know,' she says, 'no matter what happens with Dan and the baby, no matter where we live, you will always see your dad. I would always make sure of that and so would your dad.'

'Promise?' Jack mumbles.

'I promise. Has your dad said anything—'

'He said the same as what you just did.' Jack sits up, looking brighter.

'Do you want to call him now?'

Jack shakes his head. 'He's away this weekend.'

'Oh, where?'

'Don't know. Somewhere with Lilly.' Jack stands. 'I'll go help Ethan,' he says then, disappearing from the room before Jenny can ask him if he's really alright.

It's natural he'll worry about seeing his dad now Dan is in their lives, Jenny knows this, but it's not this she's thinking of now. It's the mention of Paul and Lilly's weekend away. A minibreak, a normal step in every relationship, and one of many steps Jenny and Dan are leaping over. She senses them racing ahead, but what are they racing towards?

Chapter 23

Dan

'They're here!' Bryony shouts, her voice bouncing with the same excitement Dan has felt buzzing inside him all day. 'Sleepover time.' She skids across the floor in her socks and beats Dan to the front door, throwing it open with a loud 'Hi.'

The sky outside is dirt-grey and it's raining. A drizzly, non-stop kind of rain.

Ethan hurries in first, arms loaded with pillows. He whispers in Bryony's ear and she laughs. Jack follows, arms equally full, but there's a reluctance to his demeanour. His eyes are fixed on his shoes and his shoulders are stooped as though he's trying to shrink himself down.

Dan opens his mouth to say something, but Jenny appears in the doorway before he gets the chance. 'Where is spring?' she grins, shaking off the droplets of rain that glisten on her curls. 'It's raining cats and dogs out there.'

'That's next door's dog called Benjy,' Bryony says, peering outside before shutting the door. 'He's always coming in our garden. Dad thinks he wants to eat Poppy.'

'It's an expression, Bry,' Dan laughs, ruffling her hair. 'It means it's raining a lot.'

'Oh yeah.' Bryony giggles. 'I knew that really.'

'How are you all? You alright, Jack?' Dan asks.

Jack looks up, body tense, eyes wide. 'Sure.' He shrugs.

Dan watches Jenny's eyes roam from Jack to Ethan to Bryony before landing on Dan and just for one moment – a millisecond really, not even worth a second thought – they stand, awkward and unfamiliar, just like that first lunch.

Anxiety floods Dan's body. It feels like a thousand tiny pinches raging through him. Sometimes he feels as though they're teetering on the edge of something, something amazing. A whole big, messy, happy life. All they have to do is jump.

If tonight doesn't go well, if the kids bicker too much, if something happens, will Jenny step away from the edge? Does he want that?

No. He wants to keep going. Dan swallows hard. He will jolly everyone along tonight, he will pull them with him. He'll do anything, everything to make this work, to make everyone happy.

'Dump your stuff, guys, let's get a drink. We're ordering Dominoes,' he says.

'Are we?' Bryony and Jenny ask at the same time.

'Jinx,' Bryony calls and just like that the awkwardness disappears and Bryony is dragging Jack towards the piano to play him the tune she's learning, and Ethan is diving towards the Lego that's out in the living room, and the house is filled with noise and commotion.

'Is Amelia in her room?' Jenny asks, glancing towards the stairs.

Dan shakes his head, stepping forward to kiss Jenny. 'She's out with Ginger on some kind of girly day. She was supposed to be back an hour ago, which means she should be home any minute.'

Jenny leans to the side, her eyes following Jack and Bryony. 'Is Jack OK?' Dan asks.

Jenny shakes her head. 'I'm not sure. He's been quiet since he came back from Paul's last weekend. I've asked him a hundred times if he's OK and he says he is, but then just before we left the house he had a bit of a meltdown about coming here and missing his dad.

'Christ, kids are hard, aren't they? No one tells you that, though. It's all about the baby stage and sleepless nights. No one talks about how hard it is when they're kids. Jack is so bright and clever and compassionate, but he has zero confidence and seems to carry the weight of the world on his shoulders.'

Dan pulls Jenny into his arms, holding her close, breathing in the scent of her apple and mango shampoo, wishing he could wave a wand and make everything alright. 'He'll be OK.'

She closes her arms around him. 'I hope so.'

It's only when they're sat around the table with four steaming pizza boxes in front of them that Amelia returns, bouncing into the kitchen with a loud 'I'm back.'

Dan breathes a little deeper, a little easier. Happy to have Amelia home despite his frustration that she's late. 'Just in time,' Dan replies, handing her a plate and ignoring the questions he wants to ask her, like why did Ginger drop her back late when he specifically said she had to be home by four? And why didn't Amelia answer her phone when he called her five times? And why didn't she reply to his text?

Amelia tilts her head, her eyes narrowing slightly as though she can hear the questions in his head and wants him to ask them, but instead he smiles and hands her a plate. No arguments tonight. Jenny is already worried about Jack. Dan needs this night to go well. He'll try harder with Jack, Dan thinks, find a way to make him feel more comfortable here.

'Did you have a nice time?' Jenny asks as Amelia pours herself a glass of Fanta and takes a seat.

'Yeah.'

'Let's see your nails then?' Dan says. 'Did you enjoy the manicure?'

'Oh, we didn't go in the end. Mum had to get her car serviced, so we hung out in the showroom and chatted.'

'What about afternoon tea?'

Amelia shrugs and Dan thinks he catches a fleeting disappointment cross Amelia's face, but then it's gone and she turns to Jenny. 'How's the pregnancy?'

'Good, thanks,' Jenny replies, swallowing a mouthful of pizza. 'Nearly twenty-one weeks' now. I feel pretty big today, to be honest.' She pats her stomach and smiles.

'Are you like, a geriatric mother, or something? Is that what they call it when you have a baby when you're old?' Amelia asks, helping herself to a slice of pizza.

Jenny snorts, taking a sip of her drink before she replies. 'I guess.'

'Amelia!' Dan's voice cuts through the warmth of the kitchen, the welcoming atmosphere he's been trying to create falling like a house of cards, flat to the ground.

'It's fine,' Jenny says at the exact moment Dan continues.

'Apologise to Jenny,' he says.

'Sorry,' Amelia huffs. 'I wasn't trying to be rude.' She drops her head, her hair falling over her face and Dan is suddenly unsure of himself.

'Well it was,' he replies, his tone softening. But it's too late and now a silence falls over them. Dan searches desperately for something to say. Anything. His mind blanks and he thinks of Jenny's comment earlier about how hard it is with kids.

'What does geriatric mean?' Ethan asks, breaking the silence.

'It means old,' Jack replies.

'Are you really old, Jenny?' Bryony mumbles through a mouthful of food.

'Er . . .' Jenny laughs, her cheeks flushing pink.

'Well if Jenny is old, what does that make me?' Dan jumps in.

'An old fogey?' Amelia grins.

'As old as a mummy?' Ethan adds.

'Ancient,' Jack nods, smiling for the first time.

There's a pause and then Amelia pushes her plate away. 'I'm done. Can I go to my room?' She lifts her head to look at him, expectant? Annoyed? Dan can't tell.

'What about film night?' Bryony asks. 'We're watching *Mrs Doubtfire*. We all agreed when you weren't here.'

'Seen it.' Amelia sighs. 'Dad, I've got homework.'

He gives in at the mention of homework. 'Come down for ice cream later, OK?'

'Maybe,' she mutters, disappearing down the hall. Dan catches the worry on Jenny's face as she watches her go and wishes he could rewind the last twenty minutes and try again.

'Jenny?' Bryony says, dropping an uneaten crust onto her plate. 'Will you bake a cake with me tomorrow, please?'

The worry disappears and Jenny smiles. 'I'd like that.'

'And how about I show you boys my guitar tomorrow?'

'Cool,' Ethan says, but it's the fleeting spark of interest on Jack's face that Dan clings to.

'I'm not an expert but I know a few Ed Sheeran songs.'

'Daddy, you haven't played the guitar for ages,' Bryony says, before turning to Jenny and the boys. 'My daddy used to be really grumpy because Mummy left and Grandad and Granny died and he was really sad, but he's not anymore because you make him happy.' Bryony beams at Jenny

164

before grabbing another slice of pizza from the box and launching into a conversation about Poppy with Ethan, completely oblivious to the bombshell she's dropped.

Dan glances at Jenny, catching the stunned look on her face as a sluice of hurt and guilt mixes with a strange sort of joy inside him. Bryony is right. He is happy. Happier than he's been for a long time.

Later, Dan finds Jenny lingering in the doorway to the living room. Jack, Ethan and Bryony are settled under duvets and sleeping bags stuffing themselves with popcorn, eyes focused on the TV.

Dan's hand slips into Jenny's and he guides her into the kitchen. They sit together on each end of the sofa, legs wrapped in the middle. He eyes Jenny's herbal tea before guiltily sipping his wine.

'Oh, you should feel guilty,' she laughs, reading his expression. She takes a sip from her mug and from the grimace on her face he guesses it tastes as good as it looks.

'Sorry.' He gives a half-smile. 'Do you miss it?'

'Wine? A bit. I think it's just knowing I can't drink, if that makes sense.'

'Umm,' he says, swigging from his glass. 'Totally.'

'Tonight has gone well, hasn't it?' Jenny says. 'It's been good.'

Dan pauses for a moment.

'What?' she asks.

'I want to say something cheesy, like – every day is a good day when we're together, but I'm worried you'll—'

'Laugh at you mockingly?'

'Exactly.' He rubs at the stubble that's forming on his face and when he looks up, Jenny is staring at him in a way that makes him want to drink her in and never stop.

'How long do you think until I can take you to bed?' he asks.

A grin spreads across Jenny's face. 'At least another few hours.'

He groans, but doesn't really mind. Yes, he wants to hold her, touch her, kiss her all over, but this right now – Jenny – it feels warm, precious.

'Is Amelia OK? Do you want to check on her?' Jenny asks.

Dan shakes his head. 'In a bit. I'm sorry about what she said to you. She always has a bit of extra attitude when she comes back from seeing Ginger. I'll talk to her tomorrow when you're gone.'

'You don't have to,' Jenny says, taking his hand. 'She needs time to adjust and it's hard for me to get to know her when she's being told off.'

'I get that.'

'But?'

Dan rubs at his face. 'It's just I don't want her thinking it's OK to talk to you that way. Ginger and I – we didn't talk to each other properly for a long time when we were married. I let a lot of comments she made pass me by and then she left and I didn't know why. I guess I don't want to make the same mistakes with the girls, if that makes sense?'

'Sure.' Jenny's fingers rub against his. There's a pause before she speaks again. 'Why did Ginger leave? I can't imagine leaving Jack and Ethan for anything. She must have been . . . really unhappy. Sorry,' she says quickly as guilt burns through Dan's veins. 'You don't have to talk about it if you don't want to.'

Dan doesn't want to talk about it. He wants to get up, to find something to do, anything but talk to Jenny, but this is 'the' conversation, isn't it? One all couples have to have when they've been married before. The 'what went wrong?' chat. The problem is, Dan has no way to answer it.

'I don't really know,' he says, adding a feeling of stupidity to the mix of emotions running through him.

Jenny waits as though he'll say more and he finds himself filling the silence. 'I know that sounds ridiculous, but she left so quickly and I was so focused on the girls . . .' His voice trails off.

'But you've talked about it since then, right? I mean it's been a few years now.'

'Four years.' Hot embers burn his face. How can he explain? 'There didn't seem any point, to be honest. I didn't want to argue with Ginger and give her a reason to disappear and never see the girls.'

'So you've never asked her why she left?'

Dan shakes his head, draining the last of his wine. 'What's the point in raking up the past now? Ginger is a bit flaky as it is with seeing the girls. Sometimes she takes my calls when I try to arrange things. Sometimes she just turns up for dinner. I get what you're saying, but it's hard enough managing the girls' expectations. I don't want to rock the boat now.'

Jenny bites her lip and Dan readies himself for another question, but then something changes in her face. Delight flashes in her eyes and she gasps.

'What is it?' he asks.

Jenny lifts his hand and presses to her stomach. 'Can you feel this?'

Goosebumps race across Dan's skin. He sits up and stares at Jenny's bump. 'Is the baby kicking?'

Jenny nods, a grin stretching across her face. 'It's faint though. I'm not sure if you—'

'There,' Dan cries out as he feels a nudge beneath his hand.

They fall silent, waiting for the next movement and Dan tries not to think about Ginger and his marriage, focusing instead on the present, on his hand on Jenny's stomach and the baby kicking inside her.

May

Chapter 24

Jenny

Jenny steps out of the car and into the warm afternoon sunshine. In the distance she can hear the shouts of children in the playing field and the sharp whistle from a teacher.

All around her there are signs that summer is almost here. From the sandals and maxi dresses of the mums walking towards the school, to the trees lining the street, now bushy and rich green. And yet Jenny has a sudden longing for winter and hiding her bump inside baggy jumpers and padded coats. Then again, if she's wishing for things then top of the list is wishing she'd looked in the mirror before jumping in the car for the school run.

She looks down at her outfit. A pair of leggings and an old t-shirt that clings to her body. She might as well be wearing one of those bright-pink maternity tops with a big arrow on it that says YES I'M PREGNANT in swirly black lettering.

Oh, who is she kidding? She's twenty-two weeks' pregnant. The baby might only be the size of a coconut, but Jenny is already feeling huge. Her shoulders are aching from the weight of her boobs pulling on her bra straps and she's pretty sure her bum thinks it's pregnant too based on its sudden growth. She'd need a tent to hide the pregnancy from the eagle eyes of the school mums. Besides, Ethan and Bryony will have told all their friends anyway. The news of the baby will have spread like head lice.

Ahead of her, parents wander into the school gates and Jenny feels her cheeks flush as she follows behind. She's been coming to this school twice a day for over six years. Why does she still find it so hard?

After the initial burn of realising that being a single parent who didn't live in Wellesley made her an outsider in every sense of the word, Jenny has built up a wall, an invisible shell that keeps her sane during drop-off and pick-ups.

Not just a wall for school pick-ups. Nicola's voice again. Is she right? Dan is the first man Jenny has dated since Paul. Eight years of single life. It's not a wall. It's what's been best for the boys. Walls are what she uses to protect herself from the cool judgement of the parents.

Except Jenny isn't the single parent from outside the village anymore. She's now the single parent from outside the village who is dating the hot single dad and is now knocked-up at thirty-nine. There isn't a wall big enough to hide that behind.

Jenny pulls out her phone and fires a text to Nicola. *Forgot to look in the mirror before the school run. Might as well have a neon arrow above my head telling the world I'm pregnant!! Save me! Xx*

A second later, Nicola's name appears on the screen and Jenny smiles as she answers.

'I've got four minutes before a meeting,' she whispers, and Jenny imagines her ducking into the stairwell at the office where Nicola works doing something with numbers that Jenny has never quite understood. 'How's the packing going?'

'Slowly. I don't know what to pack and what to leave. I feel like I'm packing too much stuff and then unpacking it again.'

'What if it works out, though?'

'What do you mean?'

'I mean, what if after four weeks you and Dan realise you're madly in love and decide to carry on living together. Surely you've thought about it?'

'That's not going to happen, Nic,' Jenny scoffs. 'This is just a one-month thing.' Jenny thinks back to Sunday morning, waking up in Dan's bed to the sound of the children getting breakfast. Jenny baking cookies with Bryony while Dan showed the boys his guitar. Ethan soon got bored and joined them in the kitchen, but Jack stayed and learned some chords. When they appeared an hour later, Jack's smile had been wide and he'd been chatting animatedly with Dan, his shyness temporarily forgotten. Jenny had stored the image away, slipping it in beside Bryony's confession the night before – both in the little file of evidence that maybe this isn't a bad idea – her and Dan – that maybe it could work out.

'If you say so.'

'And anyway,' Jenny adds quickly, pushing the conversation on before Nicola can question it further. 'I'm clearing loads of stuff out too. For every one thing I'm packing, ten things are going in bin bags or to the charity shop. I'm surrounded by bin bags. I can't believe I have so much crap.'

'I've always said you were a secret hoarder,' Nicola laughs. 'I'd offer to help later, but I daren't leave Rebecca. One week until her exams and it's like walking through a minefield in our house. She wants me and Ryan there for moral support and to tell her to get studying, but explodes whenever we do, screaming at us that we're terrible parents for putting so much pressure on her. I don't know how many times I can tell her that we love her no matter what. She's the one who wants to go to college to do A levels in science and become a vet. I'd be happy whatever she decides.'

'And to think I've got all that to look forward to,' Jenny grimaces.

'Times five,' Nicola says with a cackle of laughter.

'Five?'

'Jack, Ethan, Dan's girls and the baby.'

'Don't,' Jenny says, suddenly feeling queasy. 'I can't think that far ahead.'

Jenny pushes the thought away. She's trying not to think about the future right now. The thought of Dan and the girls, her and the boys, plus a baby. Everything has been going well. The boys had a great time at the sleepover. So did Bryony. Jenny just wishes she could read Amelia a little better, find some common ground. It's impossible at the moment though. Every snide comment she makes, Dan is telling her to apologise or sending her to her room, and she leaves with a strange smile on her face. It's half Bryony – sweet and open, and half something else. Something knowing, something that makes Jenny feel inexplicably nervous and sad too.

It can't be easy for Amelia having her life invaded by Jenny, Jack and Ethan, plus the news of a brother or sister on top of that, but she wonders if there's more to it. What does it do to a child to have a mum flit in and out of their lives? It must make Amelia feel insecure. Jenny wishes she could tell Amelia that she's not trying to replace her mum, but would like it if they could be friends eventually. There hasn't been the time to say it, and right now Jenny isn't sure Amelia would listen.

Jenny has no idea how it will work when they're all in the same house, but surely there will be moments where Jenny can be there for Amelia a little more. Or maybe there won't be. Maybe it's a terrible idea. How is it going to work?

It's the kind of question, Jenny has fixated on for weeks now. What will happen then? And that's just the immediate future. Whenever Jenny considers what life will be like in five years' time, it feels like she's back in Maths class staring at a question she doesn't understand let alone know the answer to.

'How are Paul and Ginger taking the news of the temporary move now the dust has settled?' Nicola asks, saying 'temporary' in a way that makes Jenny think Nicola is wiggling her fingers in quotes.

Jenny sighs and steps to her usual spot in the corner of the playground. She catches Ruben's mum staring at her before hurriedly turning back to talk to her friends.

'Ginger apparently laughed and wished us good luck,' Jenny says. 'So, I've no idea what that means. I seriously do not understand that woman. I haven't actually met her yet and I can't say I'm in any rush to.'

'And Paul?' Nicola asks.

'You know Paul. He was fine.'

'I did wonder if Paul might start trying to win you back,' Nicola laughs.

'Paul? You're joking. That ship has sailed.'

'You're probably right, but watch out for any moves. It's like a dog getting a whiff of another dog's piss on a lamppost and having to cock his leg too.'

Jenny laughs. 'What? Am I a dog now?'

'Nope. You're the lamppost.' Nicola's laughter rings in Jenny's ear.

'Oh great. An old grey post that stinks of piss. That sounds about right.'

'A very kind and beautiful lamppost. Shit, I'd better go. I'll text you later, assuming my tapping on the phone doesn't disturb revision.'

'Wish Rebecca good luck from me.'

Jenny slips the phone into her back pocket just as Ethan's class appears from around the corner, his teacher leading the way. She spots Ethan at the back of the line playing rock paper scissors with another boy. She's just about to wave when there's a tap on her shoulder and Jenny turns to find Ruben's mum smiling at her.

'Congratulations, Jenny,' she sings, her perfectly made-up eyes moving from Jenny's face down to the swell of her bump. 'How are you?'

'Er . . . fine, thanks. How are you?' Jenny glances to the huddle of other mums watching and wonders if they drew straws to decide which one would come to talk to her.

'So, you and Dan Walker then, ay? You sly thing. I always wondered what his type was. Great that you've locked him in too,' she adds with a nod to Jenny's stomach.

His type? What does that mean? What type is she? Whatever it is, it is the opposite of Ruben's mum with her straightened blonde bob and Joules wardrobe.

Jenny shrugs. 'I guess it's me.'

'Oh look, there's Ruben, better dash. Just wanted to pass on my congrats. You look great, by the way. I was saying to Lisa a few months back that I thought you looked pregnant, but now you really do.' She smiles and steps back to her friends leaving Jenny with the same bitter taste in her mouth that she always gets talking to that group of mums.

Ruben's mum didn't say anything nasty. She didn't wave her pitchfork in Jenny's direction and chant 'witch' at her,

176

and yet the way she approached Jenny, just to comment on her relationship with Dan and the pregnancy; there wasn't a shred of kindness in the gesture.

Jack appears in front of her and Jenny smiles, focusing on her son. 'Hey, how was your day?'

'Really good. I got the highest marks in the Maths test today.'

'Good for you.' She pulls him into a reluctant hug that he wriggles out of before she's even got her arms around him.

'Mumeeee,' Ethan shouts, weaving his way towards them. His bag is over one shoulder and he's dragging his rain mac across the playground. 'Can Bryony come play?'

'Not today, baby. We've got packing to do. Another week and every day will be a playdate with Bryony.'

'Will she come home with us after school instead of staying at the after-school club? I mean to Dan's house.'

'Dan's house will be our home for a month, Ethan,' she says, wondering if it will actually feel like that. 'And I don't know. I guess so.'

A wave of nerves pushes through Jenny's body and she adds the question to the hundred other things she and Dan have yet to talk about.

Chapter 25

Dan

Dan casts his eyes a final time around the house and wonders if it will ever be this clean, this tidy again. He bites his lip and wonders if he should tell Jenny that he hired a cleaning team to do it? Even now it feels extravagant, and yet he wanted the house to feel new for them and while Dan might be able to tackle a washing pile with gusto and has finally mastered ironing the teenie tiny pleats in girls shirts, cleaning just isn't something he has conquered.

He does it. Of course he does. But it's always a quick wipe, a run round with the hoover. Every month or so he'll make the mistake of looking up to the ceiling to find cobwebs hanging like garlands, and he throws some pocket money at the girls and they spend a few hours spring cleaning together.

Dan heads to his car, squinting at the bright spotlight of white-yellow sun. He turns his face towards it, breathing in the scents of the lavender tree now in full bloom. The sun is hot on his skin. It's not Mediterranean hot, but enough to make Dan think of the summer ahead of them.

His phone vibrates in his pocket and he pulls it out as he climbs into the car. It's Amelia:

Don't let anyone in my room until I get back!! Mum asked if we were having lunch with her. I said yes. She's taking us to McDonalds!!!! X

He sends a stream of silly emojis in reply that he knows will elicit an eyeroll, but a smile too. She's just nervous about Jenny coming to stay. 'It's going to be really noisy all the time,' Amelia said last night when he'd asked her if she was alright. He'd found her in the kitchen before bed, smearing a thick layer of butter onto a slice of toast. 'Like, I don't mind them, but the noise, Dad, come on.'

'I like the noise,' he told her. 'The house feels more alive with Jenny and the boys in it. And there will be a lot of cakes. Plus, you've always got your bedroom, Amelia. That's always going to be your space.'

'S'pose,' she said, although he could tell she wasn't sure yet.

'Give it some time, please Amelia,' he said as she took a large bite, spraying crumbs over the floor. 'I think you'll like it if you give it a chance. And it's only for a month.'

'Sure,' she shrugged. 'But if I had the loft room, it would be soooo much quieter. And you did say you'd think about it.' She finished her mouthful and dipped her head, looking at him with Bambi eyes.

'And I am.' It was a lie. He hadn't thought about it at all.

He's not sure what's holding him back from letting Amelia have the loft room. He wants to believe it's as simple as not wanting her to be on a separate floor, but there's more to it than that. Maybe it will feel easier in a few weeks when Jenny and the boys have been here a while. The house doesn't feel so much like his parents' house when they are here. More his, theirs.

Dan takes the turning for Mortan and two minutes later he pulls into Jenny's road. Her driveway is a hive of activity. He sees Ethan running into the house and Nicola handing a steaming mug to a man in a dusty black t-shirt standing beside a van with a plumbing logo on it.

Jack appears at the door, lugging a suitcase with him. He gives Dan a quick smile before dropping his gaze to the ground.

'Hey, Jack,' Dan says, jogging towards the boy. 'Let me get that.'

Jack smiles a thanks at Dan but doesn't say anything.

'How's it all going here?' Dan asks as he carries the suitcase towards Jenny's car.

'Well, Ethan is bonkers and getting in everyone's way. Aunty Nicola is shouting at Mum to stop trying to carry stuff and bossing Uncle Ryan around.'

Dan laughs. 'Where do you want me?'

There's something in Jack's posture that changes at the question as though he's just remembered something. His smile drops and he shrugs.

'Jack,' Dan says, placing a hand on the boy's shoulder.

'I know this is a big change, but I'm really looking forward to all of us living together. I've got a present at home for you and Ethan. I hope you're going to really like it.'

'Thanks,' Jack mumbles. 'It's only for four weeks. We'll still see our dad all the time.'

'Of course you will.'

Ethan appears then with a pillow under each arm and a stack of baking tins wobbling precariously with every bounce of his feet.

'Hi, Dan,' he shouts.

'Hey. Need some help with that?' Dan asks, hands out to catch the tins.

'Nope. I got it. See?' He grins, jiggling his arms.

'Hey, Dan,' Nicola waves.

'Hi, Nicola. Good to see you again.'

'And you.' Her smile is warm and she reaches out to hug Dan before pushing him in the direction of the house.

'Come on. I'll show you where the hutch is. That's going in your car, I'm afraid.'

'No problem. Lead the way.'

'Ryan is currently standing guard over Jenny to make sure she doesn't try to carry anything herself.'

Their footsteps echo slightly on the laminate floor as they step into the house. The coat rack is bare, the walls too, and Dan feels a sudden longing to hold Jenny. This might only be temporary, but it still can't be easy leaving her home in the hands of builders for a month.

Nicola leads them into the living room. There's a tall fair-haired man standing by a pile of boxes who Dan guesses is Nicola's husband, Ryan.

'Where's Jen?' Nicola asks, eyeing her husband.

He holds up his hands in defeat before pointing to the downstairs toilet.

'For goodness, sake. All you had to do was watch her.'

'I tried,' Ryan says before turning to Dan. 'I'm Ryan, by the way. Nicola's lesser half.'

Dan grins. 'Nice to meet you. I'll go.'

In three paces, Dan is outside the toilet door. He's grateful for the sound of Nicola's commands. A moment later both boys and Ryan start carrying more things to the cars.

'Jenny?' Dan knocks gently on the door.

'Just a minute,' comes a watery reply.

'Can I come in?'

'In here?'

He tries the handle and when it moves freely, he finds himself stepping into a toilet room with white tiles and a sloped ceiling. Jenny is sat on the toilet with the lid down, a ball of tissue in her hands. She's wearing a pair of dungarees over a white t-shirt. Her hair is tied up on top of her head and stray curls are falling over her face, and even though her cheeks are streaked with tears, she still takes his breath away.

'Jesus, this is the smallest toilet room in the universe,' Dan says as he squeezes himself in and shuts the door.

Jenny barks a laugh and nods. 'It used to be a cupboard.'

'I wouldn't be surprised to hear it used to be a shelf.' Dan kneels down in front of Jenny and places his hands over hers. 'You OK?'

'Yes. Totally fine. Ignore this,' she sniffs, waving a hand at her face. 'It's hormones. I'm just having a little freak-out because the plumber is here to make a start and I didn't think they'd be here until Monday and I'm not ready, and I know it's stupid and that we'll be back here in no time, but . . .' She waves her hands at her face.

Jenny gasps, a shuddering breath, before she continues. 'And I'm worried about the boys. This upheaval on top of the baby and us. It's so much to deal with. So now I'm in here, trying to hide the fact that I'm a total mess because my hormones are going mad.'

Dan smiles and squeezes her hands in his. 'This is the house you've lived in for a long time. This is where you've raised your boys, where you've been happy, where you've coped completely on your own, and now you're leaving it for a little while and moving in with me, which is a big deal for us as well as the kids.'

Jenny's eyes well with tears. She blinks and they fall one, two, three drops onto her face. 'How do you do that?'

'Do what?'

'Get me?'

Dan smiles. 'The same way you get me, of course.'

A smile touches Jenny's lip and she leans down, folding herself into Dan's arms. He feels the bump of their baby pressing again him and he holds her tight, ignoring the wave of panic now circling him. This will work. He'll make sure of it.

Chapter 26

Jenny

With Dan's hand, calm and soothing, rubbing her back, the nerves seep away and Jenny has the sudden urge to laugh. What is she doing in here?

This here – this man who'll squeeze himself into the smallest toilet in the world, who understands her tears and doesn't try to fix them, or sweep them away, who understands – this is what she's moving to. Not the house or the garden or the village, but this right here. She's doing it for her, for the boys, and for the baby. It might only be temporary but it's a huge leap too.

'And for what it's worth,' Dan says, tucking a stray curl behind her ear, 'I was bawling like a baby when I moved out of our house on Dove Street into my parents' house. I know that was permanent, but I get it.'

'You weren't?' Jenny snorts, swiping him with the back of her hand. 'You're just trying to make me feel better.'

'No, honestly, I was. It felt like such a change. The removal men thought I was downsizing to some dump because I was so upset. They couldn't believe it when they turned up at the house.'

'Really?'

'Yep,' he nods. 'Proper sobbing. Ask Amelia. She thought I was crackers too.'

Jenny runs a hand over the fabric of Dan's navy t-shirt, fiddling with the sleeve for a moment before looking into the depths of his eyes. 'Thank you.'

'Anytime.' His smile is crooked and warm, his eyes crinkling in the way that makes Jenny's stomach disco dance.

'Shall we get out of here then?'

Dan exhales. 'Yes please. I can't feel my legs anymore.'

They laugh as they squeeze themselves out of the toilet and find the bags are gone, the house empty. With some manoeuvring and a few unhelpful 'pivot' shouts from Nicola that sends her into a fit of cackling giggles, Dan and Ryan get the guinea pig hutch into his car.

Everything is ready. They're ready.

'Hey.' Dan touches her arm. 'Why don't the boys jump in with me? You can stay and have one final look around. We can meet you at the house.'

Jenny glances back into the empty hall. The walls look lifeless somehow. She knows she could wander around this house for another hour, touching the dent in the wall in Jack and Ethan's room where Ethan tripped and banged his head and the three of them spent the evening in A&E.

She could sit on the third step up of the stairs and remember all the times she's sat there crying after putting the boys to bed because . . . because of a hundred different things. Money. The boys. Loneliness.

Or wander into the kitchen and remember the beautiful cakes she made and how each one had the power to lift her spirits, no matter what. The next time she walks into this house the dents will be filled and the kitchen will be new. Hot water, warm radiators, taps that don't drip. She wonders if it will still feel like home.

'I'm ready.'

It's only when they arrive at Dan's house, Ryan and Nicola in one car, Jenny and the boys together in hers, Dan following behind in his, that Jenny wonders if she'd have been so ready to leave, knowing what was waiting for them.

The front door flies open as Jenny parks beside a white soft-top Fiat. Bryony rushes down the steps, waving frantically and grinning as the sunlight bounces off her blonde hair.

'Jenny,' she cries out. 'You're here.' Bryony throws herself into Jenny's arms, fidgeting with excitement as Jenny squeezes Bryony's little body against hers.

'Hey, Bry,' Jenny grins. 'I wasn't expecting to see you until later.'

'Bryony?' Dan calls out, jogging over. 'What's going on? Is everything alright?'

Bryony nods and skips over to Jack and Ethan, tugging them both towards the house. 'Come see your room. It's all ready. Daddy bought you both a present too. I picked the colours.'

Jenny catches a 'yesss!' from Ethan as the boys are dragged towards the house.

There's a sweetness to the moment, an excitement in the air that Jenny wishes she could take hold and never let go, but as the boys disappear into house, Jenny can't stop the sinking in the pit of her stomach.

It's the white Fiat. It's Bryony being here now and what that means.

Jenny's gaze lands on the open front door as Amelia appears wearing a purple t-shirt that falls off one shoulder. She's laughing, her head turning back to the person behind her.

Ginger.

She's prettier than Jenny imagined. All straight blonde hair and shimmering skin. Her clothes are tight, showing off an amazing figure. Jenny bites her lip and looks down at the dungarees she thought were cute but now seem frumpy and stupid.

'What are you guys doing here?' Dan calls out, running up the steps to the house as Nicola appears by Jenny's side, shooting her a WTF look. Jenny shakes her head. How the hell should she know what Dan's ex is doing in Dan's house, the house Jenny will be living in for the next month.

'Bryony was sooooo excited about you coming,' Ginger says, looking at Jenny with an amused smile. 'She wants to see the guinea pigs meet so we thought we'd surprise you with lunch and help unpack. Hi,' she says to Jenny then. 'I'm Ginger.'

'Hi.' Jenny gives her brightest smile. 'Nice to meet you. I've heard so much about you.'

'Er . . . right.' Dan runs a hand through his hair, turning his back on Ginger and mouthing a 'sorry' to Jenny before striding to the cars to unpack.

'Lampposts and dogs,' Nicola says in Jenny's ear when they're back at the cars.

It takes nearly an hour to get their things unloaded – bedding, suitcases, the toys Jack and Ethan couldn't be without, and Jenny's precious KitchenAid. So much stuff, but it's in the house now, and Jenny finds herself lingering on the driveway, feeling unsure what to do or where to put herself.

She catches Nicola and Ryan walking towards their car and jogs over to them. 'You will stay for lunch, won't you?' Jenny aims for peppy, but her question lands desperate.

Nicola hugs Jenny tight. 'Sorry. We need to get back. You'll be fine,' she whispers, reading Jenny's thoughts.

'Thanks so much,' Dan gushes to them both. 'You guys are awesome. Come to us for a BBQ next weekend so we can say a proper thank-you.'

'Sounds good,' Ryan says, shaking Dan's hand before hugging Jenny. 'God knows what Nicola is going to do without you in Mortan, Jen. She'll actually have to go running instead of just jogging round to your house.'

Nicola gasps incredulously before cackling with laughter. 'Busted.'

Jenny watches them leave and tries to fight off the feeling of being abandoned.

Come on, Jenny. You're not a bloody orphan!

'I'm so sorry that Ginger is here,' Dan says to Jenny when it's just the two of them. 'I had no idea she'd do this. I thought she'd drop the girls back after lunch.'

'It's OK,' Jenny says, although she's not sure it is. It's weird Ginger being in the house, making them lunch as though she is the host and Jenny the guest.

'Mum.' Jack appears at the open front door, running down the drive with a small black guitar gripped in his hand. 'Dan bought us ukuleles. He's going to teach me to play.' Jack beams at Jenny and she forces herself to stop fixating on Ginger's presence.

'That's amazing. Thank you.' Jenny stretches up to kiss Dan's cheek. He pulls her close and hugs her to him and they walk arm in arm into the house.

Ethan and Bryony rush in from the garden as Jenny steps into the kitchen.

'Dan put Hulk's hutch next to Poppy's and they're popcorning,' Ethan says, voice breathless.

'That means they like each other,' Bryony adds.

'Great,' Jenny smiles, feeling herself relax a little. 'Just don't put them in the same hutch,' she adds. 'I think one new arrival is enough.' She touches her bump, pushing out from her dungarees and feels a swell of love.

'Ooh lunch,' Bryony says, skipping to the table where a buffet has been laid out. 'Can we start?'

Jenny's tummy rumbles at the sight of fresh bread cut into chunky slices, sausage rolls, cuts of deli counter meat, dips and crisps and the little olives soaked in garlic. 'Wow,' Jenny says, turning to Ginger. 'Thank you for this.' She smiles brightly, trying to paste over the wooden tone to her voice and the awkwardness lurking inside.

Having someone make you lunch on the day you move, welcoming you to a new house, is nice, isn't it? Thoughtful? And yet, this is Dan's ex-wife.

'It was Amelia's idea,' Ginger replies with a wave of her hand. 'She thought it would be a nice surprise for us all to be here as a welcome. Hope it's not weird,' she adds, pulling a face as though she thinks it might be.

'That's really sweet, Amelia. Thank you,' Dan says, but Jenny thinks she can detect a hesitance to Dan's praise as though he's questioning Amelia's motives.

'Yes, it really is, thanks, Amelia,' Jenny adds quickly before Dan can say anything more. She wonders for a moment if she should hug Amelia before deciding against it. It's hard enough getting her own children to hug her these days.

Amelia lifts her head and smiles at Jenny. 'Anytime.'

'Can we start?' Jack asks, looking from Jenny to Dan to Ginger as though he's not sure who to ask and Jenny feels herself cringe inside. All Jenny needs now is Paul and Pam to turn up and her day will be complete.

'Yes,' they say in unison and a moment later everyone is tucking in.

It's only later when Ginger has gone and the boys are playing football in the garden with Dan and Bryony, and

189

Amelia is upstairs in her bedroom, when Jenny is unpacking the last of her toiletries, sliding them into the cabinet beside Dan's, that she thinks about Amelia. How she hung on Ginger's every word, stuck to her like a shadow.

The lunch wasn't easy for any of them, but maybe having her mum with her was Amelia's way of coping, and Jenny can't hold that against her. Jenny wonders about talking to Dan about Ginger and how often she sees the girls.

How can he not have asked her why she left? It's not Jenny's place to talk about parenting arrangements between Ginger and the girls, and yet she can't help worrying that her relationship with Dan, this oh so tentative life they're trying to build, is fragile enough without whatever unresolved issues Dan and Ginger have.

Chapter 27

Dan

Dan rinses the last mixing bowl under the tap before balancing it upside down with the others. Finally the kitchen is tidy again. Obviously he knew Jenny baked. It's her business and she's very good at it, but he hadn't stopped to consider how much baking Jenny did, and how much mess it created. In less than a week his kitchen has been taken over with a bright-red mixer, cooking racks, bowls, icing blocks and more sprinkle types than Dan knew existed.

And that's before Dan even considers the sheer volume of cakes in various stages of creation stacked along the counters and on the table. His new kitchen with the gleaming surfaces and everything in its place now looks more akin to a *Bake-off* episode mid-bake.

'Oh, hi.' Jenny walks into the kitchen, pressing a warm hand to his back and Dan pushes aside his annoyance. 'You didn't need to wash those bowls.'

'No problem. Happy to help.' Dan doesn't tell Jenny that the cake clutter was getting to him, doesn't tell her how he came in to start cooking dinner but there wasn't any space to chop an onion.

'I was just coming to do it myself,' Jenny says, grabbing a tea towel to dry them. 'I had a last-minute order for chocolate orange muffins I had to send the invoice for.'

'It's fine, honestly. I needed a break from the marking.'
That last bit is true at least.

'By the way, have you seen the boys' school shirts? I
thought I left them on the line to dry.'

'Ironed and hung in the wardrobe.' He grins.

To Dan's surprise, he catches a flicker of annoyance cross
Jenny's face. It vanishes instantly but whatever it was, it
wasn't the thanks Dan had expected.

'You really didn't need to do that,' she says, sounding
tired now.

'I wanted to. I was doing the shirts for the girls anyway.
It seemed silly not to do the others while I was at it.
Besides, it feels like the least I can do considering you're
taking Bryony to school now and bringing her home while
you're here. Are you sure that's OK, because the breakfast
and after-school club is—'

'Dan, it's fine,' she says. 'Honestly, I want to do it and
it's crazy for you to pay for the clubs if you don't need
them.'

He nods. 'Thanks. Bryony is really happy about it.'

'You don't need to say thank you. I'm looking forward
to it too. She's becoming my little helper in the kitchen.'

Dan smiles, his earlier annoyance at the kitchen mess
dissolving. 'Why don't you put your feet up and I'll bring
you a cup of tea.'

Jenny casts a final glance around the kitchen before giving
a reluctant nod. 'If you're sure.' She looks at him then
and for a moment it feels awkward, like there's a distance
between them. Dan thought Jenny being here would bring
them closer together, but he hadn't bargained for how hard
they would find adjusting to living together. He's trying
so hard not to let things get to him, but the moments of
fun between them are fewer than he'd like.

It's the shouting that draws Dan out of his thoughts. He catches Bryony's squeaking voice carrying in from the garden, and hurries outside, hoping Poppy isn't under the summer house again.

The sky is grey, the air cool. More like October than the last week in May, not that his mum's Camellia bushes that cover an entire side of the garden seem to mind. The flowers are in a full bloom of pinks and yellows, the leaves rich green.

No time to admire them now though, Dan thinks as Bryony screams. 'It's my turn. Jenny said so.'

'No, it's mine,' Ethan replies, his voice just as high.

Dan moves into a jog and rounds the corner to where the guinea pig hutches sit.

'Hey, what's going on?' he calls.

'Poppy is bullying Hulk.' Ethan's voice is laced with emotion, his face tight and red. He's clutching Hulk in his arms, pushing the little guinea pig up to his shoulder and kissing the fur on the top of its head. 'We thought they were friends and could play together but they're not.'

Bryony kisses the top of Poppy's head, a ginger ball of fur in her arms. 'Poppy is not a bully. She likes Hulk.'

'He doesn't like living so close to her. I'm going to move his hutch over there.' Ethan points to a spot in the middle of the lawn.

'OK, OK,' Dan says, holding up his hands and wondering if UN negotiators feel this same pressure. 'One at a time. Ethan can go first.'

'I came down here to clean out the Hutch Hotel, that's what I call Hulk's hutch.' He gives a loud sniff and wipes the sleeve of his arm under his nose before he continues. 'I found Hulk hiding right in the corner. He's really upset.' Ethan holds up Hulk as though Dan will be able to read the little rodent's mind.

'Right,' Dan nods, his face serious. It's the Friday of half term. He's just sent Jenny off to rest after a morning walking along the beach with the kids and then the baking she's done. She needs to know she can rely on him. He needs to sort this out. 'Bryony, your turn.'

'Poppy isn't a bully,' Bryony says, bursting into a fresh round of tears, hiding her face in Poppy's fur. 'She loves saying hello to Hulk through the cage where they can see each other.'

Dan looks between the two children, wondering suddenly if this is about something more than guinea pigs. But out of everyone, Bryony and Ethan have been the most excited about being together. They've settled so well into a friendship.

'It's been less than a week. Maybe they're having teething problems,' Dan begins.

'Hulk's teeth are fine,' Ethan interrupts. 'He has loads of Timothy hay.'

Dan laughs as two confused faces stare up at him. 'It's an expression. It means that when two guinea pigs, or two people for that matter, start living together, there is a time at the beginning when it's very new and both guinea pigs might find it difficult at times to live with each other or next to each other in this case, but after a little while they get to know each other better and become happy.'

Both kids grumble a response before putting their guinea pigs back in the hutches. 'Can I watch TV?' Bryony asks.

'Sure. Just for half an hour though, please. I think your dad will be here soon to collect you for the weekend, Ethan.'

'Are you watching *Miraculous Lady Bug*?' Ethan asks.

'Yes. Wanna watch it with me?'

'Sure.'

They walk up the garden together, heads bent and talking as though the last ten minutes never happened.

Dan pokes his head into each hutch and looks at the two guinea pigs in turn. Both stare back with their little black eyes. 'Come on, guys,' he says, feeling stupid for talking to the two creatures. 'I'm relying on you to work it out.'

Chapter 28

Jenny

Jenny pushes the cake tray into Dan's oven and sighs. It's Sunday afternoon and after a week and one day of living here she didn't expect to feel so much like a house guest. It's not like she thought it would feel like home or anything, but she doesn't feel settled either.

She sets a twenty-five-minute timer and sinks onto the sofa in the far corner of the kitchen. It faces the window into the garden and from here Jenny can see Dan fighting a losing battle with an overgrowing fir tree.

His brow is furrowed with concentration and his t-shirt damp from the exertion. He looks achingly sexy, she decides with a smile, remembering how her body reacted to his touch last night.

One week gone. Three to go.

Maybe she's not settled because it's been half term; day trips and film nights in PJs with popcorn and sweets. Maybe when the boys get back from their weekend at Paul's later today and they all settle back into the routine of school tomorrow, things will feel more normal.

She has a sudden longing for Jack and Ethan, a pull in her stomach. Her eyes stray to the clock. Another hour and they'll be here.

Jenny rests her head on the back of the sofa cushion

and listens to the sounds of the house. The shhhhh of the washing machine when the water drains away, the soft hum of the dishwasher, the clonk of the pipes when the hot water is running. The beat of music that drifts from Amelia's room when she's doing her homework, and Bryony's American accent as she clomps about the living room in Jenny's high heels, pretending to be at a Paris fashion show. They've yet to become familiar, these sounds.

Nicola and Ryan's visit for lunch today helped. Jenny enjoyed watching Nicola and Dan's banter, bonding over their mutual love of coffee and Jenny's cakes. Nicola hit it off with the girls too and even made Amelia laugh with a joke about Dan's pink apron.

'Baby steps,' Jenny whispers. 'Isn't that right, little cauliflower?' Jenny runs a hand over her protruding bump and is rewarded with the soft nudge of a kick.

If only Dan didn't insist on doing all the washing and folding, all the cooking, all the cleaning. She knows he's trying to make life easy for her, but it only makes her feel more like a visitor.

And there's the illogical positioning of Dan's kitchen items. Cutlery in the bottom drawer instead of the top, plates behind bowls, Tupperware sharing space with baking equipment. Her favourite mixing bowl has been relegated to the top shelf of the boot room with the unpaired gloves and outgrown hats. Dan said she should reorganise the kitchen however she wanted, but this is all so temporary. She can't launch into reorganising his kitchen for the sake of three weeks here.

There's a sound from the kitchen. Jenny glances over to see Amelia at the sink, gulping back a glass of water.

'Hey,' Jenny says. 'Your dad suggested heading to the park when the boys get back, if you fancy that?'

'Fine.' The one word is sighed, the 'n' overly punctuated leaving Jenny in no doubt that their plans are anything but fine. Amelia disappears upstairs without another word and Jenny tries not to let Amelia's rudeness bother her.

'She's testing you,' Nicola said when they caught a private moment together after lunch yesterday. 'That's what tweens do. Are you going to let her get under your skin? Are you going to let her win?'

'If she wins, will she stop so we can be friends?' Jenny sighed in a moment of weakness.

Nicola roared with laughter. 'Oh Jenny. Poor, innocent Jenny. You have a lot to learn about teenage girls.'

Jenny doesn't really mind the attitude. She wishes Dan would lay off Amelia a little, give her and Jenny a chance to move on from the snide comments at their own pace. Jenny is grateful Dan isn't ignoring it, but a little more balance is needed, she thinks, promising herself she'll talk to Dan later.

Things have been . . . Jenny struggles for the word. Strained? Weird? Between her and Dan. Sometimes they're laughing, and talking and talking like they used on FaceTime, and last night was amazing, but there are other times too when it feels like they should be talking and instead it's all so polite.

A desire to get up and move itches under Jenny's skin. If she was at home right now, she'd be cleaning or tidying or doing one of the hundred little jobs she leaves for the weekends when the boys are away. Her eyes roam the kitchen for something to do, but Dan has already cleaned it. Again.

Washing, she realises suddenly. Jenny leaps up with far too much excitement at the thought of being busy, distracting herself from her thoughts and the gnawing worry that things don't feel quite right here.

She heads for the airer in the utility room where she hung the boys washing earlier, but it's gone, and suddenly Jenny knows without looking that the clothes will be already folded and neatly packed away in the boys' drawers. A niggle of frustration wends through her body. She pushes it aside, tells herself she's being stupid, but it's there anyway.

'Hey, gorgeous,' Dan says, poking his head around the door.

'Hi,' she smiles.

'I'm a bit sweaty and feeling very manly and wondered if you wanted a cuddle.' He slips into the room and closes the door, eyes twinkling with mischief, lips puckered as he steps towards her with his arms out.

'No,' she laughs. 'You can keep your sweat and your manliness to yourself until you've showered. Have you seen the boys' washing?'

He stops moving and grins, bowing a little as though he's a servant. 'Folded and put away. I did it earlier while you were playing hairdressers with Bryony.'

Jenny touches the top knot of her curls and pulls a face. 'When do you think it's an acceptable time to take this out without causing offence?' She enjoyed plaiting Bryony's hair and listening to the girl talk at a hundred miles an hour about school and friends and the fairy books she loves, but walking around with a tangled bun on the top of her head, not to mention the three glittery JoJo bows stuck on the sides, is a new experience.

'At least two days,' Dan replies with a grin.

'You didn't need to fold their washing,' she says a moment later, trying to keep her tone light, trying not to make a big deal out of it.

He shrugs. 'I was doing some other folding anyway.'

'Sure, but I like to leave the clothes on the boys' beds for them to put away so they're not growing up to think the wash basket is a magical portal where clothes appear back in their drawers. I just . . . it sort of makes me feel like a guest here with you doing everything.'

'And that's a bad thing?' Dan pulls a quizzical face.

'I'm used to doing this stuff on my own.'

'You're not alone anymore, though. I'm here to help.'

'But I don't want to feel like a guest and I don't want the boys to get used to having everything done for them.'

Dan pauses for a beat. 'Got it.' The two words are tense, annoyed.

'I know I sound crazy.'

Dan sighs, rubbing at the back of his neck. 'You don't sound crazy,' he says, his voice softer now. 'I want you to feel at home here.'

They fall silent and it feels to Jenny like they should be talking more about this, arguing even, and instead Dan has accepted it.

'A magical portal?' A smile twitches on Dan's face and it's then that Jenny catches a whiff of something. Burning. It takes her a few seconds to register what the smell means. Her cakes. She pushes past him and throws open the door.

'What?' he asks. 'Do I smell that bad?'

'My cakes.' The smell of burned sponge fills her senses and she knows before she opens the oven that all thirty of the cupcakes will be ruined.

'What's up?' Dan asks, following her into the room.

'The cakes are burned.' She checks the timer on her phone. Still five minutes to go. These cakes shouldn't be burned. They shouldn't even be ready. Jenny grabs the oven gloves and pulls out a tray of chocolate sponges, black and hard on top.

'They look OK to me.'

'They're not. They're ruined,' she snaps. An anger surges through her, burning like the cakes, and Dan's bright optimism is not what she needs right now. She stomps on the bin pedal and the lid flies up just in time to catch the cakes she shakes in.

Thirty cakes in the bin. Tears of anger and frustration build in her eyes as she snatches up her phone and checks the time. It's Sunday, late afternoon, the boys will be back any minute and she should have been finished by now. Should've done it earlier instead of playing with Bryony.

Shit! This would never have happened at her old house. She grits her teeth, fighting to keep the comment from flying out.

Chapter 29

Dan

Tension hangs in the air alongside the smell of burned sponge. Dan watches helplessly as Jenny scrubs at the pan, clattering it against the sink so hard he worries it will scratch.

'Hey, it's OK,' Dan says, resting a hand on her shoulder. 'It's only cake.' The second the words are out he knows they were the wrong ones.

You idiot, Dan!

Jenny shrugs his touch away. Her face is tight, her eyes swimming with the threat of tears. He wants to take it all away, fix it, but how?

'It's not only cakes to me,' she says, her voice sharp. 'It's my business. It's how I earn money. I was supposed to drop these cupcakes off to a client tomorrow straight after school drop-off for a networking lunch she's organised. I don't understand it.' Jenny turns to the oven, frowning as she stares at the dials. 'I don't think I set the oven that high. I thought it was one-sixty, but it's two-fifty now.'

He wants to tell her that it's only cake again, only flour and eggs, but he keeps it in this time. He has a sense there are the right words and there are the wrong words that he could speak and giving any suggestion that Jenny is over-reacting, hormonal, pregnant or tired would definitely fall into the wrong word category.

'You're right,' he says. 'I'm sorry. Of course this is important. You've used the oven quite a lot. I don't see how you could've made a mistake.'

She shakes her head. 'Me neither.'

There's a moment between them, a light bulb that seems to ping on in both their minds. Amelia.

'It doesn't matter,' Jenny says first, pulling her mixer towards her on the counter. 'I can make two more batches now. They won't cool in time to decorate tonight so it will mean an early start, that's all.' Dan watches Jenny stifle a yawn, a hand on the small of her back.

But it does matter because Dan has a horrible suspicion that the oven didn't turn up all on its own. He's about to say something when Amelia appears in the kitchen, looking tired, bleary-eyed from too long on her phone, but there's a curiosity there too. He's sure of it.

'Ewww, what's that smell?' Amelia pulls a face and for a moment Dan thinks she'll go as far as to hold her nose. 'It's gross.'

'Some cakes burned in the oven,' Dan says just as Jenny says, 'It's no big deal.' Her voice is sing-songing, trying too hard.

'The oven was set too high,' Dan continues, watching Amelia's face for a reaction and seeing a defiance in the way she returns his gaze. He takes a breath. 'Did you do it, Amelia?'

'Dan,' Jenny exclaims. 'It doesn't matter. I'll make more.'

'It does matter.' He turns to Amelia. 'This is Jenny's business. It's not just for fun.'

'I know that,' Amelia snaps. 'I mean, how could I not? There are, like, cakes everywhere, all the time.' She waves a hand across the kitchen.

'Did you do it?' he asks again, anger rising in him.

'No,' she shouts. 'Why are you always having a go at me?' Her eyes dart between Dan and Jenny and then she spins around, flying out of the room. A few seconds pass before he hears the door of bedroom slam shut.

'Thanks for that,' Jenny sighs.

He starts. What the hell has he done except try to help? 'What?'

'We don't know it was Amelia. Maybe it was me who made a mistake, but now you've accused her, she's angry and upset and is going to blame me. We're never going to get along if you keep butting in.'

Dan grits his teeth. 'Right,' he nods. 'Got it.'

Jenny leans against the counter and folds her arms. 'That's all you're going to say? Got it?'

'Yep.'

A moment passes between them. A stalemate. Neither of them willing to move on.

It's Bryony who breaks the tension, hopping on one leg into the kitchen. 'What's going on?'

'I was very silly and burned some cakes,' Jenny says, her voice soft again. She pulls a silly sad face that makes Bryony gasps.

'Oh no. Not the muffins for the breakfast meeting?'

Jenny nods.

'I can help,' Bryony says, hands on hips, reminding Dan of a mini warrior preparing for battle.

'So will I,' he adds.

'It's fine. I can't ask you to do that,' Jenny says, already pulling ingredients out of the cupboard. 'I can handle it.'

'You're not asking,' Dan says, 'we're offering. Just tell us what to do.'

Jenny turns to face them, and smiles at Bryony who grins back. Dan is filled with warmth at the sight of the closeness growing between Bryony and Jenny. It strikes him then how hard it will hit Bryony when Jenny and the boys leave in three weeks' time.

For a moment it looks as though Jenny will protest again, but then she nods and starts giving orders. In no time at all, Dan and Bryony are grating chocolate, weighing and mixing. When the cakes are in the oven, Jenny leans down and hugs Bryony. 'Thank you so much.'

'It was fun,' she says.

Jenny straightens up, a hand on the small of her back again, looking beautiful and more relaxed than Dan's seen her in days. He pulls them both towards him and kisses the top of Jenny's head. Her hair smells of the conditioner in the blue bottle that she keeps in the shower that Dan likes to open when he's washing and breathe in her smell just because he can, because she's here with him.

The doorbell rings and Jenny steps away. 'The boys,' she grins, heading down the hall. Dan watches her go and thinks how Bryony won't be the only one who'll miss Jenny when she's gone. The thought sends a bolt of nervous energy straight through him.

June

Chapter 30

Jenny

The cafe is noisy with the clatter of cutlery, the hum of voices. Jenny drops into the seat opposite Nicola and sighs. 'Sorry. Mad parking. How long have you got for lunch?'

Jenny takes in her friend. Nicola's bobbed hair is razor sharp and she's wearing a smart black suit and subtle make-up. For the smallest of moments, Jenny feels intimidated by her friend. Jenny's clothes are stretched and tired, and she doesn't need to look in the mirror to know how ridiculous she looks.

The moment passes in a flash and Jenny remembers that this is Nicola. They've seen each other at their best, their worst, and a million in-betweens.

Nicola grins. 'Don't worry. My boss is on a course so I've got a full hour. What's up? You sounded a bit stressed on the phone the other day. And you look . . .' She pulls a face.

'Like I'm auditioning for *The Only Way is Essex*?'

'Or you're just trying to recreate the 1995 look,' Nicola quips.

Jenny howls with laughter, covering her hands with her face. 'Is it that bad? My make-up bag has disappeared.'

'What do you mean disappeared?'

'I opened up the bathroom cabinet this morning to put my make-up on and it was gone. I've searched everywhere for it. I found this foundation in my bag from the summer. I know it's a few shades too dark—'

'By a few, you mean four, right?'

'Trust me, it's still an improvement on my washed-up face.'

'And the pink lipstick?'

Jenny shakes her head. 'Bryony lent it to me. I think she got it free in a magazine.'

'Oh, Jenny,' Nicola laughs. 'Things don't just disappear on their own though, so if you didn't move your make-up bag, could Dan have? Or one of the kids borrowed it to play a game with? When Rebecca was little she was always diving into my make-up. Did you ask Bryony?'

'Yes. I asked everyone. Practically interrogated poor Bryony.'

Nicola laughs. 'OK, so I have images now of you pointing a lamp in her face.'

'Not far off.'

'Don't tell me – you lined up their favourite teddies and stood over them with a pair of scissors until one of them talked.'

'Ha, I should have done.' Jenny pulls a face, remembering how she'd dashed around the house earlier, yelling at the four children, asking them if they've touched her make-up. It wasn't her finest hour.

'Could the beautiful Amelia be to blame?'

Jenny groans. 'I don't know. I'm trying not to think that.'

'Why? It's the first thing I'd be thinking. If she went near my Bobbi Brown mascara I'd have ransacked her room.' Nicola grins wickedly and Jenny can't help but laugh.

'Amelia is so clearly struggling to adjust to me being in the house, and Dan's response is to call her out on every little comment she makes. I'm pretty sure she hates me for it. She spends nearly all her time in her room hiding from me.'

'All teenagers spend most of their lives in their rooms, but I get your point.'

'I just feel for Amelia. She's not had it easy. Ginger is . . . I don't really know what she is. Not a very mumsy mum, I guess.'

'Ah, I bet she's the be-their-best-friend type of mum.'

'Yes, that's exactly it. But Amelia, and Bryony too really, they need more from Ginger than that.'

'But there's nothing you can do about that. All you can do is keep being the lovely kind person you are. How is everything else going? How are you and Dan getting on living together?'

Before Jenny can reply, a waitress arrives and they order their favourite paninis – mozzarella and tomato for Jenny, ham and cheese for Nicola.

'Dan and I are fine,' Jenny says when the waitress leaves them.

'Just fine?' Nicola narrows her eyes, seeing straight through Jenny's reply.

Jenny pulls a face. 'You're going to think this sounds nuts, but it's like he's trying to be this perfect guy all the time.'

'That's not nuts at all,' Nicola says with wry look. 'One of my pet peeves is when Ryan does nice things for me.'

'Ha ha.' Jenny smiles.

'Go on then, what's he doing?'

'Everything. Literally everything. He cooks nearly every night. He does most of the washing. He cleans. I've got nothing to do, which is stupid because I used to run around like a headless chicken with the boys and foot-ball and baking and keeping on top of the house and the washing, and I would fantasise about having nothing

211

to do all the time, but it's weird having someone do so much for you.

'I've told him it makes me feel like a guest and that I don't need him to do so much but he still is.' Jenny sighs. Is this about her and not Dan? Is the thought of relying on another person so alien that she can't trust it?

'Ah, I see what you mean,' Nicola says.

'Living together, even just for these few weeks, has been harder than I thought it would be.'

'When will your house be ready?' Nicola asks.

'The four weeks is up next weekend. I'm expecting Mrs Hannigan to call any day and confirm that we're all set.'

'And you're sure about coming back to Mortan?'

Jenny bites her lip and nods. 'It's been great for a lot of the time and Dan and I know each other better now, but we're not ready to live together. It's too soon.'

Nicola fixes Jenny with a look as though she disagrees, but says nothing, and Jenny is grateful for that. Whenever Jenny thinks about her living situation, a panic swirls through her. Nothing feels right anymore. Leaving. Staying. It's all cloaked in a messy uncertainty.

Their food arrives: two heaped plates of paninis, crisps and a token pile of rocket doused in vinaigrette that Jenny doubts either of them will touch. She takes a bite of crispy bread; the tang of tomato and warm mozzarella makes the baby dance inside her.

'How's my favourite bump, anyway?' Nicola asks, digging in to her own plate of food, and Jenny is grateful for the change of subject. 'What are you now – twenty-six weeks?'

'Yep.' Jenny slides her hand across her stomach and feels the nudge of a foot. 'This little one has started dancing on my bladder at night. I spend more time getting up for a wee than I do sleeping.'

'Still, only fourteen weeks to go.'

'Only.' Jenny gives a long sigh.

'What's up?' Nicola prompts, reading Jenny as well as she can read herself.

'Does it make me a bad person that there are some evenings when I think I could actually murder someone for glass of wine. Dan's got these amazing bucket glasses and I just want to fill one to the top with some hideously expensive white wine and guzzle it back.'

Nicola laughs. 'Oh my god, I'm so glad you've said that. I was feeling a bit broody when you were talking about the baby, but you've just reminded me why I stopped at one child. The wine!'

They collapse in a fit of laughter.

'How are the boys?' Nicola asks.

Jenny nibbles on her crisps and considers the question. 'OK, I think. Jack is still pretty quiet, but then he always has been. Sometimes it feels like there's something on his mind and other times he's bright and happy, playing on the ukulele Dan got him. He's getting pretty good.'

'And what about the tornado boy?'

Jenny snorts a laugh. 'Ethan is his usual happy self. Although he keeps talking about Hulk being upset, which I don't know if that is some psychological way of him dealing with his own feelings?'

'Are we talking about the same Ethan? That boy is an open book. If he was upset, he'd tell you.'

'You're probably right. Anyway, how's Rebecca doing? Exams all finished?'

'Yes, and now suddenly she's dating.'

'What?' Jenny cries. 'She's too young.'

'That's what I thought until I remembered that we were dating those brothers when we were Rebecca's age.'

'No, we were older, weren't we?'

'Nope. Fifteen.'

'Crikey.' Jenny cringes at the thought.

'He's a nice boy. A bit daft but he treats Rebecca like she's a queen, which counts for a lot.'

As Nicola launches into a description of Rebecca's dates, Jenny's phone buzzes from her bag. 'Sorry,' she says, pulling it out in case the school are trying to reach her. 'It's Mrs Hannigan.'

'Answer it,' Nicola says, nodding at the phone. 'I need to check my work emails anyway.'

Jenny accepts the call but it takes her a moment to realise the strange sound in her ear is crying.

'Mrs Hannigan?'

'Oh, Jenny,' Mrs Hannigan wails. 'I'm so sorry.'

'What is it? Are you OK? What's happened?'

'He's run off with the mon—' The rest of Mrs Hannigan's sentence is lost to sobbing.

'Who's run off?'

'The builder. I hired this contracting firm, you see. Two men working together who were going to project manage the whole thing and sort out all the jobs for me. One of them asked for the money upfront and I stupidly gave it to him.' More sobbing takes over and Jenny sinks back in her chair, already knowing what's to come. Her house – her home – isn't ready.

'Mrs Hannigan, it's OK,' Jenny soothes.

There's a sniff and then, 'It's all such mess. He's done a bit of the work – ripped out the boiler and half the kitchen, and then he's left. Dumped his partner right in it too. The partner is going to finish the job, thank goodness, but it's going to take some time because he has to find new people to do it at short notice. The police are involved, of course. It's all such a mess.'

'How long do you think before the house is done?' Jenny asks, dreading the answer.

'Another month at least. Maybe two. I'm so sorry, Jenny.'

'It's alright,' she lies. 'It can't be helped.'

They say their goodbyes and Jenny drops her head into her hands.

'I'm guessing that wasn't good news,' Nicola says.

'My house won't be ready for another few months. The builder did a runner with Mrs Hannigan's money.'

'Oh.' The one word is bright, happy even.

Jenny lifts her head and looks at her friend. 'This isn't good news.'

'It could be, though,' Nicola says. 'For you and Dan, I mean. It gives you a bit more time to get to know each other and get over the little bumps of living together. Honestly, I think this will be good for you.'

Jenny gives a slow nod, wishing she shared Nicola's confidence. Is it a good thing? How will the boys react to staying at Dan's? How will Dan react for that matter? The nerves return to Jenny's stomach, flapping and swooping like bats hunting for moths. Jenny can't find the words to tell Nicola how she's feeling. That her and Dan – however great it is – are still so new. Jenny isn't sure living together for another few months will make them stronger. She isn't sure their relationship will survive it.

Chapter 31

Dan

Dan sinks onto the bed and loosens his tie as he wonders if he could get away with having a few beers before sitting down to mark the mountain of essays he's brought home with him. It is Friday after all. Except if he has two beers then he'll have two more, which means leaving the marking until the weekend and he really doesn't want it hanging over him.

Jenny is on the other side of the bed, folding towels. He senses her gaze on him. 'You OK?' he asks, a shadow of uncertainty clouding his thoughts.

'Yeah, of course. I just want to check you're really alright with us staying a bit longer?' Jenny pulls a face like she's asking him to pull the girls' hair out of the plughole in the bathroom, a job that makes him gag every time no matter how much of a grown-up he tries to be about it.

'Not only do I not mind,' he says, 'I'm happy.' It's the truth. One hundred per cent. They've had their teething problems. It hadn't quite been the romance and togetherness he'd expected it to be. Dan thinks of cakes overtaking his kitchen, the cosmetics spread across the bathroom, Amelia practically barricaded in her bedroom. Not to mention the constant niggling pressure he feels to do something, do more, do everything. Then Dan thinks of Bryony and how happy she is with Jack, Ethan and Jenny living here. Dan thinks of the time he spends teaching Jack the ukulele – that shyness that almost always disappears by the end of their sessions. Then there's Ethan bringing a smile and laughter to everyone's faces.

It's not a smooth journey they are on. It's more like negotiating an unmade road in an old Mini with no power steering, never knowing where the next turn is going to lead them, but it's a journey Dan is certain he wants to be on.

'Thanks.' Jenny smiles and it lights him up inside.

'Plus it means I can rope you and Jack into helping with Bryony's party.' He waves a stack of RSVPs in the air. 'Sixteen are yes and two are no so far, and one that I found in Bryony's school bag today which has both the yes and no boxes ticked and no name written on it. Plus, half a dozen replies by text.'

Jenny laughs. 'Sounds about right.'

Dan grabs the notebook he keeps by the bed and jots down the names of the children attending, before double, triple-checking the email confirmation for the bouncy castle. Right day. Right time.

He looks down at the list.

Buy party food
Buy tat and sweets for party bags
Buy sweets for piñata
Buy piñata
Construct party bags
Remind Ginger!!!!

'Is that a to-do list?' Jenny grins, peering over his shoulder.

He makes a face, holding the notebook to his chest. 'It's very manly to write to-do lists I'll have you know.'

She laughs. 'I love a list. I think it's great. And don't forget I'm doing the cake. I can help with the food too.'

'You're a lifesaver,' Dan says. 'Do all parents feel this stressed about their kids' parties? It's five weeks away and I'm already having sleepless nights. Do mums get the same fear in the pit of their stomachs that I get? I don't even care if it's not perfect. I just don't want it to be shit.'

'That's totally normal.' Jenny sits down beside him on the bed and kisses his cheek. 'It'll be great, don't worry.'

'Thanks.'

'Hey, is Amelia alright? I thought I heard her shouting something?'

Dan sighs and rubs a hand over his stubble. 'It's nothing new. She wants to move up to the loft room because it's bigger and has its own bathroom.'

'That sounds like a good idea. What's the problem?' Jenny's gaze is questioning and he feels himself bristle the same way he does when Amelia asks.

'It's hard to explain, but the loft room was my dad's study. It's the place I remember him best and it just feels hard going up there. I don't know if it's that or I'm scared to change the room itself because I'll be losing a part of him if I do that. It just doesn't feel right.'

Jenny slips her hand into his. 'Does Amelia know how you feel?'

Dan shakes his head. 'I don't want her to know it's about my dad. I just need a bit more time, I think. Am I being an idiot?'

'No,' Jenny smiles and squeezes his hand. 'You can only do what feels right as a parent, can't you? We're all just trying to do our best. I'm sorry I never got to meet your mum and dad. They sound like really nice people. If they were here right now, what would they say?'

Dan exhales a laugh. 'My dad would tell me I'm being an idiot and what good is a room if it's not used.'

'Have a think about it then. I don't think changing a room is going to change your memories though.'

He nods and Jenny pushes off from the bed, scooping up a pile of washing and heading downstairs.

He'll think about the loft room another day, Dan decides, arching his back and stretching his arms above his head. Christ, he's tired. Fridays used to be his bung it in the oven dinner night with whatever he can unearth from the freezer. Not anymore. There's some chicken in the fridge. He'll make a stir fry and rice. It's not bung it in the oven easy, but it's not gourmet rocket science.

He glances at the clock by the bed. Five-thirty.

Come on, Dan. Time to crack on.

Dan strips off his work shirt and throws on a clean t-shirt. He catches sight of the *What to Expect when Expecting* book on Jenny's bedside table and feels the usual flood of excitement and nerves.

It's enough to shake off the tiredness and he pads through the house, checking on Amelia who is in her bedroom messaging with her friends. Ethan and Bryony are in the garden playing with the guinea pigs, which just leaves Jack, who he finds in the front room.

'Hey, you alright?' Dan says with a wave.

Jack jumps at the sound of Dan's voice, dropping the phone that's in his hand. It lands on the base with a clatter.

'Oh sorry,' Dan adds. 'I didn't realise you were on the phone.'

'Sorry.' Jack's face flushes pink and he dips his head as though he's been caught doing something wrong.

'You're allowed to call people, Jack,' Dan says, leaning against the door frame. 'Assuming they're people in this country, that is,' he adds with a smile.

Jack gives a furtive nod. 'Yeah, I know. Just calling my dad.'

'Great. How's he doing?'

'He . . . he didn't answer.' Jack shifts his feet from side to side, his gaze dropping to the floor. Dan wonders what Jack would've said if his dad had answered. There's a worry to the boy's expression, like he still thinks he's in trouble.

'Well, anytime you want to call him, go ahead. You're seeing him at the weekend, aren't you?'

'Yeah, I think so.'

'Are you . . .' Dan pauses. Should he ask the question forming in his thoughts? Is it crossing a line into Jenny's territory? Jack looks up then and his eyes are brimming with worry, with fear too, Dan thinks, and before he can think about it anymore the words are out. 'Are you happy staying here, Jack? Is there anything you want? Anything I can do?'

'I'm good.' Jack runs a finger over the piano keys, pressing one so gently it doesn't make a sound.

'You've got a real talent for music,' Dan says. 'You know, Bryony's piano teacher comes every Monday. If you want to start having lessons too, you can.'

Jack face whips around to look at Dan. 'Seriously?'

'Of course.'

'But what about when I go home? We don't have a piano?'

'You can still come back here anytime for lessons and practice. I guess it must be pretty weird staying here. You must be homesick?'

Jack nods but says nothing. A pang of sympathy hits Dan's chest. They'd told all four kids over dinner last night about the extra time Jenny and the boys would be staying here for. Dan had been focused on Amelia's reaction, waiting for a comment, but she'd shrugged and gone back to eating her food without a word. Dan hadn't even seen how Jack had taken the news.

'And if there's ever anything on your mind, you know you can talk to me, don't you?' Dan pushes off from the door frame, about to turn away when Jack speaks.

'Dan, why did you and Ginger break up?' Jack's question seems to burst out of him, surprising them both, Dan thinks.

There's a beat, a pause, where Dan huffs a laugh – surprise, not humour. He pulls himself together and tries to find the words. 'It's . . . well it's complicated.'

Jack's eyes are on him now, pressing him to continue. It's the same question Jenny had asked a few weeks back, and yet he's not sure 'I don't know' is an answer he can give Jack.

'We wanted different things,' Dan says eventually.

Jack frowns and for a moment it looks as though he's going to ask another question, but then the back door slams and footsteps clatter through the house. 'I get the TV first,' Ethan shouts.

'You both want to watch the same thing,' Jenny laughs.

A moment later she appears by Dan's side, a hand on his back, a smile for Jack.

'Hey, guys, all OK?'

Jack nods before hurrying out, taking the stairs two at time. A moment later, his bedroom door closes.

'Is Jack alright?' Jenny asks.

'A bit homesick, I think.'

A crease forms on Jenny's brow. Dan wonders if he should mention Jack's question about Ginger, but decides against it. Jenny has enough going on right now. He doesn't want to add to the worry she already has for Jack.

'I'll get started on some dinner,' he says.

'I'm happy to do something.' She draws in a long yawn and loops her hair into a ponytail that a dozen curls immediately spring free from. Dan pauses, taking her in. The bump is now the size of a small football. Perfectly round and pushing out of Jenny's t-shirt. 'Why don't I—'

'I told you, I'm doing it. You put your feet up and relax. I'll do us a stir fry?'

'Fish fingers and oven chips is fine some nights, you know? It's what I was planning to cook. I know it's not exciting, but it's easy.'

Dan grins, pulling Jenny into his arms. 'I like the sound of fish fingers too. How did I get so lucky?'

'Because I like fish fingers,' Jenny asks, her voice muffled in his chest.

'Because you're you.'

Chapter 32

Jenny

It's the following week and Jenny is getting used to being in the house alone during the day. It's so very quiet without Dan and the kids and she finds herself switching on her favourite podcast, letting the howling laughter of the two hosts fill the silence.

No orders to complete today so Jenny is trying out a new blueberry and white chocolate muffin recipe.

'Yes,' Jenny says to the empty room, laughing with the hosts and forgetting for a moment that this is a podcast, these people are not her very best friends (even if it does feel like it some days), they are strangers. Strangers who love baking as much as Jenny does, but strangers none the less.

The voices cut dead as Jenny's phone buzzes with an incoming call and she sighs as she brushes the flour from her hands.

'Hello?' she says.

'Jenny?'

'Yes?'

'It's Ginger.'

'Oh, hi.' Jenny finds herself forcing a bright smile, dropping it when she realises no one else is here. She doesn't need to pretend to be delighted to hear from Dan's ex-wife.

223

'Big favour to ask,' Ginger says. 'Amelia has fallen over and hurt her wrist. The school have phoned and think it needs a trip to A&E and an x-ray but I'm at meetings in Peterborough today and one of my sister's kids is sick so she can't do it. Of course it's the day when Dan is out on a class trip to some boring castle. Would you mind?'

'Me?' Jenny splutters. 'Collect Amelia and take her to A&E?'

'Brilliant. Thank you. I've told the school you'll be coming. Tell Amelia I'll call her later. I've got to dash into this meeting now.'

She's gone before Jenny can say another word, although what those words would be, she isn't sure. Dan is on a school trip. Ginger is miles away. Amelia needs someone and Jenny is that one. Isn't this what being a blended family is all about?

Jenny covers the mixing bowl and finds a space in the fridge before grabbing her bag and heading for the door. Maybe this is the chance her and Amelia need to form a bond of some kind, Jenny thinks as she steps into a day that is overcast but warm. Jenny shrugs off her cardigan as she reaches her car and drives the ten minutes to the senior school where Jack will be starting after the summer, the same school Jenny went to once upon a time.

The school looks the same as when Jenny last walked through the gates two decades ago. A four-storey rectangular building with blue window frames, a huge playing field, and a row of netball courts. Although they've added a sports hall and given the reception area a revamp. Jenny wonders if the science block still has the wooden benches and the most uncomfortable stools ever.

There is something familiar and yet strange about being back after so many years. Jenny half expects Nicola to be walking by her side, skirts rolled up, jumpers tied around their waists. Jenny can remember it so vividly, walking beside Nicola, feeling like they owned the school, like they were unstoppable.

Jenny laughs to herself. They must have looked ridiculous. She fishes out her phone from her bag and takes a discreet selfie before sending it to Nicola.

As Jenny pushes open the door to reception, the smell of school dinners and books hits her senses. How can twenty-something years have passed and it still smell exactly the same?

'May I help you?' A woman asks from behind a glass partition. She has spikey white hair and a blouse the same pink as Bryony's bedroom walls.

'I'm collecting Amelia Walker. She fell over.'

'Are you Mum?'

'Am I a mum?' What a strange question. Jenny snorts. 'Yes.'

'No. Are you Amelia's mum?' The woman slows down her words, mouthing each one as though Jenny is lip-reading.

'Oh, sorry. No, I'm not. I'm her . . . her . . .' Jenny frowns. What is she? It feels way too soon to say stepmum and there's no way friend would be apt here either.

'She's my dad's girlfriend,' comes a voice from behind her.

Jenny's face turns red. Why does she care that Amelia refers to her like that? It's the truth after all, but the tone, the way she said it, like she was talking about an ingrowing toenail or a hairy wart of the end of an old man's nose.

'Ah yes, Mum did call to tell me,' the reception says to Jenny, sliding a clipboard across the counter for Jenny to sign.

'Are you alright?' Jenny asks, taking Amelia's backpack. Bloody hell, it's heavy. Jenny never used to carry this many books around with her, but then Jenny was never in the top sets like Amelia is. They walk through the gates towards the car and Jenny eyes Amelia's left wrist. She's cradling it against her body and there's an ice pack resting on top.

'What are you doing here?' Amelia says, ignoring Jenny's question. 'Where's Mum?'

'In a meeting. I offered to come instead.'

'Of course you did,' Amelia mutters.

Jenny ignores the comment, glad Dan isn't here to step in for once. She wants Amelia to see that she is completely unfazed by the rudeness.

Amelia's mood clogs up the car, making Jenny's skin itch. Whatever is going on, it's more than just Jenny here instead of Ginger.

A&E is surprisingly busy for a Tuesday lunchtime. Jenny spots a toddler with a bandage around her fingers, a baby in a carrier and a boy around Jack's age, ghostly white and leaning his head against his mum's shoulder.

'I'm bored,' Amelia says after five minutes of sitting.

'Me too.'

'Why did you come, then?'

'Because I was worried about you and because you needed someone to take you for an x-ray.'

Amelia huffs, shrinking further into her chair.

'How's your wrist feeling?' Jenny asks.

'It hurts.'

'What happened?'

'Nothing.'

'OK,' Jenny says, turning to her phone. She's not going to make Amelia talk.

A moment passes before Amelia sighs and Jenny puts down her phone. 'We were playing netball and me and Chelsea both went for the ball and she knocked into me.'

'Must have been a pretty hard knock.'

'Yeah.'

'Did she say sorry?'

'Miss Garner made her. She got detention too.'

'I thought Chelsea was your friend?'

Amelia shakes her head as though Jenny is the dumbest person on earth before pulling out a history book from her bag. For a moment Jenny thinks that's the end of it, but then Amelia looks up from her book. 'I don't know if Chelsea is my friend,' she says in a quiet voice. 'Sometimes she's really nice to me, but other times she's not, and she's like really popular, so . . .' Amelia's sentence trails off.

'So when she's a cow, others do the same?' Sympathy pulses through Jenny's body as Amelia nods, tears brimming in her eyes.

'Have you said anything to your dad?' Jenny asks.

A huff and then, 'He's not exactly on my side much at the moment. And don't tell him. It'll only make it harder at school.'

'What about your mum?'

'Yeah, I will when I see her next.'

'I know it's not all black and white, but if someone is making you feel rubbish about yourself, Amelia, then they're not your friend.'

'Yeah, maybe.' Amelia's gaze returns to her book and she flicks the page leaving Jenny to worry alone. Is her presence making everything harder for Amelia and Dan?

It takes two hours to receive the diagnosis of a sprain and to be told they can go.

'Ready?' Jenny sighs, craving fresh air and natural daylight.

Amelia nods and even though she doesn't look at Jenny or say so much as a thank-you, Jenny senses a truce between them. She hopes it lasts.

Chapter 33

Dan

'Hey.' Dan grins as he steps into the kitchen, striding straight to Jenny and wrapping his arms around her waist and the growing bump of their baby. 'Something smells good.'

'It's only a pasta sauce,' Jenny says, leaning her body into him.

'You OK?'

'Just tired . . . and . . . I don't know, a bit meh. It's probably hormones or Monday night blues. And this heat doesn't help.' Jenny waves a hand to the open back door and the bright-blue sky, the hot sun. The garden has bloomed into summer. Perfect yellow roses dot the bushes beside blue hydrangeas. The lawn needs cutting again and the flower beds are already out of control. It's a battle Dan seems to lose every summer.

'And,' Jenny continues, sliding a piece of paper across the counter for Dan to read. 'I found this in the living room today.'

To Bryony from Ethan
DO NOT FEED HULK.

He doesn't like you feeding him.

To Ethan from Bryony

DO NOT FILL UP POPPY'S WATER BOWL. You fill it up too much and she spills it.

To Bryony from Ethan

DON'T TALK TO HULK. He is scared of Poppy and you.

To Ethan from Bryony

NO HE IS NOT

'Crikey,' Dan says as his eyes scan the wobbly handwriting of Bryony and Ethan. 'But they're getting on alright, aren't they?'

'Who? Ethan and Bryony or Hulk and Poppy?'

'The kids? The guinea pigs are in separate hutches.'

Jenny nods. 'I think so.'

'They did have a little bicker last month about the guinea pigs, but I didn't think much of it.'

'Ethan has said a few times that he thinks Hulk is unhappy living next to Poppy.'

Dan watches Jenny's face, waiting to see if she says anymore. He has that feeling again, that not quite right feeling that gnaws in the pit of his stomach. Are they talking about guinea pigs? He and Jenny are happy, he's sure of it. And yet, it's like there's a wall between them.

A familiar urge presses down on him to change the subject, make a joke, gloss over the moment. He desperately wants this to work – for the baby, for him and Jenny and the kids too. But wanting isn't enough and he can't keep hiding from the truth and expect things to work out.

'Jenny.' He takes her hand and turns her towards him. 'I really want us to be together, you know that right?'

'Sure.' She frowns, a half-smile touching her lips.

'Not just because we're having a baby.'

'I know. Me too.'

'I'm not very good at saying how I feel or what I'm thinking. I know I need to work on that.'

Jenny bites her lip in the way she does when she's thinking. 'Sometimes I feel like you're annoyed about something but you don't say what it is, which I find hard because it makes me second guess everything. I wish you'd just say it. Like last night when you were making dinner. Was something wrong?'

Dan makes a face, cringing inwardly.

'Say it,' Jenny demands. 'Come on.'

'I was . . .' He pauses, wishing he'd not said anything. 'It's not a big deal, but sometimes there are so many cakes on the surfaces in the kitchen that there's not enough space to cook. I get annoyed sometimes but, really, it's no big deal. I know it's important to you.'

Jenny nods. 'OK, I can understand that. I'm not used to having to share a kitchen. How about we clear some space in the utility room? There's a whole worktop in there that is basically a dumping ground for odd socks. I can use that space to cool and store the cakes.'

'That would work. Thanks.'

'See,' she smiles. 'That was easy. What else?'

'So . . .' Dan starts and this one is harder to say. 'It feels sometimes like there's a wall up between us, like an invisible shield and you won't let me in, like we're not really together in this.'

Silence fills the kitchen. He's gone too far. Dan's about to take it all back when Jenny speaks. 'I guess maybe I've only had to rely on myself for so long, and after Paul, I just . . . it's hard to trust. But I'll get there,' she says with less conviction than Dan would like.

'What about me?' he says. 'I know I'm pretty perfect.' He winks and Jenny swipes his arm.

'OK, OK, I'm kidding. Seriously, what about me?'

'Lay off Amelia,' Jenny says without needing to think about it. 'It's tough for her, all this change. Last week when I took her for the x-ray she opened up a bit to me. It felt like progress between us. I think she needs a bit of breathing space though and to feel like you're on her side.'

Dan nods. 'I know. I've been thinking.' His stomach knots, emotion scratches his throat. 'It's probably time I cleared out my dad's loft room. Maybe it will help Amelia to have more of her own space.'

'I think that will make her really happy.' Jenny slides her arms around him and they kiss, softly at first, then more, stirring a heat inside him, and he thinks maybe this talking stuff isn't so bad after all.

Chapter 34

Jenny

It's Dan that pulls away from their kiss. He clears his throat and grins. 'Can I take a rain check on the rest of that kiss until tonight? We do have dinner to get ready here.'

Jenny laughs. 'Deal.'

They finish making the dinner together and Jenny calls the kids to the table. Within minutes the kitchen is filled with noise. Ethan and Jack are talking about a fantasy football team and arguing over whether a lion can be in goal.

'It's fantasy,' Ethan says. 'So it can.'

'It's not what it means. Fantasy football is about real players from different teams making up your fantasy team.'

'I'm still having a lion.'

Bryony is nattering away at a hundred miles an hour about the layers of birthday cake she wants, and Amelia and Dan are talking about school.

Dan catches Jenny's eye across the table and smiles and she can tell from his expression that he's silently asking her if she's OK? If they're OK. She nods. She is. It feels like something has cleared between them today. If only Jenny didn't feel so hot, so sticky, so yuck. Her face feels puffy in the heat. She still has ten weeks to go and has no idea how she'll get any bigger.

The clatter of cutlery dropping to a plate brings Jenny's thoughts back to the table.

'This tastes funny,' Amelia says, pushing her plate away and screwing up her nose.

'Tastes fine to me,' Ethan says, shovelling another forkful into his mouth.

'And me,' Dan adds. 'Give it another try, please, Amelia.'

'Fine.'

Jenny catches Dan's eye and shakes her head. He gives a nod of understanding. She watches Amelia scoop up a single twist of pasta on her fork and spend at least a minute scraping off the sauce. When she finally puts it in her mouth, she chews it right on her teeth like it's Bush Tucker Trial from *I'm a Celebrity Get Me Out Of Here*. Fish eyeballs or crocodile anus instead of Jenny's pasta sauce that the boys love so much. The same pasta sauce she made two weeks ago that Amelia had a second helping of.

Amelia swallows the pasta, washing it down with three long gulps of water before sitting back in her chair with her arms folded.

'I've got some news, actually,' Dan says.

'Are you and my mum having another baby?' Ethan asks.

Jenny barks a laugh. 'I think one is enough. There is definitely no space for two in here.'

Ethan leans over and pats her stomach. 'Hello, baby. Have you got enough space?'

They all laugh, even Amelia, and then Dan says, 'I'm going to clear out the loft room at the weekend.'

Amelia's head shoots up. She looks at Dan with wide hopeful eyes. He grins back. 'Maybe you want to pick a paint colour for it?'

'Really?' Amelia squeals, jumping up and hugging Dan. 'Thank you, thank you, thank you.'

'Don't thank me. It was Jenny that made me realise it was a good idea.'

Amelia freezes. Her gaze moves to Jenny. There's a pause. 'Thanks,' she mumbles before sitting down and, without a word, picks up her fork again.

It's a small victory, a moment when everyone is happy. Jenny tucks the feeling into the imagery folder in her head and smiles.

July

July

Chapter 35

Jenny

Voices in the kitchen drag Jenny out of her doze. She lifts her head from the sofa cushion and blinks in the living room. The TV is still on but *Miraculous Lady Bug* has been replaced with the garish pinks and yellows of *My Little Pony*, and the only sign of Bryony and Ethan are two empty snack bowls and the sprinkling of breadstick crumbs on the rug.

Jenny only meant to close her eyes for five minutes after the school run, but she feels bone-achingly tired today, like she could sleep for twenty-four hours and it still wouldn't be enough. She's thirty-one weeks' pregnant now and has no idea how on earth she managed her pregnancy with Ethan while also running around after Jack.

The answer stares Jenny in the face as she pulls herself up and glances in the mirror above the fireplace. She was in her early thirties when she was pregnant with Ethan, late twenties for Jack. Pregnancy at thirty-nine is a whole different experience.

Jenny frowns at herself, taking in the extra lines that seem to have appeared on her forehead recently, the pasty tone of her skin and the three red spots on her chin. If she had even an ounce of spare energy right now, she'd splodge on a generous helping of make-up.

A peal of laughter carries through the house. Adult laughter. It penetrates the last fog of her sleep and self-pity. Who the hell is in the kitchen? And how did she not hear the doorbell?

Jenny tugs her fingers through her curls and smooths her hand over her summer dress where it's bunched and wrinkled from falling asleep on the sofa. She steps into the hall and takes in the scene in the kitchen – all four children are standing around the owner of the laugh – and Jenny's heart sinks.

Why today? When she has no make-up on.

Why now? When she's just woken up and feels so crappy. So huge.

Why, why, why is Ginger here? And why the hell didn't one of the kids wake her up?

Amelia spins around, a huge smile plastered on her face as Jenny enters the kitchen. 'Mum's come to say hi.'

'Great.' Jenny forces a smile and ignores the desire to turn and flee, to hide upstairs. They've met a few times since that first lunch on moving day and Ginger has always been friendly, but there's an air of something about Ginger that makes Jenny feel awkward. Awkward and fat, she adds, eyeing Ginger's skin-tight jeans.

'Hi, Ginger, good to see you,' Jenny says brightly before filling a glass of water and taking a long drink.

'And she's staying for dinner,' Amelia says.

Jenny freezes, glad her back is to the room and she has a second to rearrange her face from horrified to relaxed after Amelia's triumphant announcement. Would it have killed Amelia and Ginger to ask first? It's not like Jenny could've said no.

Jenny turns, flashing a smile as wide as Amelia. 'Brilliant.'

This isn't weird, Jenny tells herself. It's just different. Dan told Jenny on one of their early dates how impossible it is to pin Ginger down to particular dates, and so he has let Ginger come and go from the house as she pleases, staying for tea or just hanging out so the girls get to spend time with their mum.

Was Jenny stupid for assuming that things would change while she was staying here? The answer is standing behind her in a pair of platform sandals and looking skinny and glamorous and everything Jenny isn't.

Another two weeks, Jenny tells herself. Then her and the boys will go home. She waits for the feeling of relief that thought normally brings her, but all she feels is a swarm of panic pushing through her. They'll be back in Mortan for the start of the summer holidays. Jenny tries to imagine it being just her and the boys again and the two weeks in August when Jack and Ethan go away with Paul and it will be Jenny alone in the house. The thought doesn't fit – a jumper that's shrunk in the wash.

'Are you sure you don't mind, Jenny?' Ginger asks. 'I don't have to stay for dinner.'

'Mum,' Amelia says. 'It's fine.'

'Amelia is right,' Jenny smiles. 'It's completely fine. I'll just text Dan and tell him to pick up some more sausages on his way home. He's cooking sausage and mash, if that's OK? It's the kids' favourite at the moment.'

An amused smile twitches at Ginger's lips. 'Sounds divine,' she says in a way that makes Jenny feel like she's offering 99p microwave lasagne.

'I'm going to change,' Amelia says, giving her mum a kiss on the cheek before slipping out of the room with Bryony following behind.

'Can we play in the garden, Mummy?' Ethan asks.

'Good idea.'

'Race you,' he calls to Jack before running to the mud room. Jack holds back a moment and Jenny wonders if he senses the awkwardness and doesn't want to leave Jenny alone.

'Go on,' she says, tilting her head towards the door. 'Go make sure your brother doesn't roll in mud or climb any trees.'

He nods and disappears into the July heat and then it's just Jenny and Ginger.

'I'll make myself a drink while you text Dan, shall I?' Ginger says.

'Great.' Jenny watches Ginger open a cupboard for a glass and another for a can of coke, then the freezer for ice. Ginger knows this kitchen better than Jenny. The thought stings more than it should.

Stop it. She tells herself. *Stop being jealous. Stop comparing. Dan chose you! You chose Dan! You're having a baby. That's way more important than flawless skin, toned abs and long blonde hair.* It's Nicola's voice Jenny hears in her thoughts and she's grateful for it even if she doesn't quite believe it. Did she and Dan choose each other? Or have they simply fallen together because of the baby? The question unnerves her. She pushes it away and grabs her phone to text Dan.

Ginger is here!!!!! She's staying for dinner. Have we got enough sausages? X

Dan:

What? Are you OK with this?

Jenny:

I guess I don't exactly have a choice.

Dan:

You do! Tell her she can't stay!!!

Jenny:

And be the wicked new girlfriend who doesn't let the girls see their mother! No way!

Dan:

Fair point. I'll tell her.

242

Jenny:

NO! They'll think I told you to. It's fine. It's one dinner.

Dan:

I'm leaving now. I'll be home in ten mins.

Jenny:

Sausages?

Dan:

There are more sausages in the freezer. xx

The message is followed by a GIF of Forrest Gump sprinting down the road. Jenny smiles as she puts her phone back on the worktop and turns to look at Ginger, who is peering at the four sponge bases coloured in red, orange, yellow and blue that Jenny made earlier. 'The person who invented rainbow cakes has a lot to answer for,' Jenny says.

'That's so funny. I've never been into baking. Too much like hard work, but look at you and all your little cakes. Dan and the girls must love these.'

'I run a cake-making business. It's what I do.' The words are short and come with a flush that burns Jenny's face. *Damn!* And she so wanted to be calm and collected.

'Oh sorry. Have I offended you?' Ginger asks, looking at Jenny in a way that makes her feel two feet tall.

'Of course not.' Jenny smiles and takes a sip of water before checking her phone. Nine minutes before Dan gets home. He'd better be running.

'Look,' Ginger says, running her hands through her hair. 'I get that this is a bit weird, but I want you to know I'm happy Dan has found someone as nice as you. It's great for the girls too.

'Umm . . . thanks?' Jenny replies, not meaning it to sound like a question.

They fall silent and Jenny has a burning desire to ask Ginger about her marriage to Dan, but she bites it back. It's not her place.

'I know you must think I'm the worst kind of mother for leaving them,' Ginger says as though reading Jenny's mind. Her smile has gone, replaced with a hollow sadness.

Jenny shakes her head. 'I wasn't thinking that.'

Ginger smiles. 'That's because you're nice. I do love them, you know?'

'Of course.'

'I genuinely thought the girls would be better with Dan than with me. I felt like I wasn't good enough to be a mum and I was so unhappy at home. Sorry,' Ginger says suddenly. 'I don't know why I'm telling you this.' There's a rawness to Ginger's expression that makes Jenny think she's not the only one good at building walls.

'Have you spoken to Dan about this?' Jenny knows the answer but asks anyway.

Ginger snorts. 'We don't talk about the past. I caused a lot of hurt. I wouldn't know where to begin.'

Ten minutes ago, Ginger was the last person Jenny wanted to spend time with, but now she finds herself stepping forward, wanting to hug this woman. Jenny is reaching out a hand when Amelia appears, dressed like she's going to a disco in short denim shorts and a sequined silver top.

'Love that outfit,' Ginger says, making Amelia beam with undiluted pleasure. Ginger flashes Jenny a smile. Whatever passed between them has gone. 'How was school today?' Ginger asks.

Amelia pulls a face and launches into a story about a class prank in Geography that meant they missed their break time even though it had nothing to do with Amelia.

Jenny leans against the counter and searches Ginger's face for the rawness she saw moments earlier. There is something so unresolved about Ginger and Dan's marriage and Jenny is so tired, so very pregnant, she isn't sure what to do about it, or if there's anything she can do.

A sudden feeling of being overwhelmed takes over – a huge wave dragging Jenny out to sea. The thought of her empty house in Mortan doesn't seem so bad after all.

Chapter 36

Dan

Dan pulls into the cul-de-sac faster than usual, still breathless from running through the school after Jenny's text. There's a blister on his right heel, rubbing against his shoe, wet and sore, and a sharp stitch slicing across his stomach. Bloody Nancy and her Friday Krispy Kreme staff room treats. Why can he never say no to them?

More importantly, what the hell is Ginger thinking?

He should have said something. Way back when Jenny first came to stay. He should have spoken to Ginger. Told her that the dinners would have to stop. But wasn't it obvious?

He's really messed this up. Poor Jenny.

He pulls into the driveway and gets out of the car. The day is warm in a British summer kind of way. Hot in the sun but cool in the shade, and he can feel damp patches forming under his shirt.

He's a few metres from the front door when a van pulls up beside him on the drive.

Dan turns, ready to accept whatever baby item Jenny has ordered, but then the engine stops and the driver's door opens and Paul steps out.

'Alright, Dan,' Paul says, reaching out a hand.

Dan gives a firm handshake, aware of how clammy his

246

hands must feel after his mad dash home. 'Hi, Paul. How's it going?'

'All good. Thanks for inviting me over.'

'Oh . . . er . . . no problem.' Invited? Who invited Paul? Surely Jenny wouldn't have done that without telling him, especially with Ginger here too. But Paul is looking at Dan with an expectant smile and so Dan motions to Paul and says, 'Come in.'

It's only as he slides the key into the lock and hears Ginger's deep laughter that Dan feels the first inkling of horror of what is about to unfold with Jenny and him, both exes and all four kids.

Chapter 37

Jenny

Jenny rushes down the hall like an eager puppy. A fat, pregnant puppy, but still she practically skips in her desperation to see Dan, her rescuer.

'What took you so long?' Her smile is strained, her eyebrows shooting up.

'Paul?' The name is out before Jenny can fully process what she's seeing.

'Hey, Jen, alright?'

'What are you doing here?' she asks, gaze flicking from Dan to Paul. It feels like a bad dream. A nightmare she'll wake from any second. She has the burning desire to look down in case her clothes have disappeared too.

'You invited me?' Paul says it like a question, like maybe he's not so sure.

Jenny barks a laugh of disbelief. 'No I didn't. When have I ever invited you for dinner?'

Paul frowns and pulls out his phone. There's an awkward moment where Paul is concentrating on his screen and Jenny is aware of Dan standing with them, bunched in the hall while Ginger waits in the kitchen, but Jenny can't move. Not until she's figured this out.

'Here,' Paul says, showing Jenny his phone screen and a message from her.

Come for dinner on Thursday at Dan's.

Jenny rubs at her forehead, wishing she could rub away the tiredness still clouding her thoughts, and the way her back aches and the dull niggle of pain in her stomach. 'Does that sounds like the kind of text I send, Paul?'

'You know, I did think it was odd, but I assumed you were in a rush. So I guess you didn't send it, which means—'

'Jack,' they say in unison.

Another awkward moment passes between them and then Paul nods to the front door. 'I'll be off then.'

But it's too late. There's movement behind them.

'Dad!' Jack's voice, that one word, is high and injected with a pure joy that makes Jenny's heart ache for a dozen reasons she doesn't have the energy to think about right now.

'Hey, Jackster, how's it going?'

'Really good. Is Dad staying for dinner?' The words burst out as Jack looks first to Jenny, and then as though realising something, they drag to Dan. Guilt glows on his face like sunburn.

'Of course,' Dan says, shooting Jenny a look that says what-choice-do-we-have? And she feels a warmth rising in her chest for Dan. Whatever happens tonight, they're in this together. 'The more the merrier.'

Jenny feels Jack's hesitant gaze on her and she pastes on her biggest smile and motions for Paul to come in.

As Jack drags his dad through to the kitchen, Jenny mouths a *WTF* to Dan.

'Shall we go out for dinner and leave them all to it?' Dan whispers with a grin, grabbing her hand and pulling her to the door.

Jenny rubs at the dull pain spreading across her stomach and smiles. 'I don't think I'm in any state to run.'

'Piggyback?'

Jenny laughs, then winces as the pain turns sharp for a second then disappears.

Dan's expression changes in an instant. Fun to concern. He steps forward. 'Jenny, what's wrong?'

'Nothing, don't worry. A kick just landed in the wrong place I think. Come on, let's get this over with,' she says with more conviction than she feels. The truth is, she'd like nothing more than to run away or hide upstairs right now, but Dan's willingness to invite Paul in, and the kids seeming so happy, especially Jack, Jenny can't ditch them all now. She'll talk to Jack later about inviting Paul. The boys are always playing on her phone. It would've been easy for him to send a text to Paul.

Worry gnaws at her alongside a familiar guilt. It's her that put the boys in this situation, who's dragged them from the only comfortable routine they've had for their whole lives and shaken it upside down, like a snow globe.

Paul is just releasing Ginger's hand as Jenny steps into the kitchen. She heads straight for the freezer to find yet more sausages. She finds burgers and chicken left over from their last BBQ, but no more sausages. Dan joins her and they stare together at the pitiful remains of the freezer.

'Shall I fire up the barbie?' he asks. 'Might be easier, anyway.'

She nods, grateful she won't be standing over a hot oven, cooking twenty billion sausages for a dinner she really does not want to sit through.

From the corner of her eye, Jenny spots Ethan racing across the garden. 'Mum,' he shouts as he enters the boot room. 'Hulk won't—' His words stop short, his train of thought changing in a split second. 'Daddy!' he says, throwing himself into Paul's arms.

'Monster,' Paul grins.

'Dad's staying for dinner,' Jack says.

'So is my mummy,' Bryony adds as she trails after Ethan.

'We're having a BBQ,' Dan announces, arms now loaded with frozen rolls.

'Why?' Bryony asks.

'Because it's too nice an evening to be cooped up inside.'

Bryony shakes her head. 'Why are Mummy and Ethan and Jack's daddy staying for dinner?'

A silence falls over the kitchen. It's the question Jenny would very much like to ask too, and yet it's taken the youngest person in the house, a sweet soon-to-be eight-year-old, to find the courage to ask it.

'Just because,' Dan smiles, trawling out the Get Out of Jail Free card of all parenting replies.

Bryony frowns, her little face scrunching up in a way that reminds Jenny of Ethan when she suggests he eat a Brussels sprout with his Christmas dinner.

Amelia laughs then and they all join in. It's awkward and stilted and not really laughter at all.

'You're looking great, Jenny,' Paul says, leaning against a worktop. 'Have you had your hair done?'

'Oh.' Jenny touches a strand of wayward curl. 'Yes. Last week.' She feels Dan's eyes on her. 'Just a trim,' she adds, shooting him a don't-worry-about-it look.

'Isn't Jenny getting massive, Mum,' Amelia adds. 'You didn't get that big when you were pregnant with me, did you? I've seen the photos.'

'Oh, I did get just as big,' Ginger says. Her voice is suddenly soft, dripped in treacle. Jenny glances across the room. There's something strangely feline about Ginger's movements, the tilt of her head, and her words almost a purr. Her gaze lingers on Paul for a moment too long.

Oh god! Jenny knows what's coming. Paul is the biggest flirt alive and Ginger has just given him an open invitation to flirt away.

'Amelia,' Dan says, a gentle warning to his voice. Jenny tries to catch his eye, to tell him not to go too far, but Dan's gaze is fixed on his daughter.

'Sorry,' she says. 'I was just saying.' She looks sheepish, her cheeks glowing red. It's not the surly attitude Amelia usually displays. Maybe she really is sorry.

'I think you look stunning,' Dan says, leaning over to kiss her cheek.

Jenny's cheeks flush hot and she laughs. 'Thanks, but can we stop talking about me like I'm a prize cow please.'

'What's a price cow?' Bryony asks.

'It's prize cow,' Dan replies. 'And it's just a saying, sweetheart. Why don't you run outside and play?'

'I don't think you're a price cow,' Bryony says to Jenny before skipping out of the room.

'Dad, can you play football?' Ethan says then, pulling at Paul's arm.

A jittery relief circles Jenny's mind as everyone moves outside. Dan to the BBQ, Paul, Bryony, Jack and Ethan towards the goal, and Amelia and Ginger to the outdoor chairs.

Jenny stands at the window, chopping salad as slowly as possible, delaying the inevitable moment she'll have to join them.

She rubs at a twinge in her side as she watches Amelia and Ginger wander across the patio. Amelia is clinging to Ginger's arm with the same intensity as a child holding a balloon. Not daring to let go in case Ginger drifts away. Jenny feels a pang of sadness watching the mother and daughter together. Ginger's confession earlier, Amelia's obvious insecurity – both dance through Jenny's head.

'Tongs?' Dan says, appearing at the back door. 'Why can I never find the tongs?' He stops and looks at Jenny. 'Are you sure you're alright?'

'I was just . . . Ginger said something earlier—'

'Oh god,' Dan cuts in. 'Whatever it was, ignore it. Ginger has this way of winding people up. I'm sorry.'

'No, it was about regrets, I think. About the past and when she left. She seemed . . . I don't know, sorry, I think, and like she wants to talk. Maybe now is the time to talk to her and find out what went wrong?'

Dan tenses beside her and Jenny knows she's overstepped, and yet someone had to say something, didn't they? She has to make Dan see that ignoring the past isn't what's best for the girls, or him.

'There's nothing to talk about.' Dan's words are clipped. 'She left.'

Jenny sighs, rubbing again at the pain snaking across her belly. 'But the girls, especially Amelia – she's so insecure about her mum, I think if you—'

'Jenny, I appreciate your concern but it's got nothing to do with you. It's ancient history.'

The anger in Dan's tones is sharp and she wants to push back, to be angry too and tell him he's being an idiot, but her mind blanks as a sharp pain slices through her. Even as she tells herself it's nothing, a crippling fear grabs her by the throat. She's seven months' pregnant. It's too soon for contractions, but this pain . . . it's so strong. Something is very wrong.

Chapter 38

Dan

'And what good is talking going to do anyway?' Dan continues. The anger is burning through him. Jenny is wrong and she's bang out of order bringing it up now of all times. The thoughts cloud his mind so it takes him a moment to notice the change in Jenny's posture. She shifts forward, doubling over as pain etches across her face.

'Jenny? What's wrong?' His anger disappears, elbowed out by fear. 'What's happening?'

'I don't know.' Her voice is small and scared and sends a bullet of panic straight into his heart. 'I think something is wrong with the baby.'

'OK,' Dan says, a cold chill spreading through his body. 'I'm taking you to hospital.'

'The kids?' Jenny says with a half sob.

'Paul and Ginger can manage.' Panic steals the breath from his lungs as he rushes into the garden.

'Dan, I scored a goal,' Ethan yells, racing up the lawn.

'Paul, Ginger,' he beckons them over. They turn towards him, moving so slowly he could scream.

Dan keeps his voice low as they reach him, but he can't hide the fear in his tone. 'Jenny's having some pains. I need to take her to hospital. Can you—'

'Go,' Paul says at once.

'We'll be fine,' Ginger adds.

'Thanks.' He tears back through the house, grabbing his keys on the way, finding Jenny already standing by the car. Her face is pale and there are tears falling onto her cheeks.

'It's going to be OK,' he says, hoping, praying he's right.

Chapter 39

Jenny

Jenny keeps her eyes shut tight, not daring to look at the screen. Not daring to see the worry in the sonographer's eyes as he scans Jenny's huge belly. Fear and hope swim, black and murky, through her body – oil and water.

Please be OK. Please, please, please.

A sound fills the dimly lit room. A soft thudding noise. A heartbeat. Her baby's heartbeat. From beside her, Dan squeezes her hand. Their touch is clammy, but she doesn't care. All that matters is the baby.

'So, everything looks fine,' the sonographer tells them, wiping away the gel from Jenny's stomach. Only then does she open her eyes and see his reassuring smile. 'Where did you say the pain is?'

'Here,' Jenny touches the lower left side of her bump. It's no longer sharp but a dull cramp-like feeling.

He nods. 'I'm going to get the doctor to take a look as well,' he says, his voice soft and calm, and like a security blanket Jenny clings to it, to what it means. The baby is fine. Whatever the pain is, the baby is OK.

'Try to relax. The baby looks perfectly healthy,' he adds, disappearing from the room.

Jenny stares up at the white ceiling tiles as a silence stretches out. Dan shifts in the plastic chair, his hand slipping out of hers and she feels the cold void his touch leaves behind. She has a sudden desire to reach for him and never let go.

Come on, Jen, say something.

'I'm sorry,' she says at the exact moment Dan says, 'I shouldn't have got angry with you.'

She turns her head, staring into those soft brown eyes of his.

'You're right. I need to talk to Ginger. I've been avoiding it for too long.'

Jenny shakes her head. 'It's none of my business. You should do what works for you and the girls.'

'That's the thing, though – I don't think it has been working.' Dan runs a hand over the back of his neck and sighs. 'Ginger and I have been tiptoeing around each other, ignoring the end of our marriage, but ignoring that has meant ignoring other things too, like what's best for the girls.'

Jenny squeezes his hand. 'It'll be alright.'

'I hope so.'

They fall silent. Dan's forehead is furrowed and she can tell he's still thinking everything over.

'I have to tell you something,' he says.

'What?'

Dan picks up Jenny's hand, threading his fingers through hers. 'I'm falling in love with you.'

The world stops. Jenny stops. Her mind blanks. And before she can say a word, Dan is shaking his head. 'No,' he says. 'I've fallen already. I'm in love with you. I think I have been since our first date. I love you, Jenny.'

'I . . .' Jenny's mind races. Her and Dan, the kids, Paul, Ginger, the house in Mortan. The baby. So many factors and yet she can't ignore the feeling inside her – fireworks and sparklers and those break-dancing butterflies. 'I love you too,' she says. And she does, she realises. Madly so. Like she's kept her feelings for Dan behind a closed door all these months, trying to protect herself, telling herself it wouldn't work, it couldn't. But now the door has been flung open and suddenly her body is swimming in it.

They grin at each other, Jenny from the bed and Dan on the chair beside her. Then the door opens and a female doctor in her late twenties appears. Dan squeezes Jenny's hand as the fear returns, pooling in the pit of Jenny's stomach.

Please, please, please let the baby be OK.

'Good afternoon, I'm Doctor Douglas,' she says with a strong Scottish accent. 'I understand you're having some pains in your side?'

'Yes, on the left side. It feels like it's moved down,' Jenny explains as she rubs at her bump.

'Well, the good news is that the baby is looking really healthy. Do you mind if I examine you?'

Jenny shakes her head. 'I don't mind. Whatever you need to do.'

Doctor Douglas pulls on a pair of gloves and moves around the bed. She presses her hands gently across Jenny's bump. 'And you say it's about here?'

A sharp pain shoots through Jenny's body and she gasps. 'Yes.'

She feels Dan tense beside her, leaning closer, and she wants to reassure him but she can't. Something is happening in her body. The pain is no longer a pain. It's a pressure.

Oh no. Oh no, no, no.

The realisation hits Jenny at the exact moment the doctor presses her fingers into Jenny's side a second time. The pressure builds and there's nothing Jenny can do to stop the release and the loud rumbling of a very clear, very obvious fart.

Not, as Jenny would have liked, a little toot, a silent shhh, but a big noisy raspberry that could rival any middle-aged man after a night of five pints, a madras and three onion bhajis.

'Oh my god,' Jenny cries out, her face flooding with heat. She scrunches her eyes shut. 'I'm so sorry.'

'Don't worry,' Doctor Douglas says. 'We've seen it all before. How is the pain now, Jenny?' she asks without a touch of amusement in her voice.

'Gone,' Jenny whispers, her face burning crimson. She can feel Dan moving beside her, the soft shake of his shoulders. She can't look at him. She'll never be able to look at him again.

'Good. Very good. So I think it's OK for you to go home.' Doctor Douglas smiles. 'Trapped wind can be very painful at this stage in the pregnancy. The baby needs all the room it can get in there, so er . . . don't hold it in,' she says, patting Jenny's hand with a smile.

Jenny nods. 'Thank you.'

Only when they're alone again does Dan let out a roar of laughter. And despite the humiliation, the desire to bury her head in her hands, shut herself in a wardrobe and never leave, Jenny laughs too as relief floods her body.

Chapter 40

Dan

Dan watches from the front door as Amelia says goodbye to Ginger. It's late now. Gone eight. Paul left ten minutes ago after taking over the BBQ, cooking dinner for the kids and Ginger, and then tidying up afterwards.

He catches the sound of Bryony from upstairs. A stomping foot, a yell of 'don't want to' to Jenny, who is cajoling her into bed, along with Ethan and Jack. They're overtired, he thinks, desperate to help, but he has something else to do now. His heart fills with love, with emotion, relief. He has been so blind to his feelings for Jenny and how much she means to him, but about Ginger too.

Dan grabs two beers from the fridge and heads out to the driveway to see Ginger scooping a strand of hair away from Amelia's face before kissing the top of her head. It's a mothering touch and fills Dan with a stab of regret so harsh that he stops breathing for a beat.

He swallows hard and steps forward, placing a hand on Amelia's shoulder. 'Go get ready for bed.'

She nods, deflated, sad, as she walks back to the house.

'See ya,' Ginger says, opening the car door and Dan almost lets her go. Almost.

'Ginger, wait. Can we talk?' He holds up the two bottles of beer and watches the surprise register on her face, a sign of how alien those words are to both of them. He nods to the steps up to the house and they sit, Dan on one side, Ginger on the other. The sun is setting in the distance, lighting the sky in a pink as bright as Bryony's bedroom.

Dan swigs from the bottle of beer. It's cold and fizzy and he swallows, feeling the heady release of the alcohol, the letting go of the day. He senses Ginger watching him, waiting.

'This is probably going to sound like a stupid question to ask now, and I realise I should – we should – have talked a long time ago, but we're both here now, so I'm going to ask – what went wrong between us? What made you leave the way you did?'

The question lands between them and for a moment Dan expects Ginger to laugh and give him her usual sassy quip. But instead he sees tears fill her eyes. She fiddles with the beer bottle, picking at the label before sliding it towards him. 'Here, I don't really want this, and I'm driving anyway.'

There's a pause and he fights the urge to fill it.

'I wouldn't change anything, OK? With the girls, I mean. I love them so much.' She takes a breath. 'But I'm not sure I ever really wanted children.'

Ginger's comment surprises Dan. 'Why didn't you ever say?'

She shrugs. 'It's stupid, but I didn't think about it. Kate was trying for a baby and having trouble and everyone was asking after the wedding when we would have a baby, and I thought that's what people did. You got married and you had a baby. I don't think I ever thought about whether I wanted to be a mum. I knew I wasn't the maternal type but I thought that would come when I actually had my own children.'

'And you never felt it? Because it always looked like you had it.'

I did a bit, I guess. I loved having Amelia as a baby, but I also felt so inadequate. I tried so hard to be this perfect mother and perfect wife, and I thought if I just tried hard enough, the feelings would come.'

'I had no idea you felt that way. You didn't say anything.'

'I tried, Dan,' Ginger says, her voice rising a little. 'You didn't want to listen.'

He starts to shake his head but stops. It's taken him four years to ask about their marriage. Clearly he has trouble facing difficult conversations. 'I'm sorry,' he says instead.

'Me too. I'm sorry I left the way I did. It wasn't fair to you or the girls. I woke up one day and knew I couldn't carry on pretending. I wanted my life back, I wanted to feel like me again. I know it sounds extreme, but I felt like I'd die if I carried on.'

'I just wish you'd told me. I wish I'd listened.'

Ginger nods. 'It felt too late by then, though. I knew you'd suggest I go back to work part time or something else and I knew you'd beg me to stay and I would've done for you and the girls.'

'But not for you.'

'Not for me.' Ginger agrees, wiping a stray tear from her cheek.

'I didn't do enough to help, did I? I realise that now.'

Ginger shakes her head. 'No, you didn't.'

They fall silent, the weight of their broken marriage hanging between them. All that hurt that feels so distant and yet so fresh. From across the drive, a dove begins its evening song and Dan finishes his beer.

'The girls still need you, Ginger. Now more than ever.'

'I want to spend more time with them,' Ginger says with a passion he's not heard for a long time. 'I love being with them.'

'Why don't you, then? I never stop you. Sometimes it feels like I'm begging you to see them and all you do is come to the house and hang out for a few hours. It's not parenting.'

Fresh tears fall from Ginger's eyes. She nods. 'I feel so guilty for leaving them. Every time I say goodbye to them it brings it all back. It's hard reminding myself that I've let them down.'

'But it's not about how you feel, Ginger,' Dan says, fighting to keep the frustration out of his voice. They've spoken more in the last ten minutes than they have done in four years and he doesn't want it to end in an argument. 'It's about them knowing that they are loved.'

'They are,' she cries.

'So show them. See them regularly. Take Bryony to her dance class sometimes. Pick a night in the week and have them every other weekend. Whatever you want.'

Ginger looks up, eyes wide, face tear-stained. 'You'd let me do that?'

'Of course,' he says.

'I just . . . I've wanted to ask if I could have something more but I didn't feel like I had the right to do that.'

'Ginger, you're their mum. They love you. I'm sorry for my part in what happened to our marriage. I'm sorry I didn't listen when you needed me to. I'm starting to see that sweeping things under the rug is my speciality.'

Another pause draws out.

'Thursday is good,' Ginger says eventually. 'I can finish work early on Thursdays and collect Bryony from school and then Amelia.'

'Thursday sounds good to me.'

'And every other Saturday night?'

Dan nods. 'No more stories of burglaries?'

Ginger shakes her head. 'I've been an idiot.'

'We both have,' Dan says.

'We should've had this conversation years ago.'

Dan huffs a laugh and it now feels like the most ridiculous thing in the world that they didn't. 'Yep.'

'So why now? I'm guessing Jenny had something to do with it.'

'You could say that,' Dan smiles.

'She's good for you,' Ginger says. 'For the girls too.'

'She is,' Dan agrees.

'So we're OK?' Ginger asks, tilting her head as she looks at him, reminding him so much of the girls.

He nods and for the first time in a long time he thinks they are.

Ginger stands, brushing the dust of the steps from her clothes. Dan stands too and they hug for a moment. It feels familiar and odd at the same time.

'Thursdays and every other Saturday?' Dan says again.

'One hundred per cent.'

'And Bryony's party?'

'Eleven this Sunday. I remember.'

He stands on the driveway for another minute, watching Ginger drive away as the last of the sun disappears from the sky. He rubs his hands over his face, drained but happy too. He thinks – no, he knows – that something has shifted between him and Ginger and that things will be different from now on.

Chapter 41

Jenny

A long yawn spreads through Jenny as she slips into her PJs. She rubs a hand over the firm skin of her bump and smiles. 'You're a monkey,' she whispers, her cheeks glowing at the thought of the hospital earlier, but she smiles too at the stupidity of it being trapped wind and thankful it wasn't something serious.

There's a fluttering again in her chest – those crazy butterflies – as she thinks of Dan and what they said to each other, the feelings it has unleashed in her.

She hopes Dan is getting on OK outside with Ginger. It won't be easy for him, but she knows he'll do it this time. Jenny has had her niggling issues with Paul – too much sugar, late bedtimes, the occasional film she thinks they're too young to watch, but they get on well enough because Jack and Ethan are their number one priority. Always.

Jenny remembers then that she needs to talk to Jack about inviting Paul for dinner. It's late tonight though. She can talk to him tomorrow.

A door creaks from somewhere upstairs. Jenny smiles, expecting Bryony and Bear Bear to appear in the bedroom, but it's Jack. His brown hair is already rumpled from bed. His black football PJs are looking too small; the t-shirt skirting the edges of the shorts waistband.

'Hey, baby,' Jenny says, sitting on the edge of the bed and patting the space beside her. 'Can't sleep?'

He shakes his head, hesitating, and then moving to sit beside her.

She's about to ask about the dinner tonight when Jack speaks, the words rushing out of him. 'It was me who invited Dad to dinner tonight. And Ginger too.'

'Oh.' His comment catches her by surprise. She guessed about Paul, but not Ginger.

'I didn't mean to make you ill and for you to go to hospital.' His shoulders slump, his head dropping into his hands.

Jenny wraps her arm around him. 'First of all, me going to hospital had nothing to do with your dad or Ginger being here, and, second of all, I'm not ill. I'm fine. It was a false alarm, that's all.'

'Really?' He looks up, face still aghast, and she nods, holding him closer.

'Why did you do it?' she asks.

'Don't know,' he mumbles.

'I think you do. Come on, Jack, you're not in trouble, but I'd like to understand.'

'It's . . .' He rubs his face as a tear falls onto his cheeks. 'It's stupid. I missed Dad and I thought you might get back together if you spent more time together. And Ginger and Dan could get back together too.'

'Oh, Jack.' Jenny doesn't know whether to laugh or cry at Jack's scheme. 'Your dad and I have been apart a long time. Longer than we were together. Sometimes people get on better when they're not in a relationship. I know it's hard sometimes not having two parents who live together, but you do have two parents who love you so, so much.'

They fall silent for a moment and Jenny takes Jack's hand and rests it with hers on her stomach as the baby moves, a wiggle, a kick right on their hands and Jack gasps before pulling his hand away. 'That's weird,' he says.

'You should try being me.'

'Mum, can I ask you something?'

'Sure.'

'What is it that made you fall in love with Dad and decide to marry him?'

'Oh, I'm not sure anymore. It feels like a lifetime ago. I remember the first time I saw your dad in the pub. He was the centre of everything, telling all the jokes, buying the drinks. He was a natural entertainer too, a storyteller. People were captivated by him. I was too for a long time.'

'Why did you break up?' There's a rawness to the question and to Jack's tone that throws a cloak of sadness over Jenny. A lump forms in her throat that she swallows away.

The boys were so young when Paul left, too young to ask the question Jenny has dreaded ever since. What can she say? The truth would cause too much hurt. She doesn't want Jack or Ethan to hate their dad. He may be an idiot when it comes to relationships with women, but he is a great dad.

'We stopped loving each other,' Jenny says eventually. 'I stopped thinking he was the most amazing man in the world and he stopped . . .' Jenny's voice trails off. 'Relationships are really complicated. I don't think I have the answers.'

'But you and Dan aren't going to break up when the baby comes? Like you did with Dad when Ethan was born?'

'What?' Jenny laughs. The sound is hollow. It's like Jack has opened up her head and shone a spotlight on an insecurity she didn't even know was there. 'Of course not.' She looks at her boy and sees the face of the man he'll be one day and the thoughtful eyes that see more than most. 'Jack, are you worried about this? I know it's been strange being here, but we're going home in a few weeks.'

'Why?' Jack asks.

'What do you mean?'

'Why are we going home if you and Dan love each other? Why don't we just stay?'

'I . . .' Jenny bites her lip. 'I don't know.' It's a ridiculous answer, but it's the truth. They haven't talked about staying and despite the fact that Jenny is now certain she loves Dan, the thought of staying here – of not going home – fills her with a shaky dread.

'Do you like living here? Do you want to stay?' she asks.

'It's OK.' He shrugs. 'I like our old house, but I like this one too. I like the garden here and being close to school.'

'And Dan?'

'Yeah, he's nice. I like my ukulele lessons with him and my piano lessons.' Something in Jacks face lights up at the mention of his music.

'I love you, Jack.'

'Love you too.'

'Go to bed now and don't worry, I'm fine. We're all fine.'

He nods and moves to stand, but Jenny pulls him in for one last hug. 'Next time you want to invite your dad for dinner, or anyone else for that matter, ask first, OK?'

'You won't say no?' Jack frowns.

She shakes her head. 'Now go to bed. It's late.'

Jenny slides into bed, shifting onto her side, feeling like a titanic of a vessel.

Nerves pop in her stomach. Jack's question about living here spins through her head as Dan appears in the bedroom looking every bit as tired as she feels.

'How did it go?' she asks.

He unbuttons his shirt and kicks off his trousers, leaving them in a heap together as he climbs into bed. His hand reaches across the gap between them and she shuffles closer until their bodies are touching and she can feel the warmth of him beside her.

Dan brushes a stray curl from her face and kisses her cheek. 'It went . . . pretty well, actually. It was hard. We both admitted to things. Apparently I'm not good at talking.'

'Noooo,' Jenny says in mock surprise. 'Really?'

'Ha ha. Well from now on I'm going to be Mr Chatty, talking about my feelings constantly, so watch out.'

'And the girls?' Jenny asks.

'I thought Ginger didn't want to see them, but I think it's more guilt for leaving them and this idea that she didn't have a right to see them that's kept her away.'

'That sort of makes sense.'

'I told her to get over herself and I think she will. She's asked to have the girls on Thursday after school and to stay over every other Saturday.'

'That's great. Amelia will be so pleased.'

'I know. I'll miss them, though. I'm glad I've got you guys with me.' He runs a hand over her bump and leans in, his lips finding hers. There's a nagging thought in the back of her mind. *But I won't be here.* She wants to say something but instead she focuses on Dan's kiss and the feel of his hands over her body.

Chapter 42

Dan

'It's raining,' Dan says, unable to hide the panic from his voice. Rain in July. Rain after days and days of sunshine. Why did it have to rain today of all days? On Bryony's birthday, when they have twenty-something eight-year-olds coming to the house.

'It'll pass,' Jenny says with such conviction that Dan could kiss her. He grabs his phone and scrolls through a website promising easy and fun indoor party games.

'Are you sure they'll want to play this stuff?'

'Are you kidding? Kids love the old school party games. We'll do musical chairs and pass the parcel and then it will stop raining and we can put the bouncy castle up and it will all be OK. The forecast says sunny all day.'

Dan barks a laugh and jabs a finger at the window and the pattering raindrops tapping against the pane. 'Does that look sunny to you?'

'Stop stressing,' Ginger calls from the living room where she's braiding Bryony's hair. It's followed by a 'Yes Daddy, stop it,' from Bryony that sounds so much like Ginger that Dan can't help laughing.

'I'm fine,' he shouts back, raking a hand through his hair and then patting it back into place. He drops his voice. 'Why do I feel so nervous about a kids' party?' he asks Jenny.

Jenny presses herself into Dan's arms. 'Because you're a good dad and you want it to go well. And it will. Ginger, Jack and Amelia are going to help out too, remember? Now look at this game with numbers,' she adds, holding up her phone. 'You hide them around the room and the kids have to run to the right number when you stop the music. Sounds doable. How many did you say are coming?'

'Twenty, maybe twenty-one.'

'Let me guess, Casey's mum didn't RSVP?'

'How did you know?' he grins.

'She's notorious. I bet Ruben's mum offered to stay and help.'

Dan laughs again. 'She did as well. I shouldn't admit this really, but that woman scares the life out of me. I taught her eldest daughter a few years ago. The woman brought an agenda with her to parent's evening. An actual agenda.'

'Nooooo,' Jenny laughs. 'Why am I not surprised?'

'And—' The chime of the doorbell cuts Dan's sentence short. 'Oh god. Are they early?' Dan is not prepared for this. Why did he agree to a party again? Why didn't he hire a soft play centre or go somewhere else, anywhere that wasn't this house?

'They're here. My friends are here,' Bryony squeals with such delight that Dan knows exactly why he agreed to this. And then he steels himself for the chaos to come.

Three hours later, Dan flops onto the sofa exhausted, dehydrated and hungry.

Just as Jenny had predicted, the rain stopped after an hour and the kids poured into the garden with the same speed and desperation as escaped convicts making a mad dash from prison.

Then Jack tried to organise the hitting of the piñata and blindfolded poor Bryony before pointing her, wooden bat and all, towards a papier-mâché unicorn dangling from a tree. She missed the unicorn and whacked Jack's arm instead, forcing Dan to hide all the blindfolds.

The noise and excitement was too much for next door's dog, Benjy, who dug a hole into the garden and joined the fun, chasing the children around the lawn and eating whatever sweets and leftover cake he could find; terrorising poor Isabelle Morris, who is petrified of dogs.

It took Dan and Jack fifteen minute to corner Benjy and push him back under the fence and that was only when Jack waved some leftover ham at him.

Dan sighs and closes his eyes. Despite Benjy and the rain, he thinks it went well. Bryony grinned the entire time and loved Jenny's guinea pig cake, an exact replica of Poppy.

There's movement in the room and he peels open one eye to find Jack standing over him.

'Hey,' Dan says. 'Thanks for today.'

''S OK.' He sits down, resting his hands on his thighs, tapping out the tune to the piano chords he's learning. One lesson and it's clear Jack is a natural musician.

'You were brilliant,' he says. 'A natural child-tamer.'

Jack smiles. 'Is that really a thing?'

'It should be.'

'Jack,' Bryony calls, skipping into the room in the glittery red slip-on shoes Jenny gave her that morning. 'I'm ready for my first lesson,' she says, holding up a brand-new pink ukulele.

Dan watches Jack for any sign of annoyance, but all he sees is a soft smile. 'All right then,' Jack says. 'First thing we need to do is make sure it's tuned. To the piano,' he points, looking nothing like the shy boy Dan met back in February.

So much has changed in the last few months, Dan thinks. And not just Jack but Dan too. Somehow Jenny has opened up a part of Dan he didn't know he had. She's coaxed and sometimes told him outright things he's needed to hear, like the loft room which he finished painting the dark blue and grey Amelia asked for. With a few finishing touches and some furniture, it's going to look great.

He thinks of his dad sitting at his desk and feels a familiar pang before realising it's the first time he's thought about his parents for ages. He corrects himself. He has thought of them often. They are never far from this thoughts, but in a happy way – memories and things he'd like to tell them. Not the cloying emotion, the wrenching sadness he's felt for so long.

It's then, as Jenny appears in the doorway with a cup of tea, that Dan catches the distant plinky-plonk of tinny merry-go-round music from outside. He groans inwardly and waits for what's coming.

As if on cue, Ethan charges into the living room with a feverish excitement. 'Ice cream van,' he pants. 'Mummy, can we get one? Please.'

'Please,' Bryony echoes. 'It is my birthday.'

'Please,' Jack adds with a smile, and it's that extra please that he sees tip Jenny over the edge.

'Alright then. Ethan, run and get my purse,' she says before turning to Dan. 'Fancy a 99?'

He smiles. 'Go on then. Twist my arm, why don't you?' He pats his pockets. 'I gave the last of my change to the bouncy castle guy.'

'Don't worry. I've got this.'

'Quick, Mummy.' Ethan pulls at her arm, his voice panicked now as the music stops, replaced with the sound of an idling engine.

'Amelia?' Jenny shouts up the stairs. 'Do you want an ice cream?'

'No, thanks,' comes the reply, and Jenny catches Dan's eye and raises an eyebrow. Dan knows what Jenny is thinking. It's the same as he's thinking. Not a 'No' but a 'No, thanks'.

They bustle out of the front door – Ethan racing ahead – and as it closes, Amelia appears in the living room surveying the pile of Bryony's opened presents. They look exactly like the same crap stuffed in the toy boxes that Bryony doesn't play with. And he's quite sure there's more wrapping, cardboard and plastic than actual present. Why do toys have to come with so much packaging? God, that makes him sound old and grumpy.

'Where is this stuff going to go?' he asks.

'The bin?' Amelia says before dropping onto the sofa.

'I wish,' he grins. 'Hey, I thought you had a few friends coming to the party? What happened?'

'I changed my mind,' she says. 'Not sure they're really my friends.'

Dan is instantly alert. It's the first time Amelia has come close to confiding in him about school. He wishes he could magic up a best friend for her, someone nice, someone who will make her feel like she can do anything, instead of teasing her and putting her down.

'If people make you feel bad, then they're not your friends.'

'Dad,' Amelia groans. 'I know. Mum said the same, and Jenny. It's fine. I wanted to hang out with Mum anyway. Did she tell you about Thursdays?' It's like a light switches on in Amelia then and Dan is filled with relief and joy that he and Ginger finally talked. But regret is mixed in with it too. They should have done it a long time ago.

'Yep. And every other Saturday for a sleepover.'

274

The smile widens on Amelia's face. 'It's going to be so cool.' She pauses then and turns to face him. 'You don't mind?'

He smiles, throwing an arm around Amelia. 'Of course not. I want you to see your mum, and—' Before he can say more, the front door flies open and Bryony's wails fill the house.

'Dadddddyyyy.' Bryony appears in the living room, her face scrunched up and wet with tears.

'What's wrong, sweetheart?' Dan stands, his eyes falling to Bryony's knees for signs of a graze. She can't have dropped her ice cream because it's in her hand, the white Mr Whippy already running in lines down the cone.

'My dress,' she sobs, pointing to a blob of white on her new red party dress.

'Oh, honey, it's only ice cream,' he says as Jenny, Jack and Ethan appear in the doorway. He smiles at Bryony before using his finger to scoop the lump of ice cream away from the dress. 'Why are you crying about ice cream?'

Dan pops his finger into his mouth just as Bryony's sobbing answer reaches his ears. 'It's not ice cream. A bird . . . a bird pooed on me, Daddy.'

'And you just ate it,' Ethan shouts, his face a mix of wide-eyed shock and joy.

A sudden silence falls over the room. Dan feels all eyes on him just as his taste buds explode with the bitter foul blob resting on his tongue. Nausea burns in his throat. His face contorts. He gags, clawing at his tongue, spitting the globule onto the floor. His eyes water as he fights the urge to retch again.

When he finally looks up, Bryony is no longer crying, but staring opened-mouthed at him. Ethan is hopping from foot to foot beside her and Jenny's entire body is shaking with laughter.

'You ate bird poo,' Jack says and suddenly the whole room is laughing. Four children howling at him and Jenny too. The sound reaches his ears and, despite the taste in his mouth, he can't help but laugh along.

'Here, take your ice cream,' Jenny says to Dan with a gasping sigh. 'Before it melts on the rug.'

'Err, Mum, you do realise that Dan has got bird poo on the rug.' Jack points to the spat out blob. 'I'm not sure ice cream really matters after that.'

They laugh again and Jenny fetches Dan a glass of water and a roll of kitchen roll.

'Are you OK?' Jenny asks with a shuddering sigh. Her face is glowing with laughter.

'To be honest,' he replies. 'My feelings are pretty hurt. I'm not sure you had to laugh quite so hard.'

'We really did,' Jack says, setting them all off again.

'I'm sorry, I'm sorry. It was just . . . and then you . . .' Tears are still falling down Jenny's face.

'I'll forgive you, on one condition.'

'Name it?' she says, standing straighter and wiping her eyes.

'Give me a kiss.' He lurches forward and grins.

Jenny gives a yelp of a scream and jumps away, moving around the house as best she can considering the watermelon bump she's currently sporting. He gives chase, laughing too now. Bryony is at his heels, squealing with delight and shouting to Jenny to run. He feels Jack and Ethan at his ankles, holding him back and a moment later he's on the floor, Amelia grabbing his arms laughing too and even though Dan can still taste the bitter tang of bird crap in his mouth, he laughs because they will always remember this moment together. All of them. They'll talk about it every year on Bryony's birthday and laugh as they remember, and that causes a happiness to buzz through him.

Chapter 43

Jenny

The following weekend dawns wet and cool. Jenny stands at the sink, gazing into the garden – a riot of greens – and wonders briefly if she's the only one in the country grateful for the respite from the summer heat. She kneads her knuckles into her lower back, returning her attention back to the phone in her hand. It's blank now. Mrs Hannigan has gone, leaving Jenny with a flurry of 'good news' and 'next week' in her head.

One more week here and then her and boys can go back to the house in Mortan. She catches herself. They can go home.

There are footsteps on the stairs. It's Dan. She can tell by the thud and soft whistling of a tune she doesn't recognise, not to mention the fact that the boys are with Paul, and Amelia and Bryony are with Ginger.

'The house is way too quiet,' Dan says, stepping up behind Jenny and wrapping his arms around her. The baby shifts at the sound of his voice, kicking her in the ribs and making her gasp. 'At least the rain means a day off from the gardening and I've been able to build Amelia's new desk.'

'How's it going up there?'

'Almost done. Your finishing touches look amazing.'

Jenny feels a buzz of pride at the spray of tiny gold and silver stars she painted in a corner of the blue of Amelia's new wall last week. It looks beautiful – a night sky. She hopes Amelia likes it.

'We're still waiting for the bed so it's going to be a few weeks before we can do the big reveal.'

'You might have to do that one on your own,' Jenny says, and something sinks inside her at what is about to come. This moment was always on the horizon, but now it's here she feels awkward, unsure.

'Why?' Dan asks, nuzzling her neck.

'Mrs Hannigan just called. The house will be ready by next weekend. I can go take a look today if I want to. She sounded really happy with what they've done.'

'Great,' Dan says, his voice flat.

A silence drags out between them.

'It's not like we didn't—' Jenny starts to say as Dan cuts in.

'Hang on.'

They stop and laugh. Nerves hit Jenny's stomach but she's not sure why. Dan takes her hand and guides her to the sofa and they sit down.

'In my mission to talk more and avoid less, I want to say something.' Dan's face is earnest and Jenny finds herself nodding despite the fear knotting inside her. 'Stating the obvious here – we are having a baby together.'

'Yes, but—'

'And even though we haven't known each other for very long,' he continues, 'we've been living together for a couple of months and it's been going pretty well, hasn't it?'

Jenny nods. She bites her lip, sensing what is coming and uncertain how she feels about it. Her heart thuds in her ears.

'And I love you.' Dan's eyes bore into hers and he gives her his George Clooney half-smile that even after the weeks they've lived together still stirs a desire in her. 'So how would it be if you stayed?'

She bites hard on her lower lip, feeling torn right down the middle. 'It's not that I don't want to,' she starts. 'It's just that it is so soon. And we've clearly jumped so many steps in our relationship with this pumpkin.' Jenny rests her hands on her stomach. 'I don't want to rush this and get it wrong.'

They fall silent, listening to the drip of rain on the windows.

Say yes, a voice shouts in her head. *Yes, yes, yes*. But she can't. She won't. It's not the right time.

If not now, then when?

She doesn't have an answer.

'I don't want to be by your side in the hospital when you have the baby and then for you to go to your house and me to come here alone. I want to be there, always.'

'It won't be like that,' she says.

'Then how will it be?'

'We'll figure it out, I promise. I just don't want to ruin what we have by rushing.'

Dan's face falls and she watches the knit of his brows as he thinks. 'I get it,' he says eventually. 'It's scary.'

'It's not that,' she says quickly, wondering briefly if it actually is.

'I won't push you. I just wanted you to know how I feel and that the offer is there for you and the boys to move in permanently.'

'Thank you.' She leans forward and kisses him, grateful he's not pressed her for more.

'When do Jack and Ethan go on holiday with Paul?' Dan asks then.

'The second of August.'

Jenny tries not to think about the fortnight every summer that Paul takes the boys abroad. This year it's Ibiza. An all-inclusive resort, water slides and beach games.

'How about,' Dan says, taking her hand, 'staying here until they get back? I know it's hard for you when they're away. Maybe being here will help.'

Tears burn the corners of Jenny's eyes and she nods. 'I'd like that.' It feels like a compromise of sorts and she's glad.

There's the beep of a car horn. Doors slamming. 'That's Ginger. The mad house is back in business,' Dan says with a grin, but there's a sadness lurking just beneath it.

'Dan,' Jenny says as Dan stands, 'I love you.'

He drops a kiss on her forehead. 'I love you too.'

It's later that afternoon before Paul drops the boys back that Jenny finds herself standing on the doorstep of her house in Mortan. The rain has stopped, leaving a dewy freshness to the air.

The key is in her hand, but she waits. For some reason she doesn't want to go in alone.

'Hey,' Nicola calls out, striding down the road towards her. Jenny's heart lifts at the sight of her friend.

Nicola is wearing an activewear set, her black bob scooped into little bunches behind her ears. She's rosy-cheeked and healthy, Jenny thinks.

'You look amazing,' Jenny says as they hug.

'I look sweaty, but thanks. It's all your fault. I've actually had to go running since I couldn't drop in and see you. Can you believe this weather? Where has the summer gone? Oh don't tell me, you're loving it.'

Jenny laughs. 'I am.'

'You look huge, by the way. Still gorgeous of course for a woman about to turn forty. Talking of which, what are you planning for your big birthday?'

Jenny waves a hand over her stomach. 'I'm planning to be massively pregnant and waddle around.' With everything going on, Jenny hasn't thought about her birthday much recently. Forty. And pregnant. Christ, neither feel real.

'And don't worry, in a few weeks we'll be back here and you can ditch the running and drop in anytime you like.'

Nicola raises a questioning eyebrow, but says nothing. She nods at the door. 'Are we going in then? I'm desperate for a nose around.'

Jenny slips the key into the front door and lets them in. The smell of fresh paint is heavy in the air as they squeeze into the narrow hall. It's smaller than Jenny remembers, as though the bright white paint has pushed the walls closer.

They take the stairs, Jenny leading the way as Nicola fills Jenny in on Rebecca's vow to steer clear of boys, and their holiday to Malta next week.

The walls in the bedrooms gleam, bright and new. There are soft indents in the carpets where the furniture hasn't been put back quite how it was, but, aside from that, it looks the same.

Downstairs, they head straight for the kitchen. The cupboards are a classic white, the worktops pale wood. There's a new stainless-steel sink by the window, but the table and chairs are the same and so is the fridge-freezer in the corner, still covered with certificates and photos. It looks . . . classic, Jenny decides, although it's not the design she'd have chosen for herself.

'It's so nice. Do you like it?' Nicola asks.

Jenny makes a face. 'Has it always been this small?'

Nicola laughs, a throaty cackle. 'Yes, but to be fair, you've grown somewhat in the last few months.'

'That's true,' Jenny grins.

Nicola leans against the worktop and folds her arms. 'Come on then, Jen, what's really going on? Why are we here?'

'What do you mean?' Jenny runs a hand over her bump, avoiding Nicola's eagle-eyed gaze.

'Why are we looking at a house that you don't even want to live in anymore?'

'That's not true,' Jenny protests. 'I love this house. And I love being close to you.'

'Wellesley is ten minutes away in the car so don't bring me into this. Seriously Jenny, I thought things were good with you and Dan.'

'They are.'

'And the kids?'

'Jack is good after his weird attempt to get me and Paul back together. He loves his piano lessons and I think he's even looking forward to senior school. Amelia has been giving him the lowdown. And Ethan and Bryony have their squabbles but are still the best of friends.'

'And how is Amelia?'

Jenny sighs. 'I wouldn't say things are perfect, but they're better than they were.'

'So explain to me why you and Dan aren't talking about living together permanently?'

Jenny sinks into a chair. 'He did ask me this morning.'

'And you said you'd love to, obviously.' Nicola makes a face as she joins Jenny at the table.

'I said it was too soon. We've known each other less than a year.'

'So?'

'I don't want to mess it up by putting extra pressure on our relationship on top of the baby.'

'Oh, Jenny.' Nicola's gaze is full of love and Jenny suddenly feels like crying. 'I could kill Paul sometimes.'

'Paul? What's he got to do with this?'

'He broke your heart, which was bad enough, but it's nothing compared to how he obliterated your ability to trust.'

'I trust Dan,' Jenny exclaims.

'Really? You seriously trust that things are going to work out? Because you have a funny way of showing it,' she says, waving a hand around the room.

Jenny falls silent. She doesn't have the answers, just the feeling that living together permanently is the wrong thing for them. She can't explain it, but she can't ignore it either.

'The irony is,' Nicola continues, 'and I'm telling you this because we promised each other when we were thirteen, after you bought that white Kappa tracksuit which was bloody awful.'

'God,' Jenny snorts. 'It was. What was I thinking?'

'And I let you buy it even though I hated it, and then you wore it to Nancy's party and everyone took the piss and I admitted afterwards that I didn't like it and we promised from that point on that we'd always be honest.'

'I remember.'

'So I'm telling you now that it's you and your determination to move out, your inability to trust that it will work with you and Dan, is the thing that will destroy your relationship and prove you right. How do you think Dan's going to feel when you leave? And when you have the baby and you are here and he is there? How will you feel?'

Jenny shakes her head. She doesn't know anymore. Nothing feels right. 'I don't know.'

They fall silent and Jenny hears the familiar drip of the tap. All this time, all this expense, and they still haven't fixed the sodding tap.

'Come on,' Nicola says. 'Let's go back to mine and have a cup of tea. I've got a packet of Minstrels I've been hiding from Ryan and Rebecca that we can eat.'

Jenny follows Nicola out of the house, glad to be back outside, gulping in the fresh air. Her head spins with Nicola's words. Is her friend right? Is Jenny going to be the thing that destroys her and Dan, after everything else – the kids, the exes, the pressure of the baby, living together – and it's going to be her?

The thought twists inside her and yet she can't change this feeling that it's all moving too fast, that going back to how things were is the right decision.

August

Chapter 44

Dan

'Two more steps,' Dan says, guiding Amelia up the stairs to the loft room. 'Keep those eyes closed.'

'Dad,' she groans, 'this is stupid.' But her eyes remain closed anyway. 'I can't believe my room has been ready for two days and you've made me wait.'

Dan smiles. It wasn't easy convincing Amelia to wait until this morning, but Dan wanted it to be perfect; he wanted it to be just Amelia, and with the boys having left this morning for their holiday with Paul, and Bryony still at a sleepover until lunchtime, now is that perfect time.

He takes a final step and opens the door, grinning at Jenny who is standing in the middle of the room, looking nervously at Amelia's face.

Dan's eyes travel across the room as though seeing it for the first time. There is no hint of the musty book smell Dan remembers, the one that always makes him think of his dad. The walls are fresh with paint; the double bed and furniture all new. The two slanted skylights dominate the room, over-looking the garden and the park. The wall with the windows is dark navy, and Jenny's stars have made the colour really stand out. The double bed is on the opposite wall next to the big closet where his mum used to keep the spare fabrics she used for making curtains and cushion covers. His dad's old desk has gone, replaced with a white IKEA piece and matching desk chair.

Only his dad's armchair remains, tucked in the corner with a grey throw over the old fabric. It's the chair where his dad would sit and the girls would scramble onto his lap and he'd read them facts from the *Reader's Digest* encyclopaedias he loved so much. Dan is glad the chair is still here. A little reminder.

Sadness tugs at Dan's chest. He's not sure that feeling will ever go away, but it's brief and quickly overtaken by Amelia's excitement; his own excitement to see her reaction.

'Can I look now?' she says, hopping from foot to foot with Bryony's level of excitement.

Dan laughs. 'Yes.'

Amelia's hands fall from her face and as her eyes take in the room, her mouth drops open. 'Oh my god, I love it,' she squeaks.

'Jenny and I did the decorating together. I was in charge of flat-pack furniture construction.' He catches Jenny's eye and they grin at each other, sharing a silent memory of the evening last week knelt on the carpet trying to decipher the instructions of the desk, which Dan is still certain was in some form of code.

Amelia steps to the wall by the windows, her fingers reaching up to touch the stars.

'I know you didn't ask for them,' Jenny says, her voice rushed. 'I can paint over them in ten minutes if you don't—'

'No.' Amelia shakes her head. 'I love them.'

'We'll leave you to get settled then,' Dan says, taking Jenny's hand.

Amelia turns to them, smiling widely. It's the happiest he's seen her in a long time and he knows it's not just the room. Seeing Ginger twice a week for the last few weeks has given Amelia a self-assurance Dan didn't know she was missing. 'Thank you,' Amelia says, looking at Dan.

He tilts his head towards Jenny in a silent plea. There's the briefest of pauses and then Amelia looks at Jenny. 'Thanks, Jenny. I guess now the boys can have my old room as it's bigger than their one.'

He feels Jenny shift beside him. 'We haven't talked about it.'

Amelia shrugs. 'Makes sense though.' She turns away, opening up the closet and the door to the little shower room.

Dan and Jenny descend to the kitchen. He knows she's thinking about Amelia's comment. It would make sense to move the boys to the bigger room and pile the baby things – the cot they've yet to build and the growing mountain of boxes stacked against the wall in their bedroom – in the smaller room. The nursery, Dan thinks. God, his mum would've loved that.

It would make complete sense if Jenny and the boys were staying, but they're not. And even though it's killing him to think of them leaving, he knows Jenny well enough now to know that he can't push her. That fierce independence, that determination he loves so much is standing between them and only Jenny can change her mind. He just hopes she will because he's not sure he can bear her leaving.

It's later, when Bryony is home and Amelia is still moving her things into her new room, that Dan finds Jenny on the sofa in the kitchen, gazing into the garden with the window open.

'How are you holding up without the boys?' he asks, sitting beside her.

Jenny gives a watery smile. 'They only left this morning.'

'But you miss them, right?'

She nods, resting her head against his chest. 'It's better this year though. I'm not alone. I've got you and the girls to keep me company.'

He wraps her in his arms. 'I'm sure I can think of some ways to keep you distracted,' he whispers, kissing her neck.

'Eww,' a voice says from the kitchen doorway.

Dan and Jenny leap apart. Amelia pads into the room and rolls her eyes at him. He waits for a comment, but nothing comes.

'If you're missing Ethan and Jack, Jenny, then I can, like, throw some Lego around the living room for you.' Amelia grins.

Jenny laughs and shakes her head. 'Thanks, but I think I'll be alright.'

Dan smiles, his gaze moving from Jenny to Amelia and for the laughter they're sharing. Dan senses a thawing between them as though the air can breathe again. It's not the closeness Jenny has with Bryony, but he hopes one day they'll find it, just as he hopes to continue getting closer to Jack and Ethan.

A piercing scream from the garden shatters the moment, and, a second later, Bryony bursts into the kitchen, eyes wide with sadness. 'Hulk won't wake up.'

'What?' Jenny cries out.

'I just went to give them dinner and Hulk didn't come out to see me like he normally does and so I lifted the lid and . . . and he's not moving,' she says with a hitching sob.

'Oh no,' Jenny's face falls and she turns to Dan.

He scoops Bryony into a tight hug. 'I'll go and see what's going on.'

Dan jogs across the garden, opening the hutch and seeing a very small, very lifeless Hulk.

Poor Ethan.

'Is he dead?' Jenny asks as she, Bryony and Amelia linger behind him.

Dan nods, watching Bryony and Jenny's faces crumble. 'I'm so sorry.'

'It's not your fault,' Jenny says. 'He was quite old for a guinea pig.'

'It's my fault,' Bryony wails. 'Ethan said Poppy was being mean to Hulk, but I wouldn't believe him, but now I think he was right because Poppy is being mean to me too and won't let me pick her up anymore.' She gives a sob and rushes into Jenny's arms.

'Hey now,' Jenny soothes, running a hand over Bryony's hair. 'I'm sure it's not Poppy's fault. And it definitely isn't your fault. Maybe Poppy isn't feeling well. I'll call the vet in a minute and we'll take her in tomorrow, just to make sure she's alright.'

Bryony nods, picking up a strand of hair and sucking it between her lips.

'Bry,' Amelia says, 'why don't we go bake some cupcakes? Leave Dad and Jenny to sort out Hulk.'

Bryony gives a sniffling nod and disappears with Amelia.

The moment it's just Dan and Jenny, Jenny covers her face with her hands and cries. 'Oh god. Is he really dead dead?'

'As opposed to just a little bit dead?'

'I mean, can he be . . . I don't know – be resuscitated?'

Dan huffs a laugh, feeling instantly bad. 'I must have missed guinea pig CPR in my first-aid class.'

Jenny snorts too, the sound ending in a sob. 'Sorry, I know that's stupid. How am I going to tell Ethan when he gets back from his holiday? And what should we do with Hulk?'

'Why don't we bury him under the oak tree?'

'Good idea,' Jenny nods before pulling a face.

'By we, I obviously mean just me.' Dan smiles.

'Thank you,' she sighs. 'I'll make us a cup of tea.'

Chapter 45

Jenny

'Pregnant?' Jenny's mouth drops open. Her eyes look between Bryony, the vet and a rather fat Poppy on the examination table.

The vet, Lesley, is a woman in her late fifties with short grey hair and an 'I've seen it all' expression.

'Is Poppy having a baby?' Bryony jumps up and down.

'More than one, I would say,' Lesley replies.

'But how?' Jenny asks. 'I mean . . .' What is she trying to ask here? '. . . how?'

Lesley cocks an eyebrow and glances at Jenny's protruding stomach for a moment. 'I imagine that Poppy came into contact with a male guinea pig.'

Jenny closes her eyes, blocking out the small examination room, the table, Poppy, Bryony and Lesley. 'But we kept my son's male guinea pig in a separate hutch.'

Lesley's head tilts slightly to the side as though clearly this isn't the explanation.

'They did have a sleepover once, Jenny,' Bryony says as though reminding Jenny, as though Jenny was complicit.

'What?' Jenny glances at Bryony's innocent little face.

'They were friends and me and Ethan thought they'd like it.'

Jenny nods. Heat creeps up her neck. 'Oh.'

'There we are then.' Lesley is triumphant in her expression and tone. 'Mystery solved,' she adds with a hint of sarcasm.

'I didn't realise,' Jenny says, catching Lesley's second glance to her stomach. She feels suddenly like a walking advert for failed birth control. 'There's been a lot going on.'

'I can see.'

'What do we do now?'

'I suggest you take Poppy home. Give her plenty of grass and lots of vegetables rich in vitamin C. She may not want to be picked up or handled until after the babies are born. I would say that'll be in around three to four weeks.'

Jenny feels slightly dazed as she walks out of the vet's office and into the grey August day. It's warm but the air is thick with the threat of a summer storm.

Guinea pig babies? She's not prepared for this. She's barely prepared for her own baby's arrival. They haven't unpacked any of the baby paraphernalia they've bought. It's stacked in the bedroom waiting to go to Mortan when she moves.

'Jenny,' Bryony says, cradling Poppy's carrier in her arms. 'Do you think Ethan will be happy when he finds out?'

'Yes,' she replies. 'He'll be very excited.'

'Even though he'll be sad about Hulk?' Bryony slips her hand into Jenny's, swinging it back and forth a little.

Jenny looks down at the little girl with her blonde hair bleached from the sun and feels a warmth spread through her.

'I think the babies might really help with the news about Hulk. They won't replace Hulk, but I think it will help Ethan to know that Hulk is living on in his babies.'

'Can I tell him, please?'

'Of course.' Jenny smiles. 'I'd love that.'

'Maybe we should bake him a cake too when he comes home?'

'Lemon,' they say together as they reached the car.

Guinea pig babies. Nicola is going to laugh her head off when Jenny tells her this.

Chapter 46

Dan

Music bounces from the kitchen; a fast beat followed by a female singer that could be Little Mix, Ariana Grande or someone else entirely.

Dan smiles as he steps through the door and finds Amelia and Bryony dancing around to the music as they pour Coco Pops into two bowls, scattering just as many across the worktop as they wiggle around.

Amelia has tied her hair back into a high ponytail that swishes as she moves. She looks older. With the black top and a pair of white leggings (the Next kind that come in packs of two, not the glossy Hype ones Amelia has been begging Dan for now for months), she looks fifteen. She looks every bit Ginger's daughter.

'Dad,' Amelia shouts over the music. 'What's the time?'

'Er . . . Dan glances at the clock on the oven. 'Nine twenty-two.' He stretches, arching his back as a long yawn works through his body. He should have a shower and throw on some clothes, but he loves these times, these lazy weekends in the summer holiday when there is nowhere to go, no clubs to dash to, no school to think about. He can stay in his PJs and read the newspaper over endless cups of coffee.

'Great,' Amelia grins. 'Chelsea's mum is picking me up at ten-thirty for our shopping trip.'

'And she's going to stay with you?'

'Yes.' Amelia rolls her eyes before returning to her breakfast.

'What are we going to do today, Daddy?' Bryony asks.

'Research how to look after guinea pig babies?' Dan suggests. He still can't wrap his head around what Jenny and Bryony told him yesterday.

'Can we go out somewhere too?'

Dan turns down the volume. 'I'm not sure yet, how about we get Amelia out the way and wait for Jenny to get up and then we'll decide. I need to test the pool water. It should be ready today.'

Bryony claps her hands and rushes to the window. Dan follows her gaze to the large blue construction now sitting in a sunny spot at the end of the garden. An impulse purchase last week. He told the girls it was because they're not having a proper holiday this summer, and that's part of it, but he bought it for Ethan and Jack too; it will be something to take Ethan's mind off Hulk's death.

Dan can't wait for the boys to see the pool. He can't wait for them to be home. The house hasn't been the same without them these last few weeks.

There's another reason Dan bought the pool. In the back of his mind he's hoping the boys will see it and it will be so exciting, so fun, that they won't want to leave and then Jenny will stay. It's stupid. They've talked about the move over and over, Dan forgetting his decision to give Jenny space and begging her to stay. But Jenny has been adamant and he's not sure what else he can do now other than accept that the love of his life is leaving him. Dan sighs and wonders like he always does what kind of relationship they'll have after this.

'Can we go to the park?' Bryony asks.

'Sounds good,' he says before turning to Amelia. 'Have you got the money safe?'

She taps her pocket and smiles. The excitement is humming around her. Bra shopping. Not crop tops or vests, but proper bras. How did they get here? Dan wonders with a stab of panic. How did Amelia go from lisping through gappy teeth to every single *Frozen* song to a young woman going bra shopping with a friend?

'I checked prices and that's enough for three or four.' He clears his throat. 'Bras, not one really expensive one.'

'I know, Dad. You've told me already. And you don't have to use your teacher voice when you talk about girl stuff, you know.'

'I don't,' he says, his voice now a high squeak as he feels the heat creep across his face.

'You do.' Bryony giggles. 'What's for dinner tonight? Can we have pizza?'

'I think we'll wait until tomorrow night for pizza when the boys are back from their holiday. How about chicken stir fry?'

'With egg fried rice?' Amelia asks.

'And prawn crackers,' Bryony adds through a mouthful of cereal.

'It wouldn't be a stir fry without prawn . . .' His voice trails off as Amelia's phone buzzes on the table. She looks at it and her face falls.

'Everything alright?' Dan asks, knowing it isn't, knowing whatever the message says, it's crushed Amelia.

'Chelsea just cancelled,' Amelia says. 'She got invited to London with someone, so . . .' She shrugs.

'I'm sorry, Amelia.' Anger flares inside him for this girl and how cruel she can be, how little she cares for Amelia.

'Doesn't matter.'

It does and they both know it.

Jenny appears in the doorway, still wearing her PJs too. The t-shirt has stretched out around her tummy, showing two inches of skin.

'How about we go instead?' Dan suggests as he steps over to kiss Jenny good morning.

'Can I come?' Bryony hops across the kitchen, patting Jenny's bump and whispering hello. 'Can we go to Smiggle? Can I get that bag I like?'

Amelia sinks further into her chair. 'Could I go into town by myself?' She lifts her head, eyes pleading at Dan.

He shakes his head. 'I'm sorry. No.'

'What's up?' Jenny asks, heading straight for the kettle.

'Amelia's friend has cancelled so now Amelia can't go shopping for bras,' Bryony says with the same mortification as though announcing a global disaster.

'I'm sorry, Amelia,' Jenny says. 'I know it's not as good as going with your friend, but I need to go into town this morning to get a few things for the baby. Do you want to come with me?'

Amelia looks between Dan and Jenny. 'Just you?'

Jenny shrugs. 'Why not? We're going to the same place anyway.'

'Yaaaay.' Bryony jumps into Dan's arms. 'Daddy Bryony day. Can we get an ice cream when we go to the park?'

'We'll see,' Dan says, blowing a raspberry on Bryony's cheeks, his gaze still fixed on Amelia, willing her to say yes. He's not stupid enough to think that one shopping trip will create a magical bond between Amelia and Jenny, but it's a start.

Amelia shrugs. 'Fine.'

'Is there anything else you think you should say?' Dan asks, fixing Amelia with a stern look.

'Thanks, Jenny,' Amelia mumbles.

'No worries. Just give me twenty minutes to have a shower and get dressed.'

'I'll make you a cup of tea,' Dan says, placing Bryony down and reaching for the kettle.

Jenny disappears and Bryony sits at the table, doodling in a colouring book.

'I'm sorry about today,' Dan says again. There's more he wants to say about Chelsea and friendship, but he's said it all before and however painful it is to watch, it's a lesson Amelia can only learn for herself.

Chapter 47

Jenny

Jenny's gaze flies around the clothes department as a slow panic starts to settle over her.

'Are you OK, miss?' a shop assistant in a garish turquoise t-shirt asks, eyes falling to Jenny's very pregnant stomach.

'My . . . my stepdaughter. I left her right here while I tried on some clothes.'

She'll be just around the corner. She'll have wandered a little too far. She's twelve not four. Don't panic.

But still the fear remains.

'What does she look like?' the assistant asks, guiding Jenny to an empty till. I'll call Security.'

'Thank you,' Jenny says, breathless now as her gaze flies left then right. 'She has blonde hair in a ponytail. Black t-shirt, white leggings and white shoes. She's twelve.'

'Oh,' the assistant frowns and the urgency disappears from her movements. 'Perhaps she's just looking in another area. I'm not sure—'

'Yes,' Jenny nods, desperate to get away now, to search for Amelia herself. 'Yes, I'm sure that's it. Thank you.'

Jenny moves as fast as she can, which for thirty-six weeks' pregnant, isn't that fast at all.

'Amelia?' she calls out as she turns the corner from Maternity Wear into Occasion Wear. An elderly couple look her way. A woman with a child in a pushchair gives Jenny a conspiratorial eyeroll. *Kids huh?*

Jenny calls Amelia's phone but she doesn't answer.

Shit, shit shit!

She should never have tried on the jeans. It took Jenny five minutes to bend down and unlace her trainers, and another five to get them back on. They'd already shopped for Amelia's bras, getting her measured and choosing two multi-packs and steering clear of anything lacey.

Job done. They should've got a milkshake and headed home. Why didn't they? Jenny could've come into town on her own next week to get the nursing bras she needs and a few extra bits.

But Amelia said it was OK. She said she didn't mind waiting. And now she's disappeared. She's run away just when Jenny stupidly, foolishly, thought they were making progress.

'Oh god,' she whispers under her breath as she reaches the escalators. Up to Homewares or down to Beauty? Jenny chooses down, her eyes scanning the shop floor and the street beyond as she descends.

How far would Amelia go? Jenny digs her phone from her bag, calling Amelia's number over and over. She doesn't pick up.

Ten minutes later, Jenny pushes her way out of the store and through the Saturday shoppers. There's a craft market up ahead and the air carries the scent of hot dogs and crêpes.

Jenny looks from face to face as she moves, but Amelia is nowhere. Hot tears fill her eyes. Dan trusted her to look after Amelia. He's always worried about her being in town alone and now Jenny has let her do just that.

Jenny's phone buzzes in her hand. Amelia. Thank God.

'Hello, Amelia? Where are you?'

There's a muffled sob. 'Jenny, I need help.'

'Where are you?'

'In the toilets at McDonalds.'

Jenny spins around, her shoulder knocking against someone as she spots McDonalds up ahead.

'Are you OK?' Jenny asks, already moving towards the yellow arches.

'I . . . I've started my period,' Amelia hisses, her words a rushed whisper filled with horror and panic.

'I'm here,' Jenny says. *Shit!* She is not equipped for this. From the moment Ethan was placed in her arms, a scrawny slippery little baby boy, she made absolute peace with the knowledge that manicures, shopping trips, ballet, and a million other things she'd watched Nicola and Rebecca do were unlikely to be in her future. And that was OK. Two healthy children. That's all that mattered.

'Er . . . I'm going to grab some supplies. I'll be five minutes.'

'OK. Hurry.'

'Do you want me to call your dad?'

'No,' Amelia cries out.

'What about your mum?'

There's a pause before Amelia speaks again. 'She's away. Just hurry. Please.'

Ten minutes later, Jenny shoves her shoulder against the door and pushes into the toilets, the bulging shopping bags in her hands knocking against her legs. She's breathless, in desperate need of a wee, and has bought way too much stuff. An entire class of girls could be in these toilets and she could supply them all with the kit they'd need for starting their periods.

Jenny doesn't care. Right now, she'd buy the entire period selection of every shop in town if it would make things even a little easier for Amelia, a little less scary.

Jenny remembers waking up to find her period had started for the very first time. She was late to the party. Almost fourteen. She'd been prepared. Her mum had given her a bag of products to keep in a drawer for when the time came, and yet nothing actually prepared her for how awful it was, how awkward. And nothing, not one goddamn thing, has changed in twenty-six years. There is nothing Jenny can do to make this any less horrible for Amelia.

Jenny waits for the door of the toilets to swing shut and takes in the dark-grey tiles, the shiny mirrors, the three sinks, the three toilet cubicles. A carbon copy of every McDonald's toilet in the country.

'Amelia?' Jenny says, stepping to the only occupied toilet.

'Jenny?' Amelia's voice is a squeak and all of a sudden Jenny thinks how young Amelia is and how all Jenny wants to do is take her in her arms and tell her it's going to be OK.

'I'm here.'

'It's gross.'

'I know. I'm sorry this has happened here.'

'I don't know what to do.' There's a muffled sob that makes Jenny's heart ache. Amelia might not always have been kind to Jenny, but she's not a bad person. She's a girl on the cusp of her teenage years having a huge change forced on her.

'I've got some things. Do you want me to slide them under the door or . . .' Jenny waits.

'I don't know what to do with any of it.'

'That's OK. How about unlocking the door and letting me in and I'll show you. I've also got a change of clothes. I wasn't sure if you might need it.'

'You can't come in. It's so horrible.'

'Amelia, please,' Jenny soothes, 'believe me when I say that this is not going to come even close to the gross stuff I have actually seen in my life. I've also had quite a few periods myself not to mention giving birth twice.'

There's a shuffle of movement and a moment later the door to the toilets unlocks.

Jenny slips in, bolting the door behind her.

'How much stuff did you buy?' Amelia sits back on the toilet, her face is pale and tear-stained, but she smiles.

'At least half of Boots. I've got all the different products as well as some period pants.'

'What are they?'

'They are the game-changer I wish I'd had when I started my period.' Jenny lifts out the products one by one and talks them through, sharing the knowledge she's learned through trial and error; a lot of error.

'I've got you some new leggings as well.' Jenny pulls out the Hype leggings she grabbed from the sports shop next door.

Amelia's face breaks into a grin. 'They're the ones I wanted,' she gasps.

'I know.'

'Dad said they were too expensive.'

'I think when you tell your dad about today, he won't care.'

'You can't tell him,' Amelia groans as she starts to get herself changed.

Jenny leans up against the door ignoring the pressure on her bladder and willing the baby to stop break-dancing for the next three minutes.

'Your dad loves you very much,' Jenny says. 'You know he's got a whole bathroom cupboard filled with products just like these, right?'

Amelia nods.

'He understands that this is going to happen and I know he's a man, but he's also a really good dad and he wants to support you through this, so I won't tell him, but I think you should.'

Amelia's eyes well with tears but she holds it together as she pulls on the period pants and Jenny shows her how to stick the pad in place.

'Can we go home now?' she asks, and then, 'Thanks for buying these leggings for me.'

'You're welcome.'

Jenny shuffles round to unlock the door. Christ, she's about to wet herself. 'I just need to—'

'Jenny, wait,' Amelia says. 'I have to tell you something.'

'OK.' The baby shifts inside her, a fist or a foot presses onto her pelvis and she clenches tight as a trickle of wee escapes.

'It was me who took your make-up bag. I hid it in Bryony's room. And I turned the oven up on the cakes. And I shouldn't have walked off just now. My stomach was hurting and I was mad at Chelsea. I'm sorry. I don't know why I've been so mean to you. I think I just . . . It was me and Bryony and Dad for ages and I thought it would always be that way and then you turned up and it was like it wasn't just the three of us anymore. It was six.' Amelia glances at Jenny's stomach. 'Seven soon.

'And you've always been so nice and it just made it worse, which I know is stupid.'

Jenny shakes her head as her chest fills with warmth and she smiles. 'It's not stupid. It's completely normal. It's been a massive change for all of us and everything has happened so fast; no one has had time to get used to it, have they? Even I've struggled.'

'Really?'

Jenny laughs. 'Really.'

'I am glad my dad met you,' Amelia says, her cheeks turning pink. 'Dad was really sad until you turned up. He tried to be happy and everything, but you could still see he wasn't. He didn't whistle and I'd forgotten that he even used to whistle before Mum left and Granny and Grandad died. It was only after he met you and started again that I remembered.'

Jenny smiles. 'I'm really happy I met your dad too. But that whistling is a bit annoying, isn't it? Utterly tuneless.'

Amelia laughs. 'Totally.'

Jenny turns to look at Amelia. 'Thank you for telling me all this. I do understand, I promise. And I think you're an amazing girl, Amelia. You are so smart and so kind to Bryony and the boys.'

Amelia pulls a no–I'm-not face.

'I see it,' Jenny grins. 'You're really amazing. Perhaps now is a good time to start over?'

Amelia nods, relief smoothing out the frown on her face.

'Great, because if I don't use the toilet in the next three seconds I'm going to . . .' Jenny's voice trails off as Amelia's sweet perfume tickles her nose. Oh god. She's going to . . . yep, she is! Jenny pinches her nose but it's too late; the sneeze hits her. Jenny draws in a long gasp before releasing a loud 'achoo' that presses down her body from her nose all the way down to her pelvis and the bladder she's been trying desperately to hold on to for the last twenty minutes.

A second later warm liquid trickles down her legs and drips onto the floor.

'Oh my god, have your waters broken?' Amelia cries in alarm.

Jenny shakes her head as she stares down at the growing puddle on the floor and clenches tight, wresting control over her bladder. 'Nope. I've wet myself.'

'What?' Amelia stares at Jenny open-mouthed before the laughter grips hold of both of them both. 'That's so funny.'

'Yes, so funny I've got wet knickers. Ha ha,' Jenny says, her voice dripping with sarcasm as she catches her breath and wipes a stray tear from her cheek. 'Now, how about letting me get sorted. Luckily I bought myself some new underwear too.'

Amelia slips out of the toilet and a moment later the sound of the running tap fills the silence.

When Jenny reappears a few minutes later she's glad to see the colour has returned to Amelia's face.

'Perhaps,' Jenny starts as she washes her hands, 'we don't need to tell your dad about this.'

A smile pulls at the edges of Amelia's lips. 'But my dad loves you, Jenny, and I know he's a man, but he's doing his best to support you and be understanding. I won't tell him, but I think you should.'

'Very funny.'

They laugh as they leave the toilets.

'Ready to go home?' Jenny asks.

'Definitely.'

This hasn't been the day either of them expected, but that's OK, Jenny thinks. It isn't going to always be smooth sailing with Amelia, but they've turned a corner and that's more than enough right now.

Then Jenny realises what she's said. *Ready to go home?*

Not back to the house, to Wellesley, to Dan's, but home.

The word sings in her thoughts, surprising her. She pushes it to one side. Tomorrow she's going to pack and move some of their things back to Morton before the boys return from their holiday. It was just a slip of the tongue, that's all.

Chapter 48

Dan

Dan sinks onto the bed and puts his head in his hands. He feels drained and grateful and overwhelmed.

'You OK?' Jenny asks, appearing from the en suite with a towel around her head and another around her body.

He nods. 'I think so. I'm just . . . what do I do now?'

'Nothing. You just get on with it.'

'But it's every month. She'll have to go through this every month. How can I help her?'

'It'll get easier. You'll learn what things she likes and doesn't like during her period. I'd probably stock up on some expensive ice cream and keep a stash of chocolate somewhere. It takes the edge off the misery of that first day.'

'Amelia is just speaking to Ginger now. She seems OK. And their Aunty Kate called asking if she could take the girls out tomorrow for lunch with the twins as a treat, which will be a good distraction, but I just wish there was something else I could do.'

'Dan.' Jenny shakes her head. 'I'm sorry, but there is nothing to do here. This is part of growing up. It's horrible, but it's also life.'

'I know. And it's mad. I prepared for it. I bought all the stuff and I've been waiting, but now it's here I feel so helpless.'

'You are an amazing dad, Daniel Walker. Amelia is lucky to have you. We're all lucky to have you.'

'She's lucky to have you too.' Dan holds out his arms for Jenny. She pads across the carpet and he pulls her gently onto his lap. Her shoulders are still glistening from the water of the shower and Dan feels himself stir as he takes in her bare skin.

He traces a line of kisses down her neck.

'How are you feeling?' he asks.

'Pretty good, actually.'

'Good enough for . . .' Dan moves his lips to her mouth. They kiss, gentle at first. His hands move to the towel wrapped around her body, pulling it away.

'God, you're beautiful.'

'I'm massive.'

'Not to me,' he whispers before kissing her again.

'Dan?'

A voice wades through his sleep. Pulling him away from the warmth, the peace.

'Dan?'

His eyes shoot open, registering the urgency in Jenny's voice.

'I'm having contractions,' she whispers.

'What? He sits up and turns on the bedside light. The room illuminates in a yellow glow and he takes in Jenny's pale features. She's pacing up and down by the bed, rubbing at the bump. 'But the baby isn't due for another four weeks. It's too soon, isn't it?'

'Jack was born at thirty-eight weeks and Ethan at thirty-seven.'

'What should I do?' He jumps out of bed, disorientated, panicked. He needs to get dressed and dig out the hospital bag. Have they even finished packing it?

311

'I've called Nicola. She's ready to drive here and look after the girls. I told her we'll give it an hour. They're still about eight minutes apart. Could you make me some warm milk please?'

'Milk?'

'Don't ask. I'm craving it.'

'On it.'

Warm milk, warm milk, warm milk. Dan repeats the instructions over and over as he tiptoes through the house and turns on the stove.

This is it.

They're having the baby. Excitement buzzes through him. It's that scary, jittery excitement, like at the funfair when the craziest upside rollercoaster starts to move and he's bloody terrified but excited and happy too.

It takes an age to heat the milk and he worries the whole time whether he should've used the microwave. But his mum always heated milk on the stove and so that's all he knows.

He paces the kitchen, pleading with the milk to hurry up and heat. His role from now on is going to be pretty minimal. All he can do is support Jenny and—

'Shit.'

Milk bubbles up, spilling over the edge and onto the hob in an angry hiss. Dan grabs at the pan, pouring what's left of the milk into the mug and hoping Jenny won't mind that it's only half full.

Dan leaves the pan to soak and hurries back to Jenny, his head filled with images of her groaning softly as the contractions pick up pace. Except that's not what he finds. Instead, Jenny is lying in bed reading her book.

She looks up as Dan walks in, proffering the drink like a trophy, like he's milked the damn cow himself.

'False alarm,' she says with a shrug. 'The contractions have completely stopped. I spoke to a midwife at the hospital and she said she thought it sounded more like Braxton Hicks.'

'Braxton what?'

'You know, false contractions. Just my body messing with me in the middle of the night.'

'Oh right. That's good.' Sort of. The adrenaline is still shooting through his body, nowhere to go now. 'I've got the milk though.'

Jenny scrunches up her nose. 'Actually, I don't fancy it anymore. Sorry.'

'Oh. That's OK. So, what do we do?'

Jenny yawns, snuggling herself into the bed. 'Forget I woke you up. Go back to sleep.'

Dan slides in beside her and turns out the light. He lays awake for a long time listening to the sound of Jenny's soft breathing and wonders not for the first time how on earth they'll do this – raise this baby, be a family, love each other – with half of them in Mortan and the other half here.

How will it work? Will Jenny come to stay at the weekends with the baby and the boys? Or will they share custody and then go on dates too?

The questions continue to fly through his thoughts.

Go back to sleep. Ha!

Chapter 49

Jenny

The sun scorches the back of Jenny's neck as she closes the boot of her car. It thuds but doesn't shut until she squishes down an overloaded bag of clothes and gives it another firm slam.

She steps back and sighs, rubbing at her belly, her eyes straying back to the house as a sadness tears through her.

What are you doing?

Her phone beeps from her pocket. It's Paul: *Just landed. Back in two hours if the traffic is good! Just checking we're heading to Mortan?*

Jenny sends a thumbs up before clambering into the driver's seat with some difficulty. Her belly is so big that she's had to push the chair back and can only just reach the pedals.

She starts the car and glances back at the house again. There is no big goodbye scene; no waving or kissing away Bryony's tears. Jenny didn't want that, and besides they'll be back tomorrow with the boys for lunch and a play in the pool. There are more things to collect – her KitchenAid and baking pans, and the baby stuff. Dan's going to drive some boxes over one evening next week when Ginger has the girls.

At least, Jenny thinks Dan will do that. They've barely spoken today. It's felt to Jenny as she's crept through the house, opening drawers and packing clothes into bags, that there is already a distance between them and she hasn't even left yet.

She closes her eyes, wishing suddenly that Dan would appear at the front door and beg her one more time not to leave. He won't. He's in the pool with Bryony and Amelia. It's why Jenny has chosen this moment to drive to Mortan.

It's not goodbye, she reminds herself. She'll see them tomorrow.

'It's the right thing,' Jenny whispers as she drives out of Wellesley.

For who? Nicola's voice echoes in her head.

Jenny is ashamed to say she's avoided her friend these last few weeks, avoided the disapproval and the questions Jenny can't answer.

The drive is easy. There's hardly any traffic. Jenny imagines everyone is enjoying the sunny Sunday afternoon in gardens and pubs or in a pool like Dan and the girls.

Jenny parks outside the terrace house in Mortan feeling weighed down, suddenly longing for Dan.

Her hand moves to cut the engine but something stops her.

What is she doing?

Jenny closes her eyes, listing all of her reasons for doing this:

- They've only known each other since November.
- The baby has added huge pressure to their relationship as it is. Continuing to live together will only add to that.
- There's no rush. A year down the line they can discuss living together again.

It all sounds so rational and yet it suddenly feels so wrong too.

Tears spill onto Jenny's cheeks. A memory bobs to the surface of her thoughts – pacing the living room, cradling a screaming Ethan, hushing and soothing while her own tears dripped down her cheeks. Paul packed and gone the previous week.

She swore she'd never let anyone hurt her like that again. Built up the wall that she thought Dan had knocked down. But sitting here, she's not so sure.

You're scared.

Terrified, more like. What if it all goes wrong?

What if it doesn't?

A sob catching in her throat. She loves Dan. She loves the girls. She loves their life together. What the hell is she doing here?

The impulse to go back grabs hold. Christ, she's been such a fool. Jenny snatches up her phone and fires a text to Paul telling him the change of plans. Then, with shaking hands, she puts the car into gear and turns around.

She's going to drive back. She's going to tell Dan she's changed her mind. She's going to kiss him and tell him what an idiot she's been.

Jenny makes it to the end of the road before Dan's car appears. He pulls over and jumps out, hair still dripping wet.

She climbs out of the car too and as they meet in the middle, Jenny catches sight of Amelia and Bryony in the back of Dan's car, still in their swimming costumes and towels. Bryony waves and Jenny waves back as she reaches Dan.

'I can't let you do this,' he says, his voice thick with emotion.

'I can't do it.'

'You can,' Dan cried out. 'We can, together.'

Jenny half sobs, half laughs. 'No I mean, I can't do this.' She waves a hand at the house behind her. 'I was driving back to you, to ask if actually . . . could we stay?'

Dan's face lights up. Their eyes meet and he takes her in his arms. 'Yes. One hundred per cent, yes.'

Emotion blocks Jenny's throat. 'I'm sorry,' she whispers. 'I was scared and I've been an idiot.'

'It doesn't matter now.' They kiss then and it feels to Jenny like their first kiss – magic and intense and full of promise.

The short toot of a car horn pulls them apart. They turn to see Amelia leaning into the front of Dan's car.

'Can we go already?' she calls out, rolling her eyes but Jenny catches the smallest of smiles too.

'Can we?' Dan asks Jenny.

She nods. 'I'm right behind you.'

Jenny climbs back into her car, heading home. There are no questions now, just a certainty that whatever happens, she and Dan are in this together. It's not always going to be fireworks and romance, but it's real life. It's messy and chaotic and everything she wants.

Chapter 50

Jenny

Excitement balloons in Jenny's chest as Jack and Ethan scramble out of Paul's car. She's already halfway down the drive, her arms out to hug them, moving as fast as her bump will allow her. Every step bounces on her bladder and she's quite sure if she could see her feet right now, they would look more like Big Foot's than her own size fours.

'You're ginormous,' Ethan shouts, running towards her. 'Like a hippopotamus.' He howls with laughter and rushes into her arms.

'I've missed you too,' she laughs. 'Hey, how was the holiday? You've grown!'

'Good,' Ethan says. 'We had ice cream every day. Even for breakfast. Have you had the baby?'

She laughs and shakes her head. Only Ethan would ask that question. 'Not yet.'

'Jack.' The smile stretches so wide on Jenny's face that her cheeks ache with it.

'Hi, Mum,' Jack says with a grin as he strolls over, looking more grown up than ever.

'Look at the colour of you. Did your dad put any sun cream on you?'

'A bit.'

'Did you have a good time?'

'Yeah.' Jack nods. 'There was this band in the evenings and this guy had a ukulele and let me play with them.'

'Wow,' Jenny says, trying to picture her shy boy up on a stage. She takes him in. Jack is no longer looking at his feet, he's smiling, he's getting on stage and playing the ukulele in front of other people. She can't believe it.

'Dad's got a video,' Jack says as though reading her thoughts. 'So are we staying then?' He nods to the house. Ethan stops dancing around, both of them waiting for her reply.

'Yes,' she says. 'If that's all right with you and Ethan?'

Ethan jumps up, punching the air and Jack shrugs. 'It's cool. I don't think we'd get a piano in our old living room.'

'Probably not,' she grins, feeling a relief sweep through her. That's it then. They're staying. She turns to Ethan, but he's already spinning away.

'I'm going to see Hulk,' he shouts, sprinting towards the garden. 'Bye, Dad.'

And then Jenny remembers. She remembers why she's rushed out here. It's not just to see the boys the very second she can, it's because of Hulk.

'Ethan, wait,' she calls out.

'What's wrong?' Jack asks as Ethan ignores her shouts and disappears around the house and into the garden.

'Hulk died,' Jenny says, hit again with emotion.

'I'll catch him,' Jack says, sprinting off.

By the time Jenny makes it to the garden, Paul has left and Dan has put the suitcases inside. He meets her by the back door and they hurry to the hutch together.

They find the boys by Hulk's hutch. Ethan's head is bent and his hands are covering his face. He looks up when

319

they approach and he rushes into Jenny's arms. 'Jack says Hulk died.'

'I'm so sorry, baby,' Jenny whispers, feeling her own tears forming. 'He died in his sleep. Hulk didn't suffer at all,' she says.

'No,' he cries, pushing himself into Jenny's side.

'We buried him in a shady spot underneath the oak tree,' Dan says, pointing across the garden. 'And when you're ready, we'll have a funeral and you can say some things about Hulk.'

Ethan lifts his head. 'Where?'

'I'll show you.' Ethan lets Dan scoop him into his arms and carry him across the garden. He leans his head against Dan's shoulder and cries.

Jenny watches them together, tears spilling from her eyes. Jack slips his hand into hers and she gives it a squeeze.

'Where are the girls?' he asks. 'We got them some chocolate if it hasn't melted in the suitcase.'

'They're with their Aunty Kate this afternoon. They'll be back soon.'

'Cool.' Jack nods. 'Got anything to eat?'

Jenny laughs. 'I'm pretty sure I can find you something. I've made lemon cake.'

'Yum.' Jack jogs over to Ethan. 'Mum's made lemon cake.'

Ethan shakes his head and runs inside. 'I want to be alone.'

Jenny starts to follow him, but Dan takes her hand. 'He's upset. Give him some time on his own. He'll come down for some cake when he's ready.'

'Wow,' Jack shouts, turning to face Dan. 'Is that a pool?'

Dan grins. 'You're probably sick of swimming though after—'

'No way. I'm going in right now.'

And despite the worry for Ethan, she can't help but marvel at Jack's ease. He's changed so much these past few months and Jenny is sure Dan and the music have had a lot to do with that.

Chapter 51

Dan

'Ethan's gone,' Jenny pants as she rushes into the kitchen, a torn piece of paper flapping in her hands.

Dan spins towards her, taking in the frantic look on her face, the panic in her voice. 'What do you mean?'

'He's run away.' Jenny pushes a note at him written in Ethan's tiny handwriting.

To Mum, Jack, Dan, Bryony and Amelia,

I am running away to live at our old house where Hulk was happy. If we hadn't moved here then Hulk would still be alive.

I will miss you all.

From
Ethan

'Where's my mobile?' Jenny gasps. 'I need to call the police.'

'We're back,' a voice shouts from the hall. A second later, Amelia and Bryony appear in the kitchen.

'Aunty Kate says hi but she couldn't stop because she has to get to the shops before they close. What's going on?' Amelia looks around the room, sensing the tension.

'Where's Ethan?' Bryony asks, jumping up and down. 'I have to tell him about Poppy.' She claps her hands, her eyes moving from Jenny to Dan.

'We don't know,' Dan says as Jenny rushes into the garden.

'Ethan was upset about Hulk and has left a note to say he's run away. I need to help Jenny find him. Can you girls search the house?'

'On it,' Amelia says, taking Bryony's hand.

'Ethan?' Jenny screeches as Dan races after her. She clutches her bump and jogs towards the tree, calling his name.

The air is warm but the sun has been swallowed by a squishy blanket of ominous rain clouds.

'I thought he'd be up there,' Jenny whispers as Dan reaches her.

'Try not to panic. He can't have been gone long.'

Dan walks a full circle around the tree, peering into the boughs and through the leaves for any flash of his red t-shirt, but all he sees is green.

There's a bang of wood hitting wood from further down the garden. Jenny and Dan glance at each other before following the sound.

Dan reaches the gate first. It's open and he stares into the park. It's quiet for a Sunday evening. The rain clouds have driven the visitors home.

'He's not in the house,' Jack shouts as he, Amelia and Bryony run down the garden to meet them.

'He said he wants to go back to the old house,' Dan says. 'How would he get there?'

'I . . . I don't know.' Jenny shakes her head.

Dan can see the stampede of panic marching through her body and he wants to hold her close and tell her to stay calm, but how can he? If it was Bryony who was missing right now, there is nothing anyone could say that would stop the wild fear from surging through him.

'He can't have gone far,' Dan says again. 'Jenny, why don't you stay here and call the police? We'll go out and look for him.'

'I'll check the park,' Jack says.

'I'll look on the high street,' Amelia pipes up.

'And me,' Bryony says.

Dan shakes his head. 'Bryony, we need you to stay here and help Jenny, OK?'

Bryony gives a serious nod and a wave of love washes over Dan, for Bryony, Amelia, for Ethan and Jack and Jenny. His family.

'Check the tunnel in the playground,' Jenny shouts over her shoulder as she hurries back to the house. 'He loves it in there.'

'We will. I'll phone or text every ten minutes,' Dan calls after her.

They race across the park, Amelia veering left towards the high street while he and Jack head for the playground. The first drops of rain start to fall as they near the railings and Dan's heart sinks again. It looks deserted. Above their heads, clouds the colour of smoke roll across the sky.

'Can you check inside the tunnel?' Dan points to the empty climbing frame.

'Yeah.' Jack races ahead.

Dan's breath is ragged and sharp, the air burning in his lungs, but he doesn't slow down as he follows Jack.

Jack jumps up the ladder and peers into the tunnel at the top of the climbing frame. 'He's not here,' he shouts.

'OK. Let's try the high street then the school.'

The rain spatters down on them; big, fat drops of summer rain that hit their faces like tiny bullets of cold.

Cars tear down the high street as they round the corner. The road is busy with people rushing to be home. A tightness pulls at Dan's chest as he imagines Ethan trying to scurry between the big Land Rovers, the distracted drivers.

Where are you, Ethan? A crushing anxiety hits Dan. He was sure Ethan would be here. Sure he'd find him and everything would be OK. But now what? He can't let anything happen to Ethan. He can't lose his family when they've only just begun to be one.

'There,' Jack points at the bus stop.

Dan's eyes fix on the tiny red of Ethan's t-shirt, and Amelia sat beside him.

His hands shake as he calls Jenny. Relief spins in his head. 'We've got him.'

'I know,' Jenny replies, voice cracking with emotion. 'Amelia just texted me. I'm on my way in the car with Bryony.'

There's a gap in the traffic and Dan and Jack jog across the road. Ethan hasn't seen them yet, but Amelia has. She holds up her hand, telling them to wait.

Dan and Jack draw close but say nothing.

'I want to run away,' Dan hears Ethan say, his little voice trembling.

'Where to?' Amelia asks.

'Home. We got the bus once when Mum's car was at the garage and this is where it dropped us off. I've got money,' he adds, opening up his palm to reveal a handful of coins.

Amelia looks from the money to Ethan's face. 'I'm confused. I thought your home was across the park with us.'

'My old home, I mean. Where Hulk was happy. No one is living there now, so I can live there.'

'All by yourself?' she asks.

'Yeah.' The defiance in Ethan's tone cuts straight into Dan. He's desperate to step forward and scoop Ethan into his arms but he knows that could scare him, and right now Ethan is listening to Amelia.

'But Hulk won't be there, will he?' Amelia keeps her tone soft and Dan can tell she's trying not to scare him into running too.

A wall of tears build in Ethan's eyes. 'Don't care. I hate living at your house. If we hadn't moved, Hulk would still be alive.'

'I'm sorry about your guinea pig, Ethan.'

'No you're not. You never liked him and you don't like me.'

'I do like you, actually,' Amelia says with one of her typical shrugs. 'You make me laugh. You and Jack do. I like playing on the rope swing and—'

'You don't like my mum though.'

Amelia sighs. 'I thought I didn't. But I was wrong. Haven't you ever been wrong about anything?'

Ethan shrugs. 'S'pose.'

'I like Jenny. She's really nice and you're lucky to have her as a mum, but she's going to be pretty sad if you're not here, don't you think? Don't you want to live with your mum anymore?'

'I do, but—' Ethan wipes his hands under his eyes. 'I miss Hulk and now I don't have a guinea pig anymore.'

'Can I tell you a secret?' Amelia asks.

Ethan nods.

Amelia leans closer to Ethan. 'You have to promise to pretend you don't know, OK? Because Bryony has been so excited to tell you.'

'What?' Ethan sits forward and stares up at Amelia. 'I promise.'

'Poppy is having babies. Hulk's babies.'

'Like my mum? No way!'

Amelia nods and Dan watches her slip her hand into Ethan's. 'And you know, one of them is bound to look just like Hulk.'

'All of them probably.'

'It would be a shame if you weren't there to see them. Your mum says you can keep one or two, but they would need someone to look after them.'

'I could do it,' Ethan says, his voice stronger.

'I thought you were running away?'

Ethan sinks back onto the bench looking sad and lost. 'I was.'

From the corner of his eye, Dan spots the bus turning onto the road. Jack nudges his side, pointing to it.

'I'm still sad about Hulk,' Ethan whispers.

'Yeah, but do you know who else is sad right now?'

'Who?'

'All of us. Your mum is really worried about you. And so is Bryony and Dad and Jack. We're sad because you're not at home.'

'Oh. I hadn't thought about that.'

'Come on.' Amelia gives Ethan's hand a small tug as she stands and he slips off the bench and stands beside her. 'Let's go get some of your mum's lemon cake.'

The bus pulls up in a blast of heat and the smell of petrol fills the air. The doors open and a man climbs down the steps.

'Getting on?' the driver calls.

Dan holds his breath again as Amelia looks at Ethan. His eyes stare up at the bus and then to Amelia before shaking his head and inching closer to her.

As it pulls away, Jenny's car appears and Dan steps forward with Jack beside him. Jenny climbs out of the car and pulls Ethan into a tight hug. She's crying but smiling too.

'I'm not going to run away anymore,' Ethan says.

'Good.' Jenny sighs before she looks at Amelia and mouths a 'thank-you'.

Bryony climbs out of the back seat and for a moment everyone is standing in the rain.

'Can we go home now?' Ethan asks. 'I'm getting wet.'

They laugh and Jenny shoos Ethan and Bryony into the car. 'I've got one more space,' she says. 'Amelia, fancy getting dry?'

Amelia looks to Dan and shakes her head. 'Nah. Jack, you take it. I'll walk back with Dad. It's only rain.'

The car drives away and Dan puts his arm around Amelia as they stroll back through the park.

'Thank you for what you said to Ethan.'

She shrugs. 'It's not a big deal.'

'It is to me.'

'Isn't it Jenny's birthday next weekend?'

'Yes,' Dan says with surprise. He hadn't realised Amelia had picked up on Jenny's birthday. He really needs to get her present sorted. He's got an idea, but he needs to talk to the kids, check what they think. Nerves hit him like a shovel.

'She's forty, right? Isn't that a big deal? Are you planning a surprise party?'

Dan stops walking and takes hold of her arm, his eyes wide. 'Do you think I should? Will she want that?'

'Dad, she's, like, massively pregnant and about to have a baby. I'm no expert but I think that means her life and yours is going to be taken over by nappies and stuff.'

Dan barks a laugh. 'Nappies and stuff. I like it.'

Amelia grins. 'Right, so I think the least you can do is throw her a surprise party and invite her friend Nicola over. Hasn't Jenny got, like, a brother too?'

'She either has a brother, or not,' Dan says, rolling his eyes. 'There's no like about it.'

'Yeah, yeah.' Amelia laughs. 'So, the party?'

'Alright. I will. We'll do it Saturday afternoon. It can be a pool party.'

'Cool. Can I invite a friend? I met her in the Maths lunch club. She's nice.'

'Of course.'

Amelia slides closer to Dan and they walk the rest of the way in silence as Dan's head spins with thoughts of surprise parties and the baby, the kids, Jenny, and just how lucky he feels to be walking in the rain with Amelia.

Chapter 52

Jenny

The light above the bathroom mirror glares into Jenny's eyes as she stares at her reflection, fingers pressing into the lines. She pulls at her skin, stretching it back to where it used to be a decade ago.

Forty.

She's forty years old today.

With the baby kicking at her insides, the ache in her back, the number of times wee has leaked out of her this week with every sneeze, every cough, every laugh, Jenny feels haggard, exhausted, old. Really old.

So, this is forty, she thinks frowning for a moment. No, no, that's worse. She must never frown. Too many lines appear on her forehead when she does that.

Gah, did she mention her back aches?

Her belly aches.

Her head aches.

Sleep is had in snatches of twenty-minute intervals before she gets uncomfortable and has to move position, only adding to the beached whale feeling. Jenny is quite sure she is the most pregnant woman ever to have existed on this earth and there are still two weeks until her due date.

The heat. Christ, the heat is insane. Of course there would be a heatwave when she is THIS pregnant. No chance of a normal slightly damp, slightly grey, British August to struggle through the dozens of Braxton Hicks she gets every day now.

Jenny pulls up Amazon on her phone at least once an hour and gazes at the extra-large pet cooling mats for sale. Surely it would work on humans too.

Jenny smiles, laughing to herself as she thinks of the gift Dan gave her in bed earlier. She unwrapped a small blue box to find a toy forklift truck that made her tip back her head and laugh.

'Until I can find you a proper one to help get you out of bed for the next two weeks,' he grinned.

She rubs the taut skin of her belly as she steps carefully into the shower, keeping the water cool as it splashes her skin. 'There's no more space,' she says to the bump.

Forty years old.

How has that happened? She swears she was twenty-five only a few years ago.

At least they have nothing planned today. She can lie on the sofa until tomorrow when it won't be her birthday anymore and maybe she won't feel so old.

'Mum?' Jack's voice calls through the door.

'Hang on.' Jenny wraps herself in a towel, the two sides barely meeting to cover her. 'Everything OK?' she asks, opening the door.

'What time are we going to get my new football boots today?'

'Football boots?' Jenny presses her fingers to her forehead, reminding herself not to frown.

'Remember you said we could do it today because I've got that tournament tomorrow and my old ones are too small.'

Jenny's head bobs up and down, her heart sinking. So much for lying on the sofa all day. It was a pipe dream anyway. 'Do you think maybe Dan could take you, if that's OK?'

'You said you'd do it. I thought we could get a milk-shake afterwards.' Jack's face changes. He looks suddenly sad. 'It will be our last chance to be just the two of us before the baby comes.' He fishes in his pocket, pulling out a crumpled five-pound note. 'I was going to buy you a milkshake as a birthday present.'

Jenny looks at the pleading eyes of her sweet boy and feels the guilt jab at her ribs, or maybe it's the baby; either way she is quick to nod. 'I would love that. I'll just get dressed. But we should get your school shoes too and any stationery you need for school.'

'OK.'

'Are you feeling alright about senior school?' she asks, biting her lip and waiting for the usual what-if questions that show Jack's worry.

He shrugs. 'Fine. Amelia says she'll sit next to me on the bus for the first few days.'

Jenny smiles with relief and makes a mental note to thank Amelia later. 'Great, let me get dressed and we'll go.'

'I'll make you a cup of tea.' He dashes off before she can shout after him to remember to leave the tea bag in for more than ten seconds this time. The last tea he made her looked like watery milk and tasted just as bad.

Dan appears five minutes later with a mug in his hands. 'I intercepted Jack and remade your cup of tea.'

Jenny grins. 'You are amazing.'

'Are you really going football boot shopping on your birthday? I thought you'd be on the sofa all day having us bring you a constant supply of cold drinks and cake.'

'I wish, but there is seriously no space for cake in my body.' Jenny rubs her back. 'Will you be alright here?'

'Sure. As long you feel fine to drive? I don't want anything to happen to you or the baby,' he says, running a hand over her belly.

'We've still got another two weeks of this. And I saw the midwife yesterday and she said the head wasn't engaged yet so no early appearance here.'

Dan's eyes widen as though he's thinking her exact thoughts from a few minutes ago.

'I know, there is no more space,' she laughs. 'How's the cot coming along?'

Dan rubs at the stubble on his cheek. 'They've only sent instructions in Japanese.'

'Really?' Jenny grins, remembering Dan's inability to decipher the simplest of diagrams for Amelia's desk.

'What would you like for your birthday dinner? A BBQ?' he asks.

Jenny frowns. The thought of meat makes her feel queasy. 'Would a bowl of Crunchy Nut Cornflakes be acceptable, do you think?'

Dan huffs a sigh, his eyes twinkling. 'You are the most demanding person I've ever met, Jenny Travis.'

They laugh and Dan kisses her gently on the lips. 'I'll take the girls and Ethan to the park in a bit. It feels like we should be celebrating more though. Do you want to go out for dinner?'

Jenny's eyes drop to her stomach and she shakes her head. 'Can we postpone dinner out until the baby is here and I feel like a human being again instead of a—'

'Hippopotamus?'

She laughs. 'Exactly.'

Jenny's eyes draw to the clock on the dashboard and wonders where the day has gone as she pulls the car into the drive. How is it three o'clock? Five hours they spent in town. Five sweaty hours with Jack trying on every single pair of boots in every single sports shop, before dragging her back and insisting on getting the very first pair they tried on. Not to mention spending a small fortune on school shoes and stationery.

Then the queue for milkshakes was huge, the town heaving, because why wouldn't people want to go shopping on the hottest day of the year?

Her skin is clammy with sweat, her feet swollen, her back aching more than ever. Her maxi dress, which she is pretty sure will double up as a tent for Bryony and Ethan after the baby is born, is sticking to every inch of her skin.

As she heaves herself out of the car, another Braxton Hicks stretches across her stomach and she winces slightly.

'I think I heard Ethan and Dan in the garden,' Jack says. 'Let's go look.'

She follows after him, a slow waddling pace, and feels a pang of regret for the no-nonsense birthday she's planned. Sure, she's massive and sweaty and exhausted, but in another two weeks her life is going to be about feeding and waking in the night. However much she doesn't feel like herself right now, it's only going to get worse when she has a tiny human attached to her nipple.

Jenny scrambles in her bag for her phone and fires a text to Nicola: *HELP! I think I've made a terrible mistake. Now I want to celebrate my birthday!! Are you free tonight? Fancy an impromptu BBQ?*

Nicola's reply is instant: *Sorry lovely, I'm out with Ryan and Rebecca in London. Tomorrow for a belated celebration? xx*

Jenny fires back a thumbs up and sighs. This is her own doing so she might as well make the best of it.

'Jenny.' Bryony appears from the garden, her cheeks flushed, voice screechingly high. 'Ethan is stuck up the tree again. Dad's been trying to get him down for an hour.'

'What?' Jenny pants as she rushes around the corner, already wondering in the back of her mind whether she can feasibly climb a tree when climbing the stairs feels like a battle.

'I'm coming, Ethan,' she shouts. 'Hold on.'

Jenny puffs her way to the oak tree, her back crying out in pain with the effort of her movements. It's only when she's underneath the tree that she registers the balloons bobbing in the middle of a long trestle table covered with Happy Birthday tablecloths.

'Ethan?'

'Over here, Mummy,' Ethan's voice calls from behind her.

She spins around and sees them. Everyone that matters in her life leaping out from beside the table. Ethan, Jack, Dan, Bryony, Amelia, Nicola, Ryan and Rebecca. Her brother Peter is here too with a new boyfriend by the looks of it. He looks at her dress and the bump and gives an eyeroll smirk that makes her laugh before she rushes over to hug him before meeting Bradley, a gym instructor who lives in the same building.

Only her parents are missing, but Jenny is glad. If they were here, she'd feel the need to make sure they were comfortable, to run around after them, ease their worries. This way, she can relax and enjoy the fuss.

Tears prick her eyes.

Dan steps forward and guides her to a chair positioned beside a small paddling pool filled with water glistening in the sunlight. 'Your throne,' he gestures. 'The paddling pool is for your feet, but I don't think anyone will mind if you just want to flop down in it, true hippo style.'

She laughs again and eases herself gratefully into the chair. Nicola bustles up next, enveloping Jenny in a hug that smells of Nicola, of Chanel Chance and nights out together, getting ready in one of their bedrooms, of lunches, and dancing and all of the times Nicola has been there for Jenny.

'I thought you were busy,' Jenny says, her voice cracking a little.

'You silly cow. As if I would miss your birthday.'

'Did you organise this?'

Nicola grins and nods her head to Amelia and Dan.

'Seriously?'

'Yep. But not the balloons. They were all me.'

Jenny laughs as another Braxton Hicks snakes across her belly. There's no way she's going to confuse them for real contractions this time and ruin her own birthday party.

Chapter 53

Dan

This is it. He's really doing this. Dan rubs the palms of his hands against his shorts. He has spent the last few hours watching Jenny sit with her feet in the paddling pool, surrounded by presents and balloons and enjoying every second of her birthday party.

Every so often their eyes meet across the group and Jenny smiles at him in a way that makes his knees feel weak and his heart thud. He swallows hard and steps up towards her. Goosebumps race across his body despite the glaring sun scorching the back of his neck.

From the far corner the sound of splashes and shrieks carry across the garden as Amelia and her new friend, Tilly, wage war in the pool against Jack and Rebecca.

A damp-haired Bryony and Ethan rush by his legs, checking every ten minutes to see if Poppy has had her babies yet.

'Thank you for this,' Jenny says as he approaches her chair. She's rubbing at her belly and looks tired but happy.

'I'll kick everyone out soon and get the wheelbarrow. I can wheel you to the sofa if you like.'

'I knew there was a reason I fell in love with you.'

'On that note,' Dan says, clearing his throat. The nerves rise up inside him until his heart is pounding in his chest,

337

his mouth dry. A hush falls over the party and he swallows hard. He's nervous, but he wants this. Dan can't live another day without the world knowing that this is it – him and Jenny, they're a team.

Besides, he's already spoken to all four kids and made sure they're happy with it. 'Jenny Travis,' he says. 'I wasn't sure what to get you for your birthday, I mean you've pretty much won the lottery with me already.'

Jenny tips back her head and laughs. 'That's the worst excuse for not getting me a present ever.'

'Well, I do have something for you.' He reaches into his pocket, his fingers fumbling for the small red box. 'I wondered . . . I wondered . . .' He can't get the box out, he realises. It's caught in the fabric of his pocket. He tugs uselessly, aware of the silence around him, the group watching. He glances at Jenny and gives a nervous laugh as he takes in the saucer shape of her eyes.

He's half a second away from taking his shorts off completely and shaking them upside down, getting the ring and proposing in his underwear, when finally the box pulls free and he drops to one knee so fast he almost topples straight into the paddling pool.

'Jenny,' he says, looking up at the woman he is head over heels in love with. 'You've shown me how important it is to say how I'm feeling, and so . . . I need to tell you that I can't carry on like this. I love you too much. We all do, and well . . . Jenny Travis, will you marry me?' Only when the words are blurted out does he remember the rest of the speech he's been practising in the bathroom mirror all week, but before he can say another word, Jenny stands.

The smile is frozen on her face and he scrambles to his feet, suddenly more nervous than before. Has he made a mistake? Has he ruined everything?

338

Dan holds his breath and Jenny opens her mouth to speak. 'I . . .' Her eyes move from him down to the ground and a second later splats of warm liquid cover Dan's bare feet.

'Errr,' Ethan shouts from behind them. 'Has Mummy wet herself again?'

'Yeah, like last week when you drank all that lemonade at the supermarket,' Bryony chirps with a squeal of laughter.

'Oh my god,' Jenny whispers. 'My waters. Your feet.'

'It's not quite the end to the proposal that I had in mind,' he says.

'I'm sorry,' Jenny groans. 'I think the baby is coming.'

Dan shakes his head, slipping the ring back into his pocket and taking Jenny's hand. 'Don't be sorry. Now, let's get you inside.'

'Sorry, folks, it looks like the baby has decided to upstage me.'

There's a spattering of laughter and an 'Oh my god,' from Nicola as she rushes to Jenny's side. 'Have you had any contractions?'

'No.' Jenny shakes her head. 'I mean, I have been having this horrible backache and the Braxton Hicks have been going crazy today.'

'Seriously, Jenny?' Nicola laughs. 'You've been in labour at your own party and didn't think to mention it. That is so you!'

'Stop fussing.' Jenny bats Nicola's hand away as she moves slowly towards the house. 'It'll be hours before anything happens.'

'Yeah right. This is your third, Jen. It'll be like a bullet from a gun.'

Dan's hand tightens on Jenny's arm as she stops dead on the lawn. Jenny bites her lip and Dan watches the pain take hold. He looks at his watch and makes a mental note of the time. It might have been years since he's done this, but he remembers the count; the wait for the contractions to be three minutes apart.

'Do you want me to stay?' Nicola asks. 'You can go to the hospital whenever you want then, and I'll be here to keep an eye on the kids. Or I can take them with me?'

Jenny glances at Dan before looking to Jack and Ethan, Bryony and Amelia who have gathered behind them. 'Guys, this is not going to be pretty, I can promise you that, but if you want to stay and be here until I go to hospital, that's OK with me, but if you want to go with Nicola that's also totally fine.'

'We're staying,' Amelia says, and the three others nod along.

'Great, then help me into the house, will you?'

Dan holds out his arm for Jenny to take and the children crowd around. His throat feels tight, but he knows he has to hold it together. They're halfway to the house when Jenny stops again, bending down and groaning in pain.

'Remember to breathe,' he says, feeling utterly helpless as he takes another look at his watch, his eyes widening in alarm. It's barely been two minutes since the last one.

'Jen,' he says as she moves through the house to the cool of the living room and starts to pace up and down. 'I think we need to go now. These contractions are coming pretty fast and I don't fancy being the guy delivering a baby by the side of the road.'

Jenny snorts, stopping suddenly and spinning around, her eyes flicking from Dan to Nicola.

'I can't do it. We're not ready,' she gasps. 'We can't have the baby today. We haven't finished building the cot and I'm supposed to be taking Jack to get his new uniform next week.'

'You're fine.' Nicola leaps forwards and rubs Jenny's back. 'You've got this.'

'We're ready,' Dan tells her, pushing away his own panic. 'And I can pop out and get anything you need.'

'What about a car? We were supposed to get a new car next weekend. We have to be able to fit in one car.'

'I know, and we will get one, but it can wait.'

Jenny takes a faltering step before stopping. 'And we don't have a name yet. You don't like anything I suggest because you've taught every single name I can think of. We're going to end up with a child called Tarquin.'

Dan pulls a face. 'Well actually, a few years ago—'

'Don't.' She shakes her head.

'Mummy,' Ethan calls from behind them. 'If you want, I don't mind if you use Hulk for a name for the baby.'

'There,' Dan smiles. 'All settled. We'll call the baby Hulk. Now come on, let's go to the hospit—'

'Arrghhh.' Jenny doubles over. Emotions explode inside Dan and the feeling of helplessness returns.

Chapter 54

Jenny

The pain stretches across Jenny's stomach; sharp like knives dragging outwards, spreading through her body. She breathes in short, quick gasps and wishes she'd signed up for the antenatal refresher course the midwife told her about.

'I've got your hospital bag,' Amelia says, rushing into the room still wearing her swimming costume and a towel. 'And Tilly's mum has just collected her. She says good luck.'

'Thanks.' Jenny fights to get the words out.

'Is Mummy OK?' Ethan's little voice carries from the doorway.

'She's absolutely fine,' Nicola says. Jenny clings to the words, the calm in her best friend's voice and tries to slow her breathing.

The contraction passes and she straightens up, feeling queasy and tired and completely unprepared for what her body is about to do.

'OK,' she sighs. 'Let's—' Before the words can leave her mouth another contraction is slicing through her and with it comes the pressure on her cervix, that desperate unstoppable urge to push.

'I need to push,' she gasps through gritted teeth.

'What?' Dan says, leaping closer. 'But we're not at the hospital.'

'That's good, Jenny,' Nicola adds and Jenny has the distinct impression that Nicola is mouthing something to Dan. Whatever it is, she doesn't care.

'I can't do it,' Jenny gasps. 'I can't.'

'You can.' Dan's warm hand find hers and he squeezes tight. 'You are the most amazing woman I have ever met and there is nothing you can't do.'

Jenny nods. Not because she believes Dan, but because there is no choice. The baby is coming and it's coming right now. She moves onto her knees, leaning against the sofa, Dan's hands still in hers.

Towels appear from somewhere and she hears Nicola speaking to someone on the phone. 'It's happening right now.'

The pain keeps coming and Jenny rocks back and forth, breathing deeply. The push comes on the next contraction, a force that takes hold of her body as though two hands are thrusting down from her insides.

'Arrrrrrrrgh.'

'That's it, Jenny,' Dan whispers. 'You're doing so great.'

'They're sending an ambulance,' Nicola adds from Jenny's other side.

Time passes. Jenny isn't sure if it's minutes or seconds but something changes. The invisible hands push down again and she feels the baby moving through her.

'The head is out now.' Nicola's voice cracks with emotion. 'One more push, Jenny, and you've done it.'

The next one happens fast. She gasps, the pain sharp but short and a second later relief floods her body as the baby slides into Nicola's hands.

'I got her,' Nicola says with a sob. 'She's beautiful, Jen.'

'Is she?' Tears blur her vision as Dan helps Jenny to move around and sit on the floor and a moment later Nicola is placing a baby girl in Jenny's arms. Her baby girl.

Big brown eyes stare up at her from the most beautiful face Jenny has ever seen.

'You did it,' Dan whispers, tears streaming down his face. 'I love you so much.'

'I love you too.'

Jenny wipes her eyes and looks up to see four worried faces in the doorway. 'It's OK, guys. Come and meet your new sister.'

Bryony and Ethan bounce in, followed by a more hesitant Amelia and Jack.

'She's a bit yucky,' Ethan says, earning a gentle swipe from Amelia.

The next hour is a blur as the paramedics arrive and check Jenny over. They help deliver the placenta and Dan cuts the umbilical cord.

Jenny's insides hurt, her outsides feel like they've been through a food processor, but no tears, no need to go to hospital. Euphoria dances through Jenny's body as she holds her little girl to her chest and lets Dan, Nicola and the kids fuss around her.

Chapter 55

Dan

'Did you know, you have the most amazing mummy in the whole world,' Dan says, sitting himself carefully against the pillows of the bed and cradling Baby Hulk in his arms. He touches her tiny hand and she reaches out and grips his fingers. 'And you've been born on a very special day, you know? Because your mummy agreed to marry me today. Well, I think she agreed. You have impeccable timing, little Hulkie.'

Dan takes a long breath and maybe it's the exhaustion, or the adrenaline, or the feel of this magical baby in his arms, but suddenly he wants to cry, to laugh, to grin madly and for ever. The emotions rise up, pushing out a tear that rolls down his cheek.

'You big softie,' Jenny smiles as she steps out of the bathroom. 'And no way are we calling her Hulkie.'

He laughs and wipes the tear away.

'Are the kids asleep?' Jenny asks, sliding into a pair of PJs. She winces as she moves, and Dan feels a rush of sympathy for her. 'You are amazing,' he says. 'I mean it. You were so amazing today.'

She grins. 'True. And the kids?'

'Bryony and Ethan are out for the count. Jack almost. Amelia promises soon. I think she's still buzzing.'

'I am too,' Jenny says.

'Are you OK?' he asks.

Jenny nods. 'The shower was heavenly. I feel almost human now.'

'You really were a superstar today.'

'So were you. I couldn't have done it without you.'

'Nicola was way calmer than me. And for the record, yes, you could have, but I was glad I could help. Can I get you anything, soon-to-be Mrs Walker?' A wave of love pushes through Dan as he sees the surprise register on Jenny's face as Dan holds out the open ring box.

'I didn't actually say yes, you know?'

He pulls a stricken face. 'I was hoping you wouldn't remember. Was the labour just a ruse to wriggle out of giving me an answer?'

Jenny laughs. 'I think the baby in your arms answers that question.'

'And what about my other question?'

A wide smile stretches over Jenny's face. 'Yes. Of course I'll marry you.'

Baby Hulk lets out a cough-like cry, her face nuzzling towards Dan's chest. 'Err . . . I think she's looking for you.'

Jenny grins and climbs into bed. 'Come on then, baby Walker.'

As she feeds the baby, Dan takes Jenny's hand in his and slides the square diamond ring onto her finger.

'It's beautiful.' Jenny grins. 'I love it.'

'You are the beautiful one. You and Hulk.'

'Oh, come on, I can't call this gorgeous girl Hulk,' she says. 'She'll have to be Baby Walker for now.'

'How about Hannah?'

'I like it,' Jenny says. 'But she doesn't look like a Hannah to me.'

346

Dan touches the soft brown hair on the baby's head. 'No, you're right, she doesn't.'

'Harriet?'

'Hallie?'

'Hulkina?

Jenny bursts out laughing. 'Hulkina? Really? That's what you're going with?'

'Nah,' he grins, 'I just like making you laugh.'

Dan moves closer to Jenny, wrapping one arm around her, the other resting on Baby Hulk's warm back. He thinks of the girls and Ethan and Jack and how full of life the house feels with them in it, of how he hadn't even known something was missing in his life until he met Jenny, and how he's pretty sure that in this exact moment in time there isn't another person in the world as happy as he is.

Chapter 56

Jenny

Sunlight creeps in at the edges of the curtains. It's early. Five am. The house is still. Jenny holds her breath and listens for the soft breathing from the Moses basket beside her.

Her breasts ache. It's been four hours since Baby Walker fed. Baby Walker – she really can't call her daughter that for much longer and if she's not careful Hulk is going to stick and she'll be that mum at the school gates explaining to the teacher on the first day that, yes, her daughter has a proper name, but since everyone has spent four years calling her Hulk, that's the only name she responds to.

There's a whimper, the tinniest gurgle of a sound that fills Jenny with so much love she thinks she might burst with it.

Her body feels alien to her as she moves. She's tender and swollen in all kinds of places, and at some point she's going to have to address the horror that is her lady garden as Nicola calls it, but Jenny is in no rush to do that. She scoops the baby into her arms, holding her close, breathing in the smell, the essence of her.

'Let's go downstairs,' she whispers. 'Just you and me.'

Jenny sits carefully on the sofa in the corner of the kitchen, wincing as she shifts position.

The baby scrunches her face up and a second later she

wails impatiently. The sound cuts through Jenny and she hurries to unlatch her maternity bra.

As the baby clamps onto her nipple, Jenny's eyes roam the kitchen. There are plates and glasses stacked up on the sides. There is glitter sparkling on the floor and strands of party popper confetti from an exploding birthday card her brother gave her. Everywhere Jenny looks there are jobs to do, mess to tidy, but she doesn't care.

'So, this is forty,' she says, leaning down to kiss her baby again and again. 'It's not so bad, you know?'

'What isn't?' Dan asks, padding into the kitchen and kissing Jenny then the baby.

'Being forty.'

'I told you.'

'Know it all.'

Dan chuckles.

'What are you doing up so early?'

'Sneaking down to surprise my fiancée with a spring clean of the kitchen and breakfast in bed.'

'Ah, sorry,' Jenny smiles.

'It's OK. This way I can talk to you while cleaning.'

'I can do it later if you want.'

'No way. You've just given birth to my beautiful baby Hulkie.'

'Hey, that name isn't staying,' Jenny laughs. Before Jenny can say another word there's a movement on the stairs. Footsteps and whispers. Jenny glances at the door, expecting one face to appear, but then a moment later all four children bustle through the doorway.

'What are you lot doing up at this hour?' Dan asks, throwing Jenny an amused look.

'We wanted to make you both a surprise breakfast,' Bryony says, frowning at Jenny and Dan for ruining their surprise.

'Aww, guys.' Tears pool in Jenny's eyes. 'That is so lovely.'

'It was Amelia's idea,' Jack says.

'We all decided,' Ethan adds. 'You're crying, Mummy. Are you sad?'

'No,' she huffs a laugh. 'I'm very, very happy.'

The baby stops suckling, her head drooping back in Jenny's arms, rosebud lips glistening with milk.

Jenny reclips her bra and rearranges her top. 'Well I think it might be a bit early for breakfast, but I'd love a cup of tea, please.'

Bryony and Ethan rush into the kitchen. 'We'll do it.'

Jack steps to the sofa first, Amelia following. Their eyes are wide as they stare at their new sister. 'Would you like to hold her?'

'Yes,' they say in unison before grinning at each other.

'You go first,' Jack says, ever the gentleman.

Amelia sits down and Jenny places the baby in her arms.

'She looks just like you when you were born,' Dan says, dropping a kiss on Amelia's head.

'Really?' A smile lights up Amelia's face.

'Yep. All rosy-cheeked and milk-drunk,' Dan says.

'Rosie,' Amelia says. 'That's a nice name.'

A strange sensation travels over Jenny's body, a chill of goosebumps, a sense of something clicking into place. She looks at Dan, her eyebrows raised in a question.

'Rosie,' he muses. 'I like that.'

'Rosie.' Jenny nods. 'I like it too.'

'Really?' Amelia says. 'I've named you,' she whispers to the baby. 'I've saved you from being called Hulk.'

Jenny wraps her arm around Amelia.

So this is forty, she thinks, taking in her family. And it's not bad at all.

Acknowledgements

If you've made it this far, then thank you so much for reading *Just The Six Of Us*! Readers are the magic beans of our stories. It's in your imaginations that the characters come to life, and I really hope you've enjoyed spending time with Jenny and Dan.

Thank you to my fabulous editor, Rhea Kurien, for taking a chance on this story and your amazing edits, which have made Jenny and Dan's world so much more. Thank you to everyone at Orion Dash for your hard work and vision!

To my lovely agent, Tanera Simons - thanks for not running a mile when I first suggested this idea, and for always having my back.

Thanks to the book community – especially the Chelmsford RNA for making me feel so welcome. Thanks also to the lovely book bloggers who do so much for authors. To the very talented Emma Cooper, who was the first person to read this book. Thank you for all the amazing advice.

Final thanks to my friends and family. My daughter, Lottie, asked me to write a romance with guinea pigs, so in some ways Jenny and Dan's story grew from two furry little bundles we call Kitkat and Cookie. And last but least, to Tommy and Andy for all of your support!!